Books by Frances Jenkins Olcott

PUBLISHED BY

HOUGHTON MIFFLIN COMPANY

THE WONDER GARDEN. Illustrated in color by Milo Winter.

THE BOOK OF ELVES AND FAIRIES. Illustrated in color by Milo Winter.

TALES OF THE PERSIAN GENII. Illustrated in color by Willy Pogany.

THE RED INDIAN FAIRY BOOK. Illustrated in color by Frederick Richardson.

BIBLE STORIES TO READ AND TELL. Illustrated in color by Willy Pogany.

GOOD STORIES FOR GREAT HOLIDAYS. Illustrated.

STORY-TELLING POEMS.

THE CHILDREN'S READING.

With Amena Pendleton

THE JOLLY BOOK FOR BOYS AND GIRLS.

THE WONDER GARDEN

SHE SANG OF BEAUTIFUL, STRANGE, FAR-OFF THINGS

THE
WONDER GARDEN

NATURE MYTHS AND TALES FROM
ALL THE WORLD OVER
for
STORY-TELLING AND READING ALOUD
AND FOR THE CHILDREN'S OWN READING

BY
FRANCES JENKINS OLCOTT

With Illustrations by
MILO WINTER

BOSTON AND NEW YORK
HOUGHTON MIFFLIN COMPANY
The Riverside Press Cambridge
1919

TO MY NIECE

ELISE YATES PHILLIPS

A bit of the Sky fell down one day;
It touched a Star and glanced away;
A spark from the Star in its breast it bore,
And fell to the earth, and was no more.

Up sprang from the grass a tiny flower
That brightly grew 'neath sun and shower: —
The bit of the Sky in its petals blue,
The spark from the Star in its bosom, too.

The Star gazed down at its happy lot,
And whispered, " Dear, forget-me-not !"

FOREWORD

HERE are 150 nature myths and short stories from all parts of the World. They are the kind that children delight in — tales of transformations of maidens into trees and fountains, of youths into flowers, and of men into birds. Blossoms, fragrance, and joy are the themes of many of these tales, while a few are tender, pathetic, or humorous.

Nature myths not only give joy, but they are educational — they clothe nature with poetic attributes. The Greek and Roman myths have been taught to many generations of English speaking children, and on the "transformations" the fancies and imaginations of our English poets have fed, from Chaucer to Swinburne. Without a knowledge of these myths, one cannot appreciate or even enjoy the classic allusions in the poems of Shakespeare, Herrick, Milton, Shelley, Keats, Lowell, Longfellow, and many other poets. Art, too, has for its themes, classic fables and myths; so to understand beautiful paintings and sculpture, it is necessary to know something of classic mythology.

But the Greeks and Romans were not the only

peoples possessing transformation tales and nature legends; the blossom-loving Japanese, the totem-worshipping Red Indians, and many other peoples have a wealth of such tales. When stripped of their repellent elements, — for all mythologies, classical or otherwise, contain such elements, — these tales are most delightful and fanciful, and invest flowers, birds, and nature as a whole with poetic charm that pleases children as does a fairy-tale.

"Mariora Floriora," "Maiden White and Maiden Yellow," the Iroquois "Legend of the Corn," and the other delicate, graceful, and symbolic nature myths, presented here, cover a wide range, coming from all over the World, — from Japan, China, Finland, Eskimo-land, Red Indian-land, Norway, Russia, France, Ireland, Wales, Friesland, Roumania, Persia, and Arabia.

In retelling the classic Greek and Roman myths, great care has been taken to preserve their classical features, as well as to emphasize their poetic elements. The tales, with few exceptions, have been retold directly from good translations of Homer, Bion, Moschus, Anacreon, Hesiod, Ovid, and other classic writers. Hence they have a freshness and vigour that could not be theirs if retold from adapted material.

A few modern tales have been added to complete the volume. It is regretted that Andersen's

Snow Queen and *The Little Mermaid*, are much too long for inclusion, but they may be easily got at any public library. However, a few of his exquisite shorter pieces are included, and lend their charm to these pages in which boys and girls may wander at will through this Garden of Delight. For here are the sweet scents of flowers, the colours of blossoms, the whisperings of trees, the springing of fresh grass, the singing of soaring birds, the murmuring of streams, — all are here, and all are transfused with a wonder element that creates a real Fairy Garden.

To make the volume of the greatest practical use to teachers and librarians, an Appendix is added, containing: —

(*a*) A Calendar — or Programme — of the nature tales arranged by the school year, as an aid in following the changing seasons — see page 446.

(*b*) A Reference List of nature stories and tales in other books, suitable to tell or to read aloud — see page 454.

(*c*) A Subject Index, referring to the myths and tales in this volume, under such headings as the names of fruits, flowers, trees, seasons, Arbour Day, Bird Day, etc., and under ethical headings like Retribution, Affection, Obedience, and Honesty — see page 469.

ACKNOWLEDGMENTS

SPECIAL acknowledgment is here made to the *New York Evening Post* for the use of the many stories included in this volume which I have written for its columns.

Acknowledgment is also due the Churchman Company, for the use of my little story "The Beauty of the Lily," that was first published in *The Churchman*.

Thanks are due the following publishers and authors, for stories or themes from their publications: —

To Messrs. Houghton Mifflin Company, for "The Garden of Frost Flowers," retold from William Cullen Bryant, *Poems;* "Girl who Trod on a Loaf," from Hans Christian Andersen, *Wonder Stories Told for Children;* "Gleam o' Day and the Princess Lotus-Flower," from George Soulié, *Strange Stories from the Lodge of Leisures;* "Green Plumes of Mondamin," from Henry W. Longfellow, *Hiawatha;* "The Robin," from John Greenleaf Whittier, *Poems*.

To the American Folk-Lore Society, for "The Turkey-Given Corn," and "The Pet Turkey whose Feelings were Hurt," from Washington

Matthews, *Navaho Legends* and "The Old Woman who was a Burr," from George A. Dorsey, *Traditions of the Skidi Pawnee.*

To the *Canadian Magazine*, for "The Maple Leaf For Ever," retold from a story by Miss Grace Channell.

To Messrs. Henry Holt and Company, for "The Mignonette Fairy," and "The Dandelion Fairies," from *Flower Lore and Legend*, by Katherine M. Beals.

To The Macmillan Company, for "The Wind in the Pine," from *Green Willow*, by Grace James.

To Miss Gladys Wolcott Barnes, for "The Colours of the Rainbow," first published in *The Living Church.*

To Mr. W. W. Canfield, for "The Legend of the Trailing Arbutus," and "The Legend of the Corn," from his *Legends of the Iroquois*, published by A. Wessels Company.

To Mrs. Julia Fish, for the French translations made purposely for this volume.

To Miss Elizabeth M. Lum, for "The Legend of the Goldenrod," from her *Ancient Legends*, published by Tuttle, Morehouse, and Taylor.

To Miss Ada M. Skinner, for the paraphrase "Prince Butterfly and Clover," from her *Turquoise Story Book*, published by Duffield and Company.

The following is a partial list of the many other sources from which I have drawn atmosphere and plots for stories: —

Japanese tales, like "Maiden White and Maiden Yellow," "The Chrysanthemum Children," "The Morning-Glory Fan," are from Davis, *Myths and Legends of Japan,* and Gordon Smith, *Ancient Tales and Folk-Lore of Japan.* Red Indian tales are from the publications of The American Museum of Natural History, Bureau of American Ethnology, Carnegie Institution of Washington, and The Field Columbian Museum. Miscellaneous legends and tales are from Barker and Sinclair, *West African Folk-tales;* Professor Basil Hall Chamberlain, *Language, Mythology, etc. of Japan;* Lizzie Deas, *Flower Favourites;* Dyer, *Folk-Lore of Plants;* Folkard, *Plant Lore,* H. A. Giles, *Chinese Fairy Tales;* Ingram, *Flora Symbolica;* Canon Horsley, *Some Folk-Lore and Legends of Birds;* Captain O'Connor, *Folk-Tales from Tibet;* T. W. Rolleston, *Myths and Legends of the Celtic Race.*

Other miscellaneous legends and tales are from such quaint authors as Angelo de Gubernatis, Madame Anais de Neuville, King Alfred's *Boethius;* Abbé Antoine Banier (1673); William Browne of Tavistock (1591), Abraham Cowley (1618), Abbé René Rapin (1621).

Among the classic authors and sources contributing myths are, Anacreon, Apollodorus, Apollonius Rhodius, Bion, Callimachus, Hesiod, Homer, the Homeric Hymns, Lucian, Moschus, Ovid, Pindar, Pliny, and Theocritus.

CONTENTS

CONTENTS

CONTENTS

xxiii

ILLUSTRATIONS

THE WONDER GARDEN

THE GARDEN OF DELIGHT

The Magic Waters gush from Speaking Rocks,
From Golden Boughs the Golden Apples fall,
And Silver Fruits, that tinkle in the breeze,
So sweetly tinkling, to the Children call: —

"Come into this Garden of Delight!
Dance hand in hand along its wonder-walks,
Where mellow sun-rays smile through tender green,
And every Branch and every Leaflet talks!

"Oh! twine a garland sweet of fragrant flowers,
And deck your head with wreaths of blossoms gay,
And listen to the tales they have to tell
Of that far-off and wondrous Wonder-Day!

"And as the mourning trees bend down their heads,
Oh! hush and listen to their tales of truth,
For they, erewhile, were happy Maids and fair,
In that wondrous Wonder-Land-of-Youth!"

The Magic Waters gush from Speaking Rocks,
From Golden Boughs the Golden Apples fall,
And Silver Fruits, that tinkle in the breeze,
So sweetly tinkling, to the Children call.

TO THE CHILDREN

COME! COME! INTO THIS WONDER GARDEN
AND WANDER THROUGH ITS MANY PATHS

VERY big and wide is this Wonder Garden.　All
sorts of marvellous things happen in it: —

Rainbows shed gold.　Beautiful youths and
maidens are changed into flowers.　Dryads peep
from the trees, and Nymphs dissolve into fountains of tears.　Birds and trees have strange
adventures.　Dandelion Fairies grow up in the
grass, and so do Fairy Peonies and Chrysanthemum Children; while Firefly Maidens, with
bright lights under their wings, flit about among
the flowers.

Very big and wide, indeed, is this Wonder
Garden.　In it are meadows and forests, blue
lakes and loud-sounding seas.　The boisterous
Boreas and his gentle brother Zephyr blow
through it.　Golden Apples and talking fruits
hang from its boughs.　Magic animals talk and
walk in its magic farm.　Shepherds and Shepherdesses keep their flocks, and dance in the
meadow grass; while great heroes like Hercules
and Ulysses have marvellous adventures by land
and sea.

Very wonderful, indeed, is this Wonder Garden; for it belongs to Dame Nature, while Old Father Time is its keeper, and they have spread out their garden until it covers the whole wide Fairy World.

ALONG THE FLOWERY WONDER PATH

FAIRY BLOOMS

Now all fair things come to light:
Lilies on a moonlit night
Lift the mould and greet the Morn
With a smile of Silence born;
Daffodils, and Fairy Blooms
Rise from all the woodland tombs,
And upon the mossy bough
Buds and blossoms lie like snow.
                                    ANON.

THE SWEET–PEAS' WINGS

Here are Sweet-Peas, on tiptoe for a flight;
With wings of gentle flush o'er delicate white,
And taper fingers catching at all things,
To bind them all about with tiny rings.
                                    JOHN KEATS

HOW MARIGOLDS CAME YELLOW

Jealous girls these sometimes were,
While they lived or lasted here:
Turned to Flowers, still they be
Yellow, marked for jealousy.
                                    ROBERT HERRICK

THE SNOWDROP FAIRY

Irish Tale

ONCE upon a time, there was a pleasant old house in Ireland, and around it was a wide flower garden where grew Roses white and red, and where Strawberries and Primroses peeped from the grass. Trees stood around the border and flowering shrubs were everywhere.

But the most delightful of all was a mound in the corner of the garden farthest away from the house. The greenest and softest grass grew on that mound, and in the Springtime it was covered with white nodding Snowdrops. So the children called it "The Snowdrop Mound."

They loved it best of all places, and when lessons were over they ran to the Snowdrop Mound and played and shouted and romped, trampling the grass and tossing about withered wreaths of flowers that they had gathered in the garden, — yes, and they even threw Strawberry hulls on the grass.

One beautiful afternoon when the golden sunlight was shining through the leaves, the children were playing as usual on the Snowdrop Mound, shouting and singing and making a great noise. Then suddenly they saw a lovely lady coming toward them. Her light hair gleamed softly and her long robe of shimmering green trailed in the grass. She lifted her drooping head, and the children saw that her face was delicate and beautiful, but that it was sad and displeased. They ran to meet her.

"Are we making too much noise?" they all cried.

Then the littlest child, Baby Rose, put up her lips to be kissed, but the lady stood gravely looking at the mound.

"Do stay awhile and play with us, dear, beautiful lady!" pleaded the children; and as they spoke they began to gather up the withered wreaths.

At this the lady smiled, and her eyes shone like stars. She caught up Baby Rose in her arms, and kissed her. Then, beckoning, she led the children to a green spot near the mound and, putting down Baby Rose, began to dance, swaying lightly from side to side; and as she danced she sang sweetly.

The children joined hands and danced with her in a circle, round and round. All the afternoon they danced and were not tired. Then the lady, still dancing and swaying, led them back to Snowdrop Mound, and they circled it once, twice, three times. Then they heard the voice of their nurse calling and calling as she came through the garden.

The lady hesitated, stopped singing, and looked grave.

"Oh, stay with us! Stay with us, dear, lovely lady!" the children all cried.

At that very moment the nurse stopped at a shrub and broke a branch. As it snapped, the lady glided away among the trees.

"Come back! Come back to-morrow!" cried all the children; but she was gone.

"Never did I know such children!" said the nurse. "Your supper has been waiting this hour! Here is baby sitting in the wet grass!"

As she spoke she picked up little Rose, who screamed and struggled and stretched out her arms toward the spot where the lady had gone.

"What's this, my pet?" cried the nurse. "You smell like the sweetest posies! You are like a little Snowdrop yourself!"

"She is, indeed," said old Dennis, the gardener, drawing near. "She has eyes that can see far! For the Good People have kissed her!"

"Do you mean the Fairies?" cried all the children. They looked at one another and thought of the beautiful lady who had danced with them.

Then they saw that the branch in the nurse's hand was a bit of the Mountain Ash — the mystic Rowan tree — which breaks all Fairy spells, and even frightens the Good People far away.

So it must have been. For every day after that the children went to the Snowdrop Mound, and laid fresh Forget-me-not wreaths upon the grass, but the beautiful lady never came back.

THE LITTLE NYMPH WHO LOVED BRIGHT COLOURS

Old Legend

ONCE upon a time, in days of yore, there was a happy little Nymph who liked to play by the side of the stream in which her mother, a lovely Naiad, lived.

She delighted to pick bright wild-flowers — the brighter the better — so that her eyes might feast themselves on their gay colours. Red and yellow were her favourites.

But though she was so pretty and gay, she was very fickle, and forgot her flowers the minute a Butterfly fluttered past. She would throw them on the ground, trample them underfoot, and away she would run after the bright insect.

One day Vertumnus, Keeper-of-All-the-Orchards-in-the-World, saw the little maiden romping by the stream while she wreathed her head with garlands. Immediately he wanted to take the pretty child home with him to live in his most beautiful orchard.

He put on his robes painted with Autumn colours, crowned himself with fruit blossoms, took in his right hand red Apples and yellow Pears, and in his left a big cornucopia heaped to overflowing with Grapes, Plums, and Peaches.

Then he sauntered along the brook until he met the little maiden.

He coaxed her in his tenderest tones to go along with him, offering her the Apples and Pears, and even his cornucopia, but she only shook her curls and laughed. And the minute that a Butterfly with blue wings flashed by, she forgot all about Vertumnus, she forgot about his beautiful orchard and his gorgeous fruits, and away she ran after the insect.

So light and nimble was she that before Vertumnus could follow she vanished behind a hedge of Wild Roses. At the same moment loud bursts of harsh laughter came from the wood near by, and he saw an old Faun dancing and capering among the trees.

"Ho! ho! Keeper-of-All-the-Orchards-in-the-World!" roared the Faun, holding his sides in merriment; "if you wish to snare the fickle heart of yon little Nymph, you must change yourself into a new shape each minute, to please her shifting fancy."

So Vertumnus, who wanted the little maiden very much, did what the Faun advised, and changed himself into a Butterfly, and a Rose, and a Bluebird. But no matter what he became, she liked him only for a minute, then forgetting all about him, away she ran after something else.

At last Vertumnus grew very angry, for he

could hear the Fauns and Satyrs making the
wood ring with peals of harsh laughter, while
they mocked at him from behind the trees.

"What!" cried he, "shall this insignificant
little maiden be allowed to scorn me and my
most beautiful orchard! I will catch her and
take her away by force!"

Just as he was speaking, the little Nymph
went flitting by, so he ran after her.

At first, as she sped lightly forward, she shook
her curls and smiled archly back at him. But
when she grew tired and saw that he was still
pursuing her with furious looks, as a hunter
chases the trembling Deer, her steps faltered, and
stretching out her arms, she cried in terror: —

"O ye Nymphs and Naiads, save me! Save
me!"

Then Vertumnus put out his hand to seize her,
but, lo! she vanished from his sight! She was
gone! and where she had stood grew up a splendid dancing flower — a gorgeous Tulip clad in a
striped red and yellow vest. There it stood swaying and nodding on its tall stem, and waving its
long green leaves like arms.

So every year, in the early Springtime, the
little Nymph Tulip dances in the garden-bed,
all dressed in Autumn colours, her favourite red
and yellow. But sometimes she puts on pink,
white, or violet to please the children.

HYACINTH

Retold from Ovid

ONCE when the golden-beamed Apollo roamed
the earth, he made a companion of Hyacinth,
the son of King Amyclas of Lacedæmon; and him
he loved with an exceeding great love, for the lad
was beautiful beyond compare.

So Apollo threw aside his lyre, and became
the daily comrade of Hyacinth. Often they
played games, or climbed the rugged mountain
ridges. Together they followed the chase, or
fished in the quiet and shadowy pools; and
Apollo, unmindful of his dignity, carried the
lad's nets and held his Dogs.

It happened on a day that the two friends
stripped off their garments, rubbed the juice of
the olive upon their bodies, and engaged in
throwing the quoit.

First Apollo poised it and tossed it far. It
cleaved the air with its weight, and fell heavily
to earth. At that moment Hyacinth ran forward and hastened to take up the disc, but the
hard earth sent it rebounding straight into his
face, so that he fell wounded to the ground.

Ah! then, pale and fearful, Apollo hastened to
the side of his fallen friend. He bore up the lad's
sinking limbs, and strove to stanch his wound

with healing herbs. All in vain! Alas! the wound would not close. And as Violets and Lilies, when their stems are crushed, hang their languid blossoms on their stalks and wither away, so did Hyacinth droop his beautiful head and die.

Then Apollo, full of grief, cried aloud in his anguish:

"O Beloved! You have fallen in your early youth, and I alone am the cause of your destruction! Oh, that I could give my life for you! But since Fate will not permit this, you shall ever be with me, and your praise shall dwell on my lips. My lyre struck with my hand, my songs, too, shall celebrate you! And you, dear lad, shall become a new flower, and on your leaves will I write my lamentations."

And even as Apollo spoke, behold! the blood that had flowed from Hyacinth's wound stained the grass, and a flower, like a Lily in shape, sprang up, more bright than Tyrian purple. On its leaves did Apollo inscribe the mournful characters: "ai, ai," which mean "alas! alas!"

And as oft as the Spring drives away the Winter, so oft does Hyacinth blossom in the fresh, green grass.

ECHO AND NARCISSUS

Retold from Ovid

LONG ago, in the ancient world, there was born
to the blue-eyed Nymph Liriope a beautiful boy,
whom she called Narcissus. An oracle foretold at
his birth that he should be happy and live to a
good old age if he "never saw himself." As this
prophecy seemed ridiculous, his mother soon forgot all about it.

Narcissus grew to be a stately, handsome
youth. His limbs were firm and straight. Curls
clustered about his white brow, and his eyes
shone like two Stars. He loved to wander among
the meadow flowers and in the pathless woodland. But he disdained his playmates, and
would not listen to their entreaties to join in
their games. His heart was cold, and in it was
neither hate nor love. He lived indifferent to
youth or maid, to friend or foe.

Now, in the forest near by dwelt a Nymph
named Echo. She had been a handmaiden of
Juno, Queen of all the Dwellers-on-Mount-Olympus. But though the Nymph was beautiful of
face, she was not loved. She had a noisy tongue.
She told lies and whispered slanders, and en-
couraged the other Nymphs in many misdoings.
So when Juno perceived all this, she ordered the

troublesome Nymph away from her court, and banished her to the wildwood, bidding her never speak again except in imitation of other peoples' words.

So Echo dwelt in the woods, and forever mocked the words of youths and maidens.

One day as Narcissus was wandering alone in the pathless forest, Echo, peeping from behind a tree, saw his beauty; and as she gazed her heart was touched with love. Stealthily she followed his footsteps, and often she tried to call to him with endearing words; but she could not speak, for she no longer had a voice of her own.

At last Narcissus heard the sound of breaking branches, and cried out, "Is there any one here?"

And Echo answered softly, "Here!"

Narcissus, amazed, looking about on all sides and seeing no one, cried, "Come!"

And Echo answered, "Come!"

Narcissus cried again: "Who are you? Whom seek you?"

And Echo answered, "You!"

Then rushing from among the trees she tried to throw her arms about his neck, but Narcissus fled through the forest, crying: —

"Away! away! I will die before I love you!"

And Echo answered mournfully, "I love you!"

Thus rejected, she hid among the trees, and buried her blushing face in the green leaves.

She pined and pined, until her body wasted quite away, and nothing but her voice was left. And some say that even to this day her voice lives in lonely caves, and answers men's words from afar.

Now, when Narcissus fled from Echo, he came to a clear spring, like silver. Its waters were un-sullied, for neither Goats feeding upon the mountains nor any other cattle had drunk from it, nor had wild beasts or birds disturbed it, nor had branch or leaf fallen into its calm waters. The trees bent above and shaded it from the hot sun, and the soft, green grass grew on its margin.

Here Narcissus, fatigued and thirsty after his flight, laid himself down beside the spring to drink. He gazed into the mirror-like water, and saw himself reflected in its tide. He knew not that it was his own image, but thought that he saw a youth living in the spring.

He gazed on two eyes like Stars, on graceful slender fingers, on clustering curls worthy of Apollo, on a mouth arched like Cupid's bow, on blushing cheeks and ivory neck. And as he gazed his cold heart grew warm, and love for this beautiful reflection rose up and filled his soul.

He rained kisses on the deceitful stream. He thrust his arms into the water, and strove to grasp the image by the neck, but it fled away. Again he kissed the stream, but the image mocked his love.

All day and all night, lying there without food or drink, he continued to gaze into the water. Then raising himself, he stretched out his arms to the trees about him, and cried: —

"Did ever, O ye Woods, one love as much as I! Have ye ever seen a lover thus pine for the sake of unrequited affection?"

Then turning once more, Narcissus addressed his reflection in the limpid stream: —

"Why, dear youth, do you flee away from me? Neither a vast sea, nor a long way, nor a great mountain separates us! only a little water keeps us apart! Why, dear lad, do you deceive me, and whither do you go when I try to grasp you? You encourage me with friendly looks. When I extend my arms, you extend yours; when I smile you smile in return; when I weep, you weep; but when I try to clasp you beneath the stream, you shun me and flee away! Grief is taking my strength, and my life will soon be over! In my early days am I cut off, nor is Death grievous to me, now that he is about to remove my sorrows!"

Thus mourned Narcissus, lying beside the woodland spring. He disturbed the water with his tears, and made the woods to resound with his sighs. And as the yellow wax is melted by the Fire, or the Hoar Frost is consumed by the heat of the Sun, so did Narcissus pine away, his body wasting by degrees.

Often he sighed, "Alas!"

And the grieving Echo from the wood answered, "Alas!"

With his last breath he looked into the water and sighed, "Ah, Youth Beloved, farewell!"

And Echo sighed, "Farewell!"

So Narcissus, laying his weary head upon the grass, closed his eyes forever. The Water Nymph wept for him, and the Wood Dryads lamented him, and Echo resounded their mourning.

But when they sought his body it had vanished away, and in its stead had grown up by the brink of the stream a little flower, with silver leaves and golden heart, — and thus was born to earth the woodland flower, Narcissus.

CLYTIE, THE HELIOTROPE

Retold from Ovid

THERE was once a Nymph named Clytie, who gazed ever at Apollo as he drove his sun-chariot through the heavens. She watched him as he rose in the east attended by Aurora, the rosy-fingered child of Dawn, and by the dancing Hours. She gazed as he ascended the heavens, urging his steeds still higher in the fierce heat of the noonday. She looked with wonder as at evening he guided his steeds downward to their many-coloured pastures under the western sky, where they fed all night on ambrosia.

Apollo saw not Clytie. He had no thought for her, but he shed his brightest beams upon her sister, the white Nymph Leucothoë. And when Clytie perceived this she was filled with envy and grief.

Night and day she sat on the bare ground weeping. For nine days and nine nights she never raised herself from the earth, nor did she take food or drink; but ever she turned her weeping eyes toward Apollo as he moved through the sky.

And her limbs became rooted to the ground. Green leaves enfolded her body. Her beautiful face was concealed by tiny flowers, violet-coloured and sweet with perfume.

Thus was she changed into a flower, and her roots held her fast to the ground; but ever she turned her blossom-covered face toward the Sun, following with eager gaze his daily flight. In vain were her sorrow and tears, for Apollo regarded her not.

And so through the ages has the Nymph turned her dew-washed face toward the heavens; and men no longer call her Clytie, but Sunflower-Heliotrope.

PANSY–BOY

Retold from Pindar

ONCE upon a time, there was loud weeping in the stately palace-hall of King Aipytos of Arcady. Every one was running to and fro among the golden pillars, searching for something. The little boy, just five days old, the son of Euadne-of-Tresses-Iris-Dark, was lost.

"The little one must be found," said King Aipytos. "He is a wonder-child, and, when he grows up, will be the wisest youth in Arcady."

So they searched night and day.

At last they found him hidden in a thicket, and lying on a cloak of scarlet web. He was cooing and laughing, and kicking his tiny feet. His mouth was smeared with honey, while on either side of him sat a green-eyed Serpent holding to his lips a leaf filled with fragrant honey.

And scattered over him, and under him, and all around him, were Pansies — great golden and purple gleaming Pansy-flowers, like a light bright blanket.

So they carried him home, and named him Pansy.

And when Pansy-Boy grew up, he was the wisest youth in Arcady.

THE BAD POPPY-SEEDS

Bengali Legend

ONCE upon a time, long, long ago, there lived
on the bank of the Ganges an old Magician.
One day a little Mouse was born in his hut of
palm-leaves. He made a great pet of her. Indeed, by his magic arts she was able to speak
like a human being.

When she grew older, she was discontented
and unhappy; so the Magician transformed her
into a Cat. Still she was not happy, so he
changed her into a Dog. But as she continued
to be discontented, he next made her into an
Ape, then into a Boar. But when she kept on
bothering him with complaints, he finally transformed her into a beautiful, fascinating maiden,
and called her Poppy-Seed.

One day while she was watering her flowers
the King passed by and saw her. He immediately
asked her hand in marriage, and made her his
Queen.

All went well, until it chanced that Queen
Poppy-Seed was standing by a well, and, be-
coming giddy, fell in and was drowned. The
King was inconsolable, and sent for the Magician.

"I cannot bring her back to you," said the

Magician, "but fill up the well with earth, and see what you shall see."

So they filled up the well with earth, and out of it grew a tall plant bearing one single bright red Poppy.

And that is how Poppies first came. And that is why the seed of the Poppy makes people as mischievous as a Mouse, as fond of milk as a Cat, as quarrelsome as a Dog, as filthy as an Ape, as savage as a Boar, and as high-tempered as a Queen.

And when you pick Poppies and put them in water, they soon hang their heavy heads for shame, because of all the doings of the bad Poppy-Seeds.

THE MIGNONETTE FAIRY

Old French Tale

ONCE upon a time, there was a young girl who was most unhappy. She was so ugly to look at that she thought no one loved her. So she shut herself up in her room, and wept.

While she was feeling very sad, an old woman suddenly appeared before her.

"My child," said she, "why are you weeping?"

"Because," sobbed the young girl, "I long to be beautiful, so that every one will love me."

Then the Fairy — for it was a Fairy — said: —

"If you will do just as I tell you for a year, your wish shall be granted. Go out into the world, and never let an hour pass without doing something to make others happier. And do not look in a mirror until I come again."

Then the Fairy vanished, and where she had been standing was a flower-pot in which grew a little green plant.

Now the little green plant was not beautiful at all. It had very plain little flowers that were just spikes of green and red; but it gave out the most delicious fragrance.

When the young girl saw the plant, she cried out: —

"Oh, you little darling!"

Then she set the pot carefully on the window-sill, and watered the flowers. After that she started out to do the Fairy's bidding, and make others happier.

Day after day she went about, showing kindness to every one, young or old; and she forgot all about her looks.

The year passed by so quickly that she did not know it was gone. One day, while she was watering her little plant that had grown all over the window-sill, the Fairy suddenly stood before her.

She held a mirror in front of her and said: — "Look!"

The young girl looked, and could not believe that it was her own face gazing at her. Her eyes, that had been dim with weeping, were clear and sparkling, her cheeks were rosy, her mouth was wreathed with smiles. *She was beautiful.*

The Fairy smiled, and said: —

"You have filled your heart with such beautiful thoughts, and your life with such beautiful deeds, that a beautiful soul shines in your face.

"As a reward, you shall be like the plant I left with you; wherever you go, you shall shed around you the sweetest fragrance."

At that the Fairy vanished; and ever since then the plant has been called Mignonette, which means Little Darling.

Katherine M. Beals (Adapted)

LEGEND OF THE HEART'S EASE

Old Legend

ONCE upon a time, Pansies had the most delicious perfume. Indeed, they smelled sweeter than the scented March Violets. They sprang up all over the fields among the Corn and other vegetables, just as wild-flowers do.

And because Pansies breathed such delicious perfume, and looked so beautiful turning up their purple and golden faces toward the Sun, every child who passed by stopped and picked a handful. So the Corn and other vegetables were trampled down and ruined.

This grieved the little Pansies very much for they had kind and loving hearts.

"Oh!" they sobbed, "how gladly would we give away our sweetness to save all the growing plants around us!"

And they wept so hard and sorrowed so much, that they lost their rich perfume. They no longer sprang up wild all over the fields, but grew only in flower-beds.

So, that is why the children find their purple and golden faces growing in flower-gardens and window-boxes.

THE DRAGON SIN

Sussex Legend

ONCE upon a time, in ancient days, a fearful
Dragon inhabited a certain forest. No one had
the courage to subdue him, for his name was Sin.
No knight, who ventured into the forest, was
strong enough of himself to overcome the
monster; and neither sword nor spear could
harm him.

It chanced one day that the brave young
warrior, Saint Leonard, was riding through the
forest. He saw the Dragon Sin stretching out
his hideous scaly length to prevent his passing
by. Down from his horse the good Saint leaped,
and crushed the monster in his arms.

Then backward and forward they struggled,
the Dragon tearing Saint Leonard's flesh with
his sharp claws. For three nights and three
days, they wrestled thus together, then on the
fourth day the Saint, breathing a prayer for
help, drove the monster before him into the
inner recesses of the forest.

And there the Dragon Sin stayed, skulking
in the darkness; and he never ventured out again
to attack the good young warrior.

Now as soon as Saint Leonard had conquered
the Dragon, there was seen a wonder. Over the

forest-ground were sprinkled drops of the Saint's blood, shed from his wounds.   From them sprang up a host of Lilies-of-the-Valley, like a holy white carpet.

Then all the little Lilies softly chimed their scented bells in honour of Saint Leonard's victory for God.

THE CUP OF THANKSGIVING

Hebrew Fable

THERE was once a good man who was pacing up and down his garden. He was thinking sadly; and, as he paused before a Rose-bush, he thought these words aloud: —

"Alas! How my enemies hate me! They surround me on every side! Oh, that God would pity me, and put an end to my miseries!"

Then the Rose-bush spoke to him thus: —

"Look at me. Am I not a beautiful plant? Each of my blossoms is a Cup of Thanksgiving to the Lord, an offering of sweetest incense unto Him.

"Now, where do you find me? Surrounded with thorns! But they do not sting me. They protect me and give me sap. This your enemies do for you. They make you more perfectly to turn to Him, and they cause you to keep your spirit courageous and more beautiful than a frail flower."

So spoke the Rose-bush.

The good Man listened reverently, and went home comforted; for his Soul was become a Cup of Thanksgiving for his enemies.

THE BEAUTY OF THE LILY

Easter Tale

ONCE upon a time, in a far-distant land, there dwelt a peasant named Ivan, and with him lived his little nephew Vasily.

Ivan was gloomy and unkempt, and his restless eyes looked out from his matted hair and beard. As for the little Vasily, he was a manly child; but though his uncle was kind enough to him in his way, he neither washed him, nor combed his hair, nor taught him anything.

The hut they lived in was very miserable. Its walls were full of holes, the furniture of its one room was broken down and dusty, and its floor unswept. The little garden was filled with stones and weeds. The neighbours passing by in the daytime turned aside their heads. But they never passed at night, for fear of Ivan.

Now it happened one Easter morning that Ivan, feeling restless, rose early and went and stood before the door of the hut. The trees were budding, the air was full of bird-songs, the dew lay glittering on the grass, and a near-by brook ran leaping and gurgling along. The rays of the rising Sun shone slanting from the tops of the distant hills, and seemed to touch the hut.

And as Ivan looked, he saw a young man coming swiftly and lightly from the hills, and he bore on his arm a sheaf of pure white Lilies. The stranger drew near, and stopped before the hut.

"Christ is risen!" he said in flute-like tones.

"He is risen indeed!" muttered Ivan through his beard.

Then the young man took a Lily from his sheaf and gave it to Ivan, saying:—

"Keep it white!" And, smiling, he passed on.

Wonderingly Ivan gazed at the flower in his hand. Its gold-green stem seemed to support a pure white crown,—or was it a translucent cup filled with light! And as the man looked into the flower's gold-fringed heart, awe stole into his soul.

Then he turned and entered the hut, saying to himself, "I will put it in water."

But when he went to lay the Lily on the window-sill, so that he might search for a vessel to set it in, he dared not put it down, for the sill was covered with thick dust.

He turned to the table, but its top was soiled with crumbs of mouldy bread and cheese mingled with dirt. He looked about the room, and not one spot could he see where he might lay the Lily without sullying its pure loveliness.

He called the little Vasily, and bade him stand and hold the flower. He then searched for something to put it in. He found an empty bottle, which he carried to the brook and washed and filled with sparkling water. This he placed upon the table, and in it set the Lily.

Then as he looked at the begrimed hands of little Vasily he thought to himself, "When I leave the room he may touch the flower and soil it." So he took the child and washed him, and combed his yellow hair; and the little one seemed to bloom like the Lily itself. And Ivan gazed on him in amazement, murmuring, "I never saw it thus before!"

From that hour a change came over Ivan. He cared tenderly for the little Vasily. He washed himself and combed his own hair. He cleaned the hut and mended its walls and furniture. He carried away the weeds and stones from the garden. He sowed flowers and planted vegetables. And the neighbours passing by no longer turned their heads aside, but stopping talked with Ivan, and sometimes gave the little Vasily presents of clothes and toys.

As for the Lily, seven days it blossomed in freshness and beauty, and gave forth a delicate fragrance; but on the eighth day, when Ivan and Vasily woke, it was gone. And though they sought it in hut and garden, they did not find it.

So Ivan and the little Vasily worked from day to day among their flowers and vegetables, and talked to their neighbours, and were happy. When the long winter nights came, Ivan read aloud about the Lilies of the Field, that toil not, neither do they spin, yet Solomon in all his glory was not arrayed like them. He read of that Beloved that feedeth among the Lilies, and of the Rose of Sharon and the Lily-of-the-Valley.

.   .   .   .

So Easter came again. And early, very early in the morning, Ivan and the little Vasily arose and dressed, and went and stood before the hut. And when the splendour of the coming day shone above the distant hills, lo! the young man came swiftly and lightly, and in his arms he bore crimson Roses.

He drew near, and, stopping before the hut, said sweetly:—

"Christ is risen!"

"He is risen, indeed!" responded Ivan and Vasily joyously.

"How beautiful is thy Lily!" said the young man.

"Alas!" answered Ivan, "it is vanished away, and we know not whither."

"Its beauty lives in thy heart," said the young man. "It can never die!"

And he took from his arm a crimson Rose and gave it to Vasily, saying:—

"Keep it fresh!"

But he smiled tenderly at Ivan, and passed on.

THE CHRISTMAS THORN OF GLASTONBURY

A Legend of Ancient Britain
Retold from William of Malmesbury
and Other Sources

THERE is a golden Christmas legend that relates
how Joseph of Arimathea — the good man and
just, who laid our Lord in his own sepulchre, —
was persecuted by Pontius Pilate, and how he
fled from Jerusalem carrying with him the
Holy Grail hidden beneath a cloth of samite,
mystical and white.

For many moons he wandered, leaning on his
staff cut from a White-Thorn bush. He passed
over raging seas and dreary wastes, he wandered
through trackless forests, climbed rugged mountains, and forded many floods. At last he came
to Gaul where the Apostle Philip was preaching
the glad tidings to the heathen. And there he
abode for a little space.

Now, upon a night while Joseph lay asleep in
his hut, he was wakened by a radiant light. And
as he gazed with wondering eyes he saw an Angel
standing by his couch, wrapped in a cloud of
incense.

"Joseph of Arimathea," said the Angel, "cross
thou over into Britain and preach the glad tidings

to King Arvigarus. And there, where a Christmas miracle shall come to pass, do thou build the first Christian church in that land."

And while Joseph lay perplexed and wondering in his heart what answer he should make, the Angel vanished from his sight.

Then Joseph left his hut and calling the Apostle Philip, gave him the Angel's message. And, when morning dawned, Philip sent him on his way, accompanied by eleven chosen followers. To the water's side they went, and embarking in a little ship, came unto the coasts of Britain.

There they were met by the heathen, who carried them before Arvigarus their King. To him and to his people did Joseph of Arimathea preach the glad tidings; but the King's heart, though moved, was not convinced. Nevertheless he gave to Joseph and his followers, Avalon, the happy isle, the Isle of the Blessed, and bade them depart straightway, and build there an altar to their God.

And a wonderful gift was this same Avalon, sometimes called the Island of Apples, and also known to the people of the land as Ynis-witren, the Isle of Glassy Waters.

Beautiful and peaceful was it. Deep it lay in the midst of a green valley, and the balmy breezes fanned its apple orchards, and scattered afar the sweet fragrance of rosy blossoms or ripened fruit. Soft grew the green grass beneath the

feet. The smooth waves gently lapped the shore,
and Water-Lilies floated on the surface of the
tide, while in the blue sky above sailed the fleecy
clouds.

And it was on the holy Christmas Eve that
Joseph and his companions reached the Isle of
Avalon. With them they carried the Holy Grail
hidden beneath its cloth of snow-white samite.
Heavily they toiled up the steep ascent of the
hill called Weary-All. And when they reached
the top Joseph thrust his Thorn-Staff into the
ground.

And, lo! a miracle! the Thorn-Staff put forth
roots, sprouted, and budded, and burst into a
mass of white and fragrant flowers! And on the
spot where the Thorn bloomed, there Joseph
built the first Christian church in Britain. And
he made it "wattled all round" of osiers gathered
from the water's edge. And in the chapel they
placed the Holy Grail.

And so, it is said, ever since at Glastonbury
Abbey — the name by which that Avalon is
known to-day — on Christmas Eve the White-
Thorn buds and blooms.

FORGET–ME–NOT!

Legend of Paradise

THERE is a sweet old legend that relates how on the green mead of Paradise there bloomed a little plant with clusters of blossoms white like driven-snow, and with tiny golden eyes.

All the other flowers of the mead had names, but the white plant had none. Adam had named them all, and given them their colours; but he had forgotten the little white plant. And when it saw that it was overlooked, it timidly lifted up its head, and cried: —

"Forget me not!"

All the other flowers of the mead were amazed at their little sister's daring, and the little white one trembled, but looked bravely up, and cried again: —

"Forget me not!"

Then — lo! — its snow-white blossoms were changed! They became bright blue like the sky, while all its tiny eyes were like gold stars set in the blue!

And ever since that day the children have called the timid little plant, "Forget-Me-Not"!

THE MAIDEN OF THE WHITE CAMELLIAS

Japanese Myth

It happened that in a village, not far from the foot of Mount Fuji, there once lived a poor lad named Yosoji. His father was dead, but his mother was still living, though she was very old and feeble. Yosoji's one thought was of his mother, and he worked hard and cheerfully from early morning until late evening to earn Rice and clothes for her. And in the night he did the work of the house, so that she should not get tired.

One Spring a terrible sickness came to the village, and many of the people caught the disease, among them Yosoji's old mother. Hour by hour she grew worse, until Yosoji thought her dying. Then his heart seemed breaking with sorrow, and he rushed from the house to find help. He remembered how the old folk of the village had often said that there was a hidden, health-giving spring of water on Fujiyama, so he ran to the mountain and began to ascend it.

Eagerly he climbed, forcing the bushes apart with his hands, so that the rosy-white petals of a hundred blossoms fell upon him, but he did not see them. The birds sang to him from the trees, but he did not hear them; for he was climbing breathlessly upward, thinking only of how to save his mother.

At last he reached a spot where three paths crossed, and stopped to consider which to take. As he did so, a lovely maiden stepped from the forest. She was clad in glistening white, and her long dark hair fell around her. In her hand she carried a branch of waxen-white Camellias.

"Yosoji," said the maiden, smiling sweetly. "Come, follow me to the spring from which gushes the Elixir of Life."

And turning, she waved her branch of Camellias for him to follow. He did so eagerly and full of wonder; and soon he found himself beside a rock from which gushed a crystal stream tinkling softly like a thousand silver bells.

"Take this gourd, Yosoji," said the maiden, "fill and drink. Then fill again, and carry the gourd home to your mother."

Wondering still more, Yosoji bent over the spring, and filled the gourd. As he touched the sparkling liquid to his lips he felt new life coursing through his veins, and his sorrow and fatigue fell from him like an old garment.

He rose up joyful, and stronger than ever before. Then the maiden led him back to the spot where he had met her.

"Farewell, O Yosoji, loving son of a good mother," said she, smiling. "After three days return here again, for you will need more of the precious water."

Having thanked her with many grateful words, Yosoji hastened down the mountain-side, and soon stood by his mother's bed. He put the gourd to her lips, and she fell into a calm and health-giving sleep. And when morning came she got up as well and brisk as she had been in her youth.

Three days passed by, and Yosoji returned to the mountain, and climbed to the spot where the three paths crossed. The lovely maiden met him, as before, and, smiling, led the way to the spring, where he again filled his gourd. Thanking her, he hastened to the village. He gave the water to some of the sick people to drink, and cured them.

Five times, in this wise, did Yosoji visit the hidden spring on Mount Fuji, and, guided by the maiden, fetched more of the Elixir of Life, and so cured all the sick in his village. Then the people began to praise Yosoji, and his fame spread to distant lands. People brought him gifts, and wherever he went they bowed before him.

But he was not happy. He knew that all the praise and thanks belonged to the maiden who had been his guide. He wished greatly to see her and thank her for what she had done.

So early one morning he set out for Mount

Fuji, carrying gifts to please the maiden. He climbed the mountain, and reached the spot where the three paths crossed. But though he waited long, the maiden did not come. At last, disappointed, he followed the path to the spring, and, on reaching the rock, found that the water no longer gushed from it. The spring was dried up, and only a few drops trickled down the face of the rock.

Then while he stood looking sorrowfully about, he saw the lovely maiden herself standing near him. She was more beautiful than ever. Her dark hair floated around her like a cloud; her robe glistened like Snow in the sunlight; her eyes smiled more sweetly than ever; while the branch of Camellias in her hand gave out a subtle and delicious perfume.

Seeing her thus, Yosoji uttered a cry of delight, and sprang forward to lay his gifts at her feet. But the maiden gently waved her branch of Camellias, and a soft, rosy cloud descended from the very top of Mount Fuji, and, enveloping her, floated back to the top again.

Then Yosoji knew that his lovely guide was none other than the Fairy Maiden of the "Never-Dying Mountain," who had taken compassion upon him, and had saved his mother.

And while he gazed upward with rapture, the branch of Camellias, giving out its delicious perfume, fell at his feet.

PRINCESS PEONY

Japanese Tale

In the long, long ago lived the Princess Aya.
She was betrothed to the son of the great Lord
of Ako, and the wedding day was set. While the
plans were being made for the marriage feast,
the Princess lived in her father's ancient castle.

She loved to walk on moonlit nights in the
garden of the castle. She often wandered along
the silvery paths, crossed the tiny bridges over
singing cascades, and rested by a clear blue lake,
near the margin of which grew beds of many
lovely, fragrant flowers. But above all, the
Princess loved the sweet-scented Peonies; and
when the moon flooded the Peony-bed with its
white beams, she lingered long near her favourite
flowers.

It chanced one evening that the Princess was
stooping over the Peonies to breathe their fragrance, when her foot slipped. Immediately a
handsome young man, in a robe embroidered
with Peonies, rose from among the flowers and
caught her in his arms. He set her safely on her
feet, then vanished as mysteriously as he had
appeared.

The Princess's maids were bewildered. Who
could he be, they asked, and how had he passed

the guard and entered the garden. As for the Princess she was very sad. She longed to see the young man, and thank him for having saved her from falling. She forbade her maids to tell any one what they had seen. They then returned to the castle.

The next morning the Princess was sick. She could not sleep or eat. Day by day she grew worse. The best of physicians could do her no good, nor discover the cause of her strange illness. At last her father sent for one of her maids, and questioned her closely. She admitted that some days before the Princess had slipped by the Peony-bed, and had been rescued by a handsome young man, who had vanished as wonderfully as he had come.

That evening, the weather being very hot, her father had the Princess carried into the garden and a musician summoned to amuse her. Scarcely had the musician begun to play when there rose up from behind the Peonies the same young man, in his Peony-embroidered robe. As soon as the music stopped, he vanished. The Princess's father had the flower-bed searched, but there were no signs of any one having disturbed the Peonies.

So it happened again the second night.

On the third night, the Princess's father stationed a guard hidden near the Peony-bed. As soon as the music began, the young man suddenly appeared, and stood motionless among the flowers. Then the captain of the guard sprang forward and seized the youth around the waist.

Instantly a warm steam filled the captain's face, and still grasping the youth, he fell fainting to the ground. The guard hurried to assist him, and as they raised him to his feet, behold, they saw that, instead of grasping the young man, he was holding a large and brilliant Peony!

Every one was amazed, and the Princess carried the Peony back to her room. She put it tenderly into a vase of water, and placed it near her pillow. It seemed to have a strange effect upon her. Day by day she grew better, and more beautiful than ever. She cared for the Peony herself, and the flower became fresher instead of fading. For several weeks it remained strong and blooming.

At last the Princess's wedding-day arrived. The marriage was celebrated, and immediately afterward she found the Peony no longer brilliant and fresh, but dead and drooping its once bright head.

And from that day people called her Princess Peony.

THE CHRYSANTHEMUM CHILDREN

Japanese Tale

IN ancient days, in Japan, a powerful noble was overthrown in battle, and fled for safety. His faithful servitor, Kikuo, went with him. They sought refuge among the mountains, where they lived in a small house surrounded by a garden.

Kikuo dearly loved his master, and endeavoured to comfort him in every way, in order to make him forget his troubles. Knowing that he loved Chrysanthemums, Kikuo planted a large bed of the flowers. His master was much pleased, but continued to grieve over his losses until he fell sick and died.

Kikuo wept night and day over the humble grave. Then, determining to make it beautiful, he began to plant and tend a border of Chrysanthemums of every colour and size. Red, white, pink, yellow, bronze, and cream-coloured blossoms made the spot lovely.

At length Kikuo had planted so many and tended them so carefully that the border was thirty yards wide, and people came from all over the country to see the wonderful sight. Every day Kikuo watered the plants, and dug about their roots, and stroked the flowers, until he began to love them tenderly and to grieve whenever a plant died or was broken by the wind.

One day Kikuo was taken ill, and feared that he must die. In the night he heard a rustling sound upon his veranda, and, looking out, saw many little children moving about in the moonshine. They were light and graceful in movement, and had large heads of curling hair. They were clad in waving robes of green, embroidered with red, white, pink, yellow, bronze, and cream-colour. They were whispering together, and their voices sounded like sighing breezes.

As Kikuo gazed upon them, he knew they were not ordinary children. Then three of them, entering his room, approached his couch.

"Beloved Kikuo," they said, "we are Golden Dew, White Dragon, and Starlit Night, the children of the Chrysanthemums that you have tended so gently. And because of all you have done for us, we wish to make you well. Therefore, drink this Chrysanthemum Dew."

And as they spoke they held out flower-cups filled with sparkling dew-drops. Kikuo took the cups and drank the Dew, which tasted fragrant and delicious.

Just at that moment a puff of wind passed through the room, and the Chrysanthemum children vanished. Then Kikuo fell asleep, and when he awoke in the morning he found himself perfectly well.

From that day forward he devoted all his time to raising Chrysanthemums, and his garden was so beautiful that it became famous throughout Japan, for nowhere else could be found flowers of such wonderful colours and shapes, nor in any other garden did they grow in such profusion.

MAIDEN WHITE AND MAIDEN YELLOW

Japanese Tale

LONG, long ago, in Japan, there grew in a green meadow two wild Chrysanthemums, called Maiden White and Maiden Yellow. They were sisters, and were very happy until one day an old gardener, who was walking through the meadow, stooped beside the yellow flower.

"Ah, Maiden Yellow," he said, stroking her petals, "I will take you with me, and plant you in my beautiful garden, where you shall have fine clothes and delicate food to eat."

So, in spite of the tears of poor Maiden White, who shed many drops of dew, the old gardener dug up Maiden Yellow by the roots, and carried her away in his arms.

Soon she found herself growing in his garden among thousands of lovely flowers. Winding paths of silver sand led to tiny bridges and musical cascades, while near by stood a small tea-house hung with tinkling silver bells. And Maiden Yellow was so happy that she forgot her lonely white sister in the green meadow. Her petals grew longer and more numerous, and curled. She became straighter, and prouder, and so beautiful that no one would have known her for the wild-flower of the green meadow.

One day the steward of a very rich noble came to the garden. His master wished a Chrysanthemum of perfect form having sixteen petals. The old gardener took him to see Maiden Yellow, and when she saw him coming she stood even straighter and prouder than before, and held her large golden head very high, for she thought, "Surely he will choose me."

But the steward said that she was too proud and had too many petals, and that he wished a perfect flower, simple and graceful; so thanking the gardener, he departed.

As he was returning to his master's castle, he happened to pass through the green meadow where Maiden White stood weeping in her loneliness. And when he saw her perfect form and her sixteen snow-white petals, he was delighted, and, picking her carefully, carried her to the castle.

When his master, the rich noble, saw Maiden White, he placed her in a transparent vase. Then sending throughout Japan, he summoned the greatest artists to his castle. They came from far and near, and sat down to paint the noble's crest.

And for this crest they used Maiden White's beautiful face in a hundred graceful poses. They painted her on the noble's armour, on his lacquer boxes, and on the great panels of his hall. She was embroidered on his robes, on his cushions, and on his quilts. Everywhere her lovely face appeared; and the noble's crest became the most admired of all crests in the land of Japan.

As for Maiden Yellow, she continued to bloom for some time in the garden among the other flowers. She grew for herself alone. Daily she became more proud and stately, and drank up the fragrant Dew.

But one day she felt stiff and dry. Her once bright head turned brown and sere. And when the old gardener found her thus, he cut her down and threw her upon the rubbish heap.

IN THE ROSE–BOWER WITH THE ROSE QUEEN

QUEEN ROSE

I will not have the mad Clytie
   Whose head is turn'd by the Sun;
The Tulip is a courtly quean,
   Whom therefore I will shun;
The Cowslip is a country wench;
   The Violet is a nun; —
But I will woo the dainty Rose,
   The Queen of every one!

THOMAS HOOD

CUPID IN THE WILD–ROSE HEART

Then came we to great breadths of shady wood,
And him, the boy, the son of Venus fair,
The apple-rosy Love, we found within.
No arrow-bearing quiver, no bent bow
Was by him. High in heavy foliaged trees
They hung. And he, the while, lay chained in sleep,
Embosomed in a Rose's heart of hearts!
And sleeping, smiled.
           And all around his head,
And all around his honey-dripping lips,
Murmured the yellow Workers of the Hive!

PLATO

ADVENTURES OF CUPID AMONG THE ROSES

Retold from Anacreon, Moschus, Lucian, and Other Sources

I

NAUGHTY LITTLE CUPID

THE most mischievous of all the dwellers in Jupiter's shining Palace on Mount Olympus was little Cupid. Rosy, dimpled, and laughing, with bright hair floating around his shoulders, and small wings fluttering, he flew about, shooting tiny darts at all whom he met. And whoever felt the prick of one of his darts straightway fell in love.

The naughty little boy did not spare even the greatest among the Dwellers-on-Mount-Olympus. Laughing with glee, he aimed at the heart of Jupiter himself; then he turned his bow against Apollo-of-the-Golden-Beams and grim Pluto, King of Hades. He even shot a sharp but tender little dart into the breast of his mother Venus the Beautiful.

"Naughty boy!" cried Venus in anger. "Unless you stop such goings on, I will break your bow and quiver, or clip your wings."

But Cupid would not listen, and still flew

about, slyly shooting at all whom he met. Though
his mother caught him by his small wings, and
whipped him with her sandal and with myrtle
rods, and even bound his eyes with a fillet,
quickly forgetting his punishment, he flew away
again to find other hearts to wound.

II

RED ROSES OF NECTAR

AT first Roses were all white. This is how they
came red: —

Cupid loved the White Roses and played
among them in the meadows of earth, where
they grew large and fragrant. Sometimes he
wreathed them into garlands for his head, sometimes he chased the Butterflies that alighted on
their petals, and sometimes he curled himself up
to sleep in the heart of a big open Rose. Yes,
Cupid loved the White Roses better than any
other flowers.

Now it happened one day that all the Dwellers-
on-Mount-Olympus were feasting together, and
Cupid was carrying Jupiter's golden cup filled
with fragrant red Nectar. The naughty boy
held the cup so carelessly that he spilled a few
drops. They fell on some White Roses, and the
flowers immediately foamed up in wreaths of
bright Red Roses.

That is how Red Roses first came.

ROSES OF NECTAR

III

HOW PANSIES CAME COLOURED

NEXT to Red and White Roses, Cupid loved the gleaming purple and golden-faced Pansies. And this is how they came coloured: —

At first all Pansies were milk-white. So they were, until one day when Cupid aimed a tiny dart at Diana-of-the-Bended-Bow.

Now of all the Dwellers-on-Mount-Olympus, the most stately and cold-hearted was Diana. She loved nobody, and cared for nothing but hunting. With her feet thrust in buskins, her robe tucked up for speed, a quiver on her back, and a bow in her hand, she rushed over the hills and through the woods, chasing the flying game; while behind her ran all her pretty Nymphs armed with bows and arrows.

So one day naughty Cupid, who wished to see cold-hearted Diana love somebody, shot a tiny dart at her. It just grazed her skin, and falling to earth, struck the heart of a milk-white Pansy.

Ever since then, Pansies have been stained a gleaming rich purple and gold.

IV

WHY VENUS LIKED DOVES

BUT Cupid liked to play more than he did to carry about cups of Nectar. Indeed, he liked to sit on the back of a Dolphin and rush through the green sea-waves, or to climb trees, or to borrow Pan's Syrinx and breathe sweet music through it. But more than all he delighted to play at soldier, and march around with a helmet on his golden hair, a pike over his shoulder, and a buckler on his arm.

Quite often he romped with his mother Venus, she holding high her bow and quiver, while he jumped to catch it. Sometimes, too, they took little baskets and went into the meadows to gather Roses and yellow Crocuses.

Now, one day Venus took Cupid, and her maid the little Nymph Peristera, to gather flowers. Around Venus's head circled a whole host of chirping Sparrows, and wherever she stepped, a carpet of bright blossoms sprang up under her feet.

"Come, my mother," cried Cupid, "let us make a wager, and see who can pick the most flowers!"

So they made a wager.

Cupid worked very hard, scratching his tiny hands on thorns, and bruising his little bare feet on stones, but at last he had an armful of blossoms, all that he could carry. But his mother Venus had a great many more than he.

Soon Cupid found out why his mother had so many more — the little Nymph Peristera had helped her pick them!

So he changed the sly little maid into a Dove.

That is why Venus always had Doves as well as Sparrows flying around her head, and why she liked to hear them bill and coo.

V

VENUS'S LOOKING GLASS

Now, Venus had a wonderful mirror that made any one who gazed into it look beautiful, no matter how ugly he really was.

One day she lost it in a meadow, and a silly shepherd-lad, with a frightfully ugly countenance, picked it up. But no sooner did he glance into it than he appeared so handsome to himself that he fell in love with his own looks.

So he kept on gazing and gazing so rapturously that he did not hear Cupid come winging his way to find his mother's mirror.

When Cupid saw it in the silly man's hands, and caught a glimpse of the grimaces he was making at himself in the glass, he snatched it away, and broke it into a thousand glittering pieces that fell among the grasses.

And each tiny bit of the mirror became a lovely bright blossom, bell-shaped, and so brilliant that it seemed to reflect the sunbeams.

Cupid called the plant on which these blossoms grew Venus's Looking Glass; and you may find it in the flower-garden to-day, standing near the Roses.

VI

CUPID'S DARTS

AT first Cupid had only a tiny bow and quiver, but no darts.

His mother Venus, who dearly loved her little son in spite of his naughty tricks, wished to give him a new plaything. So she decided to ask her husband, Vulcan-the-Smith, to make him some darts.

Now Vulcan lived in his forge in a cavern under the roots of Mount Ætna. There the flames roared upward and the noise of his hammer, anvil, and bellows was heard night and day. So Venus, in her car drawn by Doves, flew down to Mount Ætna and entered the cavern. When Vulcan knew what she wanted, he laid aside the gold and silver Dogs he was making for King Alcinous, and fashioned some tiny darts just the size for Cupid's bow.

Now, Venus did not wish her little son to kill any one, so she dipped the points of the darts in honey. But Cupid shyly dipped them in gall. After that they could wound though they could not kill.

Then the naughty little boy hung garlands of fresh Roses around his neck, put a crown of them on his head, and flew down to earth. There he wandered about, riding on the back of a fierce Lion, that at his touch grew as tame as a Dove.

As he rode about he shot at every one that passed by, both young men and maidens. And whoever felt the prick of his dart straightway fell in love.

This is why Cupid's darts wound the heart, but do not slay.

VII

LOST! LOST!

Now while Cupid was riding about on his tame Lion wounding young men and maidens with his honey and gall-tipped darts, his mother Venus missed him from the Shining Palace on Mount Olympus. Wringing her white hands she ran to and fro, looking for him everywhere.

"Lost! Lost! My child!" she cried. "To him who finds my little boy and brings him safely home, I will give kisses three!

"But let whoever searches for him beware! Cupid's voice is honey-sweet, while his heart is full of gall! Bright are his clustering curls, but a brighter quiver hangs upon his back. His hands are tiny, but very far can they shoot his wound-giving darts. Like a winged bird he flutters up and down, nestling in the hearts of young men and maidens. He holds a little bow, and an arrow ever ready to fly; but most dangerous of all he grasps a small blazing torch.

"If you find him, catch him, hold him, bind him! If you see him weep, do not pity him, hold him very fast! If he offers to kiss you, flee, for his kisses burn like fire!

"Lost! Lost! My child! My child!"

VIII

CUPID PUNISHED

THUS cried his mother Venus, and getting into her car drawn by Doves, she flew down to earth. There among the Roses she found poor little Cupid, weeping bitterly.

Wringing his tiny hands, he ran to meet her.

"I'm lost! I'm lost! my mother!" he cried. "And — oh! — oh — I'm dying! See my finger! I lay down to sleep in a big Rose-heart, and a little Snake — a Bee they call it — stung me! Oh! — oh — how it hurts! — I'm dying!"

"Naughty boy, mischievous child," said his mother, smiling, "if a Bee's sting hurts you so much, tell me, how much do the hearts suffer that you so cruelly wound with your darts?"

IX

WHY ROSES HAVE THORNS

THEN to comfort her little son, Venus caught all the buzzing Bees that were sipping honey from the Roses, and strung them on Cupid's bowstring like a chain of brown and yellow beads.

Then she took the Bees' sharp stings and placed them along the stem of the very Rose in whose heart Cupid had been sleeping.

That is why Roses have thorns, — so the Wonder Story says.

LEGEND OF THE ANEMONE AND THE ROSE

Retold from Bion and Ovid

ONCE upon a time, in the wonder days of old, little Cupid, the Winged Love, was playing in the lap of his mother Venus the Beautiful, and while he was giving her many sweet kisses, his arrow chanced to prick her white skin.

Now when Cupid's arrow wounds any one, even slightly, love enters one's heart. So Venus, pricked by Cupid's arrow, pushed her little son away. Then she looked down from her throne on Mount Olympus, and saw a handsome youth, named Adonis, hunting in the Idalian Grove of Cyprus.

Straightway she was charmed with his beauty, and, getting into her car drawn by white Swans, descended to the Grove. She took a bow and arrow in her hand, and joining Adonis, cheered on his Dogs, and helped him kill swift Hares and Deer with branching horns.

Day after day together they hunted the harmless wild things of the wood. But it happened one morning that Adonis was going to hunt by himself.

"Beware, sweet lad," said Venus; "follow only the gentle wild creatures. Avoid the fierce Boars and the ravening Lions, lest they turn and devour you."

Thus she warned him; then getting into her swan-drawn car, she flew away to Mount Olympus.

No sooner did Adonis reach the Idalian Grove than his Dogs started the fiercest Wild Boar of the wood. It turned upon him with foaming tusks and rolling eyes. He struck it with his spear, but it rushed against him, thrusting one tusk into his side. Then Adonis fell upon the soft green grass, and sighing died.

The flowers in the Grove withered with pain, the leaves of the trees rustled with grief, and the birds ceased singing and drooped their heads. Swiftly Cupid came, winging his way to the spot where Adonis lay dead.

And with Cupid were all the little Loves his companions. They wept, they wrung their tiny hands, and they hovered and fluttered above Adonis. One Love broke his feathered arrow, one cast away his bow and quiver, one loosened Adonis' sandal, another brought water in a golden urn and bathed his head, and still another with his soft wings fanned his white forehead.

Venus heard the sighing and lamenting. She turned her swan-drawn car, and hastily descended to the Grove. And when she saw her Adonis lying dead, she groaned, and beat her bosom, and tore her crimson robe.

And for every drop of blood that fell from Adonis's side, she shed a tear like a pearl. Then, lo! as the tears touched the soft grass, they were changed into wind-blown Anemones! And the drops of blood grew up into glowing red, red Roses!

So, says the old Greek wonder tale, Anemones and Roses came into the World.

THE ROSE–TREE QUEEN

Old Legend

OH, long, long ago there lived a beautiful maiden named Rhodanthe. She was Queen of Corinth, and gave her people such wise laws that her fame spread to many lands. From the east, from the west, from the south, from the north, kings, princes, and warriors came to woo her.

But though Rhodanthe was wise and beautiful, she was proud and cold; so she haughtily bade her suitors go back at once to their own lands. This they refused to do, and wandered about the palace in such great numbers that she commanded them all to appear before her throne.

"Oh, ye Kings, Princes and Warriors," said she, "why do you remain here in idleness? Are you cowards that you shun war and valorous action? Go back at once to your lands and seek fame in courageous deeds; then may you return to Corinth."

At these words the suitors hung their heads with shame, and, hastening from the palace, mounted their steeds and galloped away — all except three, who determined to remain and win Rhodanthe's hand.

Every day these three lovers pressed around her throne, or shouted in the corridors, or followed her through the streets clamouring to be heard.

"No rest shall you have day or night, Queen Rhodanthe," they cried, "for by day will we dog your footsteps, and by night will we sigh under your window. No rest shall you have until you choose one of us for a husband."

So it was, night and day Rhodanthe had no rest, for the three followed her everywhere with cries and shouts.

At length she could endure it no longer, and, guarded by her attendants, hastened to the temple of Diana-of-the-Bended-Bow, for she thought that her suitors would not dare to enter there.

But scarcely were she and her people safely inside when the three came bursting in, and, lifting her up, placed her on Diana's shrine, crying: —

"Let Rhodanthe be as great as Diana! Let Diana's image give place to her!"

Now Rhodanthe looked so beautiful as she stood there, her silken robes trailing, her golden crown glittering, and her eyes sparkling with pride and pleasure, that all her attendants shouted: —

"More beautiful than Diana is our Queen!"

Now these words reached Diana's brother, Apollo-of-the-Golden-Beams, as he was sitting in his Palace in the Sun. In anger he turned his scorching rays on Rhodanthe.

Her feet cleaved to the shrine, and took root there. From her stretched-out arms and finger-tips sprouted green leaves and twigs. Her body was changed into a stem and her head became a large blushing Rose. And there she stood, no longer a maiden, but a tall, stately Rose-Tree, the Queen of all flowers.

Her attendants still guarded her, for they had been transformed into sharp thorns, and were set round about her stem.

Her three lovers were become a Worm, a Bee, and a Butterfly.

THE BLUSH–ROSE AND THE SUN
Roumanian Legend

IT was early morning, and a Princess came down into her garden to bathe in the silver waves of the sea. The transparent whiteness of her complexion shone through her blue veil like the Morning Star through the azure Sky

She sprang into the sea, and played among the golden rays of the Sun, that sparkled in the dimples of the laughing waves.

The Sun stood still to gaze upon her. He forgot his duty. He covered her with warm kisses.

Once, twice, thrice, Night took up his sceptre, and returned to rule over the earth, but found the Sun still there, making all things bright with his rays.

Then the angry Night changed the Princess into a Rose. And this is why the Rose always hangs her head and blushes when the Sun gazes on her.

HOW MOSS–ROSES CAME

Legend of Paradise

THERE is a lovely wonder tale of Paradise, telling how, on a sweet Spring day, the Angel who takes care of the flowers lay down to rest beneath a fragrant Rose-Bush. All the quiet night she had been sprinkling the grass and flowers with Dew, so she was very tired. She rested her head among the Roses, and slept. When she awoke, she said:—

"Most beautiful of all my children, I thank you for your refreshing shade and delicious perfume. If you could only speak, and ask me for a favour, how gladly would I grant it!"

"Adorn me with a new charm," said the Rose-Bush.

So the Angel adorned the Roses with a delicate veil of green moss.

THE SULTANA OF THE FLOWERS

Persian Tale

AT first the Lotus was Sultana of all the flowers. But she would fold her petals at night, and sleep. This the flowers did not like, so they demanded another Sultana.

The White-Rose was then given them to rule over their Kingdom. Very beautiful was this maiden White-Rose. She was tall, majestic, and robed in snowy garments, while her stem was encircled with a protecting guard of sharp thorns.

The poor little Nightingale fell in love with her charms. He pressed his heart so recklessly against her cruel thorns that his blood trickled over her white petals, and stained them crimson.

Are not the petals of the Crimson-Rose white near her heart, where the blood of the poor little bird could not reach?

KING SULEYMAN AND THE NIGHTINGALE

Persian Tale

ONCE upon a time, the birds of every colour and every kind appeared before King Suleyman's throne to complain of the Nightingale.

"He disturbs our slumbers," they said, "with his plaintive warblings. All night long he presses his breast against a rose-thorn, while he pours forth his sorrowful melody."

So King Suleyman sent for the Nightingale, and questioned him.

"Alas! wise King!" sobbed the Nightingale, "do you not know that at the sound of my voice the Rose first bursts from her bud? Indeed, it is my distracting love for her that makes such melancholy notes gush from my bosom, until, overpowered by her perfume, I fall swooning at her feet."

Then King Suleyman, pitying the poor little bird, commanded him to return to his garden, and sing whenever he pleased to his Love the Rose.

THE NIGHTINGALE AND THE ROSE

Retold from Sa'di

ONCE upon a time, in a certain beautiful garden, a Nightingale had built his nest in the branches of a Rose-Bush. It so happened that a poor little Ant had fixed her dwelling at the root of this very bush, and was managing as best she could to store her wretched hut with food.

The Nightingale fluttered around the bush, singing melodiously to his love the full-blown Rose, while the Ant, night and day, was industriously gathering up grains of food for Winter.

So the thousand-voiced bird, fascinated by his own sweet song that echoed among the trees, sang ravishingly by day; but when the moonlight silvered the garden, he whispered his sad, sweet secrets to his love.

The poor Ant could not help admiring the airs and graces of the beautiful Rose and the blandishments of the Nightingale, but she murmured to herself: —

"Time alone can show what will be the end of all this frivolity and talk."

After the flowery season was passed away, and the bleak time of Winter was come, sharp thorns alone remained upon the Rose-Bush, for its flower and leaves were gone. The Raven sat on the branch where the Nightingale's nest had been.

Storms howled through the garden in their fury, and the yellowed leaves of the trees were whirled to the ground. The breath of Winter chilled and blasted all things, while the clouds poured down hailstones like pearls, and flakes of snow like camphor floated on the air.

Then suddenly the Nightingale returned to the garden to seek his love. But the bloom of the Rose was gone, and the fragrance of Spikenard was vanished. In spite of his thousand-voiced tongue, he stood stupefied and mute.

Then a Thorn turned to him, and said: —

"How long, silly bird, will you watch for the Rose to come back? This is the season when you will have to sing to a Bramble in the absence of your charmer!"

The Nightingale cast down his eyes upon the ground in sorrow, but he perched upon the bush and waited.

There was nothing for him to eat, and he was hungry. He was too delicate and helpless to earn even a small livelihood. Then he recalled the Ant, and said to himself: —

"Surely she used to have a dwelling under this Rose-Bush; and she was very busy storing up food for Winter. I will lay my wants before her. Maybe she will take pity on my distress, and bestow a little charity upon me."

So, like a poor beggar the half-famished Nightingale stood at the door of the Ant's house, and said: —

"Generosity is the bringer of prosperity! I was wasting my precious life in idleness, while you, toiling hard, were laying up a hoard of food. How good and kind you would be if you should spare me a little of it!"

The Ant replied: —

"Night and day you spent in idle talk, while I was attending to the needful. You were taken up with the fair blandishment of the Rose, and were busy in admiring the blossoming Springtime, while I laboured hard.

"Did you not know that every Summer has its Winter, and every road an end?"

WITH THE SOARING TALKING BIRDS

THE ROBIN

A Welsh Myth

My old Welsh neighbour over the way
   Crept slowly out in the sun of Spring,
Pushed from her ears the locks of gray,
   And listened to hear the Robins sing.

Her grandson, playing at marbles, stopped,
   And, cruel in sport as boys will be,
Tossed a stone at the bird, who hopped
   From bough to bough in the Apple-tree.

"Nay!" said the grandmother, "have you not heard,
   My poor, bad boy! of the fiery pit,
And how drop by drop, this merciful bird
   Carries the water that quenches it?

"He brings cool dew in his little bill,
   And lets it fall on the souls of sin:
You can see the mark on his red breast still
   Of fires that scorch as he drops it in.

"My poor Bron rhuddyn! My breast-burnt bird,
   Singing so sweetly from limb to limb,
Very dear to the heart of Our Lord
   Is he who pities the lost like Him!"

"Amen!" I said to the beautiful myth;
   "Sing, bird of God, in my heart as well;
Each good thought is a drop wherewith
   To cool and lessen the fires of hell."

Prayers of love like rain-drops fall,
   Tears of pity are cooling dew,
And dear to the heart of Our Lord are all
   Who suffer like Him in the good they do.

JOHN GREENLEAF WHITTIER

BIRD CALLS

WHY THE OWL CRIES HOOT! HOOT!

Breton Legend

ONCE upon a time, there was no fire. Then the little Wren flew up to the Sun and brought some down. But the poor little thing's feathers were so scorched and burned that she was quite naked.

Then all the birds came together, and each gave her a feather, except the Owl.

"I will not give her a single feather," said he. "I have only enough for myself. Winter is coming and I shall be cold."

"Very cold indeed shall you be!" cried the King of the Birds. "From this time on you shall shake and shiver with cold. And if you leave your home by day, all the birds of the air shall tear off your feathers."

That is why the Owl, during the day, sits at home in his hollow tree; and why, when he flies about by night, he cries: "Hoot! Hoot!" for he is shivering with cold.

WHY THE LITTLE BIRD THAT BRAGS CRIES CUCKOO!

Friesland Legend

ONCE upon a time, the Cuckoo sang a queer song of his own. He was very proud of it, although the song was not much to brag of.

One day he flew into a town, and asked the people: —

"What do you think of the Nightingale's song?"

"Melodious," said the people.

"What do you think of the Lark's?"

"Delightful," said the people.

"What do you think of the Blackbird's?"

"Very sweet," said the people.

"Then pardon my blushes," said the Cuckoo, "but what do you think of *me?*"

"To tell the truth," said the people, "we never hear your name mentioned."

"What! my name never mentioned!" cried the Cuckoo. "Then I will fly about and sing it instead of my song, so that every one shall know my name."

That is why the little bird that brags cries:

"Cuckoo! Cuckoo!"

WHY CROWS CAW

Eskimo Legend

ONCE upon a time, there were some little Eskimo children. In the Moon of the Falling Leaves, their mother took them to a forest by the sea to gather spruce boughs.

After they had gathered a heap, and piled them up on the beach, their mother told the children to stay there, and watch the boughs carefully, while she went to catch some Salmon.

The children stayed, but they forgot to watch the boughs, and ran up and down the beach playing with the waves.

By and by their mother came back. The children were gone! She called each by name, but instead of their voices she heard only the hoarse cawing of some Crows that were flying in circles above her head.

So it was! Those disobedient children had all been changed into Crows! And to-day they go flying about the world, crying hoarsely:—

"Caw! Caw!"

WHY THE PEWEE LOOKS FOR BROTHER

Mohammedan Legend

ONCE upon a time, the Pewee was a lovely Princess. She heard that her beloved brother was coming to see her, so she caught up a pot of boiling milk to refresh him, and, placing it on her head, ran out to meet him.

But, alas! her brother was not coming at all, and the boiling milk blistered and burned her head. Then she started out to find him. Night and day, over mountains and desert wastes, she sought him, crying: —

"Brother!   O Brother!"

At last Allah the Compassionate, the Merciful, pitying her grief, changed her into a bird, so that she might the more easily go to and fro over the earth.

So still she wheels in her long flights, and cries: —

"Brother!   O Brother!"

And all good women, when they hear her sad cry, throw cold water into the air to cool the burn on her head where her black crest grows.

THE GREEDY BLACKBIRD

Old French Tale

ONCE upon a time, the Blackbird was pure white. One day he saw the Magpie hiding away a store of gold and jewels.

"Where did you get those? How can I get some?" he asked.

The Magpie did not like being found out; but he said: —

"You must go into the depths of the earth, and find the palace of Pluto, King of Riches. Offer to sing to him. For your pay, he will let you carry off all the riches you can hold in your beak. You will have to go through cave after cave, each more full of treasure than the last. But you must not touch anything until you have seen the King of Riches and sung to him."

Off flew the Blackbird that was a Whitebird. Down a tunnel, through cave after cave, he flew, until he came to one with silver walls, and piled with silver coin. But remembering what the Magpie had said, he passed on.

Lo! the floor of the next cave was covered with gold-dust, and piled high with gold coin. The Whitebird stood still and looked about him with greedy eyes, then forgetting what the Magpie had said, he thrust his wide-open bill into the gold-dust.

Immediately, with a rush and a roar, a terrible Demon appeared, snorting fire and smoke. He leaped at the Whitebird, who with a shriek of fear, turned and flew from the cave, and out into the daylight again.

But the thick smoke had changed the Whitebird black. And so he is to-day, while his beak is stained the colour of the gold-dust he had tried to steal.

And whenever he sees a boy creeping along a hedge with a stone in his hand, he utters a terrified shriek, for he thinks it is the Demon coming back.

THE SPICE BIRD

Retold from Pliny and Other Sources

IN ancient days, in Arabia, the land of gold and spices, there lived a wondrous bird called the Phœnix.

So very wondrous was he that his purple body gave out rays of light like sunbeams. He wore a ruffle of brilliant golden plumage about his neck, and a crest on his head. His wings were red and yellow, while his long tail, blue and rose-coloured, swept behind him as he flew to and fro above the Date-palms.

Five hundred and forty years he lived, then he built himself a nest of Cassia and sprigs of Incense, and filled it with fragrant spices and perfumes. On these he lay down to die, mournfully singing his own funeral dirge.

Then from his bones and marrow sprang a tiny Worm, that grew larger and larger until it became another Phœnix, with bright rays like sunbeams issuing from his purple body, and a long tail, blue and rose-coloured, sweeping the air.

This new Phœnix took a quantity of Myrrh, and shaped it like an egg, and in it placed the remains of his father. Then he carried the egg carefully to Egypt, and laid it down in the City of the Sun.

Back to Arabia, the land of gold and spices, he flew, and after another five hundred and forty years built himself a nest, as his father had done, of Cassia and sprigs of Incense, and filled it with fragrant spices and perfumes.

On these, singing sadly, he lay down and died; and another Phœnix flew up from the nest.

And so it was, in those ancient wonder days, every five hundred and forty years a Phœnix died, and a new Phœnix flew up from his spicy nest, and carried the remains of his dead father in an egg of Myrrh to the City of the Sun.

KING PICUS THE WOODPECKER

Retold from Ovid

ONCE upon a time, there was a handsome young King named Picus. So handsome was he that even the Naiads rose from the streams, and the Dryads peeped from the trees, to watch him as he passed by.

But, though he was admired by everybody, he never looked at any one except his own wife, a lovely Nymph. Sweet Voice was her name, for so wondrous was her voice that at the sound of her sweet singing, wild beasts were tamed, rocks and trees danced, and birds paused in their flight to alight upon her shoulders.

One day King Picus put on his purple cloak, fastened on his collar of yellow gold, and taking two lances in his hand, mounted his horse, and rode forth into the wood. Soon he was chasing the Wild Boars and piercing them with his lances. But he did not see the wicked Enchantress Circe, who was hiding among the trees.

She gazed at King Picus and was astonished at his beauty. The herbs and plants she had been gathering, to mingle in her evil potions, fell from her hands. She muttered a magic spell, and straightway a phantom Wild Boar rose up in King Picus' path, and plunged into a thicket.

The King sprang from his horse and followed the animal; while Circe, uttering strange words, darkened the Sky and sent up a thick mist from the ground. So King Picus lost his way, and soon wandered to Circe's Palace-hall.

The wicked Enchantress came out to meet him. She was clad in crimson robes, and held a golden cup in her hand.

"Welcome, King Picus," she said, in softest tones. "Welcome to my happy hall! Here rest, and feast, and live without sorrow. Perfumed garments, mingled wines, and rich viands shall be yours, and music and dance shall sooth you night and day. Drink, then, O King Picus, from this cup I hold, and be welcomed to my hall!"

But King Picus answered her roughly: —

"Woman, whoever you are, I abhor you! Think not to hold me by offers of riches and happiness! Sweet Voice, my wife, awaits me in my palace, and of her only I think night and day! I will not drink from your cup, nor will I enter your hall!"

"Ungrateful wretch!" cried Circe. "Take then your doom!"

And hissing like a snake, she turned herself first twice to the west, then twice to the east. Thrice she touched King Picus with her wand, and three times she repeated a charm.

He fled, but wondered to feel himself rising

lightly in the air. Feathers covered his body,
wings sprouted from his shoulders. He was not
a man, but a bird. His wings took the purple
colour of his robe, and his neck wore a collar of
yellow feathers. Flying to a tree, he clung to
its trunk, and pecked its wood with his long
hard beak.

As for Sweet Voice, all in vain she awaited
his coming. Day after day she wandered through
the wood calling his name, and singing sadly as
does a dying Swan. With grief she pined and
pined, until little by little she melted away and
vanished into air.

Only her voice was left, and it sang and sighed
among the trees — even among the very trees
where King Picus the Woodpecker was tapping
the bark in the shadow of the cool, rustling
leaves.

THE MAGPIE MAIDENS

Retold from Hesiod and Ovid

THE NINE SISTER MUSES

OH, most lovely of all mountains in those golden wonder times was Mount Helicon in Greece. On its sloping sides stood mighty trees; laughing rivers ran through its valleys; flowers of every hue smiled up from its grass. No poisonous thing grew in its meadows; while the air, crystalline and pure, enwrapped the whole mountain like a cool, transparent veil.

But the most beautiful of all was the Grove on its summit, where statues gleamed like snow amidst the pale green shade of vines and trees. For this Grove was the abode of the Nine Sister Muses, the daughters of song, and the loveliest of all Olympian maidens.

Daily, with delicate nimble feet they danced in the Grove, or bathed in the violet-hued spring of Aganippe. Sometimes, hand in hand, they climbed to the Fountain of Hippocrene, from whose bubbling waters the winged horse Pegasus was wont to drink long sweet draughts. And always, as they climbed upward, they uttered such musical notes that the birds paused in their flight to listen, the Bees ceased their humming, and Pegasus, tossing his head, waved his silvery wings in delight.

And always the Nine Sister Muses sang about the Dwellers-on-Mount-Olympus. They sang of stately ægis-bearing Jupiter, of Minerva the grey-eyed and wise one, of Venus the Beautiful and her naughty little son Cupid, of Aurora the rosy-fingered child of Dawn, who, clad in saffron robe, each morning flung open the purple Gates of Day. But more often they sang of Apollo-of-the-Golden-Beams, dwelling in the Palace of the Sun that was raised high on columns of radiant gold, with ivory polished roof, and folding doors like brightest silver. And so the Nine Sister Muses, singing together, made Mount Helicon ring with their entrancing voices.

But, alas! one day harsh, discordant noises, and the rustlings of strong wings, came from the trees that swept with their boughs the Fountain of Hippocrene. Then there sounded a dreadful chattering among the leaves, and the Nine Muses, fled back in disgust, to their Grove.

And this is how that dreadful chattering came to disturb Mount Helicon: —

THE NINE SISTER PIERIDES

OVER the lands of Pella ruled King Pierus, and in his richly adorned palace dwelt his daughters, the Nine Sister Pierides. Very haughty and foolish they were, and proud of their voices. They grew prouder and prouder, until one day the eldest said: —

"We, and not the Nine Sister Muses, should inhabit the delightful Grove on Mount Helicon. Come, let us go thither, and put the Muses to shame with our melodious voices."

So they hastened away to Mount Helicon, and climbed to the Fountain of Hippocrene, where the Nine Sister Muses were singing sweetly to Pegasus, while he drank deeply from the sparkling water.

"Cease, O ye vain Muses, your empty vulgar noises," cried the eldest of the Nine Sister Pierides. "We are come to have a contest with you. Let us each sing, and if our charming voices make us the victors, you must retire at once and forever from this spot. But if you overcome us, — which is not at all likely, — we will return to our snow-capped mountains. Let us now to the contest, and do you call the Nymphs of the streams of Helicon to be our judges."

Now the Nymphs of the streams of Helicon heard these words as they were peeping from the water, and quickly came crowding to the Fountain of Hippocrene and sat down on the rocks to listen.

Then the eldest of the Nine Sister Pierides opened wide her mouth, and with harsh, discord-

ant sounds sang mockingly of the Dwellers-on-
Mount-Olympus. She scoffed at ægis-bearing
Jupiter; she sang scornfully of Diana-of-the-
Bended-Bow and of Diana's brother, Apollo-of-
the-Golden-Beams. And as her voice rose higher
and higher, and became noisier and noisier, the
sky darkened, and gusts of wind shook the trees.
And so it was until she had ended her song.

Then rose up one of the Nine Sister Muses,
Calliope-of-the-Silver-Voice. Her long hair was
wreathed with ivy, and her robe swept the
dewy grass. Her sweet voice soared like a bird
through the air. She sang of Daffodils and
Roses. She sang of little Proserpina romping
with her playmates in a flowery meadow. She
sang of grim King Pluto and his plunging steeds,
and of Mother Ceres the Keeper-of-all-the-Corn-
fields-in-the-World. And such wondrous silvery
melody poured from Calliope's throat, that the
Sun shone brightly forth, and the very Moon and
Stars seemed to stand still to listen. And then
Calliope ceased her singing.

"O ye Nine Sister Muses," cried the Nymphs
of the streams of Helicon, "never before have
we heard such entrancing, melodious strains!
To you, and to you alone, belongs the victor's
crown, and not to these stupid Nine Sister
Pierides who disgust all nature with their loud
noises."

At this the Nine Sister Pierides burst into abuse

and clamour. But the Nine Sister Muses looked silently and sternly upon them.

Then Calliope said: —

"O ye mockers! Your insolence and pride alone merit reproof. But now to these you add abuse and violence. Therefore receive your just punishment."

And even while she was speaking, the Nine Sister Pierides, menacing her with their hands, tried to grasp her long hair. But, lo, wonder of wonders! quills sprouted from their fingers; their arms were covered with feathers, and became wings!

In despair they beat their breasts with their wings, for they felt their feet change into claws; and each saw the others' faces shoot out into long hard beaks. And, behold, the Nine Sister Pierides were no longer maidens, but were become Magpies, the scandal of the woods, for their pride and love of chattering still remained.

Then they rose into the air with a rushing sound, and settled in the trees whose boughs swept the Fountain of Hippocrene. And so dreadful was their chattering and their harsh, discordant clamour, that Pegasus, stretching his silvery wings in fright, soared into the sky, while the Nine Sister Muses fled in disgust back to their Grove.

THE BOY THAT THE EAGLE STOLE

Retold from Lucian and Other Sources

THERE was great excitement in the Shining Palace on Mount Olympus. Hebe, the royal cupbearer, had fallen and spilled the fragrant Nectar. It had gushed in a rich tide over the golden floor of the banquet-hall.

Yes! rosy, dimpled Hebe, the youngest and most charming of all the Dwellers-on-Mount-Olympus, had stumbled awkwardly as she was running about carrying a great golden goblet, and had fallen. So Jupiter, her father, said that she should be royal cupbearer no longer.

"I'll serve the Nectar. Let me be your butler," growled Vulcan-the-Smith, rising from the banquet-board.

So just as he was, all covered with soot and sparks, for he had come straight from his forge, he laid aside his tongs, and went limping around the hall, a golden goblet in either hand. But when he served Nectar to Jupiter, the goblet was so dirty with soot that everybody burst out laughing, and Jupiter looked about for another cupbearer.

Now on leafy Mount Ida, a beautiful boy with pink cheeks and flowing hair was hunting the wild Stags. Prince Ganymede was his name.

And the minute that Jupiter saw him, he changed himself into a mighty Eagle, and swooping down caught him up in his talons, and carried him off.

In vain did Prince Ganymede's attendants stretch out their hands to save him. In vain his Dogs bayed angrily, pointing their noses toward the sky. Jupiter bore him up and up to the Shining Palace on Mount Olympus. There he clad him in unfading Olympian garments, and made him royal cupbearer.

So ever after that Prince Ganymede ran about the banquet-hall carrying in his rosy finger-tips great golden goblets filled with honey-sweet Nectar.

THE ROBE OF FEATHERS

Japanese Myth

IT was Springtime, and along the pine-clad shore there came the sound of birds. The blue sea danced and sparkled in the sunlight.

A fisherman was sitting on the shore. He chanced to glance up at the Pine-Trees, and saw a beautiful robe of pure white feathers hanging on a bough. He took it down, and as he did so, a lovely maiden came toward him from the sea.

"Oh! restore that robe to me, dear fisherman," she pleaded.

He gazed at her in wonder. Then he shook his head. "This robe," said he, "I have found, and I mean to keep it. It is a marvel, and should be placed among the treasures of Japan. No, I can't possibly give it to you."

"Oh!" cried the maiden pitifully, "I cannot go soaring up into the sky without my Robe of Feathers. If you keep it, never again may I return to the Palace of the Moon. O good man, I beg of you to restore my robe!"

But the fisherman was hard-hearted, and refused to relent.

"The more you plead," said he, "the more determined I am to keep what I have found."

"O dear fisherman!" cried she again, "say not

so! Without my Robe of Feathers I am like a helpless bird with broken wing. Without my wings I cannot soar to the blue plains of the sky, and to the Palace of the Moon."

Then the fisherman's heart was softened. "I will restore your Robe of Feathers," he said, "if you will dance for me."

Then said the maiden: "I will dance here the dance that makes the Palace of the Moon turn around so mysteriously. But I cannot dance without my Robe of Feathers."

"What!" cried the fisherman, "do you think I'm such a fool as to give up this robe? If I do, you will surely fly away without dancing."

"The pledge of mortals may be broken," answered the maiden sternly, "but the Moon Folk never lie."

At these words the fisherman was ashamed, and quickly gave her the Robe of Feathers. Straightway she put on the pure white garment. Then she struck the strings of a lute, and began to dance to the sweetest music, such as the fisherman had never heard before.

And while she danced and played, she sang of beautiful, strange, far-off things. She sang of the mighty Palace of the Moon where thirty monarchs ruled, fifteen in robes of white when the orb was full, and fifteen robed in black when the Moon was waning.

Then soon her dainty feet ceased tapping the

sand. She rose into air, the white feathers of her robe gleaming against the Pine-Trees, and against the blue sky itself.

Up, up, she went, still singing and playing, until her song was hushed — until she reached the glorious shining Palace of the Moon.

PAN'S SONG

From Britannia's Pastorals (retold)

Hark to the Pipes of Pan! This is a song of the Golden Age on fair Britannia's shores.

The all-drowsy Night, in car of jet with steeds of iron grey, was coursing through the darkened sky, when the silver-footed Thetis, Queen of the Ocean Wave, left her coral palace beneath the sea.

She mounted her silver car, inlaid with Pearls and precious stones, and urged her foaming steeds through the rolling billows. Singing Naiads, garlanded with seaweed, and riding on sporting Dolphins, were her guides.

Onward they rushed through the blue Ægean Sea, then past the happy shores of Cyprus, and from thence toward Britannia's snowy cliffs. So runs my song away!

. . . .

In those golden days, on Britannia's meads, Shepherds fed their bounding flocks. On oaten reeds they piped their songs to maids who danced upon the green, wreathed in chains of flowers, in which were twined the Daisy and the scented Violet, the Lily and the Primrose, too, the orange-tawny Marigold, the wind-blown Columbine, the fragrant Honeysuckle, and the Kingcup yellow as true gold.

And in those far-off happy days, Marina was the fairest maid to whom the Shepherds sung. But wretched fate! On a time when none was nigh to succour her, Limos, savage caitiff, gaunt with hunger, seized the trembling maid and bore her to his den.

There in the Cave of Famine he locked her behind iron bars. Then, laughing in his evil heart, he went by night to a distant sheepfold to steal the Shepherds' choicest lambs.

So in the Cave of Famine, Marina lay, sighing and lamenting. She heard the cruel sea waves beat against the walls, and saw the Sun's feeblest rays creeping through the bars. Thirst and Hunger were her jailers there; and the pangs of Famine darted through her tender sides. But Heaven, that lends a hand when human helpings fail, did not forget the gentle maid.

A little Robin Redbreast, in the clear day, sat singing sweetly on a thorn-bush near her cave. Then Marina, pitying the dear bird, fearing lest Limos should return and kill him, rose and tried to frighten him away.

"Poor, harmless creature," said she, sighing, "go seek some brook, and to its tinkling fall sing with your happy fellows. Or better still, do this, you loving bird: fly to the good greenwood and grassy mead, and tell the Shepherds of my cruel fate. Or, if instead you tarry here, do me a deed of charity. When my soul shall have left this form, cover my poor body with a green sheet of leaves gathered in some sweet valley!"

When Robin Redbreast heard this plaint, he sang no more, but flew away.

Then in a trice back again he came to the thorn-bush by Marina's bars. And from his beak hung by its slender stem a red ripe Cherry. Through the bars he flew, and nestled in Marina's bosom, and there he laid the Cherry, and straightway was gone again.

Soon he returned with a cluster of fragrant Strawberries. These, too, he laid in Marina's bosom, and hasted away.

And so he fed her. No sweet or toothsome fruit grew in all the wood, but the kind bird knew it and brought it to the maid.

Then to the seashore he hastened, and flew to and fro above the sand, until he found an Oyster with shell half open, yawning in the Sun.

The wily Redbreast took a little pebble, and pressed it between the pearly lips, and the Oyster tried to close its shell, but could not. Then the bird thrust in his head and pulling out the Oyster, flew with it to Marina's cave, and put the morsel between her lips.

And so he fed her with juicy fruits and refreshing meats.

When the tide rolled out, and many shells were left high upon the shore, Marina, looking through her bars, saw — oh, wondrous sight! —

Doves and Eagles, Hawks and Ospreys, standing on the sand, and before each lay an Oyster, yawning in the Sun, and each bird held in his beak a pebble, as he had seen Redbreast do.

But the birds were not so wise as he! Some put their pebbles too far within the shells, others used stones too small and smooth. And when they thrust in their heads between the pearly lips, the shells closed tight and cut their necks in two.

"Unhappy birds!" Marina sighed, "thus to meet your deaths! Not wise you were, like little Robin Redbreast!"

The feathered hours flew by, and ten days and nights came and went, and still the kind bird fed Marina, and still the caitiff, Limos, came not. He, too, had met his death.

In the distant sheepfold the angry Shepherds found him ere he could steal their choicest lambs. With many shouts they pursued him across the plain. Seizing him, they bound him with iron chains to a rock, and left him there to die. His eyes flashed with flames; he ground his teeth and tore at his chains, and died.

So in the Cave of Famine Marina lay with none to free her. Alas! her wretched state!

.   .   .   .

While Aurora, rosy-fingered Child of Dawn, touched the Sky with opal lights, swiftly to fair Britannia's shore the car of Thetis came.

Near to the Cave of Famine drew the car, and the silver-footed Queen heard Marina's plaint — unhappy maid! — in fear of grief and hunger. For on that same rosy day, — oh, mournful chance! — the willing little Redbreast had flown too swiftly through the thorns, had pricked his tender breast, and so had died.

When the silver-footed Queen heard the maid's lament, her heart was moved by such dire distress. To her she called great Triton, and bade him free the sorrowing maid.

Meanwhile, the Naiads caught Marina's tears in Oyster shells. Those sparkling briny drops changed into rare pearls of Orient, and the Naiads strewed them on the shore and in the clefts of Britannia's snowy rocks.

Then the Ocean Queen drew Marina into her silver car, and swiftly urged her foaming steeds through the leaping billows toward the coral palace underneath the waves, where joy and bliss for ever reign.

The all-drowsy Night, in jetty car, drove his iron-grey coursers through the darkened sky.

So the song of Pan is ended!

WHERE FLORA REIGNS THE QUEEN OF FLOWERS

FAIR FLORA'S FLOWERS

The Daisy scattered on each mead and down,
A golden tuft within a silver crown,
(Fair fall that dainty flower! and may there be
No Shepherd graced that doth not honour thee!)
The Harebell, for her stainless azured hue,
Claims to be worn of none but those are true.
The Yellow Kingcup Flora them assigned
To be the badges of a jealous mind.
Flora's choice buttons of a russet dye,
Is Hope even in the depth of misery.
The Pansy, Thistle all with prickles set,
The Cowslip, Honeysuckle, Violet,
And many hundreds more that graced the meads,
Gardens and groves, where beauteous Flora treads,
Were by the Shepherds' daughters (as yet are
Used in our cotes) brought home with special care.

WILLIAM BROWNE OF TAVISTOCK (*condensed*)

QUEEN FLORA'S GLOVES

The Foxglove on fair Flora's hand is worn,
Lest, while she gathers flowers, she meet a thorn.

ABRAHAM COWLEY

WHY CROCUS HOLDS UP HIS GOLDEN CUP

Retold from Ovid

IN the bright Springtime, in those days when golden-beamed Apollo shed his happiest rays upon Earth, Flora, the bride of the gentle West Wind, Zephyr, walked in her garden, where streams of sparkling water sang among the trees.

"Beloved," said Zephyr, "rule now the Empire of Blossoms! Be Queen of all the Flowers!"

And he breathed through the garden, and from the soft grass sprang up dew-washed Violets, Lilies, and Daffodils; while from Flora's lips Red Roses fell to the ground, and, taking root there, bloomed again.

So Flora, Queen of all the Flowers, tended the plants and unfolded the buds. The birds burst into song, the streams sang more gayly, while Apollo with his golden beams dissolved the Dew upon the leaves. And Flora's four maidens, Spring, Summer, Autumn, and Winter, arrayed in their painted robes, ran hither and thither among the flowers, gathering the blossoms into light baskets.

Then from among the trees came dancing the Three Graces, swaying hand in hand, — Aglaia, Thalia, and Euphrosyne. And they, too, ran hither and thither among the flowers, plucking

Violets and Daffodils, and twining delicate garlands for Flora's head.

Now in all that wide and beautiful garden only two people were unhappy, — a youth and a Nymph. And very unhappy they were, for the Nymph loved the youth, but he mocked at her love.

Flora heard them disputing and hurried to their side.

"Crocus and Smilax!" she cried. "Unhappy ones, who are disturbing the peace of my garden! Become flowers at once!"

And straightway the youth pined and grew smaller, until he peeped from the grass, no longer a youth, but a slender green stem holding up a golden cup.

The Nymph, she sank to the grass and was changed into a delicate trailing vine.

And so it is to-day. Crocus stands in the fresh, green grass holding up a golden or a purple cup, while Smilax trails upon the ground.

LEGEND OF THE FRAIL WINDFLOWER

Old Legend

WOULD you like to know why the pale-tinted buds of the frail Windflower tremble so in the breeze? And why its delicate petals are so cruelly torn by the cold North Wind?

Once upon a time, at the court of Queen Flora,

there dwelt a little Nymph called Anemone. She was of such rare and delicate beauty that no flower in all Queen Flora's garden was so lovely. Even the gentle West Wind, Zephyr, liked to ruffle her soft hair and fan her pink cheeks with his wings.

But though Anemone was beautiful, she did not always obey Queen Flora, who grew displeased at her little Nymph's naughty ways. So she touched her with her wand, and changed her into a frail Windflower with tightly closed pink and lilac buds. Then, to punish her still further, she took her out of the garden, and planted her along the forest-walks.

But Zephyr, pitying the lonely little flower, hurried to the forest, and, breathing gently on her folded buds, coaxed them to unclose.

Then, because he was such a fickle Wind, blowing this way and that just as he chose, he soon forgot about sad little Anemone. He flew back to Queen Flora's garden; while his rough brother Boreas, the cold North Wind, came rushing down from his icy home, and tore her frail petals with his rude breath.

That is why — so the Wonder Story says — little Anemone is called the Windflower; and why, in the early, early Springtime she stands trembling, and waiting for Zephyr to coax open her tight buds; and why, when Zephyr has flown back to Queen Flora's garden, she bows her

fragile blossoms before the rude cold blast of
Boreas his brother.

THE PRIMROSE SON

Old Legend

OF course you have heard how, in those golden
wonder days of old, Flora the Beautiful was
Queen of all the Flowers.

In her garden grew tall proud Tulips, slender Daffodils with drooping golden heads, and
Hyacinths that softly rang their scented bells.
And everywhere along the paths, Crocus held
up his yellow and purple cups; while Smilax
trailed delicately around the trees and upon the
ground.

In the Spring and Summer time, Queen Flora
walked joyously through her garden, shedding
glowing Red Roses from her mouth; while
everywhere she stepped, whole troops of little
flowers came crowding from the mould, and,
lifting their radiant heads, smiled up at her.

But in all that wide and lovely garden there
was no Primrose to sweetly tremble in the breeze,
when the gentle West Wind, Zephyr, stirred its
leaves.

Now, it was by Flora's magic art that Crocus,
a troublesome youth, and Smilax, a quarrelsome
Nymph, had once been transformed into the
flowers that bear their names. So when Flora

saw that there was no Primrose, she walked about her garden to find a youth to change into one.

Soon she found her own pretty son, Paralisos, stretched out in the soft grass, where he was weeping and wailing for a maiden he had loved and lost. And, because he would not be comforted, and was mourning himself to death, Flora touched him with her wand.

Instantly he was changed into a green Primrose Plant, holding up its staff of pale sweet blossoms. And there, night and day, Paralisos stood, drinking the dew from his flower-cups; folding his petals when the Sun shone too brightly, and opening them again in the cool of the day to scent his mother's garden.

Then, because she loved her Primrose Son so dearly, she planted him in meadows and woods, so that all the world might see him.

THE LILIES WHITE

FAIR was the day, but fairer was the maid who wandered through the good greenwood. Sweet was the air, but sweeter was her breathing perfumed with Roses. Bright was the Sun, but brighter were her eyes.

A green silk frock she wore. Loose from her waist fell a mantle stitched with gold and green, and lined with rich carnation silk. Around the mantle's edge hung a deep fringe of twisted gold, as if on the margin of a brook a thousand yellow flowers did fringe its course. Upon her feet she wore a pair of buskins soft, studded with Orient Pearls and Chrysolite. A silver quiver she hung upon her back, and in her hand she held a bow of scented wood. All lovely was she, with heavenly Roses in her face.

But her slender hands were whiter than all else on earth. Yes, whiter than the snowy Swans that float upon the bosom of the lake. So dazzling were they, that when she stooped to pick the meadow-flowers, they shone like white stars fallen in the grass. No bloom on earth was half so white as they.

Sweet Flora, Queen of all the Flowers, saw them, and was ravished at the sight.

"I must," she said, "make blossoms as lovely as her hands."

Now all the Lilies, in those days, were black. Often the dancing Fairies left their happy play, and, pulling the black flowers, filled their cups with honey from the hollow trees. Then to the banquet of the Fairy Queen they hastened, bearing the jetty cups.

These Queen Flora saw, and said, "Such unsightly blossoms will I change to flowers that shall vie for beauty with this maid's fair hands."

She touched the black Lily cups, and straight

their jetty petals grew pure and crystalline, and set with tiny golden crowns within.

Yet these new flowers, so stately with their crowns, were not half so snowy as the maid's dazzling hands, but were of a transparent whiteness, — shadowy, like the breasts of Venus' Doves.

WILLIAM BROWNE OF TAVISTOCK (*retold*)

THE CORNFLOWER YOUTH

Old Legend

A VERY foolish youth was Cyanus. He loved the bright Cornflowers more than he did his father and mother. When the Cornflowers were in blossom, he neglected his duties, and spent all his time wandering among them.

One day he put on a fringed robe of bright silk, blue like his favourite flowers, and went to walk in Queen Flora's Cornfields. He wandered about, picking the blue blossoms, and wreathing them into garlands and chains.

He forgot his home, he forgot to sleep, he forgot to eat. Day after day and night after night he wandered to and fro, growing weaker and weaker, until he sank down fainting among the Cornstalks.

Then lovely Flora, Queen of all the Flowers, came to walk in her fields. She found Cyanus lying there among his scattered blossoms, that he had loved so dearly and so foolishly. And, as she liked to change youths into flowers, she waved her wand above him.

Straightway he grew smaller and smaller. His body became a stem rooted in the ground, while his robe was changed into little, bright blue Cornflowers.

And there he is to-day, dressed in emerald green leaves and sky blue blossoms, standing among the growing Corn.

Very busy is Cyanus, holding high his florets, like Fairy vases filled with rich Nectar for Queen Flora's thirsty Bees. And when his florets are faded away, the Fairy vases become beautiful green cradles filled with little Winged Children, whose tiny pinions are adorned with delicate jet-black plumes.

Then comes rollicking Zephyr, blowing through the Corn. First he rocks the cradles. Then — *puff! puff!* and all the little Winged Children go sailing away before Zephyr's breath. And wherever a Winged Child falls in the Cornfield, another little Cyanus springs out of the ground. All this you may see for yourself, if you will watch in the Cornfield.

THE LITTLE NYMPH WHO RANG THE BELLS

Old Legend

VERY wonderful and beautiful was the Garden of the Hesperides on the edge of the world. In it grew a magic fruit-tree on which hung Golden Apples that looked like little suns shining on its branches.

Three lovely sister-maidens watched the tree, dancing hand in hand about its trunk. And their clear-voiced singing rang through the garden, and livened the heart of their father, old Giant Atlas, who was holding up the heavy sky on his head and hands. Indeed their sweet singing soothed the temper of the terrible Dragon with a hundred heads, who lay around the roots of the magic tree, coiling and uncoiling his glittering scales.

Morning, noon, and night the three Hesperides, as the sister-maidens were called, sang and danced, while they watched lest any rash mortal should enter the garden.

Morning, noon, and night the hundred heads of the Dragon vomiting flames, watched with all their two hundred eyes lest the Hesperides themselves should pluck some of the Golden Apples.

And there was still another watcher, for the Dragon had a little Nymph to wait upon him. Campanula was her name. She carried a bunch of tiny silver bells to ring if any mortal tried to enter, or if the Hesperides drew too near the tree.

One day Campanula was weary and forgot her duty for a moment. Just then a thief came leaping over the wall. She ran for her bells, but before she could reach them he thrust his sword through her heart.

Ah! then what weeping and wailing there was in the garden! All the flowers drooped their heads and shed tears of dew. The Butterflies folded their wings and quivered with grief. Even the Hesperides stopped their clear singing, and old Giant Atlas groaned louder than before.

Lovely Flora, Queen of all the Flowers, heard the weeping and wailing, and came hurrying into the garden. She pitied poor little Campanula so, that she touched her with her wand. Immediately the little Nymph was changed into a Bluebell swinging its bright blossoms in the wind.

And each Summer since then little Campanula, standing in the garden-bed, announces the coming of the hot days by ringing her silver-sweet amethyst bells.

THE MARIGOLD ARROWS

Retold from Abraham Cowley and Other Sources

ONCE upon a time, when Queen Flora reigned over the flowers, a maiden named Caltha lived in Flora's garden.

Caltha loved to look at the bright Sun, and all day long she sat with her eyes fixed on his shining disk. At night she did not sleep, but sat watching for him to rise again.

So she gazed and gazed, until one morning she

melted under his hot beams, and vanished away. And in her place grew up an orange-coloured Marigold, dew-washed with tears.

All day long the Marigold turned her face toward the Sun as he moved through the sky. At night she closed her petals, only to open them again at the first touch of his morning beams.

When at last her blossom faded and withered away, she still stood there holding up her calyx, shaped like a little quiver filled with tiny painted arrows.

So Queen Flora, walking in her garden, saw the quiver. She plucked it and hung it on her shoulder. Then she put on buskins made of Lady's-slippers, and drew Foxgloves on her slim white hands; and, holding a small bow, she went to hunt Butterflies among her flowers.

Soon a large pale yellow Butterfly flew past her, alighting on the stem of a pale yellow Rose. And there he hung motionless with closed wings, hoping that Queen Flora would mistake him for a Rosebud. But Zephyr breathed upon him, and made him flutter. So Queen Flora knew that he was not a flower, and shot a bright Marigold-arrow straight through his body.

Then she took the Butterfly home to her palace, and made a wee yellow fan of his wings.

FRUIT ON THE ROSE–BUSH
Old Legend

SINGING birds, humming Bees, blooming flowers, and bubbling water-springs, all these were in Queen Flora's lovely garden. Above them towered giant Oak-Trees rustling and whispering secrets. Inside each Oak-Tree dwelt a little Dryad with nut-brown hair wreathed in oak-leaves.

One day Queen Flora found her largest tree blasted, and its little Dryad lying dead among the ferns; while all the other Dryads stood about, crying and wringing their hands.

"Do not weep, my children," said Queen Flora, "for your little companion shall reign over all my flowers."

Then Queen Flora sent out her messengers the Bees, to invite the Dwellers-on-Mount-Olympus to come to the garden.

Straightway through the air came flying Apollo-of-the-Golden-Beams, trailing his long purple robe, and Venus the Beautiful in her car drawn by Swans. While through the lush green meadows came walking Bacchus, Keeper-of-All-the-Vineyards-in-the-World. After him followed Vertumnus and Pomona hand in hand, he bearing aloft his big cornucopia filled with Pears, Plums, and Peaches, and she clasping a basket of bright red Apples.

Then Zephyr the West Wind breathed gently through the garden, and Flora touched the little Dryad with her wand. Lo! the little maiden's body became a lovely green bush; but there were no flowers growing on it.

Apollo warmed its roots with his bright beams. Bacchus poured nectar of dew-drops over it. Vertumnus anointed it with his choicest perfumes, while Pomona scattered her smallest, brightest, and reddest Apples upon its branches.

Then Flora touched the bush with her wand, and from each small red Apple sprang a blossom like a diadem of crimson perfumed petals.

After that Venus stepped forward, set many tiny thorns along the stems of the bush; — and she called its flowers *Roses*.

That is how the little Dryad of the blasted Oak came to reign over all the flowers in Flora's garden; and why, in the Autumn, little bright red Apples grow on Rose-Bushes.

PLUCKING MEADOW WONDER BLOSSOMS

THE TROOPING FLOWERS

The air is soft, the dale is green,
The Kingcups troop in golden sheen,
And nod the Windflowers gaily;
The meadow-ground
Is bright around,
And waxes brighter daily.

The Rivulet tumbles down the rock,
And thrills and shudders to the shock,
Sings on through shady places;
Where'er it goes,
The Pale Primrose
Runs with it little races.

The Roving Cowslips, born at night,
Steal forth into the early light,
Beside a stubble meadow;
And there the cold
Dark stream in gold,
Melts murmuring out of shadow.

ANON. (condensed)

FAIRY CLOTHES

Next followed on

The Fairy Nobles, ushering Oberon
Their mighty King, a prince of subtile power,
Clad in a suit of speckled Gillyflower.
His hat, by some choice master in the trade,
Was (like a helmet) of a Lily made.
His ruff, a Daisy was, so neatly trim,
As if of purpose it had grown for him.
His cloak was of the velvet flowers, and lined
With Flowers-de-Luces, of the choicest kind.

WILLIAM BROWNE OF TAVISTOCK (condensed)

LEGEND OF THE TRAILING ARBUTUS

Iroquois Legend

MANY, many Moons ago, in the far Northern Land beside the Lakes, there lived an old man alone in his lodge. His locks were long, and white with Age and Frost. The fur of the Bear and the Beaver covered his body, but none too warmly, for the Snow and Ice were everywhere.

Over all the Earth was Winter. The North Wind rushed down the mountain-side, and shook the branches of trees and bushes as it searched for song-birds to chill to the heart. But all living creatures had crept into their holes, and even the bad Spirits had dug caves for themselves in the Ice and Snow.

Lonely and halting, the old man went out into the forest seeking wood for his fire. Only a few fagots could he find, and in despair he again sought his lodge. He laid the fagots on the Fire, and soon they were burned; and he crouched over the dying embers.

The wind moaned in the tree-tops, and a sudden gust blew aside the skin of the Great Bear hanging before the door. And, lo, a beautiful maiden entered the lodge.

Her cheeks were red like the petals of Wild Roses. Her eyes were large, and glowed like the eyes of the Fawn at night. Her hair was black like the wing of the Crow, and so long that it trailed upon the ground. Her hands were filled with Willow buds, and on her head was a crown of flowers. Her mantle was woven with sweet grasses and ferns, and her moccasins were white Lilies laced and embroidered with petals of Honeysuckles. When she breathed, the air of the lodge became fragrant and warmer, and the cold wind rushed back in affright.

The old man gazed on her in wonder. "My daughter," said he, "you are welcome to the poor shelter of my cheerless lodge! It is cold and desolate, for I have not wood enough to keep my Fire burning! Come, sit beside me, and tell me who you are, that you wander like a Deer through the forest. Tell me also of your country, and your people who gave you such beauty and grace. Then I, who am the mighty Winter, will tell you of my great deeds."

The maiden smiled, and the sunlight streamed forth from the grey clouds and shot its warmth through the roof of the lodge. Then Winter filled his pipe of friendship, and when he had put it to his lips, he said: —

"I blow the breath from my nostrils and the waters of the rivers stand still, and the great waves of the lakes rest, and the murmurings of the streams die away in silence."

"You are great and strong," said the maiden,

"and the waters know the touch of your breath. But I am loved by the birds, and when I smile the flowers spring up all over the forest, and the meadows are carpeted with green."

"I shake my locks," said Winter, "and, lo, the Earth is wrapped in a covering of Snow!"

"I breathe into the air," said the maiden, "and the warm rains come, and the covering of Snow vanishes like the darkness when the Sun awakens and rises from its bed in the morning."

"I walk about," said Winter, "and the leaves die on the trees, and fall to the ground. The birds desert their nests and fly away beyond the lakes. The animals hide themselves in their holes."

"Oh! great are you, Winter," said the maiden, "and your name is to be feared by all living things in the land! Cruel are you, Winter! More cruel and cunning than the tortures of the Red Men! Your strength is greater than the strength of the forest trees, for do you not rend them with powerful hands?

"But when I, the gentle maiden, walk forth, the trees burst into leaves, and the sweet birds build again their nests in the branches. The winds sing soft and pleasant music to the ears of the Red Man, while his wife and papooses sport in the warm sunshine near his wigwam."

As the maiden ceased speaking, the lodge became very warm and bright. But the boasting

Winter heeded it not, for his head drooped upon his breast, and he slept. The maiden passed her hands above his head, and he grew smaller and smaller.

The Bluebirds came and filled the trees about the lodge, and sang; and the rivers lifted their waves and foamed and leaped along. Streams of water flowed from Winter's mouth, and he vanished away, while his garments turned into glistening leaves.

Then the maiden knelt upon the ground, and took from her bosom a cluster of delicate flowers, fragrant and rosy-white. She hid them beneath the leaves, and breathing on them with love, whispered: —

"I give you, O precious jewels, all my virtues and my sweetest breath. Men shall pluck you with bowed head and bended knee."

Then she arose, and moved joyously over the plains, and among the hills, and through the valleys. The birds and the winds sang together, while the flowers everywhere lifted up their heads and greeted her with fragrance.

So always in the early Spring, wherever the maiden stepped, grows the Trailing Arbutus.

WILLIAM W. CANFIELD (adapted)

THE WOOD–VIOLET THAT WAS A MAIDEN

Old Legend

WOULD you like to know why the little blue Wood-Violet peeps so shyly up from under her broad green leaves, and why she hides away so modestly in the woods and beneath shady hedges?

This is what the Wonder Story tells: —

Once upon a time there was a charming modest little maiden named Ianthis. She was one of the attendants of Diana-of-the-Bended-Bow. Often she and her companions, Arethusa and Syrinx, wandered about the woods picking flowers and berries.

But unlike her two companions, who went bare-armed the better to use their bows when hunting, the modest little Ianthis wrapped herself in a dusky blue veil, and tended a herd of Cows that were gently browsing in a fragrant meadow.

Now it chanced one day that Apollo-of-the-Golden-Beams was looking from his Palace in the Sun, and caught a glimpse of Ianthis's sweet eyes gazing shyly up at him through her blue veil. Straight he flew down to the meadow.

But Ianthis saw him coming, and timidly ran away.

"O Diana!" she cried piteously, "whither shall I flee from Apollo? Shall I hasten to the mountains, and there hide my head?"

Then came Diana's answer calm and clear: —

"Sister, little Sister, do not go near the mountains, for on their tops Apollo likes to sit and watch the open sky. Hide, instead, in some shady nook, for Apollo dislikes cool shadows."

So Ianthis ran into the wood, and hid herself in a cool thicket beside a brook.

And there Apollo found her. He parted the branches, and when he saw her shy, blushing face gazing at him, he stretched out his arms to carry her off to his Palace in the Sun.

But Diana, who loved her little maiden well, touched her face in its dusky blue veil, and it became a modest, lovely Violet; while her body sank down among the stones and leaves, and was a green-spreading Violet-plant.

That is why to-day — so the Wonder Story says — Ianthis, the little blue Wood-Violet, hides by the sides of streams and beneath shady hedges, peeping timidly up from under her broad green leaves.

THE DANDELION FAIRIES

Old Tale

ONCE upon a time, there was a meadow inhabited by Fairies. Brownies and Elves skipped about in the grass. Wood-Gnomes lived in the trees. The cheerful little Flower-Sprites, in their gay gowns, flitted about in the sunshine.

Suddenly human children ran into the meadow. They trampled down so many flowers and shouted so loudly that all the Fairies were frightened, and scampered hither and thither looking for some place to hide in.

The Gnomes hid themselves deep in the earth. The Elves curled themselves up in the cracks of the rocks. The Brownies jumped into the hollow trunks of trees.

But the little Flower-Sprites loved the sunshine, and did not wish to live in the dark ground and in hollow trees. Indeed, the poor little things did not know where to hide; so they clung to the stems of plants. Then the Fairy Queen changed them all into flowers, the colours of the gowns they were wearing.

Now, a number of the Flower-Sprites were wearing new frocks made of bright yellow Sunbeams. And when the excitement was over they found themselves huddled together on one stalk and staring straight up at the Sun. All the littlest Sprites were in the centre, while the oldest and strongest were formed into a circle to protect the littlest ones.

They were a Dandelion Flower!

KATHERINE M. BEALS (*adapted*)

THE STORY THAT THE BUTTER-
CUPS TOLD

THE Buttercups were glittering amongst the fresh green leaves, like bright little suns. How gaily they sparkled! And could they sing? Well, listen to the story they sang:

"*Chime! Chime!*

"The bright warm Sun shone on a little garden, on the first warm day of Spring. His beams rested on the white walls of a cottage. Close by bloomed the first yellow Buttercup of the season, glittering like gold in the Sun's warm ray.

"An old woman sat in her arm-chair at the cottage-door, and her granddaughter, a poor but pretty servant lass, came to see her for a short visit.

"When she kissed her grandmother, there was gold everywhere! — gold of the heart in that holy kiss; it was a golden morning; there was gold in the beaming sunlight; gold in the leaves of the little Buttercup, and on the lips of the maiden.

"There, that is our story!" sang the Buttercups.

Chime! Chime!

HANS CHRISTIAN ANDERSEN (*adapted*)

LITTLE PRINCESS WHITE CHICORY

Old Legend

OH, very, very sad indeed is the reason why the little White Chicory stands patiently waiting by the roadside; and why around her nod the little Blue Chicory flowers watching in all directions.

Once upon a time, the little White Chicory was a lovely Princess. She was most happy, for she was wedded to a Prince so handsome that there was none like him in the whole wide world.

But his heart was vain and fickle. So one day he left his lovely Princess without saying farewell, and, mounting his horse, rode out of the kingdom.

And when she knew that he was gone, and that she was forsaken, perhaps for ever, she wept night and day. The rose-colour fled from her cheeks, and she grew whiter and whiter. But always she sat at her bower window watching for him to return.

Her strength became so spent with weeping that she could sit up no longer.

"Alas!" cried she, "I would rather die; but if I do, no more can I watch for my Beloved!"

"Alas!" cried all her maids of honour, "we would rather die with you; but if we do, we cannot help you watch for him!"

And behold! even as they were speaking they were changed!

The lovely Princess was become a little White Chicory flower waiting by the roadside. Her maids of honour were little Blue Chicory flowers standing about her, and watching in all directions.

That is the sad, sad reason why to-day the little Blue Chicory maids stand guarding their Princess and watching; while she, the little White Chicory, is still patiently waiting for her Beloved to return.

WHY THE FROGS CALL THE BUTTERCUPS

Old Legend

WHEN the long cold Winter is passed away, and the warm Sunbeams of Spring touch the meadow-brooks, the Frogs sing: —

> *"Ranunculus!*
> *Ranunculus!*
> *Ranunculus!"*

And at their call up grow from the fresh green grass hundreds and hundreds of glistening yellow Buttercups.

This is why — so the wonder story says — the Buttercups bloom when the Frogs sing.

Of all the lads who roamed the Libyan plain, Ranunculus was the brightest, sauciest, and merriest. Each morning he put on a robe of shining yellow satin, and sat down in a meadow, where the Nymphs of the flowers and trees came every day to dance.

Now Ranunculus had a very sweet voice, so it chanced one day, while sitting in the meadow, that he began to sing. At first his song was soft and low, then it rose clearer and louder, filling the air with delicious notes like a flute's.

The Nymphs stopped dancing and drew near. They pressed close around him, in wonder and delight, fixing their starry eyes on his face. Ranunculus was so filled with joy, and felt such pride at his own sweet singing, that he sang louder and louder, until a great flood of musical sounds gushed from his throat and burst his heart-strings. Then, swooning, he lay down in the grass, and died.

His body, yellow satin robe and all, melted into the ground, and in its place sprang up a delicate branching plant, its tiny twigs crowned with dancing yellow Buttercups.

That is why every Spring, when the long cold Winter is passed away, and the warm Sunbeams touch the meadow-brooks, the Frogs sing: —

> *"Ranunculus!*
> *Ranunculus!*
> *Ranunculus!"*

And at their call, up start from the fresh green grass hundreds and hundreds of bright Buttercups.

LITTLE WHITE DAISY

Old Legend

In the long, long ago, in the golden wonder time, there were no Daisies. Snowdrops bloomed under the Snow, Crocuses opened their yellow and purple stars on sunny banks, Violets looked timidly up from the grass, and Daffodils bent their silvery heads over the whispering streams. But the little white Daisy was not there.

In the Springtime, in those golden wonder days when the Sun shone warm, and the fragrant breezes blew, and the trees put forth their most beautiful tender green, out of every tree trunk in the whole wide woodland peeped a smiling Dryad-Maiden. There they had all been sleeping the cold Winter through.

Then each Dryad-Maiden laughed a laugh like the rustling of the leaves, and tiptoed out of her tree. Then all joined hands, and skipped to a meadow where the Shepherd lads were watching their flocks. And together they danced, the Dryad-Maidens and the Shepherds, in the meadow-grass bright with flowers. But the little white Daisy was not there.

Now it happened one Springtime, that all the Dryad-Maidens were dancing in the meadow with their Shepherds. Their green robes were trailing, their slender arms were tossing, and garlands of oak leaves were twined in their hair. But the loveliest and most graceful of all, was the pretty Bellis. Her trailing robe was white, and a crown of yellow Crocuses was on her hair.

So pure and white was she, so sweet and winsome, that all the Shepherds wished to dance with her. But she would dance with none except a red-cheeked Shepherd lad. So merry was he, so lithe and nimble, that she danced all the happy day with him.

Now it chanced that Vertumnus, the Keeper-of-all-the-Orchards-in-the-World in those golden wonder-days, heard the laughter, and left his orchards and his pink fruit-blossoms, and came rushing to the meadow. He saw the Dryad-Maidens dancing with the Shepherds, and he, also, wished to dance. And he would dance with none except the pretty Bellis. But her Shepherd lad would not give her up.

Now, when the pretty Bellis saw the flaming eyes of Vertumnus, she trembled for the life of her Shepherd lad. Pale and smiling she drew back, and stood apart among the grasses. Then her hair changed to white petals, and her crown became a yellow disk; her hands turned into green leaves; and she sank into the grasses a little white Daisy!

So ever since that time, among the tall grasses, when the Crocus and the Narcissus

have faded away, the pretty Bellis, the little
white Daisy, blooms modest and sweet.

LEGEND OF THE GOLDENROD

Old Legend

In the long, long ago, there lived a beautiful
maiden who had lost her lover. Very dear he
was to her; so she wandered night and day
through meadows and by-ways calling and calling his name.

The birds sang sorrowfully to her; the flowers shed tears of dew; and the gentle Summer
breeze caressed her long golden hair that fell in
gleaming ripples about her slender form.

But though all things pitied her, she could not
find her lover; so she sank weeping and fainting to the ground, for she had had no food. From
sheer weariness she slept.

Then came the Autumn Wind, rustling and
rustling through the trees. He saw the lovely
maiden sleeping on the ground; and he shook a
bright blanket over her of red and yellow leaves.

Then came the Winter Wind, roaring, roaring through the sky. He saw the bright leaves;
and he spread a white blanket of Snow over the
maiden.

Then came the Fairy of Spring, wafting and
wafting sweet perfumes through the meadows.
She saw a lock of the maiden's shining hair

straying from under the leaves and melting Snow; so she planted her wand in the earth, and wreathed the lock around it.

And, lo! when the Autumn came again the wand was a wand no longer, but a tall green stem; and the golden lock had become the Goldenrod flower.

THE OLD WITCH WHO WAS A BURR

Skidi-Pawnee Tale

THERE was once an Indian boy who lived in a village on a plain. He was handsome and rich. He owned Ponies, blankets, robes, buckskin shirts, and leggings, and was well dressed every day. He was a very generous boy, and gave his Ponies and clothes away to any one who asked for them, but he was fortunate enough always to get more wealth.

One day he visited another village, and on his way home came to a wide stream. He sat down and took off his moccasins, so that he might wade across. Just then he heard a voice call his name. He looked up, and saw, standing close beside him, a pretty Indian girl dressed very nicely.

"Take me on your shoulders," said she, "and pack me across the stream."

"You are too heavy to pack," he answered; "I'll help you over."

But that would not do at all! She wanted to

be packed, and she wept so hard and begged so prettily that at last he consented.

She climbed on his shoulders, and he waded slowly across, for she was very heavy. When he reached the other side, he told her to get down, but she laughed and said: —

"Keep on walking, for I am going to stay with you for ever. I am your wife now!"

Then the boy grew very angry, and tried to shake her off, but he could not. She had grown into the flesh of his shoulders, and stuck fast to him. So he was forced to carry her into his lodge.

His father sent for the Medicine Men, but they could not take the girl off the boy's back. Then the chief Medicine Man called a Crow that lived on a tree near the village, and the bird came quickly to the lodge.

It flew in, and sang a magic song; and instantly the pretty girl turned into a bony old Witch with pointed chin and red eyes. But she stuck as fast as ever, and no one could pull her off.

Then the Crow said, "She is not a human being, so you must send for the Medicine Woman and her four daughters, who live in a tepee west of this village."

They sent a swift runner to the tepee; and when the Medicine Woman knew what they wanted her for, she called her four daughters.

She told them to comb and braid their hair and to paint themselves with magic red ointment, for they were going to the village to pull an old Witch from the shoulders of a handsome young man.

So the four girls sat down and combed their hair and painted themselves, and their mother did the same. Then each took in her hand a magic stick with a crook at the end.

They went to the boy's lodge, and when the Witch saw them come in she began to hiss. They ran around the fireplace. Then the eldest girl pointed her magic stick at the Witch and sang a magic song. The stick grew, and grew, and grew, until its crook passed around the Witch's neck, and her head fell off.

The second daughter pointed her stick, and it grew, and grew, and grew, until its crook passed around the Witch's arms, and they both fell off.

The third and fourth daughters did the same, and the Witch's legs fell off.

Then all four girls took hold of the Witch's body with their sticks, and the mother kept tapping between the body and the boy's shoulders; and they pulled, and pulled, and pulled, and they pulled *a big prickly Burr* off the boy's back!

Then he got up, and carried the Burr out and threw it in a field.

That is why Burdocks grow everywhere, and why Burrs get into children's hair and stick to their clothes.

FAIRY COWSLIPS

Folklore

THE yellow Cowslips, hanging their sweet heads, are Fairy Cups, you know. And Fairy Palaces they are too, for whenever the pattering raindrops begin to fall, the little Fays and Elves climb up the stalks, and rush into the yellow bells. There they swing and sing until the rain is over.

The Cowslips are the Key Flowers, and find where the Fairy Gold is hidden. So if you discover a door overgrown with Cowslip blossoms, just pick one and touch the door. It will open softly. Slip in, and you will find a Fairy Hall. A lovely Fairy Lady is sitting there, who will show you treasure-crocks ranged along the wall covered with yellow Cowslip blossoms.

Lift the blossoms, and take out all the treasure you wish. Fill your apron and pockets with the sparkling precious things. Then cover the crocks again with the blossoms; but do not forget the little Key Flower that opened the door for you.

If the crocks are not neatly covered, and if you forget to take away the Key Flower, you may never find the Fairy Hall again. And when you get home all your treasure will turn to withered leaves.

THE FOX IN GLOVES

Celtic Folklore

OH! the Fairies are a frisky folk. Very wily, indeed, are the Little People. They are friends of bad Master Fox, and help him in his adventures.

When he starts out at night to steal poultry, they lend him Foxgloves, to make his feet velvety and noiseless. So with Foxgloves on his four paws he creeps silently into the barnyard, and carries off the fattest Chickens and Ducks. That is, of course, if the farmer's wife has not laid out four little mittens where he can find them; for Master Fox is a gentleman, they say, and he will not steal your poultry if you give him little mittens as pretty and speckled as the Foxgloves.

But you must not tell this out loud, or even whisper his name, for if you do Master Fox will be so offended that he'll not take your mittens; but he will carry away all your best hens.

PAN'S LOVELY MAID

WHILOM great Pan, the father of our flocks,
loved a fair lass so famous for her locks. To
keep her slender fingers from the Sun, Pan
through the pastures oftentimes hath run, to
pluck the speckled Foxgloves from their stem,
and on those fingers neatly placèd them.

The Honeysuckles would he often strip, and
lay their sweetness on her sweeter lip.

Some say that Nature, while this lovely maid
lived on our plains, the teeming earth arrayed
with Damask Roses in each pleasant place,
that men might liken somewhat to her face.

WILLIAM BROWNE OF TAVISTOCK (*condensed*)

LISTENING TO THE MAGIC WATERS

ARETHUSA

Arethusa arose
From her couch of snows
In the Acroceraunian mountains, —
From cloud and from crag,
With many a jag,
Shepherding her bright fountains.
She leapt down the rocks,
With her rainbow locks
Streaming among the streams; —
Her steps paved with green
The downward ravine
Which slopes to the western gleams;
And gliding and springing
She went, ever singing,
In murmurs as soft as sleep;
The Earth seemed to love her,
And Heaven smiled above her,
As she lingered towards the deep.

PERCY BYSSHE SHELLEY

THE STONE THAT SHED TEARS

Retold from Ovid

OF all the women of Lydia, Niobe might have been the happiest of mothers but for her pride. And great was her pride! for whenever she walked through the streets the people shouted, "Lo! Niobe comes!"

One day she stepped proudly from her house surrounded by her attendants. Her curling hair hung down upon her robe of woven golden threads. Holding her graceful head high she haughtily lifted her eyes.

"Ye people of Lydia," she cried, "worship me! I am Niobe! My grandfather is the mighty Atlas who holds up the sky. My mother is the sister of the Pleiades. In my palace are my seven sons and seven daughters, all beautiful and stately. Greater and more fortunate am I than Latona, the mother of Apollo-of-the-Golden-Beams and Diana-of-the-Bended-Bow. I am well worthy to be worshipped!"

Now Niobe's proud words were heard by golden-beamed Apollo himself. Quickly he took in his hand his darts bright like the Sun's rays. Down to earth he flew, and near him flew his twin sister, Diana, her robe tucked up and her

bow shaped like the silver crescent moon, ready
to shoot.

Together they entered Niobe's palace. And
Apollo with his golden darts smote and killed
her seven sons; while Diana shot her silver-
white arrows into the bosoms of her daughters.

Niobe sat weeping among her dead children.
She wept night and day. Her face grew color-
less. No breeze could move her hair. Her eyes
became fixed. Her tongue congealed and her
heart was without motion. She could not bend
her neck nor move her limbs, for she was hardened; she was turned into stone. Yet she wept
on.

Then a mighty whirlwind arose and carried
her off to the top of a high mountain. And there
her soul was dissolved into tears within her
stony body.

Still ever from the stone distilled a stream of
pure tears that trickled sadly through the grass
and down the mountain-side.

THE WEEPING WATERS

Retold from Ovid

ONCE upon a time, when Magic Waters gushed
from Speaking Rocks, and maidens were transformed into flowers and trees, in a clear blue
pool dwelt the lovely Nymph Cyane.

Often she rose to the surface, and floating

there, plucked the fragrant Water-lilies. Sometimes she sat on the green bank, and combed her azure hair, singing sweetly all the while.

Now, on that day when little Proserpina danced with her playmates in the flowery meadow near the pool, Cyane watched her through the veil of clear blue water. And so it was that she saw Pluto, the grim King of Hades, standing in his chariot when it came leaping from the chasm where the Hundred-Headed Daffodil had been. And when he grasped the shrieking Proserpina to carry her off, Cyane saw that too.

Quickly she rose to the surface of her pool.

"O gloomy Pluto," she cried, "you cannot have that child against her will! No farther shall you go."

And stretching wide her arms, she stood in King Pluto's path.

But he, furious at the Nymph, hurled his sceptre straight into the depths of her water. And where it struck a great abyss opened, down which his horses plunged, while the abyss closed over his head.

Cyane wept. She wept because the little Proserpina was stolen from her mother. She wept because the clear blue water of her pool was muddied by the feet of King Pluto's horses.

She wept night and day. Her limbs softened. Her nails melted. Her bones waxed away. Her azure hair, her white fingers, her snowy shoulders, all dissolved and vanished in little streams of water. Lastly only pure water flowed through her veins.

She became transparent, and was changed into a Fountain of Weeping Waters — a fountain that for ever sheds clear azure tears for little Proserpina.

ARETHUSA

Retold from Ovid

Now on that happy day when little Proserpina returned to earth, her mother Ceres, Keeper-of-all-the-Cornfields-in-the-World, sought the fountain of the Nymph Arethusa, to listen to her tale.

She sat down by its waters, and called: —

"O unhappy Nymph, why do you always wander? Why do you gush from this spot as if in fear?"

Then from her murmuring fountain the Nymph Arethusa raised her head, and tossed back her dripping hair.

"Once," said she, "I was a Nymph of the lovely Arcadian meadows, and an attendant of Diana-of-the-Bended-Bow. With light step I roamed the woods, and set my nets for the fish. And though I surpassed all the other Nymphs in looks, yet I modestly blushed if any one spoke of my beauty.

"I remember one day returning tired from the chase. There was no breeze, and the trees drooped from the heat. I came to a smooth river that glided noiselessly along, and through its clear waters the pebbles gleamed like silver. The hoary Willows swept its surface with their weeping boughs, while the Poplars spread their refreshing shade above its watery mirror.

"I sat upon the shelving bank, and bathed my feet in the cool tide. Then suddenly I heard a murmuring noise in the midst of the stream. Frightened I sprang to the top of the bank. Then from the river, Alpheus, the mighty King of its waters, raised his foam-covered head.

"'Whither dost thou hasten, O Arethusa?' he cried from his waves. 'Whither dost thou hasten?' cried he again in hollow tones.

"I fled, and he pursued me; even as the Dove with trembling wings is wont to flee from the Hawk, and as the fierce Hawk pursues the trembling Dove.

"I ran over fields and over rocks and crags, and where there were no paths. Alpheus hastened after. I heard the sound of his feet close behind me, and his breath fanned my hair. Wearily I stretched out my arms to the Moon that rode pale and serene in the sky. Then Diana took pity on me, and flung a soft white cloud about me.

"Alpheus looked and I was gone. I was

hidden by the cloud. Then twice he cried out,
'O Arethusa! O Arethusa!' and I trembled as
does the Lamb concealed from the Wolf.

"Yet Alpheus did not depart, but remained
watching the cloud that hid me.

"Fright shook my limbs. Cold azure drops
distilled from my body. Wherever I moved my
foot was a pool of blue water. Bright drops
trickled from my hair. And in the twinkling of
an eye I was changed into a fountain.

"Then Alpheus saw my form in my transparent stream, and quickly he became a river,
and pursued me again.

"Diana in pity cleft the earth, and I sprang
through a chasm. Down, down through the
dark underground caverns went my rushing
waves, while behind me, bounding and roaring,
came the waters of Alpheus' river.

"And at this spot, O Ceres, Keeper-of-all-the-
Corn-Fields-in-the-World, I rise as a fountain,
gushing from the earth. And Alpheus, rushing
upward, mingles his cold dark stream with mine."

So sighed the Nymph Arethusa, and ending
her tale, again hid her dripping form in her
fountain.

LITTLE HYLAS

Retold from Theocritus and Other Sources

THROUGH the blue salt waves the good Ship
Argo bounded. On her deck stood Jason and

all his brave comrades. Eagerly they gazed across the water, for they were going on a wonderful adventure, to fetch home the Golden Fleece from Colchis.[1]

Among those famous heroes was the Mighty Hercules wrapped in his lion-skin. By his side stood his favourite lad, little Hylas, beautiful little Hylas, his yellow hair blowing in the wind.

Onward bounded the good Ship Argo, and when evening came it anchored near a strange shore. The heroes leaped out upon the sand. Some hastened to build fires, others killed an Ox for roasting, and still others ran about gathering wild fruits. But Hercules wandered off by himself to find a tree to make into a knotted club.

Then thought little Hylas: —

"I will go and bring some fresh cold water to surprise Hercules when he returns."

Night was falling. The Moon was risen, and by her white light little Hylas, carrying a brazen urn on his shoulder, hastened along a path through the wood. Soon he saw before him a hollow in which shone a bright pool set round with Ferns and Rushes.

He stepped down into the hollow. Tinkling laughter sounded at his side. He looked about. No one was near him, but he thought that he saw shadowy maidens in flowing garments, swaying hand in hand among the moonlit trees.

[1] See page 383.

He knelt down among the Ferns on the margin of the pool, and thought again that he saw lovely faces of shadowy maidens smiling at him from its brightness. He plunged his urn into the gurgling water. Mischievous laughter came rushing upward. Then, wonder of wonders! many white arms shot up from the water, and, clinging around his neck, drew him down headlong into the pool. He gave one wild cry, and the cold ripples closed over him.

Then, lo! he found himself on a bright pebbly floor, while many laughing Naiads were pressing their lovely faces close to his, and were holding him tightly in their white arms. They took him in their laps, and, drying his tears with kisses, bade him weep no more.

Now, the mighty Hercules, wandering in the wood, had heard the cry of his beloved boy, and knew his voice.

"Hylas!" he shouted, "Hylas!" and again, "Hylas!"

Then, like a roaring Lion, he rushed through the wood, breaking down bushes and crashing through trees. Over trackless ways he raged, through valleys and across mountains; but little Hylas was gone, and gone for ever.

The beautiful boy was with the Naiads, who were feeding him on ambrosial scented cakes and honey-dew.

CATCHING INSECTS GREEN AND BLUE

HOW ENDYMION MADE A GOLDEN BUTTERFLY

A Wild-Rose tree
Pavilions him in bloom, and he doth see
A bud which snares his fancy. Lo! but now
He plucks it, dips its stalk in the water: how!
It swells, it buds, it flowers beneath his sight;
And, in the middle, there is softly pight
A Golden Butterfly; upon whose wings
There must be surely character'd strange things!

JOHN KEATS

CHANT OF THE INDIAN CHILDREN TO WATASEE, THE FIREFLY

Firefly! Firefly! Bright little thing,
Light me to bed, and my song I will sing.

Give me your light, as you fly o'er my head,
That I may merrily go to my bed.

Give me your light, o'er the grass as you creep,
That I may joyfully go to my sleep.

Come, little Firefly, — come, little beast —
Come! and I'll make you to-morrow a feast.

Come, little candle, that flies as I sing,
Bright little Fairy-bug, Night's little King;

Come, and I'll dance as you guide me along,
Come, and I'll pay you, my bug, with a song!

HENRY SCHOOLCRAFT

GLEAM–O'–DAY AND PRINCESS LOTUS–FLOWER

Chinese Tale

ONCE upon a time, in the days of the Shining Dynasty, there lived a wise young man named Gleam-o'-Day. One night he was sleeping, and the moonlight was playing on his bed, when he saw a strange man stand beside him.

"Who are you?" grumbled Gleam-o'-Day, not wishing to be disturbed.

"The Prince is asking for you," said the man.

"What Prince?"

"The Prince of a near-by land."

Gleam-o'-Day grumbled more, got up and put on his court robe. The man then led him outdoors, where a beautiful palanquin was waiting, borne by a retinue of richly dressed servants.

Gleam-o'-Day reclined in the palanquin, which was carried swiftly along. At length he arrived at a strange land, and found himself amid numerous pavilions with towers and pointed roofs. The air was filled with a pleasant humming sound, but he could not tell from whence it came.

The palanquin was set down in the courtyard

of a large palace. Immediately twenty young
girls, dressed in shining yellow garments, came
hurrying to greet Gleam-o'-Day, and escorted
him into a large audience chamber. There on
the throne sat a handsome Prince.

The Prince descended from his throne. "Welcome, Gleam-o'-Day," said he. "You perfume
the neighbourhood! We have heard of your
wisdom and knowledge, and have longed greatly
to see you."

Thereupon he led Gleam-o'-Day to the seat
of honour, and the young girls brought wine of
honey and little cakes, and served him.

"Tell me, Gleam-o'-Day," said the Prince,
"among the flowers which do you prefer?"

"The Lotus-Flower," said Gleam-o'-Day,
without hesitation.

"The Lotus-Flower!" exclaimed the Prince.
"Strange! That is my daughter's name! You
must know the Princess."

Then he made a sign, and the young girls hastened away, and soon returned with the Princess.
She was sixteen years old, and of a beauty sur-
passing anything that Gleam-o'-Day had ever
seen. Her brown robe was embroidered with
yellow silk, and a golden girdle confined her
slender waist. Indeed her waist was so very
slender that it seemed to Gleam-o'-Day that
her body was almost divided in two.

Gleam-o'-Day looked at her and was troubled.

Her beauty bewildered his mind and made his heart beat with both pain and joy. But before he could speak, the twenty young girls rushed in, crying out: —

"A monster has entered the palace! It is a Serpent twenty feet long! It has devoured some of our people! It's head is like a mountain peak!"

Then the Prince and his retainers began to run hither and thither seeking some place to hide in. And the Princess and the young girls were crying for help.

"Come to my house," said Gleam-o'-Day to the Prince. "Come, fly thither with the Princess Lotus-Flower. You will be safe there!"

"Yes! Yes!" cried the Prince, seizing his daughter's wrist. "Let us go as quickly as possible."

So all three ran from the palace; and in an instant Gleam-o'-Day found himself, with the Prince and the Princess Lotus-Flower, standing in his own room. The Princess cast herself weeping upon the pillow of his bed; and at the same moment Gleam-o'-Day moved, and woke. The room was empty.

It was a dream!

Just then Gleam-o'-Day heard his father crying out in terror from the next room. There was a struggle and a blow. Gleam-o'-Day sprang up, and rushed in. The old man was pushing away the dead body of a huge Serpent that he had killed with his stick.

Gleam-o'-Day returned to his room, and, wonder of wonders! a swarm of Bees covered his bed, while the Queen Bee herself had alighted on his pillow!

PRINCE GOLDEN–FIREFLY

Japanese Folktale

ONCE in the moat of an ancient castle in Japan, there floated a rose-colored Lotus-Flower. Deep in its fragrant heart dwelt the King-of-All-the-Fireflies, with his beautiful daughter, the Princess Firefly.

Very wonderful was the Lotus-Flower Palace to the little Princess! Often on warm summer nights she sat on the edge of one of its pink petals, and peeped out at the lovely world around her. She longed to fly across the moat and play in the flower-garden of the castle; but she knew that her father would not allow her to leave the Lotus.

As she grew older, the beautiful white light that she carried under her wings became so brilliant that she looked like a golden lamp shedding silvery rays. Then, as she sat on the Lotus petal, and watched the other Fireflies darting and wheeling in the air, and flashing past in joyous dance, she wept to think that she

could not show her wonderful white light to all
the world.

Now, the Princess Firefly had many suitors,
but none of them carried a firefly light.   Prince
Hawk-Moth, Prince Beetle, Prince Dragon-Fly,
and many others laid their gifts at her feet, and
humbly sought her heart.   But her only answer
was: —

"Never will I marry a Prince who is not as
luminous as the brightest Star!   Go and bring
me white fire, and then I will be your bride."

Immediately, all the suitors set out to search
for the white fire.   Prince Hawk-Moth flew into
a temple, and circled around and around the
flame of a tall candle, hoping to get some of its
fire for the Princess, at length he flew clum-
sily into the flame, and fell scorched and dying
to the ground.

Prince Beetle, who had been watching, like-
wise flew into the flame, and was burned and
died.

But Prince Dragon-Fly first sunned his red
burnished wings, then hastened away to Mount
Fuji to steal some of the fire from its bosom.

But he, too, perished.

So it was with all the suitors, they sought the
white fire in vain, and strewed the way with their
dead bodies; for not one could find and bring
the great gift to the Princess.

Now, in the castle-garden, in the heart of a

White-Lily palace, there lived Prince Golden-Firefly. The light he carried under his wings was so dazzling that on dark nights it illumined the whole garden, and when he flew over the still water of the moat, his beautiful form was reflected in it, so that it seemed as if a sheet of golden flame spread over the water.

When the Prince heard of the beautiful Princess Firefly and her suitors, he flew swiftly to the Lotus-Flower Palace. As he entered, a flood of golden light filled the flower, and so overcame the heart of the Princess that she at once consented to become his bride.

Soon the two were wedded, and away they flew to the castle-garden to hold their marriage feast. All the Fireflies for miles around came darting like a thousand sparks through the air. And when the moonlight flooded the garden, the revels began.

The flowers gave out their richest perfumes, the wind breathed low, and like a gold and silver cloud the Fireflies danced through the garden. But the most happy and brilliant of them all were the little Princess and her bridegroom, Prince Golden-Firefly.

PRINCE BUTTERFLY AND CLOVER BLOSSOM

Louisa M. Alcott

In a quiet, pleasant meadow, where green old trees waved their branches as the Summer winds went singing by, bloomed a sisterhood of flowers. A neighbouring brook rippled musically, and passing clouds cast shadows upon the waving grass below.

The flowers were very happy together in this pleasant spot. No cold winds came to blight them, no rude hands tore them from their stems. Warm Sunbeams smiled on them all day long, and the Dewdrops refreshed them at night with a cooling drink.

One morning when the flowers awoke, fragrant and fresh, a little Worm came creeping by.

"Oh, pity and love me," sighed the little Worm. "Give me shelter, dear Flowers. I am lonely, poor, and weak. A little spot for a resting place is all I ask. Only let me lie in the deep, green Moss, and weave my little tomb, and sleep my long, unbroken sleep, until Spring's first flowers come. Then will I come forth in Fairy dress, and repay your gentle care for a poor Worm. Kind Flowers, let me stay!"

But none of the proud flowers would give shelter to the poor Worm.

Wild Rose showed her little thorns, while her soft face glowed with pride.

Violet hid beneath some drooping Ferns; and the Daisy turned her face away.

Little Bluet laughed scornfully as she danced on her slender stem; while Cowslip bent down and whispered the tale to the brook.

A Blue-Eyed Grass looked down on the poor Worm as She silently turned away.

"You will harm our delicate leaves," she said; "that is why you may not stay."

At that moment a sweet voice called from a distance: —

"Come here, poor Worm, come to me. The sunshine lies warm in this quiet spot. I will share my home with you."

The flowers all looked in wonder to see who had offered the Worm a home.

To their surprise they found Clover Blossom, with fluttering wings, beckoning him to come. From her snug little nook, where the cool winds rustled by, and the murmuring Bees and Butterflies loved to come, her rosy face smiled kindly down as the friendless Worm drew near.

"Poor thing, you are welcome here," she said in a soft voice. "In the green Moss close at my side you may sleep until Spring comes. I will spread my leaves over you, and guard you through the long Winter."

Then, deep in a Moss-bed, the grateful Worm spun his winter home, and lay down for his long rest.

And well did Clover Blossom keep her watch. Autumn came and took all her sister flowers. Then, when it was time for her to go, she spread her withered leaves softly over the sleeping Worm, and bent her faithful little head beneath the Winter Snow.

Spring came again, and the flowers arose from their Winter sleep. How gaily they danced on their slender stems, and sang their songs with the rippling waves of the brook. The warm winds kissed their cheeks, as one by one they came again to dwell in their summer homes.

Little Clover Blossom bloomed once more, and watched patiently by the mossy bed where the Worm still lay quietly sleeping.

Her sister flowers cried scornfully, as they waved in the Summer air:—

"Come and dance with us, little Clover. That ugly Worm was poor and friendless. He will not come again in Fairy dress. Don't believe what a Worm tells you. At any rate he lies in the green Moss dead. So come and be happy with us."

But little Clover kept watch, for she did not doubt the poor Worm's truth. She trusted that he would come as he had said.

At last she felt the Moss at her side move.

Then a small cell opened wide, and out flew a glittering Butterfly, that soared up to the Summer sky on golden wings.

Then the flowers cried out: —

"Clover, your watching was in vain. It is as we told you. He will never come again."

And the unkind flowers danced for joy, as they watched him silently soar away.

Little Clover bowed her head in silence. As she drooped, she heard a Daisy say: —

"O sisters, look, I see him now! He is floating back from Cloudland. Spread wide your leaves, that he may choose the one he deems most fair."

Then Wild Rose glowed with a deep blush, as she proudly waved on her stem.

Cowslip bent to look at herself in the rippling brook.

Little Bluet merrily danced, and spread out her leaves wide.

And Daisy whispered her joy and hope to Violet, who peeped out from the tall green Ferns to watch the glittering form of the Butterfly, that shone in the Summer sky.

Nearer and nearer the bright form came, and fairer and fairer grew the blossoms. Each welcomed him in her sweetest tones, and each offered him honey and dew.

But in vain did they beckon and smile and call. He floated past Violet, Daisy, and Rose, and went straight to the pleasant home of Clover Blossom, the flower most truly fair.

"Dear Flower," he said, "when I was alone and friendless you watched over me, and cared for me. Now I will try to show the thanks the poor Worm could not tell. And you shall find, dear faithful Flower, a loving friend in me."

Then through the long bright Summer hours, through sunshine and rain, lived happily together Clover and Prince Butterfly.

Paraphrased by ADA M. SKINNER

ANANSI THE SPIDER–MAN '

Stories from the Gold Coast

THESE are stories about the Spider-Man, Anansi, which the African Grandfather tells to the children of the Gold Coast: —

Come, comrades, listen to a tale. Once upon a time there was a man named Anansi. He was a cunning and deceitful creature, who liked to get the better of his neighbours; but he was punished for his badness. Listen now to

WHY SPIDERS LIVE IN DARK CORNERS

THERE was a time when Anansi was a very industrious farmer. One year he and his wife and son planted a large farm with Yams, Maize, and Beans. The crops flourished.

When the harvest came it was ten times greater than any Anansi had ever had before. And very well pleased he was, as you may believe, to have such a store of Corn, Beans, and Yams for the Winter. But the more he thought about all the nice vegetables, the less he wished to keep them for Winter.

Now, Anansi was greedy and bad-hearted, and did not like to share anything with anybody, not even with his wife and son. So when he saw that the crops were quite ripe, he called his wife and son, and said to them:—

"We have worked hard raising our vegetables. They have repaid us well. Let us gather the harvest into our barn."

So they gathered in the harvest.

Then Anansi said: "Now we three need a rest. Go home to the village and have a good time for three weeks, while I am away on business. When I get back we'll come to the farm and have a great feast."

His wife and son thought that this was a good plan, and went to their house in the village.

But the cunning Anansi did not go away on business; oh, no! He stayed there on the farm and built himself a nice little thatched hut with everything to cook with in it. Then each night he crept softly from the hut, and fetched a great quantity of vegetables from the barn, and feasted greedily all by himself.

It happened in about two weeks that Anansi's son said to his mother: "I will go and weed the farm, and surprise father when he returns."

So he went. But what was his wonder when he looked into the barn to see that half the rich harvest was gone!

"Robbers have been here!" thought he. "I must hurry and catch them before they steal everything!"

So he went back to the village and told the people, and they helped him make a Rubber Man, black, grinning, and very sticky. This they carried to the farm, and set down in the middle of the field to frighten the robbers. Then some of the young men stayed with Anansi's son to watch in the barn.

When it was quite dark Anansi came out of his hut to fetch more food. As he was creeping through the field he saw the figure of a strange man in front of him. At first he was very much frightened, but seeing that the man did not move, he went up to him.

"What do you want here?" said he.

But there was no answer.

"What do you want here?" said he again, getting angry.

But still no answer.

So Anansi, in a rage, hit the man a blow on the cheek with his right hand. And his right hand stuck fast in the rubber.

"Let me go," cried he, gnashing his teeth, "or I'll hit you again!"

And he hit the man a blow on the other cheek with his left hand. And his left hand stuck fast in the rubber.

"How dare you hold me!" cried he, foaming with rage. "Let me go or I'll kill you!"

Then he put up his right foot to kick himself free. And his right foot stuck fast in the rubber.

Then he kicked with his left foot, and pressed with both his knees against the man. And his left foot and his knees stuck fast in the rubber.

So there Anansi had to hang helpless until daybreak. Then his son and the young men came out of the barn to catch the robber, and very much astonished they were, as you may well believe, to find that the evil-doer was Anansi himself!

After that Anansi was so ashamed that he changed himself into a Spider, and hid away from sight in a dark corner of the ceiling. And ever since then Spiders have been found in dark places, where people are not likely to see them.

WHY SPIDERS LIVE UNDER STONES

THIS is another tale of Anansi, the greedy Spider-Man. Once there was a sore famine in the land. The villagers were thin and pale for

lack of food. Only one family was fat and well.
This was the household of Anansi's cousin, Kofi.
So Anansi was determined to find out how his
cousin got food.

Now it had happened this way: —

One morning when Kofi was hunting, he found
a wonderful Mill-stone. It ground flour of its
own accord, heaps and heaps of rich yellow corn-
flour. Near it ran a stream of honey.

Kofi was delighted. He sat down by the
Stone, and made cakes, and ate them, and drank
all the honey he wanted. Then he carried away
enough flour and honey for his family. So this
is why his wife and children were fat and well,
while the other villagers were thin and hungry.

Well, as I said, Anansi was determined to find
out how Kofi got food, and he gave his cousin
no peace until he told him about the Stone, and
promised to show him the wonderful spot where
it was. Kofi said that he would take him there
the next day.

So in the morning, about the time when
women begin the day's work, they both set off
for the forest. And as soon as Anansi saw the
Stone he cried out in a loud voice: —

"Ho! ho! Here is plenty of food for me! I
need never go hungry again!"

"Hush!" said his cousin. "You must not
shout here! It is a magic spot. Sit down quietly
and eat your fill."

So they sat down. But when they had eaten all they wanted, and had drunk enough honey, Anansi shouted again:—

"Ha! ha! Now I'll take the Stone with me!"

And in spite of all that Kofi could say, he lifted the Stone on to the top of his head, and went staggering through the forest toward the village.

But as he went the Stone cried out:—

"Spider! Spider! Put me down!
The Pig came, ate enough, and left me!
The Antelope came, ate enough, and left me!
Kofi came, ate enough, and left me!
Greedy Spider! Put me down!"

But Anansi only laughed scornfully, and went staggering along, and would not put the Stone down.

Then the Stone began to grind and grind the top of Anansi's head.

He tried to throw it onto the grass, but it stuck fast to him, and went on grinding. It ground, and it ground, and it ground, around and around, until at last Anansi was ground into a thousand little pieces lying in the grass under the Stone.

That is why to-day, whenever one lifts up a big Stone, one finds so many small Spiders under it.

LADYBIRD! LADYBIRD!

Folktale

ONCE upon a time, there was a poor little girl, who liked to play with Ladybirds, and to sing to them: —

> "*Ladybird, Ladybird, fly away home,*
> *Your house is on fire, your children will burn.*"

One day while she was playing in the wood, a lovely little carriage, drawn by a hundred red Ladybirds drove up. She stepped into it, and was carried through the air straight to a cottage, in front of which sat a beautiful lady spinning.

The lady rose when she saw the little girl, and, taking her by the hand, led her into the cottage, saying: —

"I sent for you, dear child, because there is a dreadful war being fought in your land. I wish you to stay with me until it is over."

So the little girl stayed with her five years.

At the end of that time, the carriage drawn by the hundred red Ladybirds, drove up again, and the lady put the little girl into it, saying:—

"Good-bye, dear child, the war is over."

The little girl was carried through the air to her parent's cottage; and they, as you may guess, were overjoyed to see her. Then they found the carriage filled with fine things for the little girl.

THE BOY WHO CAUGHT FLIES

Old Legend

ONCE upon a time, there was a boy named
Campion.   He was an idle, worthless fellow, and
would never have worked at all, if he had not
been afraid of his mistress Minerva,—Pallas-
Athena as some folk call her, — who was the
wisest of all the Dwellers-on-Mount-Olympus.
She kept him busy every minute catching Flies
for her pet Owl.

He was afraid of her frown; and very good
reason he had, for she was stern and awful.
Large, steadfast, and grey were her eyes.   Over
her ringlets she wore a helmet.   On her arm she
carried the fearful ægis — or shield — in the
centre of which was graven the snaky head of
the Gorgon Medusa.

But, though she was usually armed like a warrior maiden, Minerva liked far better to be clad
in homespun, and to sit weaving and spinning.
Many were the beautiful gifts, made with her
own hands, that she bestowed on good and
happy mortals.   But when people were lazy,
idle, or wasteful, she frowned so terribly that
they shook and trembled for fear of her wrath.

Wherever she wandered about the world be-
stowing her gifts or punishments, the pet Owl
went with her, rolling his wise eyes and flapping

his dusky wings. And a ravenously hungry bird
he was, gobbling Flies every minute of the day.
So, to satisfy his enormous appetite, Campion
had to run around the meadows, catching handfuls of Flies, and putting them into a little
bladder he carried.

One day Campion thought that Minerva was
too far away to see him, so he curled up under a
tree to take a nap. But she did see him. For
her Owl grew hungrier and hungrier, and she
came with stately stride into the meadow, to
find why Campion was not bringing Flies for her
pet's dinner.

There she saw him curled up comfortably,
the empty bladder lying by his side.

Frowning her most awful frown, she touched
him. Instantly he was transformed into a plant
holding up clusters of white flowers, the stems of
which were covered with a sticky substance. The
Flies came buzzing around, and in a second they
were caught and held tight in the sticky juice.
So the Owl had all that he wanted for dinner.

After that the little plant, Bladder Campion
— or Fly Catcher — had to stand night and
day catching Flies for the Owl. And you can
find him for yourself in the garden, with all his
children around him. Night and day they are
busily catching Flies and other insects.

TITHONUS, THE GRASSHOPPER

Retold from the Homeric Hymns and Other Sources

AURORA, the Rosy-Fingered Child of Dawn, arose from her couch in the eastern Sky and donned her saffron robe. Then mounting her rose-colored car she threw back her flowing veil and opened the Gates of Day. She urged her white steeds through the Sky. Night and Sleep fled before her, while her maidens, the happy Hours, floated by her side.

High above the earth the white steeds bore the car, and Aurora scattered Roses and refreshing dew on the grass beneath. And as she looked down she saw Prince Tithonus of Troy standing in the royal garden. A very beautiful youth he was, with golden curls clustering on his white forehead.

Swiftly Aurora guided her steeds to earth, and lifting Tithonus into her car carried him off to her golden palace beyond the Gates of Day. And there in the Land of Dawn she wedded him.

Years passed, and Tithonus grew older. Then Aurora, who loved him tenderly, trembled at the thought that he might die. So she flew in her car to Mount Olympus and begged Jupiter to grant him immortal life. Jupiter consented; and Aurora, returning joyfully to her palace, fed Tithonus on Ambrosia and red Nectar to make him live forever, and clothed him in unfading Olympian garments.

More years passed by, and still more years. Tithonus grew grey and decrepit, and his voice became feeble, because — alas! — Aurora had forgotten to ask for the gift of Eternal Youth. So the wretched Tithonus could not die, but grew older and older. He became smaller and smaller, and Aurora wrapped him in swaddling clothes and laid him in a cradle.

At last, when he was many hundreds of years old, Aurora, out of pity, changed him into a Grasshopper and carried him back to earth.

That is why to-day Tithonus, withered and small, goes chirping and hopping about in the grass.

THE MORNING–GLORY FAN

Japanese Tale

In the Island of the Dragon-Fly, the Land of the Rising Sun, where the Cherry-Blossoms lie like snow clouds on the Cherry-Trees, and the Peach Blooms fall pink on the grass, there once lived a little Japanese maid. She was called Morning-Glory, and why she was called that, listen, and you shall hear.

It happened one warm Summer night that the Little Maid went down to the river and saw her companions, the village maidens, sporting on the water in their small boats.   And as the maidens darted here and there, they tried to catch with their hands the sparkling Fireflies that sailed past in the air like strange Fire-Flowers or hosts of wandering Stars.

The Little Maid climbed into her boat, and soon she, too, was catching Fireflies with the gay throng.   She held the shining insects on her fingers, or laid them against her soft black hair, laughing with glee.

While she played thus on the river she met and loved a stranger youth, whose name was Miyagi.   And when they parted she gave him her fan, on which were painted trailing Morning-Glories.   On his own fan Miyagi wrote a song about the Morning-Glories, and gave it to the Little Maid; then he went his way and returned to his home in a distant land.

But alas! when the Little Maid reached her home she found that her parents had betrothed her to a man whom she had never seen.

At the thought of Miyagi her heart seemed to burst.   So she left her home, and started out in search of him.   Many weary days she went up and down the world, weeping great salt tears. And little by little the tears quenched the light of her eyes, and she became blind.

But still she wandered on from village to village, from town to town, singing the little Morning-Glory song Miyagi had written on the fan, for she thought: "If he hears it, he will come to me." So people called her "Morning-Glory."

It happened one day that Miyagi rested himself in a tea-house, and saw the song he had composed written on a screen. Eagerly he questioned the master of the tea-house.

"It was written," answered he, "by a blind maiden, who left her home because her parents betrothed her to a man she could not marry. Now she is searching the world over for the youth she loves. To him belongs this song. Therefore she ever sings it, hoping that some day he may hear her."

Miyagi could hardly control his joy.

"Bring her hither to me," said he, "and let her sing before me."

The Little Maid came, and sang so sweetly that his heart was strangely moved. And as he gazed on her beautiful, sad face and sightless eyes, he longed to declare his love, but kept silent because of the strangers present.

"I will come back another day," thought he.

But before leaving, he presented her with the fan on which were painted trailing Morning-Glories.

Scarce was he gone when the Little Maid eagerly felt of the fan with her soft fingers; and she knew it for the one she had given her lover so long ago.

"Oh, tell me," she cried to the master of the tea-house, "oh, tell me if there are trailing Morning-Glories on this fan!"

And he answered, "Yes, Morning-Glories are painted on it."

Then the Little Maid cried out with joy; and, wonder of wonders! the tears of joy healed her eyes, and her vision returned clearer than it was before.

And she rose up and followed the way her lover had taken. All night long she travelled over rough and stony roads, and when the morning was breaking she climbed with bleeding feet a high mountain. As she reached the summit the day dawned in all its glorious colours. And she heard a voice calling, and calling sweetly:—

"Morning-Glory!"

She looked and saw Miyagi waiting for her. Then what happiness was theirs! How gladly she let him lead her to his home, where the wedding feast was preparing!

As for the Morning-Glory flower, it lasts but a short time, while the love of little Morning-Glory and Miyagi lasted years and years.

WANDERING THROUGH THE EN-
CHANTED FOREST

UNA AND HER LION

Her angel's face
As the great eye of Heaven shined bright,
And made a sunshine in the shady place.
Did never mortal eye behold such heavenly grace!

The Lion would not leave her desolate,
But with her went along, as a strong guard
Of her chaste person, and a faithful mate
Of her sad troubles and misfortunes hard.

He kissed her weary feet,
And licked her lily hands with fawning tongue,
As he her wronged innocence did weet.
Oh, how can beauty master the most strong!

.   .   .   .

The day is spent, and cometh drowsy Night,
When every creature shrouded is in sleep.
Sad Una down her lays in weary plight,
And at her feet the Lion watch doth keep.

EDMUND SPENSER (*arranged*)

THE WHITE HARE OF INABA

Japanese Legend

Once upon a time, there were eighty-one brothers who were Princes. Eighty of the brothers were jealous of one another, and were always quarrelling. But the youngest was good and gentle and did not like their bad ways.

Now each of the quarrelsome brothers wished to marry the Princess of Yakami in Inaba. So they decided to visit her, and persuade her to choose one of them for a husband.

After quarrelling very hard, they set out, taking their youngest brother to carry their bag. The eighty brothers went on ahead, for the youngest could not travel fast because the bag was so heavy.

By and by the eighty brothers came to the seashore, and on the sand they saw a little white Hare with most of its fur torn off. The brothers laughed very hard at the poor little thing.

"If you wish your fur to grow again," they cried, "go bathe in the sea; and after you have done so, run to and fro on the top of yonder high hill and let the hot Wind blow on you!" And they laughed again and went on.

The little Hare limped down to the sea, and

jumped into the water and bathed. Then it limped up the hill and lay down to let the hot Wind blow on it. The hot Wind blew and blew, and the poor Hare's skin, all wet with salt water, dried, cracked, and split open. And there the little creature lay, moaning with pain, when the gentle youngest brother drew near.

"Where is your fur? Why are you suffering so?" asked the youngest brother.

"Please wait a minute, and I'll tell you," said the Hare, weeping. "I was in the Island of Oki, and wished to cross to this place, so I said to the Crocodiles: 'I want to know how many Crocodiles are in the sea. Arrange yourselves in a row, and let me count you.'

"Then the Crocodiles formed a long line with their horny bodies from the Island of Oki to this beach. I hastened across, leaping from back to back; and when I reached the last Crocodile, I cried out: 'You silly beasts! As if I cared how many Crocodiles are in the sea! I only wished to use you for a bridge!' And immediately that last Crocodile raised its head, and tore off my fur with its sharp teeth."

"Well! Well!" said the youngest brother. "It served you right, for you lied to them. But is this all of your story?"

"No," said the Hare. "Your eighty brothers passed by, and laughed. They told me to bathe in the sea, and to let the hot Wind blow upon me, and I did. My skin dried, and cracked, and split open."

"Ah, my poor little Hare!" said the youngest brother pityingly. "Bathe in fresh water, and roll in the pollen of the sedges, and your fur will come again."

So the little Hare limped down to the river, and bathed in fresh water. Then it rolled in the pollen of the sedges; and immediately its skin was healed, and its fur came again, white and handsome.

Then the grateful Hare ran after the youngest brother, crying: "Your eighty quarrelling, wicked brothers shall never get the Princess. It is you she will choose, and you will reign over Inaba."

And so it was. For the eighty brothers quarrelled so hard that the Princess turned them out of her kingdom. But she chose the gentle youngest brother; and they were married and ruled happily over Inaba.

STORY OF THE TIGER AND THE MAN

Tibetan Folktale

ONCE upon a time, there was a Father Tiger who lived in a certain forest, and had a family of three children. He grew old and began to fail; so just before his death he sent for them, and said: —

"Remember, my children, the Tiger is the lord of the jungle. He roams about at will, and makes a prey of the other animals, and none can gainsay him.

"But there is one animal against whom you must be on your guard. He alone is more powerful and cunning than the Tiger. That animal is Man. And I warn you solemnly, before I die, to beware of Man, and on no account to hunt him or kill him."

So saying, the old Tiger turned on his side and died.

The three young Tigers obeyed him for some time; and if they came within sight or scent of any human being, made off as fast as they could from so dangerous a neighbourhood.

But the youngest Tiger, as he grew older and stronger, thought to himself: —

"What, after all, can be this creature Man, that I should not slay him? I am told that he is a defenceless animal, and that his strength cannot be compared with mine, and that his claws and teeth are quite blunt. I can pull down the largest Stag, or tackle the fiercest Boar, — why then should I not be able to kill and eat Man also?"

So after a while, in his conceit and folly, he set out to search for Man.

He had not gone far when he met an old Ox, thin and sick, with marks of scars on his back. Walking up to him, he said: —

"What sort of an animal are you, pray? Are you Man?"

"No, indeed," said the creature, "I am only a poor Ox."

"Ah!" said the Tiger. "Well, perhaps you can tell me what sort of an animal Man is. I am hunting for one, to kill him."

"Beware of Man, young Tiger," replied the Ox. "He is a dangerous, faithless creature. Just look at me. From the time I was young, I was Man's servant. I carried loads for him on my back, as you may see by these scars. I slaved for him faithfully and well. But as soon as I was old and weak he turned me out into the wild jungle to seek my food. He gave no thought for me in my old age.

"Therefore I warn you to beware of Man, and not to try to kill him. He is very cunning and dangerous."

But the young Tiger only laughed, and went his way.

Soon afterward he met an ancient Elephant feeding with its trunk on the grasses and leaves it loves so well. The old animal had a wrinkled skin, and one small bleary eye. Behind his ears were cuts and scars, showing where the iron goad had struck him.

"What sort of an animal are you?" said the young Tiger, walking up to him. "You are not Man, I suppose?".

"No, indeed," replied the old creature. "I am only a poor worn-out Elephant."

"Is that so?" answered the Tiger. "Perhaps you can tell me what sort of an animal Man is. I am hunting for one to kill him."

"Beware how you hunt Man, young Tiger," replied the old Elephant. "He is a dangerous, faithless creature. Look at my case. Although I am lord of the jungle, Man tamed me, and made me his servant. He put a saddle on my back, and struck me often with an iron goad. When I was young and could serve him, he fed me and cared for me. I had a groom who used to wash me and tend to all my wants. But when I became old and too feeble to work, Man turned me out into the jungle to find food for myself.

"So take my advice, and leave Man alone, or it will be worse for you in the end."

But the young Tiger only laughed again, and passed on.

After a while, he heard some one chopping wood, and creeping near, saw a Woodcutter felling a tree. Then going up to him, he said:—

"What kind of an animal are you?"

"Why, you ignorant Tiger," said the Woodcutter, "can't you see that I am a Man?"

"Oh, are you?" replied the Tiger. "What a piece of good luck for me! I am just looking for Man to kill and eat him. You will do nicely."

THE TIGER FOLLOWED THE MAN TO HIS HOUSE

On hearing this the Woodcutter began to laugh.

"Kill and eat *me*," he cried. "Why, don't you know that Man is much too clever to be killed and eaten by a Tiger? Come a little way with me, and I will show you some of the things Man knows. It will be very useful for you to learn."

The Tiger thought this a good idea, so he followed the Man to his house, which was built of strong timbers and heavy logs.

"What is this place?" asked the Tiger, when he saw it.

"This is called a house," said the Man. "I will show you how we use it," and he went inside and shut the door.

"Now," said he, speaking from inside, "you see what a foolish creature a Tiger is compared with Man. You poor animals live in holes in the forest, exposed to rain, and cold, and heat; yet with all your strength you cannot make a house like this.

"Whereas I, although I am so much weaker than you, can build myself a fine house, in which I live comfortably in all weathers."

On hearing this, the Tiger flew into a rage.

"What right," he roared, "have you — an ugly, defenceless creature — to possess such a lovely house? Look at me with my beautiful stripes, and my great teeth and claws, and my long lashing tail. I am far more worthy than you to have your house. Come out at once and give it to me."

"Oh, very well," said the Man, and out he came, leaving the door open.

The Tiger stalked in.

"Now look at me!" he called from inside. "Am I not nice in my fine house?"

"Very nice indeed," answered the Man — and he bolted the door on the outside, and walking off, left the young Tiger to starve to death.

WHY RABBITS HAVE YELLOW HAIRS

Sioux Myth

ONCE upon a time, Master Rabbit lived with his grandmother in a little lodge. Every morning he got up early to set his traps to snare game. But no matter how early he got up, he found that some one with a *very long* foot had been before him, and had frightened away all the wild creatures.

One morning he rose earlier than ever to see who the mysterious stranger was, but all that he saw was the trail of the *very long* foot. The stranger had been there, and the wild creatures were gone.

Well, Master Rabbit was mad! He jumped

all the way home, stopping now and then to thump the ground with rage.

"Grandmother," he shouted, "give me my strongest snare. I will set it and catch the stranger."

"What has he done to you, my Grandson?" asked she.

"He has made me mad," grumbled Master Rabbit, "and I intend to punish him."

Well, Master Rabbit took his strongest bowstring, and set it for a snare. Then he hid in the bushes and waited. It grew dark and no one came, so at last he had to go home.

The next morning he got up *very early*, and went to look at his snare. And what should he see but Master Shining Sun himself caught in the snare and struggling to escape.

Master Shining Sun was in a violent passion. "What! Ho!" cried he. "You miserable little creature, how dare you hold me this way? Come and untie me at once."

Well, Master Rabbit trembled with fear, you may be sure, and he ducked his head and crept near. He whipped out his knife, and cut the bowstring. And up sprang Master Shining Sun, soared into the sky, and was gone.

As for Master Rabbit, all his children since that day have had yellow hairs between their shoulders, because Master Rabbit's hairs were scorched by the great heat of Master Shining Sun.

WHY THE DEER HAVE ANTLERS

Hopi Tale

ONCE the Deer had n't any antlers and his head was smooth like the Rabbit's. He was a fast runner, while his friend the Rabbit was a great jumper.

All the animals were curious to know who could go the faster, the Deer or the Rabbit, so they decided to hold a race. They made a beautiful pair of antlers for a prize.

Well, the day for the race came, and all the animals got together in front of a thicket, and laid the antlers on the ground to mark the starting point. They told the Deer and the Rabbit to run through the thicket to the other side, and back again; and they said that the first to return and pick up the antlers, might keep them.

While every one was admiring the prize, the Rabbit said:—

"I do not know this part of the country. I wish to take a look through the bushes where I am to run."

The animals thought this fair, so the Rabbit jumped into the thicket. But he was gone so long the others began to suspect that he was up to one of his tricks. So a messenger went to look for him.

He crept softly along, and there was the Rabbit

gnawing down the bushes and throwing them aside, so as to clear a path. Then the messenger returned to the others, and told what he had seen.

The Rabbit came back at last, and the angry animals held a council, and agreed that such a trickster had no right to enter the race.

So they gave the antlers to the Deer because he was an honest runner. As for the Rabbit, they told him that since he was so fond of cutting down bushes, he might do so for a living — and so he gets his living to-day.

WHY THERE ARE NO SNAKES IN IRELAND

Irish Folktale

In ancient days, when Saint Patrick came to Ireland, the land was filled with Snakes, and Serpents, and Toads. Some flew in the air, and others crawled and hopped on the ground. They were in very bad company, indeed, these creatures, for with them were many Demons who darkened the air with their sooty wings.

Well, Saint Patrick determined to rid Ireland of them all. So he gathered the Snakes, Serpents, Toads, and Demons together in one place, and bade them go to the top of Crochan Acla.

Now the creatures did not wish to go there at all, at all, for they knew that the other side of the mountain hung over the sea. So some of them went up very slowly, and others twisted and turned and wriggled about, hoping to escape.

But Saint Patrick had a watchful eye, and what is more, he had something much better — a sweet tinkling magic bell. Of all the sounds in the world the creatures dreaded the most, it was the sound of this bell. So when Saint Patrick saw that they would not obey him he uncovered the bell and rang it gently.

At the first tinkle, Snakes, Serpents, Toads, and Demons rushed forward in a body up the side of the mountain, and hurried to the top.

The good Saint clambered after. He pointed to the sea, and in a minute Snakes, Serpents, Toads, and Demons rushed helter-skelter over the edge of the mountain, and, before the bell could be uncovered again they were half way down to the water. There they stopped, and hid themselves in a deep hollow, feeling quite safe under the shadow of the cliff.

But Saint Patrick leaned over the edge, and rang his bell again, so gently that the roaring of the surf beneath drowned the tinkling, and the creatures refused to stir. Rising to his feet, the Saint swung the bell around and around his head, and flung it with all his force over the cliff.

Down it went, booming and ringing, on to the shivering creatures' backs. And in the twinkling of an eye, Snakes, Serpents, Toads, and Demons rushed downward and plunged into the sea, and disappeared under the foaming waves.

And never since that day have Snakes been seen in the land; and some folk say that the good Saint's bell lies hidden under the earth in the hollow on Crochan Acla.

THE LAST OF THE SERPENTS

Irish Folktale

AFTER Saint Patrick had driven the Snakes and Serpents out of Ireland, there was just one cunning old Serpent left, who had hidden away in a hole by a lake.

Well, the good Saint did not know what to do about it at all, at all, for the old one was making a lot of mischief. The Saint thought about it for a long time, then he got a strong iron chest with nine bolts on it. And one fine morning he took a walk to the hole where the Serpent was.

The old one did not like Saint Patrick, small blame to him, and began to hiss and show his teeth.

"Oh!" says Saint Patrick, "where's the use of making such a noise when a nice gentleman like myself is coming to see you? It is a fine house I have got for you against the Winter," says he, "and you can come and look at your house whenever you please."

The Serpent, hearing such smooth words, stuck his head out of the hole, and came wriggling up fair and easy to see the house Saint Patrick had brought. But when he saw the nine bolts he was terribly frightened, and began to wriggle away.

"Stop! stop!" says Saint Patrick. "'T is a nice warm house as ever you saw," says he.

"Thank you kindly, Saint Patrick," says the Serpent, "but it's entirely too small for me," says he, wriggling away still farther.

"Too small is it?" says Saint Patrick. "I am sure it will fit you completely. If you'll only try, there's plenty of room," says he.

"I don't like to contradict you, Saint Patrick," says the Serpent, "but it's altogether too small, it is," says he.

And with that the Serpent swelled himself out as big as he could, and crept into the chest all except a bit of his tail.

"There now, see," says he, "the house is much too small for me. I can't get my tail in," says he.

And what did Saint Patrick do but quick as a wink slap down the heavy lid of the chest with a bang like thunder?

When the rogue of a Serpent saw the lid coming down, in went his tail like a shot, for fear of its being whipped off him. And Saint Patrick began to bolt the nine bolts.

"Oh! murder! won't you let me out, Saint Patrick?" cries the Serpent.

"Let you out, my darling!" says Saint Patrick. "To be sure! to be sure! But you must wait until to-morrow," says he.

And with that the Saint heaved up the chest, and pitched it right into the lake, where to this hour it certain is. And 't is the Serpent struggling down at the bottom that makes the waves boil so.

And many a living man has heard the Serpent crying out, within the chest under the water:

"Is it to-morrow yet? Is it to-morrow yet?"

Which it sure never can be, for it is always *to-day*.

And that's the way Saint Patrick settled the last of the Serpents.

GATHERING FRUITS STRANGE, RICH,
AND RIPE

SONG OF THE HESPERIDES

The Golden Apple, the Golden Apple, the
*   hallowed fruit,*
Guard it well, guard it warily,
Singing airily,
Standing about the charmèd root!

. . . . . .

Keen-eyed Sisters, singing airily,
Looking warily
Every way,
Guard the Apple night and day,
Lest one from the East come and take it away!

. . . .

Golden-kernelled, golden cored,
Sunset-ripened above on the tree.
The World is wasted with fire and sword,
But the Apple of Gold hangs over the sea.
Five links, a golden chain are we,
Hesper, the Dragon, and Sisters three,
Daughters three,
Bound about
The gnarlèd bole of the charmèd tree.
The Golden Apple, the Golden Apple, the
*   hallowed fruit,*
Guard it well, guard it warily,
Watch it warily,
Singing airily,
Standing about the charmèd root!

                From LORD TENNYSON'S *The Hesperides*

THE MAGIC STRAWBERRIES

Folktale

ONCE upon a time, a poor woman lived in a little hut near a mountain on which was a wide forest. She had one little child whom she loved dearly.

Now, in that forest grew many Strawberries very large and juicy, and one Midsummer Day the woman took the child to pick some. They climbed the mountain-side, and presently lighted upon vines that were covered with berries larger, redder, and more luscious than any they had ever seen before.

These they picked. But no sooner had the woman put them in her basket than she saw the door of a large cavern open before her. Great heaps of gold lay glittering on the floor, while three White Maidens sat there guarding the treasure.

"Come in, good Woman," called the White Maidens. "Take as much gold as you can grasp at once."

The woman, holding her child by the hand, entered eagerly. She stooped and grasped a handful of gold and put it in her apron. But the touch of it filled her with greed, and, forgetting her child, she gathered up two more handfuls. Then she turned and ran out of the cave.

Instantly a loud rumbling sounded behind her, and a voice cried out: —

"Unhappy Woman! You have lost your little one until next Midsummer Day."

The door of the cavern closed, and the child was shut inside.

Well, the poor woman wrung her hands and wept, but it was of no use, and she had to go home without her child. And though after that she often visited the place where the cavern had opened, she never could find the door.

Early on the next Midsummer Day she hurried to the spot; and what should she see but the door wide open! The great heaps of gold lay glittering on the floor, while the three White Maidens sat there guarding the treasure. And near them stood her little child holding a big red Apple.

"Come in, good Woman," called the White Maidens. "Take as much gold as you can grasp at once."

At that the woman ran eagerly in. She forgot all about the gold, and clasped her dear child in her arms.

"Good Woman," said the White Maidens, "take the little one home. We give it back to you, for now your love is greater than your greed."

So the woman took her child home with her, and loved it better than gold all the days of her life.

THE GOLDEN STRAWBERRIES
Folktale

Now, near that same mountain lived another poor woman who had a little daughter.

One day the woman fell ill of a fever, and longed for Strawberries. So the little girl took a jug and went to gather some. She climbed the mountain-side, and entered the forest, where she found vines covered with big, red, luscious berries.

She had gathered her jug nearly full, when she saw a tiny woman come tripping toward her. A very strange tiny woman she was, all gold-coloured and dressed entirely in golden moss.

The little girl remembered how her mother had told her about the Fairies, called Moss-Women, who inhabited the forest, so she knew this must be one of them.

The Moss-Woman drew near.

"My dear child," said she, "I see that your jug is full of delicious berries. Will you not give me some to quench my thirst?"

"Take all you want," said the little girl gladly, "and I'll pick more for my mother."

So the Moss-Woman ate, and ate until the jug was nearly empty; then away she tripped, and vanished among the trees.

The little girl quickly filled her jug again,

and went home. And, lo, when she took it to her mother's bedside, every Strawberry in it was turned to pure gold!

From that day she and her mother were very rich.

WHY THE POMEGRANATE WEARS A CROWN AND ROYAL ROBES

Old Legend

ONCE upon a time, in Tyre the City-that-Crowns-a-Rock, there lived a proud young girl.

Now the King and Queen of Tyre, and all the Princes and Princesses, wore robes of Tyrian purple; not the dark colour we call purple to-day, but a deep rich crimson, glowing ruby-like in the sunshine, and, in the shadows, gleaming like ripening Grapes.

More beautiful was Tyrian purple than any other colour in the world. So this young girl gazed and gazed with rapture and longing, every time one of the royal family went by. Indeed, she could think of nothing else, but of this wonderful colour.

At last she could neither eat nor drink; and since she could endure this condition no longer, she consulted a Wiseman. He told her that she was destined to wear a crown and royal robes. So of course she thought he meant that she was to

wed a King. After this she refused all humble
suitors who asked for her hand, and waited for
her King to come and woo her.

One day she heard a great noise in the street,
and rushed from her house. A procession was
passing by. First came goat-legged Pan piping on his Syrinx. After him pressed a great
crowd of Satyrs and Fauns prancing around on
their shaggy legs, and shouting wildly.

Behind them, seated in a huge car drawn by
Leopards, came Bacchus, Keeper-of-All-the-Vineyards-in-the-World. He was dressed in purple
garments, and wore a crown of Grapes and leaves.
Behind him followed captives chained together,
and many Elephants laden with rich stuffs, spices,
gold, and silver. For Bacchus was returning from
India, which country he had conquered.

Well, as soon as the young girl saw his purple
garments and crown, she thought: "There is
my King!" and, rushing forward, threw herself in his way.

Bacchus, who was good-natured and merry,
lifted her into the car, and took her along; for
he was pleased to have such a pretty girl sitting
beside him.

But, when she began to insist that he should
make her his Queen, he was so annoyed that he
changed her into a big ripe Pomegranate hanging on a low tree. And her rind glowed ruby-
like in the sunshine, and in the shadows gleamed

like ripening Grapes, while she wore a tiny yellow crown.

So there she hung, peeping out of her glossy leaves in order that all the world might see her crown and royal robes.

THE TANTALIZING FRUITS

Retold from Homer and Pindar

OH, a very wretched man was King Tantalus the father of Niobe the Proud. He lived in the golden wonder days when maidens were transformed into trees, and youths were changed into flowers. Though he was the son of ægis-bearing Jupiter, he did not dwell in the Shining Palace on Mount Olympus, but reigned over the rich and powerful kingdom of Lydia.

Now King Tantalus was a favourite of the Dwellers-on-Mount-Olympus, and they often invited him to their banquets, and even visited him in his palace. But he was so vain and puffed up by these favours that he became very presumptuous.

Some people say that he told the secret things he heard at the banquets, and others relate that he stole some of Jupiter's Nectar and Ambrosia, and fed his friends; and still others accuse him of having killed his son Pelops, cooking and serving him up at a feast to the Dwellers-on-Mount-Olympus. But whatever his wickedness was, he was well punished; for Jupiter cast him into Tartarus, that dreadful place of punishment in grim King Pluto's underground kingdom.

Over King Tantalus' head was suspended a huge rock that was always threatening to fall and crush him. He stood in a lake up to his chin, while above him drooped branches of trees laden with the most delicious fruits — crimson Pomegranates, luscious Figs, yellow Pears, and crisp Olives.

But though all this food and drink was close at hand, King Tantalus was always hungry and thirsty. Whenever he bent his head to drink, the water fled from him. Whenever he lifted his arm to pluck a fruit, a great Wind arose that whirled the branches, fruit and all, high up into the shadowy clouds.

So the wretched King stood there night and day, stretching out his arms toward the food and drink, and suffering the most terrible hunger and thirst, in punishment for his pride and presumption.

THE GOLDEN APPLES OF THE HESPERIDES

Retold from Apollodorus and Other Sources

THE LABOURS OF HERCULES

In those ancient golden wonder days, the most unfortunate of men was the mighty hero Hercules; for by evil Destiny he was forced to serve and obey King Eurystheus of Mycenæ.

A cruel man was King Eurystheus, and twelve labours — or tasks — he set for Hercules to perform. Fearful adventures they were. And in order that Hercules might win over all dangers, the Dwellers-on-Mount-Olympus armed him with Olympian armour.

Mercury gave him a bright sword; golden-beamed Apollo bestowed a bow upon him, Vulcan the Smith made him a golden breast-plate; and Minerva, with her own hands, wove him a robe of the finest web.

Then Hercules cut for himself a huge club, and started on his adventures. The fierce Nemean Lion he choked to death, and made a cloak of his skin. With fiery darts he slew the hundred-headed Hydra-monster. He tamed the Stag-of-the-Golden-Horns, and the Wild Boar of Erymanthus. He cleansed the great Augean stables, and even stole grim King Pluto's three-headed monster Dog, Cerberus.

All these labours did Hercules accomplish, and others as fearful. But the most wonderful of his tasks was his search for the Golden Apples that grew in the Garden of the Hesperides.

THE SEARCH FOR THE GOLDEN FRUIT

FAR, far away, beyond the bright ocean, at the very edge of the world, lay the Garden of the Hesperides. There the most beautiful flowers bloomed, and the sweetest birds sang. Every kind of tree grew there, and streams of crystal-clear water moistened their roots.

In the centre of the garden stood a magic tree on whose boughs hung the glittering Golden Apples. Very marvellous they were, for they belonged to Juno, Queen of all the Dwellers-on-Mount-Olympus. Fair Earth had given them to her for a wedding gift. And to keep them safe, Juno had planted them in the garden and had set the three sister-maidens, the Hesperides, to watch over the tree on which they grew, and had placed a fierce hundred-headed Dragon around its roots to guard it from the sisters lest they should pluck one of the magic fruit.

And it was to fetch back some of these wonderful Golden Apples that King Eurystheus sent Hercules. Many and dangerous were the hero's adventures. Some men say that he went to the Land of the Hyperboreans, those strange folk who dwelt beyond the glittering ice palace of the North Wind Boreas. They lived for a thousand years. On sweet grassy herbs they fed, and drank ambrosial dew. No shadow of care ever touched their radiant brows, nor were they ever sick.

Thither some men say Hercules went, sailing beyond the bright sea in the Golden Bowl of the Sun. And as he drew near to the Garden of the Hesperides, he shot and killed with his sharp arrows the mighty Eagle that was hovering on outstretched wings and devouring the liver of Prometheus. For that wretched one was still bound to the pillar where Jupiter had placed him because he had given the untiring Fire to men.

So Hercules set Prometheus free, who in gratitude bade him seek out his brother, old Giant Atlas, who was holding up the sky, and send him for the Golden Apples.

Then Hercules sought out old Giant Atlas, and found him groaning under his burden. And very glad the old Giant was to be rid of the weight of the sky for a while, while Hercules took it on his own shoulders. He hastened to the garden where his daughters, the Hesperides, were dancing hand in hand, and singing their clear-voiced songs while they circled about the magic tree. From them he received some of the glittering fruit, and carried it back to Hercules.

So was Hercules able to fetch home, at last, the Golden Apples to King Eurystheus of Mycenæ, who returned them to him as a gift, in honour of his bravery.

But the hero did not wish to keep them, so Minerva-the-Wise-One carried them back to the Garden of the Hesperides.

And there they are to-day, glittering on the magic tree around which the three sister Hesperides are still circling hand in hand, singing their clear-voiced songs, while the hundred-headed Dragon is keeping watch and ward over the Golden Apples.

THE APPLE OF DISCORD

Retold from Euripides, Ovid, and Other Sources

THE WOOING OF THETIS

In those ancient golden days, came handsome King Peleus of Thessaly a-wooing of the silver-footed Thetis, loveliest of the Nereids. She dwelt beneath the ocean-waves, in clear green depths where the silvery sand was strewn with Pearls and Coral.

Often she was wont to rush through the deep water, seated on the back of a swift, well-harnessed Dolphin. Sometimes she rose to the surface of the sea, and, rocking on a billow, combed her long hair while she sang softly to the fishes.

But more often she slept in a little cave on the shore. Around it was a grove of Myrtle. Inside it, the sand was whiter than camphor,

while the cool green light from the sea played
on its lichen-covered walls.

One day, King Peleus found Thetis, in her favourite retreat, sleeping with her head pillowed
on the Dolphin. He gathered her up in his
arms, and, lo! she changed herself into a bird
with sharp claws and beak. He held her fast,
and she became a thorny tree. He clasped her
still closer, and, behold! she was a spotted
Tiger tearing at his bosom. In terror he opened
his arms, and she slipped from them into the
water.

"Alas!" he cried, "how have I lost her!"

"Listen, Peleus," said a voice from the waves;
and Proteus, the Old-Man-of-the-Deep, raising
his head from the brine, shook the foam from
his long hair and beard. "Listen, Peleus, and
I will tell you how to win yon ocean-maid.
When again she sweetly sleeps in her cave, bind
her with cords. Then hold her fast. Let her not
deceive you, no matter how many terrible
shapes she takes. So will you win, if you are
bold to the end."

Thus saying, old Proteus hid his face in the
sea, and sank beneath the waves.

Now when the Sun was setting, the silver-
footed Thetis, gayly shaking the reins of her
Dolphin, came riding into the cave, and laid
herself down to sleep in that cool place.

Then King Peleus saw her, and, creeping close,

bound her with strong cords, and grasped her
tightly in his arms.

Many and fearful were the forms she took, —
shapes of wild birds, savage beasts, and horrible
creatures, — but King Peleus held her in a vice
like iron and would not let her go. At last, with
a sigh, she returned to her own form, and said: —

"King Peleus, daring man, you have conquered. But not without the aid of old Proteus
of the sea!"

And that is how the handsome King Peleus
of Thessaly won his bride.

THE MARRIAGE OF PELEUS AND THETIS

JOYOUSLY through the groves and caves of
Mount Pelion sounded Apollo's lyre, and Pan's
reedy Syrinx, while the fair-haired Muses,
striking their golden sandals on the ground
with musical ringing, came dancing from among
the trees to attend the marriage of King Peleus
and the silver-footed Thetis.

Richly was set the banquet table, around
which were seated the Dwellers-on-Mount-Olympus. With rosy finger-tips, Ganymede the Cupbearer poured out the Nectar into the golden
depths of the goblets. Along the white sand the
Nereids, the fifty daughters of Old Ocean,
twined their arms in a circling dance. Then
with arrows of fir and crowns of pine, the horse-

mounted troop of the Centaurs came galloping from their dark cave to the feast.

Now all the Dwellers-on-Mount-Olympus were there except one. Discord alone had not been invited. A malevolent creature she was, sowing anger and strife wherever she went. So Jupiter had banished her from the Shining Palace on Mount Olympus.

When the marriage feast was nearly over, Discord herself suddenly appeared among the guests, her face ghastly pale, and her garment rent, while the handle of a naked dagger protruded from her bosom.

She cast upon the banquet-board a beautiful Golden Apple; then, her eyes sparkling with malicious fire, she vanished.

The Apple went rolling along the board until it stopped at the place where Juno, Venus, and Minerva were reclining. Mercury, the wily one, picked it up, and read aloud the inscription written on its side: —

"Let the most beautiful take me."

Then arose a violent quarrel, for Juno, Venus, and Minerva each claimed the Apple for her own. And had not Jupiter separated them, they would have come to blows.

"Make haste, take this golden fruit of Discord," said Jupiter to Mercury. "Hie to leafy Mount Ida, to the place where Paris, the son of King Priam of Troy, is watching his flock. Say to the youth that Jupiter bids him decide which is the most beautiful, Juno, Venus, or Minerva."

So to leafy Mount Ida Mercury, with the Golden Apple of Discord in his hand, flew quickly, and descended to the spot where Paris was sitting.

THE JUDGMENT OF PARIS

THE handsomest of all Shepherd-lads on Mount Ida was Paris. He knew not that he was the son of King Priam; for when he was born an Oracle had declared he should be the destruction of his country. So King Priam had exposed the babe on Mount Ida to die. But a Bear had suckled the little one, and a Shepherd had found him, and, adopting him, had named him Paris.

So now to where Paris sat, playing on his flute of reed while watching his sheep, came Mercury; while behind him, still loudly quarrelling, hastened Juno, Venus, and Minerva.

Mercury delivered his message, and the bewildered youth rose to his feet and gazed in wonder. So magnificent and noble was Juno in her royal raiment and crown, so stately and tall was Minerva in her rich armour, so rosy and dimpled was Venus in her shining robes, that he could not decide on whom to bestow the Golden Apple.

Then Juno stepped forward, and said: "O

royal Youth, if you will award the Apple to me, you shall be Lord of all Asia."

"Good Youth," said Minerva, "give me but yon Apple, and I will make you a great warrior. You shall always win in battle."

"Dear, fair Youth," said Venus, smiling, "bestow on me yon prize of Beauty; and I will give you the most beautiful wife in the world, even Greek Helen herself. Pale and fair she is like a Swan, and of rare and delicate beauty. There is none in the whole world to compare with her. Give me the prize, and I will send my little son, Cupid, to guide you to Sparta and to Helen."

So Paris bestowed the Golden Apple upon Venus.

Alas! time is too short in which to relate all the woes and sorrows that Paris brought upon his native land; how his father King Priam found him; how Paris himself stole Greek Helen away from Sparta; how the army of the angry Greeks assembled, in many swift ships, and sailed to Troy; how they, with the help of Juno and Minerva, besieged and destroyed the city, and carried Helen home.

These were some of the baleful miseries and strifes brought about by ghastly Discord and her Golden Apple.

IDUN AND THE MAGIC APPLES

Norse Myth

Retold from the Younger Edda

THIS is a wonder tale of the Northland, the land of the Midnight Sun, where the cold grey sea beats and foams against dark crags, and where, by night and day, are heard the thunder of snowslides and the crash of rending ice in the mountains.

High above this land, among the clouds, once dwelt the mighty Asa Folk. Asgard, their abode was called. In Asgard were many lofty halls and palaces, whose gold and silver roofs, seen through the pale mists, burned like sheets of white and red flame.

In Valhalla, the loftiest palace of them all, that had five hundred and forty windows and a roof shingled with heroes' golden shields, sat Odin-the-One-Eyed, the father of all the Asas. On a high seat he sat, with his wife Frigg by his side, and his two Ravens, Hugin and Munin, croaking loudly on his shoulder.

Often he called all the Asas to a banquet. At his summons came Thor-the-Strong, standing up in his chariot, and furiously urging on Goats instead of Horses. Around his waist was girded the Belt of Strength, into which was thrust Mjolner the Thunder-Hammer.

Near Thor's chariot rode Freyja the Fair in
her car drawn by Cats. She was singing sweetly
to her brother Frey, as he galloped along at her
side on his golden Boar Gullinburste.

So all the Asas but one came to the banquet —
Brage the Poet-Singer, Balder-the-Beautiful, the
gentle Nanna, Hoder-the-Blind, Loki-the-Evil-
One. But the happiest of all, rosy, young, and
beautiful, was Idun, bearing her locked casket.

These came to the banquet, and one only did
not come, for Heimdal-the-White-Asa remained
behind to guard Bifrost, the Rainbow Bridge,
that stretched its bright arch from Asgard to
earth. There he stood watching night and day,
and guarding the Asas from the attacks of the
terrible Mountain-Giants who lived on earth.

But the other Asa Folk sat with Odin and his
heroes in Valhalla, drinking from the flowing
mead-horn, and eating the flesh of a Magic Boar
that was cooked every day, and every night became alive again.

Of all the good things at the feast, the best
and most desired were the Magic Apples of
Youth — kept by Idun locked safely away in
her casket. Just a taste of one of these was
enough to make an Asa grow young and handsome again, no matter how old, weary, and
wrinkled he was. So this wonderful fruit was
very precious, and Idun hid it away under lock
and key, and always carried the casket with her.

And this is what happened at last to those Magic Apples: —

One day Odin wrapped his blue cloak around him, pulled down the rim of his broad-brimmed hat well over his one eye, and journeyed across the Rainbow Bridge to earth. With him went Loki-the-Evil-One, and together they wandered over mountains and meadows.

At length they saw a herd of cattle grazing in a valley. These belonged to Thjasse a Mountain-Giant, but they did not know it. So they killed an Ox, and began to make broth of its flesh. They boiled it, and kept boiling it from early morn to noon, but still it was red and raw.

And while the two were talking about this wonder, a voice above them cried out: —

"O foolish ones! That meat shall never be cooked, until you give me all that I can eat at one meal."

Odin and Thor looked up, and saw an Eagle perched on a bough.

"A bird cannot eat much," they said, so they consented.

Now the Eagle was really Thjasse the Mountain-Giant, but they did not know it. Down he dropped, and snatched the two thighs of the Ox, then both of its shoulders. But before he could fly away, Loki picked up a pole, and began to beat him. Immediately one end of the pole fastened itself to the bird's body, and the other end to Loki's hands.

Up the Eagle flew, but only high enough to drag Loki's feet over sharp stones, and almost to pull his arms from his shoulders. Loki pleaded and cried, and at last the Eagle said: —

"If you will promise to bring me Idun and her Apples, I will release you."

Loki promised gladly, and the Eagle set him free and flew off.

Now of course Loki did not tell Odin what he had pledged himself to do. And as soon as he reached Asgard, he tried to coax Idun away.

"In a forest on earth," he said, "I have found some Apples much more wonderful and fragrant than your Apples of Youth. Let us go and gather them."

So he coaxed her across the Rainbow Bridge into a forest. Then came Thjasse, in his dress of eagle-feathers, and, swooping down, bore her off, casket and all, to Giantland.

Ah, then there was sorrow and lamentation in Asgard! Idun was gone and so were her Magic Apples. The Asas grew grey, wrinkled, and old. They no longer feasted, but mourned.

But when they learned that Loki had been last seen with Idun, they threatened him with death. So he confessed what he had done, and offered to fetch Idun back, if Freyja would lend him her dress of falcon-feathers.

He put on the falcon-guise, and away he flew northward over raging torrents, icy mountain peaks, and cold glaciers, to Giantland. There he found Idun sitting alone in her hall, for the Giant Thjasse was gone fishing.

Quickly Loki changed her into a Nut, and holding it firmly in his claws, flew off toward Asgard. But the Giant Thjasse saw him winging his way along, and, putting on his eagle-feathers, pursued him.

Now Heimdal-the-White-Asa, standing guard at the Rainbow Bridge, saw them coming, — first the Falcon flying slowly and feebly, for it was very tired, then the fierce Eagle rapidly pursuing. He called all the other Asas, and they came running.

Then the Asas saw that the two were flying nearer and nearer. And just as the Eagle was about to pounce upon the Falcon, the exhausted bird flew over the walls into Asgard and dropped panting on the ground.

But Thjasse, unable to stop in his mad flight, passed through a great fire the Asa Folk had kindled, and fell burning to the earth. So they slew him there, where he fell.

That is how Idun and her locked casket came back to Asgard, and why the Asa Folk grew young and handsome again after once more tasting the Magic Apples of Youth.

DIVING THROUGH THE GREEN SEA
WAVES

THE PEARL

A Drop of Rain was falling
From forth a summer cloud,
It saw the Ocean under it
Roll billows large and loud;

And, all-ashamed and sore-dismayed,
It whispered, "Woe is me!
O Allah, I am naught! What counts
One Rain Drop to the Sea?"

But while it mocked and mourned itself —
For littleness forlorn —
Into a Sea-shell's opened lips
The Drop of Rain was borne,

Where many a day and night it lay,
Until at last it grew
A lovely Pearl of lucent ray,
Faultless in form and hue.

From Sa'di ; *trans. by* Sir Edwin Arnold

FAIRY SONG

Full fathom five thy father lies;
Of his bones are Coral made;
Those are Pearls that were his eyes:
Nothing of him that doth fade,
But doth suffer a sea-change
Into something rich and strange.
Sea-Nymphs hourly ring his knell:
Ding-dong,
Hark! now I hear them, — Ding-dong, bell!

William Shakespeare

THE FISHERBOY URASHIMA

Japanese Folktale

ONE day a fisherboy, named Urashima, left his little village and went out to fish. He caught a Tortoise. Now Tortoises are said to live a thousand years, so the kind-hearted boy dropped it back into the sea. Then, rebaiting his hook, he sat patiently waiting for a fish to bite.

The sea gently waved his line to and fro. The Sun beat down upon his head. He fell asleep.

He had not slept long, when he heard a voice call: —

"Urashima! Urashima!"

It was such a sweet, haunting voice that he stood up in his boat, and looked about. Swimming near him was the very Tortoise he had restored to its watery home.

"Urashima," said the Tortoise, "get upon my back. You have been kind to me, so I will take you to the Dragon-King's palace."

Urashima eagerly stepped on to its back, and away the Tortoise glided with tremendous speed through the water. He was amazed to see that his clothes were dry, for not a single drop touched him.

As they drew near a Magic Island, out of the palace of the Dragon-King came Red Bream,

Flounders, Soles, and Cuttle-fish. After welcoming Urashima, they escorted him to an inner apartment in which sat the beautiful Princess Otohime. She was arrayed in robes of red and gold, which looked like waves with the sunlight on them.

"Urashima," said she in the same sweet haunting voice that he had heard before, "I was the Tortoise who brought you hither. I took that form in order to test your kindness of heart. Because you restored me to the sea, instead of selling me for food, I will reward you. If you wish it, I will become your bride, and you may dwell with me for ever in this Land of Eternal Youth and Everlasting Summer."

Urashima joyfully consented, and immediately a great troop of fishes appeared, robed in long garments, and bearing in their fins coral trays laden with plates of delicious food.

The happy pair together took the wedding cup of Saki, and, while they drank, some of the fishes played softly, others sang, and still others, standing on the tips of their gold and silver tails, danced upon the white sand.

After the wedding festivities were over, the Princess led Urashima out of the palace to show him the marvels of the Dragon-King's land. Everywhere around him were trees with emerald leaves and ruby fruits, while on all sides of the palace the four Seasons — Spring, Summer,

Autumn, and Winter — stretched out their wide domains.

Looking toward the East, Urashima saw Plum and Cherry trees in full bloom, with bright-winged Butterflies skimming over the blossoms.

To the South, all trees were in their Summer glory, Bees humming and Crickets chirping.

To the West, the Autumn Maples were flaming in gold and scarlet, while Autumn flowers painted the meadows yellow and purple.

But when Urashima looked toward the North, he saw only broad stretches of cold white Snow, and a mighty lake covered with glistening Ice.

Now after Urashima had been in the Dragon-King's palace for three days, he remembered his poor old father and mother, and longed to see them. But when he told this to the Princess she wept.

"Indeed, I must see my old parents," said he. "It will be only for a day, after which I will return to you, dear wife of mine."

So he pleaded; and when she saw that he was determined to go, she placed in his hand a jewel-set box, saying: —

"Promise me that you will not open this, no matter what happens."

So he promised.

Then getting on the back of a large Tortoise, he soon found himself in his own village.

But everything was changed. His father's

cottage was gone; only the little stream re-mained.   He questioned a strange fisherboy, and found that he had been in the Dragon-King's palace, not three days but *three hundred years*.

His parents were dead.   His little house was torn down.   His heart was filled with grief and despair.   Then he heard the low murmuring of the sea, and it seemed to be whispering of the land where Spring, Summer, Autumn, and Winter reigned eternally, the land where the trees had emerald leaves and ruby fruits, and where the fishes wore long robes, and danced, played, and sang.

He wandered on the shore.   He thought that he heard his wife's sweet, haunting voice calling to him from the waves, but no Tortoise appeared to carry him to the Dragon-King's palace.

"The box! the box!" he cried.   "Surely it will help me!"

With eager fingers he untied the red silk strings that bound the jewel-set box, and lifted its cover.   Out rushed a small white cloud, that rolled away over the sea and was gone.

Alas! Urashima's sacred promise was broken! His form was changed.   He was no longer a hand-some fisherboy, but a grey, wrinkled, old man. He was *three hundred years old*.

He staggered forward, his white hair and beard blowing in the wind.   He looked out at the sea. Then he fell down dead upon the shore.

PRINCE FIRESHINE AND PRINCE FIREFADE

Japanese Myth

IN Japan, in days long gone by, there once dwelt two brothers. The elder was named Prince Fireshine and the younger Prince Firefade.

Prince Fireshine liked the sea, and daily caught fish of all kinds. Prince Firefade was a hunter, and shot much game, big and little.

One day Prince Firefade said: —

"My brother, lend me your fish-hook, and to-day I will go fishing. Do you take my bow and arrows, and hunt in my stead. So shall we find out who is the luckier."

At first Prince Fireshine refused, but when his brother pressed him hard, he consented, and lent him his fish-hook. Then taking the bow and arrows, he went hunting.

At night, when they returned home, Prince Fireshine, who had shot nothing all day, gave up the bow and arrows sullenly, and demanded back his fish-hook. Now poor Prince Firefade had had no luck, and had lost the fish-hook into the bargain.

"You promised to return my hook," said Prince Fireshine in a rage, "and my hook I will have."

So Prince Firefade, much grieved at his

brother's harshness, broke his sword into bits, and made five hundred bright hooks, and offered them to him. But he refused them all.

Then Prince Firefade made a thousand hooks, and offered them to him, but he said angrily: —

"My own hook I will have, and no other."

Thereupon Prince Firefade, weeping bitterly, went down to the shore. As he stood by the sea, there arose from the water an old man with a long white beard and flowing white hair.

"Prince Firefade," said he, "why do you weep?"

"Because I borrowed my brother's fish-hook," he answered sadly, "and lost it. I have offered him a thousand and five hundred bright ones instead, but he has refused them all, saying, 'Give me back my own.'"

The old man then plaited a boat of sea-weed, and setting it on the waves, said: —

"Get into this, Prince Firefade, and your journey will be pleasant. Soon you will see a palace built of silvery fish-scales. It is the abode of the Sea-King. Near its gate is a well, over which droops a Cassia Tree. Climb into the tree, and wait until the Sea-King's daughter finds you."

So Prince Firefade sprang into the boat. Immediately it dived beneath the foam, and, descending deeper and deeper, rested on the ocean-floor. Then he got out of the boat, and walked

until he beheld the Sea-King's palace glittering
like a thousand fishes. Over the well bent
the Cassia Tree, and into its branches he
climbed.

Soon the handmaidens of the Princess Rich-
Gem came bearing jewelled vases with which to
draw water. They saw the handsome youth in
the tree, and ran and told their mistress. She
hastened to the spot, and, after giving Prince
Firefade one look, exclaimed: —

"Why, he is handsomer than my father!"

So she hurried to her father, and said that a
beautiful young man was sitting in the Cassia
Tree. The Sea-King went to look for himself,
and liked Prince Firefade's face so well that
he invited him into the palace. There the
servants seated him on a pile of silken carpets,
and prepared a fine banquet for him.

After which the Sea-King gave him the Princess Rich-Gem in marriage. So he dwelt in the
Sea-King's palace for three years.

Now, at the end of that time, Prince Firefade
suddenly thought of his brother and the lost
fish-hook, and sighed deeply.

"Why do you sigh, my Son-in-law?" asked
the Sea-King. "Tell me, too, what brought you
hither to my Kingdom."

So Prince Firefade told him how his brother
had pressed him to return the hook as he had
promised.

Thereupon the Sea-King hastily summoned all the fishes of the world to appear before him. They came swimming up, thousand and thousands of them, gold and silver fishes, red, green, blue, and yellow ones, and assembled respectfully before his throne.

The Sea-King asked them if they had found Prince Fireshine's hook.

All the fishes replied: —

"The Tai-Fish has complained lately of something sticking in her throat, so that she cannot eat. Doubtless it is the hook."

Then the Sea-King commanded the Tai-Fish to open her mouth. She did so, and there was Prince Fireshine's hook all safe and sound.

So they took it out, and gave it to Prince Firefade, who immediately made preparations to depart.

As he was leaving, the Sea-King pressed a flashing jewel into his hand, saying: —

"This is the Jewel-of-the-Flowing-Tide. If at any time your elder brother attacks you, hold this in your hand, and the tide will advance and drown him."

Then he pressed another flashing jewel into his hands, saying again: —

"This is the Jewel-of-the-Ebbing-Tide. If, when your brother is drowning, he repents, hold this in your hand and you will save him."

After which the Sea-King called a Crocodile,

and commanded him to take Prince Firefade on his back, and carry him safely to his home.

He did so, and in a few minutes Prince Firefade was standing before his own house. Prince Fireshine met him sullenly, and, snatching the hook from him, carried it into the house.

Strange to say, from that very time ill-luck attended all that Prince Fireshine did, and soon he became so poor that he had nothing to eat.

"This is all your fault!" he cried one day to Prince Firefade. "It is you who have brought all this misfortune upon me!" And drawing his knife, he attacked him.

Then Prince Firefade took the Jewel-of-the-Flowing-Tide into his hand. Then the great waves came rolling in, and began to drown Prince Fireshine, who cried out: —

"Save me! Save me, oh my brother! I have done very wrongly!"

So Prince Firefade took the Jewel-of-the-Ebbing Tide in his hand, and the waves drew back into the sea again.

When Prince Fireshine saw that he was saved, he fell at Prince Firefade's feet, saying humbly:—

"You have rescued me. Henceforth I will serve you faithfully. Night and day will I be your guard."

ARION AND THE DOLPHIN

Retold from Herodotus and Ovid

WHAT sea has not known, what land does not know, Arion? With his sweet songs he used to stop running brooks. Often the raging Wolf stood still, while Arion charmed men and beasts with his lyre.

Listen, then, and I will tell you how he tamed a Dolphin: —

Arion had a great heap of gold and silver that he had gained as prizes for his singing. One day he set out from Italy on a voyage to Corinth. All his treasure was in the hold of the ship. When she reached open sea, the sailors said to one another:

"Come, let us destroy this Arion, and divide his wealth."

So they called him to the deck and ordered him to jump overboard. In vain he pleaded for his life, and even offered them all his gold and silver; they threatened him with their swords, and ordered him to jump without delay.

Then he begged that he might put on his finest robe, and, standing in the poop, sing and play for the last time. To this they consented, for they were delighted to hear such a great singer.

So he clad himself in a bright mantle twice steeped in Tyrian purple, and put a chaplet on his flowing hair. Standing in the poop, he struck his lyre, and sang like a dying Swan his last, low, mournful lay.

The Dolphins in the sea heard him, and came rushing through the waves. Charmed by his song they pressed against the ship close under the poop. Then, all clad as he was in bright garments, he leaped overboard, splashing the blue ship with foam and spray.

The sailors, when they saw him spring into the sea, quickly raised all sails, and made for the port of Corinth.

But, wondrous to tell, a Dolphin had arched its back, and caught Arion as he leaped. Then the other Dolphins had formed a ring around him so that the sailors should not see him; and all were swimming toward the land of Greece.

As they passed rapidly through the billows, Arion struck his lyre, and sang of green ocean-grottoes, pearl and coral strewn, and of the long-haired laughing Naiads. So they reached the shore before the ship, and Arion sprang safely upon the sand.

But his perilous adventures were not over, for when he went to Corinth and told the King how the Dolphin had rescued him, no one believed his strange tale. So he was cast into prison to await the coming of the sailors.

Soon after this, the ship entered port, and the King summoned the sailors to appear before him. He asked them where Arion was.

"He is safe in Italy, where we left him," they answered. "He is well and flourishing."

At that Arion, dressed in the same bright garments that he had worn when he leaped into the sea, stepped from behind the throne and stood before them.

The wicked, terrified men fell on their knees, and, confessing their crime, begged for pardon. But the King condemned them to severe punishment; after which he restored all the stolen wealth to Arion.

As for the people of Greece, they set up a statue of a Dolphin with Arion on its back, and called a cluster of Stars after the good fish that had saved one of the sweetest and greatest of ancient wonder-singers.

THE JEWEL TEARS

Japanese Folktale

IN far-away Japan, in ancient days, there lived by the sea a youth named Totaro. One day, as he was about to cross a bridge, he saw a strange creature lying upon it. The creature had a body like a man's, with a black skin, and the head of a Dragon. Its eyes glowed like Emeralds, and its long green beard swept the bridge.

At first Totaro was afraid, but, on looking closer, he saw that the eyes of the creature were filled with tears.

"Who are you?" exclaimed Totaro.

"I am Samebito," said the monster mournfully. "I am a servant of the Eight Dragon Kings who live in the depth of the sea. For a small offence I have been banished from the Dragon Palace, and may not return. Now I am lonely, and without food and shelter. Pity me, good Totaro, and give me a home and something to eat."

"You certainly are in a sad plight," answered Totaro. "Come with me to my home, and I will provide for you."

So the creature followed his new master to his garden. There Totaro placed him in a clear blue lake on which floated rose-coloured Lotus flowers, while on its banks grew gay Azaleas bending to look at themselves in the water. And there he left Samebito and fed him daily. So for nearly a year the strange creature lived in the clear blue lake.

Now one day when Totaro rode forth to enjoy the festival of Cherry-blossoms, he saw a beautiful maiden sitting beneath the Cherry-trees. And, as the breezes blew the white-pink petals from the boughs, they dropped in showers upon her dark hair and richly embroidered kimono. And as Totaro gazed he fell in love with the maiden.

He inquired who she was, and learned that her name was Tamana, and that she had many

suitors. Yet none would she wed unless he presented her with a casket containing ten thousand
jewels.

When Totaro learned this he was filled with
despair, for, though he was wealthy, yet not all
his riches were sufficient to purchase ten thousand rare gems.

He returned to his home, and became so ill,
that the doctor shook his head and said that
nothing could cure him.

Now Samebito, in the clear blue lake, heard
the servants say that his master was ill and
dying. So he crept from the water and hastened
to Totaro's chamber.

"Oh, Samebito," cried Totaro, when he saw
him enter, "who will feed you when I am gone?"

"Alas! Alas! My good master!" cried Samebito.

Then, uttering a wild yell, the creature began
to weep great tears of blood. And as the tears
fell on the floor they changed into glowing
Rubies.

When Totaro saw the bright jewels sparkling on the floor, he shouted with delight, and
his health came back. He sprang from his
couch and began to gather up the Rubies.

Seeing this, Samebito stopped weeping, and
asked in astonishment why his master had re-
covered so suddenly.

"It is because of your tears!" cried Totaro.

"I was dying of grief since I could not procure ten thousand jewels for the maiden Tamana. Now that your tears have turned to Rubies, she will consent to become my bride!"

Then Totaro counted the jewels, but there were not ten thousand.

"Not enough! Not enough!" he cried. "Weep! Samebito, weep!"

"What!" said Samebito angrily; "do you think I can weep at will? I wept only because you were dying. Now that you are well, it is a time for laughter, not for grief."

"But unless you weep," replied Totaro, "I cannot get ten thousand jewels, and the beautiful Tamana will not marry me. What, then, am I to do? Weep, dear friend, weep!"

"Master," answered Samebito, sorrowfully, "I cannot cry unless I am sad. Let us, therefore, return to the bridge where you found me. Perhaps as I sit and gaze toward the Dragon Palace, and as I think of my lost home, I may weep."

So to the bridge by the sea they went, and Samebito sat and gazed into the green water, and as he did so his eyes filled with great tears of blood. As the teardrops fell on the bridge they changed into glowing Rubies.

Shouting with delight, Totaro gathered up the jewels, and found that he now had many more than ten thousand.

At that same moment sweet strains of music

came from the sea. And from the waves arose a Rainbow mist that shaped itself into a wonderful palace. And when Samebito saw this he gave a cry of joy.

"Farewell, my master!" he exclaimed. "The Dragon Kings are calling!"

Then, plunging from the bridge, the strange creature disappeared for ever beneath the ocean foam.

Totaro hastened to place his jewels in a magnificent casket and present them to Tamana. Soon afterward their marriage feast was celebrated with great joy.

THE FAIRY SWAN SONG

Celtic Myth

BEAUTIFUL was the Fairy Palace on the Boyne, and through its glittering halls the magic music rose and fell and died away.

In the largest and most glittering hall, on silken cushions, Angus, the Fairy Prince of Love, lay sleeping. Over his head hovered four bright-plumaged birds, which were his gentle kisses. And when the bright birds sang, the strains of their melody pierced the green earth, and mortal maids and mortal youths loved one another.

Now, while the Fairy Prince was sleeping, the birds began to sing a song so low and tender that it failed to pierce the earth, and falling

like a mist, softly stole into Prince Angus's
dream.

And lo! he thought he saw a lake great and
wild, and by its margin walked a maiden robed
in white and crowned with yellow gold. And as
he gazed, she turned luminous eyes upon him,
and his heart grew sad with love, and he awoke.

Then through East, through West, through
South, through North, rode Prince Angus, the
bright birds fluttering above his head, and he
searched the world over and found not the
maiden.

Then to his aid he called the Red King of the
Fairies, and bade him seek for her throughout
the land. For a year and a day the Red King
searched, and then, returning, said: —

"Shining One, the maiden of your dream
dwells at a lake called the Lake of the Dragon's
Mouth. Thither must you go with me to find
her."

So over bog and moor, over valley and mountain, over brook and meadow, fared Prince
Angus and the Red King, till they reached the
shore of the Lake of the Dragon's Mouth, a lake
great and wild.

And on its margin walked two by two thrice
fifty gold-crowned maidens, trailing their white
robes through the lush green grass, yellow with
blowing Lilies. And the maidens were linked
two by two with golden chains, and one of the

maidens was taller and fairer than the rest. And as they passed Prince Angus, the fairest one turned luminous eyes upon him.

"That is she," cried he to the Red King, "that is the maiden of my dream! Tell me by what name she is known."

"Her name is Caer," answered the Red King. "She is the daughter of the Fairy Prince of Connacht. But so powerful is she that we shall not be able to take her by force. Let us then seek her father and ask for his aid."

So to the Fairy Prince of Connacht they went.

"I cannot give you my daughter Caer," said he, "for she is more powerful than I. She is a Swan-Maiden, and in the form of a Swan does she dwell on the waters of the Lake of the Dragon's Mouth. When the Moon is at the full you will see her, together with thrice fifty other Swans save one, crowned with yellow gold."

So when the Moon was at the full, to the Lake of the Dragon's Mouth went Prince Angus; and the four bright birds sang low and witching notes as they flew above his head. And when he drew near, he saw that the lake was no longer wild, but smooth like glass, and on its surface, mirrored in the moonlit waters, floated two by two thrice fifty snow-white Swans, each crowned with yellow gold. And the Swans were linked two by two with golden chains, and one of the Swans was whiter and larger than the rest.

"Caer, most beautiful of Swan-Maidens!" cried the Prince. "Oh, come and speak to me!"

"Who calls me?" said Caer.

"'T is I, Angus, the Fairy Prince of Love," he answered. "And hither am I come to the world's end, seeking you, O Maiden of my dream."

And even as he spoke, his form was changed into that of a Swan, large and snow-white and beautiful. Uttering a joyous cry he plunged into the lake to join Caer.

Then from the water together they rose on their swan-wings, circling higher and higher, and toward the Fairy Palace on the Boyne they flew, making as they went such delicious music that all mortals who heard their song straightway fell into a magic slumber for three nights and three days.

And above the heads of the flying Swans hovered and fluttered the four bright-plumaged birds shedding sweet melody upon earth — a gift for mortal maids and mortal youths.

ON THE WINGS OF THE WIND IN
THE RAINBOW SKY

THE SONG OF THE CLOUD

I bring fresh Showers for the thirsting flowers,
  From the seas and the streams;
I bear light shade for the leaves when laid
  In their noonday dreams.
From my wings are shaken the Dews that waken
  The sweet buds every one,
When rocked to rest on their mother's breast,
  As she dances about the Sun.
I wield the flail of the lashing Hail,
  And whiten the green plains under,
And then again I dissolve it in Rain,
  And laugh as I pass in Thunder.

.   .   .   .

That orbèd maiden with white fire laden,
  Whom mortals call the Moon,
Glides glimmering o'er my fleece-like floor,
  By the midnight breezes strewn;
And wherever the beat of her unseen feet,
  Which only the Angels hear,
May have broken the woof of my tent's thin roof,
  The Stars peep behind her and peer;
And I laugh to see them whirl and flee,
  Like a swarm of golden Bees,
When I widen the rent in my wind-built tent,
  Till the calm rivers, lakes, and seas,
Like strips of the sky fallen through me on high,
  Are each paved with the Moon and these!

From PERCY BYSSHE SHELLEY'S *The Cloud*

WHY THE IRIS WEARS RAINBOW COLOURS

Old Tale

A VERY marvellous family had Wonder, the son of Pontus, and the Nymph Brightness, the daughter of Old Father Ocean.

Four daughters were theirs, three of whom were called the Harpies or Snatchers. Most dreadful winged-monsters these three were, with bodies like birds', and faces like women's, and breath that rushed from their nostrils like the blast of stormy winds.

Over the heaving seas they flew, now seizing a ship and whirling it far out of its course, and now swooping down and snatching food from its deck or plundering everything on which they could lay their sharp claws.

Though these three children of Wonder and Brightness were such horrible creatures, their fourth daughter was good and beautiful. Iris was her name, — swift-footed Iris-of-the-Golden-Wings.

When Iris passed like a flash through the air, so rapid was her flight that her burnished golden wings shone like sunbeams, while her long robe, of brilliant blended colours, lay like a bright scarf against the grey sky.

So wise was Iris that Juno, the wife of Jupiter, took her to live in the shining Palace on Mount Olympus, to be her attendant and messenger. Iris joyfully waited upon her night and day, making Juno's bed, and harnessing her Peacocks to the royal chariot. She even slept in sandals and robe by the side of Juno's golden throne, ever ready to start up and bear her mistress's commands over the Rainbow Bridge to any part of the world.

One day Juno, to reward her faithful Iris, called for a golden goblet filled with Nectar, and sprinkled a few drops of the precious liquor over the earth.

They fell into the flower-cup of a stately white Flag growing by a river. Then they foamed up in beautiful colours, — red, orange, yellow, green, blue, indigo, and violet, — and, overflowing, stained the petals of the Flag with all the hues of the Rainbow.

So Juno named the flower "Iris."

FLOWER OF THE RAINBOW

New Tale

IN the long, long ago, in those wonder-days when Daphne became the Laurel and Clytie the Heliotrope, at the foot of Mount Helicon there dwelt a Shepherd-lad, named Chrysos.

Each day he led his flocks along the grassy

bank of a stream that gushed cold and pure from the mountain-side. When he was hungry, he plucked the ripe fruits that hung from the boughs above his head. When he was thirsty, he drank of the sparkling water. And if the hot rays of the noonday Sun beat upon the earth, he sat beneath a shady tree, and played upon his pipes while his flock gambolled about him.

Now there were Shepherdesses near that stream, but Chrysos would not walk with them. He preferred to wander alone by the water, and to dream.

"Come, Chrysos," the Shepherdesses would call. "Come, dance with us among the flowers. Come and be merry."

But he would only shake his head, and driving his flock farther on, would sit upon a bank and dream.

And Chrysos dreamed of gold!—always of gold heaped up and glistening! Rich gold, red gold! Night and day he longed for gold! The purple Crocus, the perfumed Violet, the silvery Narcissus bending over the stream, the caressing airs, the laughing waters leaping down the mountain-side, none of these did Chrysos see or hear.

And when the Sun broke through the gentle rains of Spring, and the Rainbow's radiant arch bent over Mount Helicon, Chrysos gazed upon the arch and sighed: —

"Ah me! Ah me! They say the Bow sheds gold! Fortunate the man who at the end of yonder arch may find the Crock that holds the gold of Iris! Oh would that I might find that gold! Ah me! Ah me!"

And sighing thus, he dreamed.

So it happened on a fragrant day, the Sun smiled behind a veil of soft Spring shower, and Chrysos sat beneath a tree watching for the Rainbow to span Mount Helicon. Then, suddenly, swiftly, the flashing, shimmering band, all rosy, yellow, violet, blue, like a path of blended lights, reached from Chrysos' feet up through the Sky, and bent in a glorious arc across Mount Helicon.

Then down this Rainbow-path there seemed to glide, to float, to wing its way, a lovely form, a maiden with robes of a thousand hues, and golden wings that burned like flames. She held aloft a herald's staff, and in her other hand a crystal vase from which distilled the drops that fed the Clouds.

So floating, gliding, down the Rainbow-path she came, and beckoned with her staff to wondering Chrysos. Up he sprang and threw his crook aside.

"Iris! The gold! The gold!" he cried.

And straight he leaped upon the Bow that trembled underneath his feet. But it held firm. And Iris, smiling, turned, and floated upward;

while Chrysos, panting, pressed on up the Rainbow-path.

Then the Sun shone forth, and the Rain ceased. The trembling Rainbow melted beneath Chrysos' mortal feet. And with a cry he fell.

The Shepherdesses saw him fall; and though, day and night, they searched the mountain-side, they could not find his broken body. But in a dewy hollow by the stream where he had sat, they saw a little flower with Rainbow-petals and golden heart. And when the Sun rose high and cast his hot rays, the flower faded and was gone.

THE BOY WHOSE WINGS FELL OFF

Retold from Ovid

A FEARFUL monster was the Minotaur of Crete, half Bull and half man, a savage monster whose daily food was beautiful youths. So horrible was he, that King Minos commanded Dædalus, a famous artisan, to build an abode strong enough to hold him.

So Dædalus laid out a Labyrinth containing so many winding passages and bewildering mazes that every one who entered became confused and could never find his way out again. In the very heart of this Labyrinth, the King shut up the Minotaur.

Now Dædalus and his young son, Icarus,

were exiles, and held as captives in the Island of Crete; and they were watched night and day lest they should try to escape. So Dædalus thought to himself: —

"If by my skill I could build the Labyrinth, why can I not invent a means of escape? The sea belongs to King Minos! But the air belongs to me!"

Thereupon he began to fashion two pairs of wings like a bird's, arranging the long feathers in order, and fastening them together with thread and wax. Young Icarus stood by his side, smiling eagerly. Now he sorted the feathers for his father, now he kneaded the yellow wax.

When the wings were finished, Dædalus attached one pair to his own shoulders, and put the other pair on Icarus. Then he beat his own wings together, and, raising himself from the earth, said: —

"My dear son, follow me with care. Fly not too low, or the water will wet your feathers. Fly not too high, or the Sun will melt the wax."

Then kissing Icarus tenderly, and trembling for his safety, he led the way over the sea. Icarus followed, beating his wings with delight. Onward and onward they flew. Under them rolled the fierce billows, and above them spread out the wide sky.

Soon Icarus forgot his father's command, and

began to long for a bolder flight. He was even filled with a great desire to reach Heaven itself. So he mounted higher and higher, until the hot Sun melted the wax, and his wings fell from his shoulders.

Then downward, like a plummet, he dropped into the dark water. In terror he stretched out his arms and called aloud for his father, but the hungry billows closed over his head.

Meanwhile Dædalus missed his son, and flew to and fro calling his name. Looking down he saw his wings floating on the water. In vain he searched and called. Then soon he perceived the waves casting Icarus's body on to the shore of an island.

Then the wretched father, winging his way to the land, lifted the body of his dear son tenderly, and mourned over it with tears. After which he buried it there in a tomb that he made. And that island was called Icaria.

THE MAN IN THE MOON

Folktale

ONCE upon a time, an old man lived in a hut near a forest. He was too lazy to gather fagots for his fire; so one Sunday, when he thought that every one else was at Church, he slipped into the forest and stole a bundle of fagots that was lying under a tree.

Softly he crept out of the forest again, with the bundle of fagots on his back, when what should he see but a stranger on a white horse galloping toward him.

"Old man," said the stranger, "since you have stolen these fagots, and stolen them on Sunday as well, you shall be punished. To what place would you rather be banished? To the Sun, or to the Moon?"

"The Sun is too hot," answered the old man. "I would rather freeze in the Moon."

Scarcely were the words out of his mouth when — *whisk* — he shot up through the Sky, and landed straight in the Moon.

And there he stands to-day with the bundle of fagots on his back. Some folk say that his wife is with him, churning and churning and churning, as a punishment, because she churned on Sunday when everybody else was at Church. And they say, too, that sometimes the Man in the Moon comes down to earth with a bag on his back, and that he carries off all the bad children.

THE STORY OF JACK AND JILL

Norse Myth

Retold from the Younger Edda

ONCE upon a time, the bright maiden, called Sun, was driving her flame-red chariot through the sky. Swiftly her horses sped along the blue arch of heaven, the fleecy clouds floating about their feet. At last they reached the place where the Sun always sets, and vanished beyond the sea.

Darkness fell, but not for long. Soon the softly shining youth, called Moon, came gently driving his flame-white chariot from the place where the Moon always rises. And silently the chariot cast its broad, silvery beams over land and sea.

Now Moon was very lonesome, for at night the world was quiet, and people slept or rested. But it happened one night that two children were wandering around in the moonlight. The boy's name was Juke, and the girl's, Bil. They carried a pail of water between them, hung from a pole on their shoulders.

Moon looked down and saw them. Gently he guided his horses to earth, and, snatching up the children, carried them into the sky. There he placed them in his flame-white chariot.

And you may see them to-day, whenever the Moon is full. There they stand, Juke and Bil, holding their pail of water between them.

THE SHEEP IN THE PASTURE

Welsh Myth

IN the ancient land of Wales there once lived two brothers, Kings of Britain. Their names were Peibaw and Nynniaw. One moonlight night they were walking together in the royal garden.

"Look! See what a fine, wide field I have," said Nynniaw.

"Where is it?" asked Peibaw.

"There above our heads — the whole wide heaven," said Nynniaw.

"But look! See, all my cattle are grazing in your field!" said Peibaw.

"Where are they?" asked Nynniaw.

"There above our heads — all the golden Stars, with the Moon for their shepherd," said Peibaw.

"They shall not graze in my field!" cried Nynniaw.

"I say they shall," said Peibaw.

"They shall not!"

"They shall!"

"They shall not!"

And they went on quarrelling and answering each other until they returned to the palace.

Then the two brothers called together their armies and went to war. They laid waste the land, burned down houses, and killed the people, until at last they both were changed into Oxen, as a punishment for their stupidity and wickedness.

THE LAZY BOYS WHO BECAME THE PLEIADES

Caddo Myth

LONG, long ago, there lived an old woman who had seven children, all boys. Those seven boys were so full of fun and frolic that they would run off by themselves and play from morning till night. Indeed, they liked to play so well that they scarcely took time to eat. And, as they never worked, their mother was always scolding them soundly.

It happened one evening they came home so late that their mother sent them to bed without supper. And though they got up very early the next morning, she refused to give them any breakfast. So they were hungry and sad.

Now their mother did not know it, but they had learned some magic songs. So they went outside, and began to dance round and round the house, singing mournfully.

By and by their mother heard them, and came rushing out. She saw their feet slowly rising from the ground; but still they kept on dancing and singing. She was very much frightened, and tried to grasp their legs, but up, up the seven boys went, circling higher and higher into the sky.

And there they became Seven Stars; and the Paleface Children call them the Pleiades.

And because those seven boys did not like to work, the Seven Stars may be seen only in Winter. But in Spring and Summer, when the time is come for ploughing, planting, and reaping, those lazy Seven-Star Brothers are gone.

THE MAIDEN IN THE MOON

Folktale from Eastern Europe

ONCE upon a time, there was a charming maiden called Twilight. She was so lovely that she delighted to admire her own face.

One evening she knelt down beside the silver looking-glass of a river, and gazed at her reflection in the quiet water. She saw her cloud-like dusky hair, her softly beaming eyes, and her smiling mouth. And so she knelt in delight, admiring her own image.

Now it chanced that the white youth, called Moon, rose high above the mountains, and glanced down into the silver looking-glass of the river. He saw the reflection of Twilight's lovely face gazing up at him.

Then quickly he descended from the Sky, and laid himself like a bright silver disc under the smooth water, and gazed back into Twilight's beaming eyes. And straightway she forgot her own lovely image, and could think only of Moon's white beauty.

So she would have knelt the whole night through, but a thick darkness fell upon the Earth, for Moon had forgotten to send his silver beams over land and sea.

And when Twilight saw the darkness, she wept with sorrow, then Moon remembered his duty. Swiftly he rose from under the water, and, gathering her in his arms, carried her back with him to the Sky.

So to-day lovely Twilight rests her head against the bright Moon, and there you may see her happy face.

THE COLOURS OF THE RAINBOW

New Tale

"CHILD," asked the Fairy, "how are you off for Rainbows?"

"Rainbows!" said the Child scornfully, "how could I have a Rainbow with my dull life? You have to have sunshine for that!"

"Ah, but, Child," returned the Fairy, "you also have to have rain. — Do you know," she continued, "what the Rainbow-colours mean?"

"No," said the Child. "What do they mean?"

The Fairy smoothed her long white wings. "Violet is For-Other-People's-Sorrows. Indigo is Troubles-of-Your-Own. True Blue is for Honest-Purposes, and Green for Happy-Memories."

"And Yellow?" said the Child softly. "I love Yellow!"

"Yellow is the Blessings-We-Forget. Orange, splendid glowing Orange, is God's Promise-of-Victory, and Red is the Richness-of-Life-After-All."

The Fairy bent to tighten her heel-wings. "So you see, Child, you need both Sun and Rain to make a Rainbow."

"I see," said the Child. "What is the Sun?"

"The Sun is the Love-That-is-in-You."

"Oh!" said the Child. "And what is the Rain?"

"The Rain is the Need-Right-Around-You."

"Oh!" said the Child. "And can *I* —"

"You certainly can," said the Fairy, smiling, and she vanished.

GLADYS WOLCOTT BARNES

A DROP OF THE WATER OF LIGHT

New Tale

ONCE upon a time, there was a Queen who had two children, — a son named Floribel, and a daughter named Coeca. They were both extremely beautiful. But, alas! when the Princess Coeca reached her sixteenth year, she became blind. Her large, soft brown eyes had no light in them.

The Queen consulted the Wisemen of the Kingdom; and they said: —

"Her aunt, the wicked Queen Pomarea, has cast a spell upon her. Nothing will break it and restore her sight except a Drop of the Water of Light."

"Where does this water come from?" asked Prince Floribel.

"It springs from the Glacier of the Mountains of the Moon," replied the Wisemen.

"Then I will go and get a drop," said the Prince.

"There are many great dangers in the way," said the Wisemen.

"Nevertheless I will go," answered the Prince, for he loved his sister tenderly.

While he was preparing for the journey, his mother entered his apartment, and, pulling a hair from her head, presented it to him.

"My son," said she, "cast this before you, and it will lead you to your sister's Fairy Godmother, who will tell you what to do next."

Prince Floribel obediently cast the hair before him, and it sailed out of the window. He leaped after it, and was carried rapidly along to a strange land, where he was dropped gently upon the ground. All around him were hedges to which clung quantities of gossamer webs, spangled with dew. He then saw that his mother's hair was caught in one of these webs. He put his finger into the gossamer threads to disentangle the hair, and instantly the web grew larger and larger, and, enveloping him like a veil, carried him off his feet, and wafted him to the Clouds.

There he found himself in Fairyland; and a kind old Fairy was standing before him.

"Prince Floribel," said she, "I am the Fairy Godmother of the Princess Coeca. I will do what I can for you, for your purpose is good. You shall go to the Mountains of the Moon. I will give you three things, — your mother's hair, a tray, and a bit of advice."

So saying, she handed him a little sandal-wood tray, and, taking the hair from him, stroked it, and stroked it, while it grew longer and longer. Then she twisted it, and reeled it on a spindle.

"When you require a boat," said she, "set this tray upon the water and step into it. As for the hair, look!"

She cast the end before her, and the spindle began to unwind rapidly as the end of the hair flew away.

"Reel this up as you follow it," said she,

"and unwind it again when you return." And she handed him the spindle.

Immediately the gossamer web enveloped Prince Floribel more closely, and wafted him down to the lower world again. As he set his feet upon the earth, he saw a rusty crowbar lying there. He picked it up and took it along with him.

Presently he came to a House that was groaning and moaning loudly.

"Why do you groan and moan so?" asked he.

"Because," said the House, "my windows and door are all on one side, and that side is turned toward the North. The bright warm rays of the Sun cannot reach my rooms, so they are mouldy and damp, and bugs live in them."

"I'll quickly change all that," said Prince Floribel, for he was very kind-hearted.

So with his crowbar he turned the House around until its windows faced the South and the warm sunshine poured into them. Then the House stopped groaning and moaning, and laughed instead.

As Prince Floribel was turning away, he heard something weeping and sobbing, and saw on a window-sill a lank little Ivy-vine in a pot. It was pale and feeble.

"Why are you weeping and sobbing so?" asked he.

"Because I have not enough soil to grow in,"

said the Ivy, "and the bright light cannot touch my roots."

"I'll quickly change all that," said the Prince.

So he took the little Ivy-vine out of its pot, and planted it by the side of the House where the bright light could strengthen it.

Then he saw that the Ivy-vine was glistening and dripping with dew as if with tears of gratitude; and he heard its little voice say: —

"Because you have been so kind to the House and to me, I will help you when you need it."

Prince Floribel then pursued his way, and soon came to the place where the River of Light rolled along. He set his tray upon the water, and stepped into it. It immediately became a boat, and he sailed rapidly up the river.

Soon he saw before him the mighty Mountains of the Moon, shining like Diamonds, and reaching halfway up to heaven. Between them rose the Glacier, flashing brighter than any Diamond, while from its side gushed a waterfall, that, as it touched the river, broke into spray whose drops sparkled like Opals, Rubies, and Pearls.

Prince Floribel caught one pearly drop in the palm of his hand, and, turning his boat around, shot down the river. But the banks were different now. They towered above him in cliffs and crags too steep and sharp to climb.

It grew dark as pitch around him. As he unreeled the spindle with his right hand, with his left he held aloft the Drop of the Water of Light that illumined the whole darkness before him.

Thus Prince Floribel sailed on for some time, until suddenly the hair rose to the top of the cliff, and at the same instant he heard the thunderous roar of a cataract toward which his boat was speeding. His heart stood still with terror, and he trembled so that the drop danced, and almost fell from his palm.

Then he saw before him the end of a frail streamer of Ivy hanging from the cliff, and waving in the draught of the river. He caught it with his right hand, and as he did so, the boat shot from under his feet, and plunged down the cataract.

Clinging to the Ivy, Prince Floribel climbed to the top of the cliff. He found himself in a wide country, and, following the hair, soon reached the Kingdom of his wicked Aunt Pomarea.

He stayed there just long enough to put his crowbar under her throne, and turn it toward the Sun, for she always sat facing the North. And when the bright sunshine streamed into the dark recesses of her heart, she saw how many mean and spiteful thoughts were hidden there. She wept so hard that the tears carried away all her bad feelings and left her heart filled with light, and with love for her sister, and for Prince Floribel, and the Princess Coeca.

After that the Prince hastened to his mother's Kingdom, and dashed the Drop of the Water of Light into the Princess Coeca's eyes. At once she sprang up with a cry of joy, for she could see again.

I need not declare the happiness of Prince Floribel, the wonder of the Princess Coeca, nor tell how glad the Queen-mother was, nor how great were the rejoicings of the people, nor how magnificent was the royal banquet that good Queen Pomarea attended with all her Court.

S. BARING-GOULD (*retold*)

THE HALCYON BIRDS

Retold from Ovid

ONCE upon a time, there was a King named Ceyx, who was very happy with his beloved wife Halcyone, the daughter of old King Æolus, ruler of the Winds.

It happened that Ceyx's brother was lost most mysteriously, so he determined to set out on a voyage in search of him. This he told his wife Halcyone; and she grew pale, and wept at the thought of their parting.

"I swear to you, Dear One," said he, "that I will return before the new Moon appears twice in the sky."

And with this promise, he bade her good-bye, and stepped into the swift, many-oared ship. She, shuddering, wrung her hands and cried:—

"Farewell! my Beloved, farewell!"

So King Ceyx's ship set out over the boundless deep. Onward and onward it sailed; and when night came on the sea began to foam with swelling waves. The boisterous East Wind blew with violence. The sea was upturned with billows that seemed to reach to heaven and to lash the Clouds. The great waves beat against the sides of the ship.

So fearfully did they beat, and with such violence, that the bolts fell from the blanks, the seams opened, and the fatal waves rushed in. The ship sank, and King Ceyx was hurled far out into the deep. He called aloud for Halcyone, but the black hungry billows closed over his head.

Meanwhile, Halcyone, not knowing what had happened to her husband, began to prepare for his return. She spun, wove, and embroidered rich garments for him, while she sat waiting morning and noon and night for his ship to come sailing back.

Then Juno, Queen of all the Dwellers-on-Mount-Olympus, looked down from her Shining Palace, and saw poor Halcyone watching and waiting for King Ceyx to return, — watching and waiting in vain. She pitied the poor wife, and straightway summoned her messenger, swift Iris-of-the-Golden-Wings. She bade her go at once to the Court of old Father Sleep, and command him to send a vision of her drowned husband to Halcyone.

Iris put on her robe of a thousand colours, and, spanning the sky with her bright Rainbow, hastened over it to the Court of old Father Sleep.

In a cavern in a hollow mountain he lived, all slothful with slumber. Silence filled that land. Fogs of darkness brooded over the cavern. Within it no sound was heard of voice, or of waving bough, or of stirring bird. Before its door was a field of Poppies drooping their languid heads, and near them grew rank herbs whose dark juices bring fatal slumber.

On an ebony couch spread with dusky pillows lay old Father Sleep, torpid and heavy-eyed; while around him reclined the pale, transparent forms of Dreams. And into that silent cave came gliding golden-winged Iris, and delivered Juno's message.

Old Father Sleep, lifting for one moment his heavy lids, murmuringly bade his son Morpheus take Ceyx's shape, and appear in a dream to Halcyone. Then back he sank in deep slumber upon his ebony couch.

With noiseless wings, and wrapped in his dark robe, Morpheus flew through the night. In the shape of her dead husband, he bent over Halcyone's bed. She saw him, and beheld his pale visage and dripping hair. She stretched out her hands to hold him, but he fled away. Wailing with grief she awoke.

Then rising from her bed, she hurried to the shore, and standing on a rock gazed out across the sea in the direction that she had seen her beloved husband depart. And, lo! as she gazed she saw something white on the crest of a distant billow. The billow rolled toward the land, and cast the white thing against the rock at her feet. It was her own Ceyx's body glimmering palely on the dark tossing water.

Tears rained down her cheeks. She stretched out her arms. She leaped to join him in the sea. And, lo! two wings supported her. She flew, beating the light air with her new pinions. She had become a bird skimming close to the water.

She touched Ceyx, kissing his mouth with her slender beak. Then, lo! he too was changed. Up he rose as a bird into the air. Two Kingfishers they were, — Halcyon Birds, — flying side by side, while sad, piping notes came from their long, slender beaks.

So they lived together, flying to and fro on the face of the water. And every year, during seven calm days in Winter, did Halcyone brood upon her eggs in a nest floating on the sea. And all those seven days were calm and peaceful be-

cause her father, old King Æolus, had shut up
his rough sons, the Winds, so that his daughter,
the Halcyon Bird, might brood in happiness and
safety.

THE BAG OF WINDS

Retold from Homer's Odyssey

Thus it happened in the golden days when the
Earth was young: —

The wise Ulysses, King of Ithaca, escaping
from Calypso's Fairy Isle, where he had been
enchanted, stretched himself upon a raft, and
hoisted sail. Night and day he sped over the
dark blue sea before a freshening breeze. But a
stormy Wind arising, he was cast speechless and
perishing upon the Phæacian shore.

Then the white-armed Nausicaa, the bright-
haired daughter of King Alcinous, found him.
She led him to her father's palace, that shone
with brazen walls, and golden doors guarded by
gold and silver Dogs. And there King Alcinous
welcomed him, and had him clad in new rich
robes.

Then, seated on a silver-studded throne, Ulysses,
sipping mingled wine and eating savory meats,
spoke thus: —

O Alcinous, large-hearted King, and wise
Queen Areta! Know that the story of my
sufferings is very fearful.

Since that time when I fought before the walls of Troy I have wandered far, searching for my native Ithaca. But never could I come unto that land, for Neptune, King of the loud-sounding Ocean, pursued me with his wrath. He was enraged because I had put out the eye of his monster son, Polyphemus the Cyclops.

Therefore he bade his stormy Winds pursue me. Night and day they drove my tossing ship across the loud-sounding Ocean. They blew her from isle to isle and coast to coast.

Fearful were the misfortunes we suffered, my men and I! For scarcely did we escape from the drowsy Lotus-Eaters before we were imprisoned in the loathsome cave of one-eyed Polyphemus, who slew and devoured some of my men. I put out the monster's eye; and those of us who remained quickly launched our swift-bounding ship and beat the hoary main with our oars. So we escaped from the Cyclops.

After other horrors had been our lot, Aurora, the rosy-fingered child of Dawn, arose from the bright morning Clouds, and we saw in the distance the Æolian Isle, the abode of King Æolus. Thither we steered, and soon landed on its coast.

It was a floating island, with walls of brass around it. And in his shining palace, day by day, King Æolus banqueted with his twelve lovely children. Faint strains of music, as though the gentle breeze did touch a Fairy harp, floated through the perfumed halls and hovered over couches spread with tapestry. And to this palace King Æolus welcomed me, and he refreshed us all with Nectar and delicious viands.

For one full month we tarried there; and then I begged the King to permit us to depart, for my soul longed for sunny Ithaca.

He consented, and went with us to our ship. He placed within the hold a huge leather bag, and bound it to the floor with bright silver chains.

"Ulysses, wise-hearted King," said he, "in this bag are imprisoned all the fierce stormy Winds. Open it not! And I will send before you my gentle son, Zephyr, to blow against your sails; and so may you come safely to sunny Ithaca."

So we departed, and the gentle West Wind, Zephyr, breathed softly on us and wafted our ship over the smooth blue sea. Not a wave rippled, nor was there a wreath of foam on the far waters.

For nine days and nine nights we skimmed over the smooth blue sea, and on the ninth day we sighted the shore of Ithaca. Now for those nine days and nine nights I had not slept, but had sat with my hand ever on the rudder. And when I saw my native fields so near, sorrow fell from me and peace enwrapped me, while all-powerful Sleep pressed on my weary eyelids. I slumbered.

Then my men talked among themselves. "See," said they, "what a rich gift of gold and silver King Æolus has stored in yon huge bag! How greatly beloved is our Chief by all men, for when he sailed from Troy they filled the hold with gifts and spoils of treasure for him, while no man gave us anything! Come, let us open this bag, and see what King Æolus has bestowed upon him!"

So they untied the bag. Alas! The fierce stormy Winds rushed forth! They darkened the Sky with their dusky wings. They tossed up the raging billows. They seized the ship and whirled her far out upon the roaring deep. And I awoke and found the Whirlwinds bearing us back to King Æolus's isle!

Despair grasped my soul, but silently I endured, and soon we were driven upon his coast.

We landed. I took a little food and wine to strengthen me, and hastened to the palace. There I found King Æolus banqueting with his children.

"What!" cried they. "Why are you here? What evil Fate pursues you, O Ulysses, wretched man? We sent you away well protected, so that you might safely reach your home!"

"It was the fault of my unthinking men," I said, "and of my weariness. For while I slept they untied the bag, believing that it held much treasure."

"Hence with you, wicked man!" cried King Æolus. "Hence, miserable wretch! Vilest of living men must you be if Fate pursues you thus!"

Lamenting and weeping, I left the palace door. Again we set sail upon the pitiless deep. Through the mounting billows we drove, only to suffer greater misfortunes, for Neptune, King of the loud-sounding Ocean, called up again his stormy Winds, and they raged around us.

Many and fearful were our adventures, until at last all my men — my comrades — perished, and I was shipwrecked on the sand of Calypso's Fairy Isle. And there I languished seven years, enchanted by the bright-haired Nymph. But when she saw me grieving, mercy moved her heart, and she sent me forth upon a raft to search once more for sunny Ithaca.

So I escaped from the enchanted Isle, but Neptune, still pursuing me, I was cast perishing upon thy shore, O Alcinous, large-hearted King! Then did the white-armed Nausicaa save me and bring me hither.

And so the bag of Winds that King Æolus gave, wrought despair for me and destruction for my men.

Thus ended his tale, the wise Ulysses, and sat in silent grief.

WITH FLASH O' FIRE AND GLINT
O' GOLD

HOW THE CYCLOPS MADE ÆNEAS' ARMOUR IN VULCAN'S FORGE

In streams the gold, the copper flows,
And in the mighty furnace glows
  The death-inflicting steel.
A shield they plan, whose single guard
May all the blows of Latium ward
Some make the windy bellows heave,
Now give forth air, and now receive.
The copper hisses in the wave.
The anvils press the groaning cave.
With measured cadence each and all
The giant hammers rise and fall.
The griping pincers, deftly plied,
Turn the rough ore from side to side.

  And the Cyclops made: —
The helm that like a meteor burns,
  The sword that rules the war,
The breastplate shooting bloody rays,
As dusky clouds in sunlight blaze,
  Refulgent from afar,
The polished greaves of molten gold,
The spear, the shield with fold on fold,
A prodigy of art untold.

                    From VIRGIL'S ÆNEID (*Condensed.*)

THE GOLDEN GIFT OF KING MIDAS

Retold from Herodotus and Ovid

ONCE upon a time, there lived a King of Phrygia named Midas. He loved gold above everything and everybody. And next to gold he loved his spacious and beautiful Rose Gardens, in which Roses grew in great pink and white masses. Everywhere the Rose-Vines trailed across walls and around statues; they climbed over the roof of the palace; they covered the ivory pleasure-houses; they wreathed the tree-trunks; and they perfumed the whole place. And every Rose blossom had sixty petals, and was larger and more fragrant than any other Rose in the world.

Inside King Midas's palace were couches of silver and ivory; cups, plates, and vases of precious metals beautifully chased; heaps of treasure; and a throne more magnificent than that of any other King on earth.

But in spite of all these riches King Midas was not happy, and wandered about his Rose Gardens, sighing for still greater treasures.

Now it happened, one day, that his servants brought to him Silenus, the attendant of Bacchus, Keeper-of-All-the-Vineyards-in-the-World. This Silenus was a stout, merry old fellow, flat-nosed and bald, who often drank more wine than was good for him. And the servants of King Midas had found him swaying about on the back of an Ass, and waving a big pot of wine in the air. So they brought him, just as he was, crowned with grape-leaves and singing loudly, into one of the Rose Gardens.

King Midas immediately gave orders that he should be taken into the palace, treated with all respect, and entertained royally. Then a few days after, King Midas himself escorted Silenus to Bacchus, Keeper-of-All-the-Vineyards-in-the-World.

Now Bacchus was merry-hearted and generous, so he gratefully said that King Midas might make a wish, and have anything he desired.

"Let it be, then," said King Midas eagerly, "that everything I touch shall instantly become gold."

"So be it," said Bacchus, laughing heartily, "though your wish is a bad one."

King Midas departed, and on his way home he gently touched an oak-twig that hung above his head. And, lo! it was instantly changed to pure gold!

Then he took up a stone, and it turned into pale gold. He seized a clod of earth, and found that he was grasping a yellow lump that crumbled into gold-dust and trickled through his fingers. He broke off some ears of Corn; they hardened, and glistened in the sunshine.

He plucked an Apple, and, lo! it was as bright and beautiful as one from the Garden of the Hesperides.

Oh, joyful, then, was King Midas! He hastened into his palace; and as he brushed past the lofty door-posts, they turned into pilasters of carven gold. He went hurrying from room to room, touching article after article; and soon all things in his palace glimmered, and shimmered, and sparkled in the sunlight.

But, alas! when King Midas sat down to eat, and his servants poured water over his hands, the drops that fell through his fingers were small golden balls. And when they set a table before him laden with sweetmeats and spiced viands, he bit with hungry teeth — not into food, but on hard lumps of precious metal. Groaning with hunger and thirst, he lifted his cup, and nothing but liquid gold passed through his lips.

And so it was on the next day, and on the next; there was nothing but gold, gold, gold, for King Midas to eat and drink. At last fierce hunger gnawed his vitals, burning thirst parched his throat, and he hated all his wealth. Then he rushed from his palace to find Bacchus again.

"O Keeper - of - All - the - Vineyards - in - the - World!" he cried. "What have I done to deserve this misery? Have pity on me! Take back your fatal gift, and give me food and drink once more!"

"O foolish man!" said Bacchus, laughing. "Did I not say that your wish was a bad one? But, in order that your treasures, which you so greatly desired, may not slay you, go to the river that flows by the great city of Sardis. Follow it to its source in the mountain, and plunge your head under its bubbling water where it bursts from the mountain-side. Then shall my golden gift leave you."

So to the source of the river King Midas hastened, and plunged his head into its cold bubbling water. And as he did so the waves of the river grew yellow, and the sand at its bottom sparkled with golden grains. Then, raising his head, he found to his joy that the fatal gift had passed from him. It was gone for ever.

So he ate and drank again, and returned to his palace and Rose Gardens a wiser and more contented man.

As for the river, from that time on it flowed over sands formed of golden grains that glinted and sparkled in the sun.

LITTLE WHITE RABBIT

Menomini Myth

ONCE upon a time, in Red Indian Land, a small lodge stood on an island in a great lake. In the lodge lived a poor old woman all alone.

One day she set a wooden bowl on the table,

and when she lifted it, under it was a little white Rabbit. She gave him some fresh leaves to nibble, and he went hopping and skipping around the lodge. Then suddenly he turned into a handsome young man.

"Oh! Ho! My Grandson!" cried the old woman with joy. "Sit down and I'll give you something to eat!"

So the young man sat down, and she fed him. After that he lived in the lodge, and his grandmother named him Manabus.

"Grandmother," he said one day, "why have we no Fire?"

"Oh, Fire is not for us, my Grandson," said she. "The only place on this Earth where there is any Fire is across the lake. There lives greedy Old-Man-Fire-Keeper, who has all the Fire in the world."

"Then I'll go and get some," said Manabus.

"Oh, no, my Grandson," cried his grandmother. "He will kill you!"

But Manabus teased her until she said "Yes."

"Have kindlings ready, Grandmother," said he, "to light when I bring the Fire home."

Then off he went. But as he ran over the threshold he turned into a little white Rabbit again, and went hopping and skipping away.

By and by he came to the shore of the lake and saw a broken-down wigwam on the beach. He lifted the mat that hung at the door, and peeped in. A wretched old woman, all in rags, sat shivering in the lodge.

"How goes it, Grandma?" cried Manabus, hopping and skipping to her feet.

"Yes, I'm here, Grandchild," said she. "But what have you come to me for?"

"I'm looking for Fire, Grandma; have you any?" asked he.

"No, indeed, I have n't any," answered she. "Across the lake lives greedy Old-Man-Fire-Keeper, who has all the Fire in the world."

"Then I'll be off and get some," said Manabus, "and I'll give you a spark when I come back."

And off he went, hopping and skipping to the water.

"May I be a Thistledown," said he, "and may a fair Wind blow me over the water!"

Then he became a Thistledown, and a fair Wind blew, and blew him over the lake to the shore on the other side. There he changed into a little white Rabbit again, and went hopping and skipping along.

And so he came to a spring, and near it was Old-Man-Fire-Keeper's lodge, that was big and covered with mats. Inside were two rooms. In one sat Old-Man-Fire-Keeper himself, in the other were his two pretty daughters.

Manabus hid under a stone near the spring. By and by the elder sister said to the younger:—

"Go fetch some fresh water from the spring."

So the younger sister took a bucket, but when she stooped to fill it at the spring, out jumped the little white Rabbit at her feet.

"Oh, you cunning little fellow!" she cried, and threw down her bucket, while Manabus, hopping and skipping, let her catch him. She put him in her bosom and ran back to the lodge.

"Look, sister," she cried, "I've caught a little white Rabbit! See how he shivers with cold!"

"Let us put him by the Fire to get warm," said the elder sister.

So they put Manabus down by the Fire.

"Now's my time," thought he. "May a fair Wind blow open the door, and may the Fire blaze up!"

Immediately a fair Wind lifted the mat at the door, and the Fire blazed up, and a spark fell on Manabus's fur. Then off he went like a flash through the door, hopping and skipping away. The girls ran after him.

"This is the way he went," shouted one.

"No, he went this way!" cried the other.

"I tell you, it was this!" said the first.

"My Daughters," called out Old-Man-Fire-Keeper from his lodge, "why are you quarrelling so?"

"Our little white Rabbit has run away," said they.

"No white Rabbit was he," growled Old-Man-

Fire-Keeper, "but a man who went off with some Fire. I heard the spark crack."

As for Manabus, he ran on, hopping and skipping, to the beach.

"May I be a Thistledown," said he, "and may a fair Wind blow me over the water!"

Then he became a Thistledown, and a fair Wind blew, and blew him across the lake to the island. Straight into his grandmother's lodge he ran.

"Heigh! Ho! Grandmother!" cried he. "Have you the kindlings ready?"

"Here they are, my Grandson," said she.

So Manabus backed up to the kindlings, and threw the spark on them. The kindlings burned, and the Fire blazed up.

Then Manabus took another spark on his fur, and away he went, hopping and skipping, until he came to the broken-down wigwam on the beach, where the wretched old woman sat shivering alone.

"Grandma, here is the Fire I promised," he cried. "May you never have to gather firewood; and may the Fire go out when you tell it to, and burn when you say so."

That is the way the little white Rabbit brought Fire in those old days. And when the people told the Fire to go out, it did; and when they said, "Burn," it blazed up; for it was Magic Fire. And they never had to gather any firewood.

THE WICKED FAIRIES

Old French Tale

ONCE upon a time, there were two young Fairies named Carabosse and Follette. They were both so malicious and wicked that the Fairy Queen banished them from her Court. So they fell to earth and wandered around, seeing how much mischief they could do to mortals.

Now it happened that they arrived at a country where there were many rich farms, on which were splendid crops of grain, and large fields of vegetables, and acres of fruit trees heavily laden. When Carabosse and Follette saw these they were filled with spite. They listened to what the farmers were saying to one another, and soon learned that the unhappy people were dissatisfied with the abundance growing on their land, and that they wished for all the wealth of the whole world.

Carabosse and Follette laughed mockingly; and when it was quite dark they touched with their wands everything that grew.

Instantly all was changed.

The ears of Corn, ripening so beautifully, no longer waved their yellow tassels, but were changed into ears studded with precious gems. Each stalk of grain was changed into a tube of gold or silver, surmounted by a cluster of Dia-

monds. The trees became columns of alabaster
or crystal, with leaves of Emerald and fruits of
Topaz, Rubies, Pearls, and Amethysts. The
grapevines were hung with bunches of Garnets
and Rubies. In fact, every growing thing
was changed into gold, silver, or precious
stones.

When the people woke in the morning and saw
their fields and orchards sparkling with a thousand coloured rays, they shouted with joy and
ran about picking basketfuls of jewels, and breaking off branches of alabaster or crystal. They
made themselves collars and girdles of Diamonds,
Rubies, and Pearls; and they plaited gold crowns
for their heads, and embroidered their garments
with every kind of gem.

The Summer passed and Autumn came.
There were no cool, spreading trees to sit under.
There were no delicate blossoms breathing fragrance. There were only stiff emerald leaves
and hard precious stones, whose brilliance burned
the eyes.

The farmer's sickle was broken against tubes
of gold and silver, and there was no grain for the
mill to grind into flour. The vines and orchard
trees, instead of being full of ripe Grapes, juicy
Apples, and velvety Peaches, broke beneath tons
of precious gems. No one could sell anything,
for everybody had so much wealth that he needed
no more.

Soon the food was all gone. The children cried for bread, and there was none.

The malicious Carabosse and Follette, not content with all this misery they had caused, flew from brook to brook and fountain to fountain, touching them with their wands. Instantly the brooks ran molten gold, and the fountains cast up silver spray.

There was no water. The children cried for some to drink, and there was none. Everybody was starving and dying of thirst.

The desperate people, in their agony, threw off their rich robes embroidered with gems, and cast away their golden crowns, and tore off their collars and girdles of Diamonds, Rubies, and Pearls.

"Oh, give us bread and water!" they cried. But there was none.

Now, there was just one poor man in all that country who was content with his lot. He lived in a little cottage surrounded by a small patch of ground. And because he was contented Carabosse and Follette had not been able to change anything that was his.

When he heard the children crying from hunger and thirst he ran into his garden and picked all his fresh fruit and vegetables. These he gave to the children, and left none for himself.

Immediately the Fairy Queen's voice was heard crying out: —

"Take thy reward!"

A great crashing noise was heard. A rushing Wind blew away all the emerald leaves and jewel-fruits. Red and yellow flames played over the brooks and fountains. The fields of grain shook violently. And in the twinkling of an eye, green leaves rustled on the trees, while ripe fruit appeared on the branches. Delicious vegetables stood in rows in the garden. The fields were yellow with waving grain. The brooks ran pure water, and the fountains cast up a cooling spray.

Then the Fairy Queen's voice was heard crying out:—

"Die, Carabosse! Die, Follette!"

And with a terrible noise the two wicked young Fairies burst into a thousand bubbles.

The people went nearly mad with joy. The mill wheels began to turn, grinding flour for bread. The children, clapping their hands, ran into the gardens to pick fruit, while the maids brought home pitchers of cold, fresh water from the brooks. In fact, everybody had all that he wanted to eat and drink.

And, every year after that, the farmers had rich and abundant crops, and were never unhappy nor discontented again.

THE MAN WHO BROUGHT FIRE

Retold from Hesiod and Other Sources

In those golden wonder days, when the earth was young, the whole world was one beautiful garden. Men knew no sorrows then, nor did they have to work, nor were they ever sick. Indeed, there was nothing to make them unhappy but one thing — Jupiter had carried off the splendour of the untiring Fire, and hidden it from men.

Now in that happy garden lived three brothers, named Atlas, Prometheus, and Epimetheus. Night and day the mighty Atlas held up the sky on his head and hands, while his two brothers lived at ease.

But Prometheus was not content to be idle, and he pitied mankind because they had no Fire to work with. So he searched until he found the splendour of the untiring Fire where Jupiter had hidden it. He put some in a hollow Fennel-Stalk, and carried it back to earth.

So he brought Fire again to men, and with it he brought the cunning of the workman's wisdom and Minerva's art of weaving.

Now when Jupiter knew what Prometheus had done, he was very angry.

"I will punish Prometheus," said he, "and I will give men a great evil that shall delight their hearts but bring sorrow to their souls."

Then he commanded Vulcan the Smith to mix water and earth, and to form a maiden fair and lovely, and with so sweet a voice that she should enchant every one who heard it.

Vulcan fashioned a living maiden. Very lovely was she. Her eyes sparkled with joy and life. In her throat were all the sweet notes of bird-voices. Venus gave her grace and beauty. Minerva arrayed her in silver-white robes, and taught her how to weave delicate silken webs. The Graces hung gold chains about her slender neck, while the fair-haired Hours crowned her with fresh Spring blossoms.

And they called the maiden "Pandora," the maiden-of-all-gifts.

Now when Pandora was finished, Jupiter commanded his winged messenger, Mercury, to take her at once to Epimetheus, for he knew that the wise Prometheus would not accept a gift from his hands.

This Mercury was a tricksy being, always delighting to make mischief. Indeed, from his very birth he had been tricksy. For he was born in the morning, at noon he slipped from his cradle and made a lute of tortoise-shell, and that same night he stole the Oxen of the Sun; then running quickly home, he climbed into his cradle again, before any one knew what he had been about.

So, now, while he was conducting Pandora

to the garden, he craftily put all sorts of wiles
and naughtiness into her bosom. Then he took
her to Epimetheus, who, as soon as he saw the
beautiful maiden, made her his wife, in spite of
all that Prometheus could say.

And so, alas! sorrow and misfortune came into
that happy garden! For at Epimetheus' door
stood a closed box, which he had been forbidden
to open. Naughty Pandora was so full of curios-
ity that one day she lifted its lid, and out flew
whole swarms of Woes, Fears, and Sicknesses.
Only Hope remained in the box, for Pandora
closed the lid before Hope could escape. As
for the Woes, Fears, and Sicknesses, they were
scattered over the garden, and blighted everything beautiful. So men were no longer happy.

As for the wise Prometheus, who out of pity
had given Fire to men, Jupiter punished him.
He bound him with chains to a pillar, and sent
an Eagle to feed without ceasing upon his liver.
And as fast as the liver was consumed, it grew
again.

As for men, by the means of Fire, and of the
cunning workman's wisdom and Minerva's art,
they had heat, food, and clothing; and they
wrought in copper, iron, steel, gold, and silver.
But they suffered all the miseries that came into
the world when Pandora opened the box.

WHY UNLUCKY IRON KILLS

Finnish Myth from the Kalevala

In the wonder garden of the World there were both Iron and Fire.

It happened one day that Iron would a-wandering go to visit his brother Fire. But when Fire saw him coming, he blazed up in fury and would have devoured him. So Iron fled far away, and hid in a bog under the ground, just where the Swans build their nests and the Eagle watches over his young.

So Iron lay deep in the moist bog, and there he kept himself for three years hidden under crooked tree-trunks and decaying leaves. But, alas! he could not always escape from his fierce brother, and he had to come again into the power of all-devouring Fire, and be forged into tools and weapons.

And thus it came about: —

Over the bog the great Wolf stalked, and the growling Bear lumbered over the moor. And where their broad footprints sunk into the ground, rusty Iron showed his face.

Ilmarinen the Cunning Smith came into the world. In the night, on a coal-heap, was he born, and in the night he grew up with a hammer in his hand and a little pair of tongs under his arm. In the night was he born, and in the morning he

was a man and went forth to find a smithy and
a place for his bellows.

He came to the bog; he saw the wet morass,
and there he built him his smithy and set up his
bellows. And there he found rusty Iron showing
his face in the broad footprints of the Wolf and
the Bear.

Then spoke Ilmarinen the Cunning Smith: —

"O unlucky Iron, what has happened to you?
Why do you lie in such an unworthy place, under
the Wolf's heavy paws, in the track of the
Bear?"

But Iron made no answer.

Then Ilmarinen the Cunning Smith whispered
to himself: —

"What if I cast unlucky Iron into the Fire,
into the burning, sparkling furnace?"

Then anguish and despair took hold of Iron
as he heard the terrible name of Fire.

Then spoke again Ilmarinen the Cunning
Smith: —

"Fear not, poor Iron. Fire surely will not
hurt his brother. If you enter Fire's red chamber
you shall come out fine and useful."

So spoke Ilmarinen the Cunning Smith, and
took Iron out of the moist bog, and cast him
into the red-hot furnace. Three days he stirred
the furious flames.

Slowly glowing Iron was melted, and boiled
up in crimson bubbles. While inside the furnace

he spread himself like softened dough within the flames of mighty Fire.

Then cried Iron in his anguish: —

"O Smith, have pity on me! Take me, take me from these flames! Take me from this burning glow!"

But Ilmarinen the Cunning Smith answered gently: —

"If I take you from the furnace, perhaps you will be hard and evil; perhaps you may hurt man or murder woman."

Then cried aloud unlucky Iron: —

"Make me into spears and axes. I will fell trees and break hard stones. I will fetch you game and fresh fish. Never will I hurt a mortal! never wound, nor harm, nor murder!"

So Ilmarinen the Cunning Smith took poor Iron from out the furnace, laid him down upon the anvil, hammered him till he was welded, and shaped him into spears and axes and many other household things.

But unlucky Iron lacked hardness; the axes all were dull and blunt-edged. Water had not tempered Iron, nor made the blue Steel flash.

So Ilmarinen the Cunning Smith prepared a bath of softened water. This he tasted, then he whispered: —

"Even yet it does not please me. It will not harden rusty Iron, nor make the blue Steel flash."

And as he spoke, a Bee came flying. High and

low it flew on light wings, and flittered above the anvil.

Then cried Ilmarinen the Cunning Smith: —

"Busy Bee, my nimble comrade, bring me honey on your light wings! Go, suck it from the cups of flowers. It alone will harden Iron, and make the blue Steel flash!"

Now the Wasp, Malicious One, peeping, peering from the rafters, heard his words and saw Iron waiting, saw the bath of water standing. Quick she darted to the forest. Back she came with many horrors. On her blue wings bore she horrors — poison of the deadly Adder, venom black of hissing Snakes, and the bitter froth of Worms. These she poured into the bath.

Ilmarinen the Cunning Smith thought that Busy Bee had flown back laden with the sweetest honey. Laughing, spoke he: —

"Ah, nimble comrade, all is ready; the bath is right to harden Iron, and make the blue Steel flash!"

So in the bath of many poisons straight he plunged poor hissing Iron, when he had drawn him from the furnace.

Then, indeed, Iron was made hurtful, deadly harmful. Then, indeed, blue Steel was angry.

Then, indeed, Iron broke his promise. He was formed into swords and lances. Forth he rushed throughout the wide world, hurting, rending, killing mortals. So he murdered sister, brother, father, mother, biting wounds with his sharp edges. So he opened springs of blood that poured out their crimson, foaming tides.

Now you know the beginning of Iron. Now you know who made him do evil.

Woe to you, unlucky Iron!

Woe to you, deceitful Steel!

So it was in ancient days, in the ancient wonder garden.

WITH SNOW ELVES IN SNOW HILLS

THE SNOW ELVES

Now you must know that in those early times,
When Autumn days grew pale, there came a troop
Of childlike forms from that cold mountain-top;
With trailing garments, through the air they came,
Or walked the ground with girded loins, and threw
Spangles of silvery Frost upon the grass,
And edged the brooks, with glistening parapets,
And built it crystal bridges, touched the pool
And turned its face to glass, or rising thence,
They shook from their full laps the soft light Snow,
And buried the great Earth, as Autumn Winds
Bury the forest floor with heaps of leaves.

. . . .

But when the Spring came on, what terror reigned
Among these Little People of the Snow!
To them the Sun's warm beams were shafts of Fire,
And the soft South Wind was the wind of death.
Away! away they flew all with pretty scowl,
Upon their childish faces, to the North,
Or scampered upward to the mountain's top.
And there defied their enemy, the Spring;
Skipping and dancing on the frozen peaks,
And moulding little Snowballs in their palms,
And rolling them to crush her flowers below,
Down the steep Snowfields.

WILLIAM CULLEN BRYANT (*The Little People of the Snow*)

SNOW–BLANCHE

Folktale from Nizhni-Novgorod

So it happened:—

The man's name was Ivan, and his wife's Marie. They lived in a little house in a village. They had no children. They were very lonesome, and their only comfort was to watch their neighbour's children playing in the street.

One Winter's day the Snow was lying knee deep, and some children were playing, while the two old people watched them from the window. The little ones were making a Snowman. Suddenly Ivan smiled, and said:—

"Wife, let us play, too. Let us make a Snowwoman."

"Why should we not?" said Marie. "But, instead, let us make a dear child — a little girl. She will be nicer than a Snow-Woman!"

"Thou art right!" said Ivan, laughing.

So the two went into their garden, and began to make a Snow-Doll. First they made a tiny body, then tiny hands and feet. On the top of this they placed a ball of Snow, and shaped it into a head with nose and chin and two holes for eyes. Then Ivan carefully drew two lines for lips; but scarcely had he finished these when he felt against his hand a puff of something warm like breath.

He started back. He looked at the Snow-Doll. Its eyes were sparkling with life, its lips had suddenly reddened, and were parted in a sweet smile.

"Look! Look, Wife!" he cried. "Is it good, or is it magic?"

The Snow-Child bent its head, and moved its tiny arms and legs.

"Oh! Ivan!" cried Marie. "God has sent us a little one at last!"

And rushing toward the Snow-Child she covered it with kisses. Then the Snow peeled off, and a little girl sprang out of it and threw herself into Marie's arms.

"Oh! Snow-Blanche! Snow-Blanche!" cried Marie with delight as she carried the little one into the house.

That was a joyful Winter for Ivan and Marie. Snow-Blanche grew more and more beautiful every hour. In a few weeks she had grown so fast that she appeared like a girl of fifteen instead of a little child.

Her form was tall and slender. Her eyes were blue like Forget-Me-Nots, her hair was yellow as gold and flowed to her knees, while her skin was pearly white and delicately transparent. She was so sweet and happy that the village girls came every evening to chat with her. They loved Snow-Blanche dearly.

"You see, Ivan," said Marie over and over again, "that God has sent us happiness instead of sorrow!"

"Alas, nothing in this world exists forever!" answered her husband, shaking his head.

So the Winter passed and the Sun of early Springtime began to pour its bright rays upon the earth, melting the Snow and warming the cold ground. Green grass sprang up; little red, yellow, and blue flowers showed their heads; birds sang merrily in the trees, and the village girls met at Ivan's cottage and sang: —

> *"Hast thou come, Sweet Spring!*
> *Sweet Spring! Sweet Spring!*
> *New life and joy*
> *To our hearts to bring!"*

But Snow-Blanche sat silent and sad.

"What ails thee, dear child?" asked Marie. "Art thou ill? Why art thou sorrowful and downcast?"

"'T is nothing. 'T is nothing, my Mother," answered Snow-Blanche.

But when all the Snow was gone, and the Sun began to shed warmer rays upon the earth, Snow-Blanche grew more and more sorrowful. She sought the shadiest parts of the wood, hiding under the trees like a shy white Lily. When it rained she delighted to walk by the margin of the lake where the Weeping Willows trailed their hanging branches in the clear water, and she gathered up Hailstones as if they were precious Pearls.

Spring passed, and Summer came. The hot rays of the Sun burned the grass and flowers. Then Snow-Blanche sat drooping and weeping all the day long.

One lovely evening the village girls came, and, taking Snow-Blanche by the hand, tenderly coaxed her with them to the wood. There they linked their arms around her and danced, and sang, and wreathed garlands for her head. Then as the Sun was gone down and it was quite cool, they built a little bonfire of dried leaves.

Snow-Blanche drew apart.

"Come, dear Friend!" they cried to her merrily. "Now we are going to run! Thou must run, too!"

Clapping their hands, they laughed and skipped through the fire. Then they heard a deep sigh behind them. They turned. Snow-Blanche was gone!

"Where is she? Where is she?" they cried. "Oh! our sweet Snow-Blanche! Surely she is hiding for fun!"

And they searched under the bushes and everywhere, but they could not find her. They wandered about, calling her name.

"Perhaps she is gone home," they said, so they went back to the village. But Snow-Blanche was not there.

That night, and the next day, and for many days after, the neighbours searched the wood in vain. Ivan and Marie were in despair. Nothing could comfort them. Marie wandered among the trees, calling and calling her darling child's name and listening for the sound of her sweet voice.

But Snow-Blanche was gone for ever.

And where was she gone? Had a fierce wild beast devoured her? Ah, no! Snow-Blanche had run through the flames her friends had kindled. She had dissolved into a thin vapour, and, rising through the trees, had mounted into the transparent evening Sky.

THE SNOWBALL HARES

Aino Myth

ONCE upon a time, the little Sky Children were playing among the Stars.

"See," they cried, "that soft, white Cloud beneath us! Let us play on that!"

They folded their wings, and dropped down upon the Cloud. But it was not an ordinary one at all; it was all of soft, white Snow. So the little Sky Children made Snowballs, and began to pelt each other.

The balls flew so thick and fast that six of them rolled over the edge of the Cloud, and fell down on the earth. And they turned into six little white Hares running about.

But they were naughty Hares, and began to quarrel. They quarrelled so loudly that Okiku-rumi, the owner of that country, came running with a burning stick in his hand.

"Oh, you bad Hares! Oh, you naughty Hares!" cried he. "What are you fighting about? You who live on this earth, in this world of human beings, must be quiet."

Then he beat each of the six Hares with his burning stick. They all ran away.

And ever since then white Hares have had black ears, because the Snowball Hares had their ears scorched by Okikurumi's burning stick.

WHY THE SNOW IS WHITE

Old Legend

WHEN the world was first made, says the Fairy Tale, everything had a beautiful colour except the Snow. The Sky was blue, the Clouds golden and creamy, the trees green, while the flowers had all the colours of the Rainbow.

But the poor Snow had no colour at all. So it was very sad and wandered over the earth look-ing for a colour. First it went to the Red Rose.

"Oh, Rose," it begged, "pray give me some of your royal red," but the Rose said "No."

Then it asked the Violet, the Buttercup, and all the other flowers for some of their colours, and they said "No."

But a humble little Snowdrop drooped its pale head and whispered, "If my whiteness pleases you, take it all!"

And since that day the grateful Snow has kept the little Snowdrop safe and warm the whole Winter through.

HOW THE FIRST SNOWDROP CAME

Legend of Paradise

As Eve sat weeping for lost Paradise, so says the golden wonder tale, and as she mourned for the many beautiful flowers that had grown in the Garden, an Angel flew down to Earth to comfort her.

Now since the Fall, no green thing had sprung up, but everywhere lay the thick white Snow, while the whole World was cold and bleak.

The Angel caught a passing Snowflake, and gently breathed upon it. It fell to earth, and, lo! it was a flake no more, but a folded bud, white and delicately fragrant.

"This bud," said the Angel, "is a promise that Summer shall come again, and bring fruits and flowers to gladden the hearts of all."

The Angel's mission done, away he flew.

"And, lo! where last his wings have swept the Snow,
A quaintly fashioned ring of milk-white Snowdrops blow!"

THE GARDEN OF FROST FLOWERS

Retold from William Cullen Bryant

THE PROMISE MADE

IN the olden time, long, long ago, there dwelt on a mountain-side a cottager, his wife, and his little girl named Eva. A lovely spot was their home, for near it was a glen through which dashed a brook fringed with many sweet-smelling Spring flowers.

But when Winter came, the little brook was fringed with other blossoms. Strange white ones with crystal leaves and stems grew there in the clear November nights. For when the Winter Winds blew hard, down from the mountain-top came a troop of Little People of the Snow. A beautiful Fairy race they were, with bright locks, and voices like the sounds of steps on crisp Snow. With trailing robes they came, some flying through the air, others tripping lightly across the icy fields.

They threw spangles of silvery Frost upon the grass, and edged the brook with glistening parapets. They built crystal bridges over the stream, and, touching the water, turned its face to glass. Then they shook, from their full laps, so many Snowflakes that they covered the whole world with a soft blanket.

Now Eva had often heard about these Little

People, but she had never seen them. One Mid-Winter day, when she was twelve years old, she dressed herself warmly to play in the Snow.

"Do not stay too long," said her mother, as she wrapped her furry coat around the child and put on her fur boots, "do not stay too long, for sharp is the Winter Wind. And go no farther than the great Linden-Tree on the edge of our field."

All this Eva promised, and went skipping from the house. Now she climbed the rounded snow-swells that felt firm with Frost beneath her feet, and now she slid down them into the deep hollows. So she played alone and was happy.

But as she was clambering up a very high drift, she saw a tiny maiden sitting on the Snow. Lily-cheeked she was, with flowing flaxen hair and blue eyes that gleamed like Ice; while her robe seemed of a more shadowy whiteness than her cheeks.

When she saw Eva, this tiny creature bounded to her feet, and cried: —

"Oh, come with me, pretty Friend. I have watched you often, and know how well you love the Snow, and how you carve huge-limbed Snow-men, Lions, and Griffins. Come, let us ramble over these bright fields. You shall see what you have never seen before."

So Eva followed her new friend. Together they slid down drifts and climbed white mounds, until they reached the spot where the great Linden-Tree stood.

"Here I must stop," said Eva, "for I promised my mother I would go no farther."

But the little Snow Maiden laughed.

"What!" cried she. "Are you afraid of the Snow? of the pure Snow? of the innocent Snow? It has never hurt any living thing. Surely your mother made you promise that, because she thought you had no one to guide you. I will show you the way, and bring you safely home."

By such smooth words Eva was won to break her promise, and she followed her new playmate. Over glistening fields they ran, and down a steep bank to the foot of a huge Snowdrift or Hill of Snow. There the Winds had carved a shelf of driven-snow, that curtained a wide opening in the hill.

"Look! Look! Let us enter here!" cried the little creature merrily. "Come, Eva, follow me."

IN THE GARDEN OF FROST FLOWERS

STRAIGHT under the shelf-like curtain Eva and the little Snow Maiden crept, and walked along a passage with white walls. Above them in the vaulted roof were set Snow-Stars that cast a wintry twilight over all.

Eva moved with awe and could not speak for wonder; but the little Snow Maiden, laughing gayly, tripped lightly on before. Deeper and deeper they went into the heart of the Hill of Snow. And now the walls began to widen; and the vaulted roof rose higher and higher, until it expanded into a great white dome above their heads.

Eva looked about her. She stood in a large white garden, where everything seemed to be spun out of delicate silent Frost.

At her feet grew snow-white plants with lace-like leaves and spangled flowers. At her side Palm-Trees reared their stately white columns tufted with frosted plumes. Huge Oaks, with ice-like trunks, waved their transparent branches in the silent air; while their gnarled roots seemed anchored deep in glistening banks. Light sprays of Myrtle, and snowy Roses in bud and bloom, drooped by the winding walks.

All these things — flowers, leaves, and trees — seemed delicately wrought from stainless alabaster. Up the trees ran Jasmine vines with stalks and leaves as colourless as their blossoms. All this Eva saw with wonder and delight.

"Walk softly, dear Friend," said the little Snow Maiden. "Do not touch the frail creation round you, nor sweep it with your skirt.

"Now, look up, and behold how beautifully this Garden of Frost Flowers is lighted. See those shifting gleams that seem to come and go so gently. They are the Northern Lights that make beautiful our Winter Palace.

"Here on long cold nights I and my comrades, the Little People of the Snow, make this garden lovely. We guide to this place the wandering Snowflakes, and, piling them up into many quaint shapes, bid them grow into stately columns, glittering arches, white trees, and lovely flowers of Frost.

"But come, now, dear Eva, and I will show you a far more wonderful sight."

THE DANCE OF THE LITTLE PEOPLE OF THE SNOW

As she spoke, the little Snow Maiden led her to a window-pane of transparent ice set in the Snow wall.

"Look," said she, "but you may not enter in."

Eva looked.

Lo! she saw a glorious glistening palace-hall from whose lofty roof fell stripes of shimmering light, rose-coloured, and delicate green, and tender blue.

This light flowed downward to the floor, enveloping in its rainbow hues a joyous multitude of tiny folk, whirling in a merry dance. Silvery music sounded from cymbals of transparent Ice skilfully touched by tiny hands.

Round and round they flew beneath the dome

of coloured lights, now wheeling and now turning. Their bright eyes shone under their lily-brows. Their gauzy scarfs, sparkling like snow-wreaths in the Sun, floated in the dizzy whirl.

Eva stood entranced in wonder, as all these Little People of the Snow, dancing and whirling in the coloured lights, swept past the icy window-pane.

Long she gazed; and long she listened to the sweet sounds that thrilled the frosty air. Then the intense cold around her numbed her limbs, and she remembered the promise to her mother.

THE PROMISE BROKEN

"ALAS!" she cried, "too long, too long am I lingering here! Oh, how wickedly I have done to break my promise! What must they think, the dear ones at home?"

With hurried step she found the snowy passage again, and followed it upward to the light; while the little Snow Maiden ran by her side, guiding her feet.

When she reached the open air once more, a bitter blast came rushing from the clear North, chilling her blood; and she shrank in terror before it. But the little Snow Maiden, when she felt the cutting blast, bounded along, uttering shouts of joy, and skipping from drift to drift. And she danced around Eva, as the poor child wearily climbed the slippery mounds of frozen Snow.

"Ah me!" sighed Eva at last, "Ah me! my eyes grow heavy. They swim with sleep."

As she spoke, her lids closed, and she sank upon the ground and slept.

Then near her side sat the little Snow Maiden, watching her slumber. She saw the rosy colour fade from Eva's rounded cheeks, and the child's brow grow white as marble; while her breath slowly ceased to come and go. All motionless lay her form; and the little Snow Maiden strove to waken her, plucking her dress, and shouting in her ears, but all in vain.

Then suddenly was heard the sound of steps grating on the Snow. It was Eva's parents searching for their lost child. When they found her, lying like a fair marble image in her death-like sleep, and when they heard from the little Snow Maiden how she had led Eva into the Garden of Frost Flowers, their hearts were wrung with anguish.

They lifted the dear child up, and bore her home. And though they chafed her limbs and bathed her brow, she never woke again. The little maid was dead.

Now came the funeral-day. In a grave dug in the glen's white side they buried Eva; while from the rocks and hills around a thousand slender voices rose, and sighed, and mourned, until the echoes, taking up the strains, flung them far and wide across the icy fields.

From that day the Little People of the Snow were never seen again. But all during the long cold, Winter nights, invisible tiny hands wove around Eva's grave frost-wreaths, and tufts of silvery rime shaped like flowers one scatters on a bier.

SECRETS OF THE WHISPERING TREES

SONG

Orpheus with his lute made trees,
And the mountain-tops that freeze,
*   Bow themselves when he did sing.*
To his music, plants and flowers
Ever sprung, as Sun and showers
*   There had made a lasting Spring.*

Everything that heard him play,
Even the billows of the sea,
*   Hung their heads, and then lay by.*
In sweet music is such art,
Killing-Care and Grief-of-Heart
*   Fall asleep, or hearing die.*

WILLIAM SHAKESPEARE

OLD–MAN–WHO–MADE–THE–TREES–TO–BLOSSOM

Japanese Folktale

ONCE upon a time, an old man and his wife were working in their garden. Their little Dog suddenly sniffed the ground, and began to bark. So the old woman brought a spade, and the old man dug and dug. And what was their surprise and delight to unearth a great number of gold and silver coins, and a heap of precious treasure as well.

They carried it into the house, and immediately gave a part of it to the poor, for they were very tender-hearted.

Now, there lived next door another old couple, who were bad-hearted and greedy. When they saw all the wealth that their good neighbours had found, they borrowed the little Dog, and dragged him into their garden.

Immediately he began to sniff and bark. The old couple dug and dug, and found nothing but dirt. Then they were so angry and disappointed that they killed the poor little Dog, and buried him under a Pine-Tree.

The good old man and woman grieved very much when they heard that their faithful friend was dead; and they laid flowers on his grave.

That night the Dog appeared to the good old man in a dream.

"Master," said he, "cut down the tree under which I am buried. Make a mortar of the wood, and think of me when you use it."

So the next morning, the old man cut down the tree and made a mortar. And when he began to grind Rice in it, every grain turned into a lump of gold or a precious jewel.

Now, when the greedy old couple heard about the mortar, they borrowed that also. But when they began to grind Rice in it, every grain turned into a lump of dirt. Then they were so angry that they burned the mortar.

Well, that night the Dog again appeared to the good old man in a dream, and said: —

"Master, sprinkle the ashes of the mortar over withered trees. Think of me as you do so, and the trees will immediately be full of blossoms."

The next morning the old man gathered up the ashes of the mortar, and put them into a basket. Then he went from village to village, sprinkling them on withered trees. Immediately the trees burst into masses of pink and white blossoms. Every one gave him gifts, so he went home quite rich.

Then a Prince heard of the magic ashes, and sent for the good old man, who quickly restored the Prince's withered trees. After which the royal treasurer heaped the good old man with gifts, so that he went home very rich.

Now, his greedy old neighbours heard about the ashes, and they scraped together all the ashes that were left on the ground where they had burned the mortar, and set off to visit the Prince.

There was just one withered tree left, and the greedy old man climbed it, and threw the ashes over its branches. But, lo! the withered limbs remained just as before, and the ashes fell into the Prince's eyes and blinded him. Then the royal servants pulled the greedy old man down from the tree, and beat him nearly to death; after which they sent him limping home, as poor as before.

When the good old man and his wife saw how ashamed the greedy old couple were, they took pity on them. They shared their wealth with them; and the greedy old couple were so thankful that they became very kind-hearted, and lived good and happy lives ever after.

THE DAUGHTER OF THE LAUREL

Roumanian Legend

"OPEN your branches, beautiful Laurel Tree, and let me forth. It is the hour when the Evening Star bathes her silver hair in the stream."

So spoke a fair young maiden shut up in the Laurel. Then the Laurel opened wide her branches, and out the maiden sprang to dance in the flowery meadow.

"Remember, my daughter," said the Laurel, "to return before the Sun rises, or you will dissolve into dew."

"I will remember, beautiful Laurel," cried the young maiden, "oh, I will remember!" And she went dancing through the meadow.

The pale Moon shone softly from the Clouds, the breeze rippled the blossoms and grasses, while the maiden went flitting down the valley. Her large eyes reflected the glow of the Stars, and her long hair floated on the breeze.

Then sang a handsome stranger who was wandering in the valley: —

> *"The Star Queen sleeps in her palace of light.*
> *The pale Moon Queen looks down.*
> *Oh! hand in hand let us dance all night,*
> *Till the cold grey Dawn doth frown!"*

So the maiden danced with the stranger. Hand in hand they danced through the valley while the Stars slept in their palace of light, and the Moon looked softly down.

All night long they danced and sang, till the cold grey Dawn frowned. But still they danced on, hand in hand.

Then above the mountain-top the Sun began to rise in a sea of opal lights. And, lo! the handsome youth was gone!

The maiden shrieked with fear, and called to

the Stars and the Moon. But they, too, were gone. She called to the birds singing in the trees, but they did not know whither the stranger had fled.

"Open your branches, beautiful Laurel," cried she, "open your branches! The night is flown, and the first rays of the rising Sun are touching the earth. Open, open, or I shall dissolve into dew!"

"Away, beautiful maiden," answered the Laurel mournfully. "Alas! the star-wreath of obedience has fallen from your brow. There is no longer a place for you here."

Then the Sun rose over the mountain, and the Daughter of the Laurel dissolved into dew.

WHITE FLOWERING ALMOND

Old Legend

SURELY you have heard the sad, sad tale of little Princess White Chicory, who stands by the roadside, patiently watching for her Beloved to return. Listen, now, to the sad but beautiful tale of Queen Phyllis and Prince Demophoon.

In those ancient golden times lovely Queen Phyllis ruled over Thrace. One day a handsome youth was cast by a storm on to the Thracian shore. He was young Prince Demophoon of Athens, returning from the siege of Troy.

When he saw Queen Phyllis, he loved her; and when she saw the handsome youth, she loved him in return. So they were wedded, and together ruled happily and joyously over all Thrace.

But after a while Prince Demophoon wished to visit his home. He promised to return within a month, and, bidding good-bye to his sorrowing Queen, sailed away to Athens.

Month after month went by, but he did not return. He had forgotten all about his beautiful bride. Poor Queen Phyllis watched day and night for him to come back. Then her grief became so great that she died, and was transformed into a leafless Almond-Tree.

At last Prince Demophoon grew tired of Athens, and returned to Thrace. When he found that Queen Phyllis had died of grief, he threw himself at the foot of the Almond-tree. He wept bitter tears, embracing its slender trunk in an agony of repentance.

Then, lo! at his touch, the tree seemed to tremble with joy. And immediately it burst into bloom, — into one glorious fragrant mass of rosy white blossoms.

ORPHEUS WHO MADE THE TREES TO DANCE

From King Alfred's Boethius (adapted)

I⊤ happened in ancient days that there was a Harper in the land of Thrace, which was in

Greece. The Harper was inconceivably good.
His name was Orpheus. He had a very excellent
wife, who was called Eurydice.

Then men began to say of the Harper that he
could harp so that the trees danced, and the
stones stirred themselves at his music. And the
wild beasts ran to him and stood as if they were
tame; and if men pursued them, they shunned
them not.

Then men said that the Harper's wife died
and her soul was led to Hades. Then the Harper
became so sorrowful that he could not remain
among other men, but frequented the woods, and
sat on the mountains both night and day, weeping and harping so that the trees danced and
the rivers stood still, and no Hart shunned any
Lion, nor Hare Hound, nor did the cattle know
any hatred or any fear for delight of the music.

Then it seemed to the Harper that nothing in
this world pleased him. Then thought he that
he would seek the King of Hades and try to
soften him with his harp, and entreat him that
he would give him back his wife.

When he came thither there ran toward him a
Dog of Hades whose name was Cerberus. He
had three heads, and began to wag his tail and
play with the Harper because of his harping.
Then there was also a very dreadful gate-keeper
whose name was Charon. He also had three
heads and he was very old.

Then began the Harper to beseech him that he would protect him while he was there, and bring him thence again safely. This did Charon promise to him, because he was well pleased with the unaccustomed sounds.

Then went the Harper farther until he met the grim ones whom people call the Fates, of whom they say that they know no respect for any man, but punish every man according to his deeds, and of whom they say they control every man's fortune. Then began he to implore their mercy. Then began they to weep with him.

Then went he farther, and all the inhabitants of Hades ran toward him and led him to their King. And all began to speak with him, and to beg for that for which he begged.

And the restless wheel which Ixion the King of the Lapithæ was bound to for his guilt, stood still because of his harping. And Tantalus the King, who in this world was exceeding greedy, and whom the same vice of greediness followed there, became quiet. And the Vulture ceased so that he tore not the liver of Tityus the King, which before that tormented him. And all the punishments of the inhabitants of Hades were suspended while he harped before the King.

When he long had harped, then spoke the King of the inhabitants of Hades, and said: —

"Let us give this man his wife, for he has
earned her by his harping."

And the King commanded him that he should
well observe that he never look backward after
departing thence, and said that if he looked
backward he should lose his wife.

But men can with great difficulty, **if at all,**
restrain love! Well-a-day! What!

Orpheus then led his wife with him till he
came to the boundary of light and darkness.
Then went his wife after him. When he came
forth into the light then looked he behind his
back toward the woman.

Then was she immediately lost to him!

ERYSICHTHON THE HUNGRY

Retold from Callimachus

ONCE upon a time, the most lovely of all gardens on earth was the one that Ceres, the Keeper-
of-All-the-Cornfields-in-the-World, had planted
for herself.

Around it was a hedge so thick that an arrow
could scarcely pass through it. Inside were tall
Pines, graceful Elms, and many orchard trees
laden with yellow Pears, red-cheeked Apples,
and juicy Peaches. In and out among the trees
glided shining brooks, while flowers of every hue
grew on their banks.

In the midst of all this stood a huge Poplar

Tree so lofty that its top touched the sky. At noontime each day the Water-Nymphs and the Tree-Dryads danced under its spreading boughs, singing sweetly, for they loved the Poplar more than any other tree in the garden.

Now in that part of the world there dwelt a bad, greedy man named Erysichthon. One day when Ceres was far away tending her wide corn-fields, he hastened from his house with twenty servants, all giant men armed with sharp axes. They rushed into Ceres's garden to cut down her trees.

They surrounded the huge Poplar and began to hack its sides. And the Poplar as it felt the blows trembled and writhed and groaned so loudly that Ceres heard it.

"Who is cutting down my beautiful trees?" she cried in anger.

And immediately she tore off her poppy-wreath, and, changing herself into an old woman, hurried to the garden.

"My Son," she said to Erysichthon, "why do you fell these trees that belong to Ceres? Stay your hand! Send away your men or the Lady Ceres will be angry and punish you!"

"Get out of my way, old woman!" exclaimed Erysichthon, fiercely, "or I'll bury this great axe in your flesh! These trees shall roof my new mansion in which I intend to eat and drink with my friends."

And as Erysichthon spoke thus, he struck a mighty blow against the Poplar's shivering side.

Straightway Ceres became herself. Her form towered upward so that her poppy-crowned head seemed to touch the Clouds. Her eyes flashed with anger, and she brandished a lighted torch.

Erysichthon's knees shook and he drew back in terror. His servants rushed from the spot, leaving their axes behind. But Erysichthon remained trembling before Ceres.

"Wretch!" cried she. "Get you gone! Roof with my trees — if you will — your new mansion! Well, indeed, shall you have need of it! For often shall you eat and drink therein! Now get you gone!" And she drove him from the garden.

From that day on a fierce hunger, burning and violent, seized Erysichthon. But the more he ate the hungrier he became. Twenty cooks prepared each meal. Twelve servants poured out his wine. But still his thirst and hunger grew.

He hid himself from his friends, and ate and drank night and day. He devoured ten thousand viands of every kind, and emptied a hundred flagons. And so he continued to eat until he had spent his last money for food and was forced to sell all that he had to get money to buy more.

But still the raging hunger and the burning

thirst consumed him. He pined and wasted
away until only his skin and bones were left.
And then he was forced to sit for the rest of
his life at the crossroads begging for morsels of
bread.

THE WIND IN THE PINE

Japanese Folktale

LONG, long ago, so long that even the White
Crane cannot remember it, in the Land of Fresh
Rice Ears, the Land of the Reed Plains, there
grew a Pine-Tree. It stood within the sound of
the sea. Great it grew, and there was not a
greater in all that land. Its trunk was rosy-red,
and beneath it stretched a brown carpet of fallen
pine-needles.

In the sweet nights of Summer the Fairy Children of the Wood came hand in hand in the
moonlight, slipping their dark feet on the moss,
and dancing on the pine-needles, and tossing
back their long green hair. And the Fairy Children of the Water came, and the sparkling drops
fell from their finger-tips. The Elfin Children
of the Air rested in the pine-branches and murmured sweet music the livelong night.

And from the sea came the Wonder Children
of the Waves, creeping, creeping up the yellow
sand. And Lovers, wandering on the beach, heard
sweet sighing above them. "Joy of my heart,"

they said one to another, "do you hear the Wind in the Pine-Tree?"

Then came the Maiden; tall and slender she was, and most lovely. By day she sat in the shade of the Pine-Tree plying her wheel or her shuttle, while her ears listened to the Wind in its branches. Sometimes her eyes looked over the sea, and she sat as one who waits and watches. Often she sang, and her voice was like the singing of birds. The music of her words, mystic and sweet, floated out over the waves.

Now concerning the Youth. He dwelt far, far from the Maiden. By day he worked in the green rice-fields. He looked upon the valley and the streams. He gazed into the sky. He saw above him the great White Crane circling in the blue.

"I hear a call," he said. "I may tarry no longer! Voice in my heart, I hear and obey!"

And straightway he said farewell to his mother and father, and to his sisters, brothers, and friends; and getting into a boat, he sped over the sea. The White Crane flew behind the boat, and when the Wind failed, she pushed it forward with her strong wings.

At last one evening, at the setting of the Sun, the Youth heard the sound of sweet singing. He stood erect in his boat, and the White Crane, beating her wings, guided it to the yellow sand. And as the Youth sprang out upon the shore, the words of the singing came mystic and sweet: —

"Comes the Lover with a gift for his Maiden?
Jewels of Jade on a silken string!
Well-carved jewels!
Well-rounded jewels!
Green as the grass!
All on a silken string.
Oh! the strength of that silken string!"

And so he found the Maiden sitting in the shade of the Pine-Tree, weaving and singing. He stood before her, waiting.

"Whence come you?" said she.

"I am come across the sea-path. I am come from afar."

"And why are you come?" she said.

"O Voice in my heart, it was your voice that sang!"

"Do you bring me a gift?" she said.

"I bring you the gift, jewels of Jade upon a silken string."

"Come," she said, and, taking him by the hand, led him to her father's house.

So they drank "the Three Times Three," and were wedded. So they lived in sweet tranquillity for many, many years.

At last the Youth and the Maiden that were, grew old and white-headed.

"Fair Love," said the old man, "how weary I am! 'Tis sad to be old."

"Say not so, Dear Delight-of-my-Heart," answered the old woman, "say not so; the best of all is to come."

"My Dear," said the old man, "I have a desire to see the great Pine-Tree once more before I die, and to listen to the Wind in its branches."

"Come, then," said she.

And she rose and took him by the hand. Together they wandered on the shore, and sat on the brown carpet under the Pine-Tree, and they listened to the Wind in its branches.

The old man closed his eyes, and when he opened them, behold! his wife was no longer old, but tall, slender, and lovely! They were again the Youth and the Maiden! He touched her hand. Lightly they left the ground. To the sound of the Wind's music they swayed, they floated, they rose into the air. They rose higher and higher. The branches of the Pine-Tree received them, and closed about them, and they were seen no more.

But still in the sweet nights of Summer the Fairy Children of the Wood come hand in hand in the moonlight, slipping their dark feet on the moss, dancing on the pine-needles, and tossing back their long green hair.

And the Fairy Children of the Water come, and the sparkling drops fall from their finger-tips. The Elfin Children of the Air rest in the pine-branches, murmuring sweet music the livelong night.

And from the sea come the Wonder Children of the Waves, creeping, creeping up the yellow sand. And Lovers wandering on the beach hear sweet singing above them.

"Joy of my heart," they say one to another, "do you hear the Wind in the Pine-Tree — the Wind, the Wind in the Pine?"

THE MAPLE LEAF FOR EVER!

Canadian Tale

I AM the oldest of the Maples of the Northland, and this is what the Wind whispered to me when the Snow lay white and thick upon the ground, and the Stars twinkled in the frosty night. This is what he whispered to me: —

.   .   .   .

Long, long ago, — long before the Red Men or White Men lived in the Northland — there were no Maples. Only dark Cedars, Pines, and Firs grew in that cold land, for there was never any Summer.

Then went the Sun complaining to Queen Nature, saying that the soil of that land was rough and wild, and that nothing beautiful would grow there. So Queen Nature called her Maiden Beauty, and commanded her to hasten and carry a message to the Northland.

Through the clear, blue sky the Maiden Beauty flew, bearing in her hand a rod that shot back the rays of the Sun. She was robed in a wonderful garment, like a Rainbow twisted and twined about her. Blue were her eyes, as the sky from which she came. Her hair shone like gold. Her skin was like the Lily-Flower, and her lips like petals of Wild-Roses.

She hovered over the Northland, and bade the Wind take the message of Queen Nature to the dark Cedars, the Pines, and the Firs.

"Say to the Queen's dark children, O Wind, that for a few months each year, I shall be with them. The Sun has been bidden to shine more warmly, and the sweet-scented flowers to bloom, and the Summer-birds to fly hither from the Southland. So shall beautiful Summer come and dwell among you."

The Wind carried this message to the dark trees, and they moaned piteously, and cried: —

"Give unto us a bright sister of our kind, whom the Sun will love and cherish!"

Then the Maiden Beauty took the rod that she carried, and planted it in the ground.

"I bid you grow great in this land," said she, "and rule over all your kind. Grow tall by looking at the Sun. Spread out your branches and cast a shade to refresh man and beast in the heat of the day. Let your juice be sweet and deliciously flavoured to delight the children. And, ere you drop your leaves for the Winter, I bid them turn yellow for the sunlight and crimson for man's blood. For in the far, far-away time there shall come a White Race to these shores, and you, my bright Child, shall stand to them for all that is dear — for Home and Country."

So saying, the Maiden Beauty turned, and, with outstretched arms, flew away through the clear blue sky.

A hush fell on the Northland. Then a faint melody was wafted to the wild creatures of the wood, and to the listening dark trees. Warm breezes blew over the land, flowers sprang from the ground, and the air was filled with the singing of Summer-birds.

The great Sun smiled on all the Northland. And the rod of the Maiden Beauty waxed strong and grew into a mighty tree, straight of trunk, and bending neither to the right nor the left. It spread wide its canopy of curved leaves, fresh green in Summer, and crimson, gold, and coloured like a sunset when the Autumn Winds blew clear.

So passed the years away, and by the mighty rivers, along the edges of the brooks, and in the forests and valleys, thousands strong the Maples stood sentinels in the land.

. . . .

I am the oldest of the Maples in the Northland, and this is what the Wind whispered to me when the Snow lay white and thick on the ground, and the Stars twinkled in the frosty night. This is what he whispered.

Grace Channell in The
Canadian Magazine (retold).

DAPHNE

Retold from Ovid

In ancient times, when Apollo left his Shining Palace in the Sun, to roam the earth, he met Cupid, who with bended bow and drawn string was seeking human beings to wound with the arrows of love.

"Silly Boy," said Apollo, "what do you with the warlike bow? Such burden best befits my shoulders, for did I not slay the fierce Serpent, the Python, whose baleful breath destroyed all that came nigh him? Warlike arms are for the mighty, not for boys like you! Do you carry a torch with which to kindle love in human hearts, but no longer lay claim to my weapon, the bow!"

But Cupid replied in anger: "Let your bow shoot what it will, Apollo, but my bow shall shoot *you!*"

Then Cupid rose up, and beating the air with his wings, drew two magic arrows from his quiver. One was of shining gold, and with its barbed point could he inflict wounds of love. The other arrow was of dull silver, and its wound had the power to engender hate.

The silver arrow Cupid let fly into the breast of Daphne, the daughter of the River-King Peneus; and forthwith she fled away from the homes of men, and hunted beasts in the forest.

With the golden arrow Cupid grievously wounded Apollo, who, fleeing to the woods, saw there the Nymph Daphne pursuing the Deer, and straightway he fell in love with her beauty. Her golden locks hung down upon her neck, her eyes were like stars, her form was slender and graceful and clothed in clinging white. Swifter than the light Wind she flew, and Apollo followed after.

"O Nymph! daughter of Peneus," he cried, "stay, I entreat you! Why do you fly as a Lamb from the Wolf, as a Deer from the Lion, or as a Dove with trembling wings flees from the Eagle! I am no common man! I am no Shepherd! You know not, rash maid, from whom you are flying! Jupiter is my sire. Mine own arrow is unerring; but, alas! Cupid's aim is truer, for he has made this wound in my heart! Alas! wretched me! though I am that great one who discovered the art of healing, yet this love may not be healed by my herbs or my skill!"

But Daphne stopped not at these words; she flew from him with timid step. The Winds fluttered her garments, the light breezes spread her flowing locks behind her. Swiftly Apollo drew near, even as the keen Greyhound draws near to the frightened Hare he is pursuing.

With trembling limbs Daphne turned to the river, the home of her father, Peneus. Close behind her was Apollo. She felt his breath on her hair and his hand on her shoulder. Her strength was spent, she grew pale, and in faint accents she implored the river: —

"Oh, save me, my Father, save me from Apollo-of-the-Golden-Beams!"

Scarcely had she thus spoken before a heaviness seized her limbs. Her breast was covered with bark, her hair grew into green leaves and her arms into branches. Her feet, a moment before so swift, became rooted to the ground. And Daphne was no longer a Nymph, but a green Laurel-Tree.

When Apollo beheld this change he cried out and embraced the tree, and kissed its leaves.

"Beautiful Daphne," he said, "since you cannot be my bride, yet shall you be my tree. Henceforth my hair, my lyre, and my quiver shall be adorned with Laurel. Your wreaths shall be given to conquering chiefs, to winners of fame and joy; and as my head has never been shorn of its locks, so shall you wear your green bay leaves, Winter and Summer — for ever!"

Apollo ceased speaking, and the Laurel bent its new-made boughs in assent, and its stem seemed to shake and its leaves to murmur gently.

WITH MARVELLOUS FARM THINGS

THE GREEN PLUMES OF MONDAMIN

All around the happy village
Stood the Maize-fields, green and shining,
Waved the green plumes of Mondamin,
Waved his soft and sunny tresses,
Filling all the land with plenty.
'T was the women who in Springtime
Planted the broad fields and fruitful,
Buried in the earth Mondamin.

. . . .

Summer passed, and Shawondasee
Breathed his sighs o'er all the landscape,
From the Southland sent his ardours,
Wafted kisses warm and tender;
And the Maize-field grew and ripened,
Till it stood in all the splendour
Of its garments green and yellow,
Of its tassels and its plumage,
And the Maize-ears full and shining
Gleamed from bursting sheaths of verdure.
Then Nokomis, the old woman,
Spake, and said to Minnehaha,
"Let us gather in the harvest,
Let us wrestle with Mondamin,
Strip him of his plumes and tassels,
Of his garments green and yellow!"
From HENRY WADSWORTH LONGFELLOW'S *Song of*
Hiawatha (condensed)

THE PROUD BUCKWHEAT

OFTEN after a thunderstorm, when one passes a field of Buckwheat, one sees the grain all blackened and singed. It looks as if a fire had passed over it. Then the farmer says, "The Lightning did it!"

But this is what a Sparrow told me about it. The Sparrow heard it from an old Willow-Tree that stood by a buckwheat-field, and stands there yet. It is quite an old tree, and crippled from age. It is burst in the middle, and grass and brambles grow out of its cleft. The tree leans forward, and its branches hang down to the ground like long green hair.

This is what the Sparrow told: —

In the fields around the Willow-Tree grain was growing; not only Rye and Barley, but also Oats, — yes, the most capital Oats, — which when ripe looked like many little Canary birds sitting on a spray. And the Oats and the other grains in the fields stood there smiling; and the richer their ears, the lower they bent in pious humility.

But there was also a field of Buckwheat near the old Willow-Tree. The Buckwheat did not bend at all like the other grains, but stood proudly and stiffly.

"I am as rich as any ear of grain!" said the

Buckwheat. "Besides, I am much handsomer! My flowers are as beautiful as the Apple-blossoms! It is quite a delight for any one to look at me or mine! Do you know anything more splendid than we are, you old Willow Tree?"

And the Willow-Tree nodded his head, just as if to say, "Yes, that's true enough!"

But the Buckwheat spread itself out from sheer vanity, and said: "The stupid tree! He's so old that the grass grows in his body!"

Now a terrible Storm came on. All the field-flowers folded their leaves together, and bowed their heads, while the Storm passed over them. But the Buckwheat stood erect in its pride.

"Bow your head like us!" said all the flowers.

"I've not the slightest reason to do so," said the Buckwheat.

"Bend your head as we do!" cried all the other grains. "The Storm comes flying. He has wings that reach from the Clouds to the earth. He'll beat you to pieces before you can cry for mercy."

"Yes, but I will not bend," said the Buckwheat.

"Shut up your flowers and bow your leaves," said the old Willow-Tree. "Don't look up at the Lightning when the Cloud bursts open. Even men do not do that. For in the Lightning one may see into Heaven; but that dazzles even men. And what would happen to us if we dared to do so — we the plants of the field that are so much less worthy than they!"

"So much less worthy!" cried the Buckwheat. "Now, I'll look straight up into Heaven!"

And the Buckwheat did so in its pride and boasting.

It was as if the whole world were on fire, so bright was the Lightning. And when the Storm was passed by, the flowers and grains stood in the still pure air, refreshed by the Rain. But the Buckwheat was turned coal-black by the Lightning, and it was like a dead weed upon the field.

And the old Willow Tree waved its branches in the Wind, and great drops of water fell from its green leaves, just as if the tree wept.

And the Sparrows asked: "Why do you weep? Here everything is so cheerful! See how the Sun shines. See how the Clouds sail by. Do you not breathe the scent of flowers and bushes? Why do you weep, Willow-Tree?"

And the Willow-Tree told them of the pride of the Buckwheat, of its boasting, and of the punishment that always follows such sin.

And I who tell you this tale have heard it from the Sparrows. They told it to me one evening, when I begged them for a story.

HANS CHRISTIAN ANDERSEN (*adapted*)

FARMER MYBROW AND THE FAIRIES

West African Folktale

ONE day, Farmer Mybrow was looking for a piece of land to make into a farm. He wished to grow Corn and Yams. He found a fine spot close to a forest. He set to work at once to prepare the field by cutting down the weeds and bushes.

Now the forest was the home of some Fairies; and no sooner had Farmer Mybrow sharpened his knife and cut down the first bush, than he heard a little voice say: —

"Who is there, cutting down the bushes?"

Farmer Mybrow was too astonished to speak, and the little voice said again: —

"Who is there, cutting down the bushes?"

Then he knew that it must be one of the Fairies, and he answered: —

"I am Mybrow come to prepare a farm for Corn and Yams."

Fortunately, the Fairies were in great good humour, and he heard one of them say: —

"Let us help the farmer cut down the bushes!"

And instantly, to his delight, all the bushes and weeds were rapidly cut down. Then he returned home well pleased with the day's work, but resolved to keep the matter a secret from his wife, who was very curious and meddlesome.

When the time came to burn the dry brush, he set off for his farm, hoping that the Fairies would help him again. He struck the trunk of a tree as he passed, and he heard the same little voice say: —

"Who is there, striking a tree?"

And he answered, "I am Mybrow come to burn the brush."

"Let us help the farmer burn the brush!" cried the little voice.

And instantly all the dried weeds and brush were burned, and the field was left clean in less than no time.

The next day the Fairies helped him again. For when Farmer Mybrow came to chop up the stumps for firewood, in a twinkling all the firewood was neatly piled and ready to be carried home. So it went on from day to day. The field was dug, sowed, and planted, the Fairies doing it all.

Still Farmer Mybrow managed to keep things a secret from his wife, although each time he left home she begged him to tell her where his farm lay.

The plants grew tall and strong, and Farmer Mybrow visited them every day, and rejoiced over the rich harvest that he should soon have.

One morning, while the Corn and Yams were yet in their unripe and milky stage, Farmer Mybrow's wife came to him weeping and wringing her hands, and insisted on knowing where his farm lay, so that she might fetch some firewood from it.

At first he refused to tell her, but when she began to scream, and to say that she should die if she did not know where it was, he said: —

"I will tell you, if you will promise not to answer any question that is asked you."

She promised this eagerly, and he told her where his farm lay. Then she set out immediately for it.

When she arrived there, she was amazed to see such wonderful fields of Corn and Yams. The Corn looked so tempting that she plucked an ear. Then she heard the little voice say: —

"Who is there, plucking the Corn?"

"Who dares ask me such a question?" she answered angrily. Then, going on farther, she pulled a Yam.

"Who is there, pulling the Yams?" said the little voice.

"'T is I, Farmer Mybrow's wife," she answered. "And I'll break off as much Corn and pull as many Yams as I choose."

"Let us help the farmer's wife pluck the Corn and pull the Yams!" cried the little voice.

And instantly all the Corn-Ears and Yams lay useless on the ground, and the whole harvest was utterly spoiled, for it was green and unripe.

When Farmer Mybrow's wife saw this, she was horrified, and ran home weeping. But she did not tell her husband what had happened.

The next morning the poor man hurried gleefully to the farm to see how his fine crops were doing. When what did he find but his whole harvest destroyed and his Corn-Ears and Yams lying on the ground! He was filled with anger and dismay.

"Alas!" cried he. "This comes of my own foolishness, and of my wife's broken promise! Next year she may weep and rage, but she shall not draw my secret from me!"

THE WITCH CAT

Scotch Folktale

ONCE upon a time, a hunter was sitting alone in his hut before a peat fire. Near him his faithful Dogs lay stretched, resting after a hard day's run. The Storm howled outside, and the hunter sat listening to the Rain and Wind.

Suddenly the latch was lifted, and a Black Cat, shivering with the cold and wet to the skin, sprang across the threshold. She stood trembling in the middle of the floor, while the Dogs rose up, every hair on their bodies bristling.

"Great Hunter-of-the-Hills!" cried the Black

Cat piteously. "Spare, oh, spare a poor creature that is so hungry, wet, and cold!"

"Come, sit by the fire," said the hunter, moved
with pity. "Nothing shall harm you."

He then tried to calm the Dogs, and they lay
down again, growling, their hair still bristling.
But the Black Cat did not move.

"I cannot come near the fire, good hunter,"
she said gently, "unless you first bind your two
furious Hounds with this hair."

And the hunter saw that she held a long black
hair in her mouth. He took it, but instead of
binding the Dogs, he threw it across a beam
near the chimney.

The Black Cat thought that the Dogs were
tied, so she approached the fire, and squatted
down before it, as if to dry herself.

When she had been there only a few minutes,
the hunter saw that she was swelling.

"Bad luck to you, Puss!" he cried. "You
are getting bigger!"

"Yes — yes —" purred the Cat, "as my hairs
dry they stand out."

But she kept on swelling, and swelling, and
swelling.

"More bad luck to you, Puss!" cried the
hunter. "You are as big as my bucket!"

"Yes — yes," snarled the Cat. "When my
skin dries, it expands."

And still she kept on swelling, and swelling,
and swelling.

"Black death to you, evil beast!" cried the hunter. "You're as big as the door!"

At that the Black Cat reared her back up until it touched the ceiling, and screeched: —

"Fasten hair! Fasten!" for she thought the Dogs were tied.

And the hair fastened itself so tightly around the beam that it cut it in two. Then up sprang the Dogs, their eyes rolling and red, and leaped toward the Cat.

But before they could touch her, she turned into a Witch, and flew yelling up the chimney.

WHY DOGS HAVE LONG TONGUES

Caddo Tale

Long, long ago in Red Indian Land, all Dogs talked just as people do. But they were great tattlers, and ran about telling everything their masters did. Of course the masters did not like this at all, and they scolded them, and even whipped them. But it was of no use, for they still ran about tattling.

Now, there was a young brave named Running Water, who was a great hunter. At first he would not own a Dog. But he was so lonely on his hunting trips, that at last he decided that he would adopt a very young one, and bring it up so well that it should not talk too much.

So he found a nice bright puppy, only a few

days old. He took him home, and brought him up very well indeed. And when the little Dog was big enough, and had learned not to talk too much, he took him out to hunt Rabbits. And after that the little Dog always went with Running Water on his hunting trips.

But this little Dog was worse than all the other Dogs. They ran around in plain sight telling what their masters did. But this little Dog would wait until Running Water was busy shooting Rabbits, then he would sneak away to the village, and boast to every one how he and his master had killed a lot of game. Then back he would hurry, and creep up very softly behind Running Water as if he had been there all the time.

Running Water, however, knew all that the bad little Dog was doing, and he whipped him, and scolded him, until he thought that the little Dog was cured of telling lying tales.

Now, one day Running Water told his mother to prepare plenty of food, because he was going to the mountains to hunt game, and would be gone for a long time.

His mother did so; and he loaded several Horses with the food and blankets, and started out, the little Dog leaping and playing by his side.

They hunted for several weeks, and killed some big animals, then they set out for home. After a day's journey, Running Water missed the little Dog. He searched for him on all sides, and even went back to the mountains, but could not find him.

And what was the little Dog doing? He had hurried on ahead, just as fast as he could, and was going about the village boasting to every one how he and his master had killed hundreds of Mountain-lions, Bears, Deer, Coyotes, and so many other animals that he could not name them all.

Well, when Running Water reached the village, and found all the people excited, he was more angry than ever before.

"Now," said he, "I will surely stop that little Dog from tattling!"

So he caught the little Dog, whipped him hard, and, taking hold of his tongue, pulled, and pulled, and pulled it out *very long*. Then he ran a stick across the little Dog's mouth.

And that is why all Dogs have long tongues and big mouths, and why they are afraid to talk.

POTATO! POTATO!

New Tale

ONCE there was a little girl. She lived all alone with her mother in a wee house in the wood.

They were very poor, and did not have much to eat; but the little girl wanted Potatoes every day for every meal. She liked them fried and crisp. She liked them mashed with butter and milk. And, better yet, she liked them baked brown and sweet in the hot ashes on the hearth.

One day her mother said: "My child, I am going to town to buy a loaf of bread. Here is a piece of cheese for your luncheon. There is just one Potato left on the shelf in the cupboard. Do not touch it. It is for our supper." Then she went away.

After she was gone the little girl swept the kitchen floor, made the bed, and fed the Pigs and Chickens. Then she felt, oh! so hungry! And she ate up all the cheese. But it was not lunch-time yet.

When lunch-time really came, the little girl was so very, very hungry that she did not know what to do. She thought and thought about the Potato on the shelf in the cupboard.

"How good it would taste fried!" thought she. "No! I would rather have it boiled and mashed! No! No! It would be perfectly delicious baked!"

And before she knew what she was doing, she ran to the cupboard and got the Potato, and buried it in the hot ashes on the hearth. Then she sat down to watch it.

By and by she heard "Puff! Puff! Puff!" and she knew that the Potato was done.

She was just going to dig it out of the ashes

with a fork, when up jumped the Potato himself! He had a mouth, and a nose, and eyes all round him, and spindle legs and arms. He went straight up the chimney and was gone.

Well, the little girl was so frightened that she ran out of the house, and looked up at the chimney. And there sat the Potato on the roof, laughing and holding his sides.

She got a ladder and climbed to the roof. She put out her hand and was just going to catch him, when — *puff!* the Potato was gone again! She looked, and there he was running along the road in front of the house. She clambered down and hastened after, crying and crying: —

> "*Potato! Potato! Come back! Come back!*
> *Or my mother will scold me. Alack! Alack!*"

And the Potato called and called: —

> "*Catch me! Catch me! And carry me back!*
> *And you shall have a Magic Sack!*"

He ran fast, but she ran faster. She put out her hand, and was just going to catch him, when — *puff!* the Potato was gone again!

Then she heard him laugh over her head. And there he sat on the branch of a tree, laughing and holding his sides.

So she climbed up. She put out her hand and was just going to catch him, when — *puff!* the Potato was gone again!

She looked, and there he was running away through the woods. She clambered down and hastened after, weeping and weeping: —

*"Potato!   Potato!   Come back!   Come back!
Or my mother will whip me!   Alack!   Alack!"*

And the Potato called and called: —

*"Catch me!   Catch me!   And carry me back!
And you shall have a Magic Sack!"*

And he ran fast; but she ran faster. She put out her hand, and was just going to catch him, when — *puff!* the Potato was gone again.

Then she heard him laugh near her feet. And there he sat at the bottom of an old dried well, laughing and holding his sides.

She put out her hand, and *caught him.*

Then — *puff!* the Potato was gone again, and what do you think? The little girl found herself standing in the door of her own wee house.

She ran into the kitchen, and there was the Potato — just an ordinary one again, brown and dirty, — lying on the shelf in the cupboard, and near it was a Magic Sack filled with new, clean, pink Potatoes!

And when the little girl's mother came home, she was delighted to find the Magic Sack. And though she cooked a great many of the Potatoes for supper, she could not empty the sack, for every time she took one out another came in its place.

So after that, every day at every meal, the little girl had all the Potatoes she wanted to eat. She had them fried and crisp for breakfast. She had them mashed with butter and milk for luncheon. And for supper she had them, best of all, baked brown and sweet in the hot ashes on the hearth.

THE DUCK–FEATHER MAN

Chinese Tale

ONCE upon a time, in a little village in China, there lived an honest old farmer called Mr. Chang. He was so kind-hearted and polite that he never said a rude thing to anybody. He had a large flock of Ducks.

Close to his farm lived a good-for-nothing beggar named Wang. One night Wang felt hungry, so he rose, and stole Mr. Chang's biggest Duck, carried it home, and ate it. Then he went to bed.

In the middle of the night he felt pricklings all over his body, and when he got up in the morning he found that he was covered with sharp duck-feathers that were growing out of his skin like so many pin-points. He was in great pain all day, and was ashamed to go out.

That night, when he was asleep, he dreamed that a man came to him and said: —

"You are being well punished for stealing

that Duck. You will have to wear the feathers until you go to Mr. Chang, and persuade him to call you a thief."

When Wang woke, he was very much worried, for he did not wish to tell that he had stolen the Duck. At last he thought of a way out of it. He went to Mr. Chang and said:—

"Sir, your Duck was stolen by old Lin who lives down the road. He does not like to be called bad names, so if you will go to him and call him a thief, he will give back the Duck."

"Ha! Ha!" laughed kind Mr. Chang. "I have no time to waste calling people bad names. No! No! Let him have my Duck, and be happy!"

Just then Wang's skin began to smart and burn. He could feel the sharp feathers growing longer and longer, so in a terrible fright he fell on his knees, and confessed how he had stolen the Duck and eaten it. Then he begged Mr. Chang to call him a thief.

"Why, my good man," said polite Mr. Chang, very much shocked, "I have never called any one a rude name, and I shall certainly not do so now."

Thereupon poor Wang, in tears, tore open his coat, and showed all those horrid feathers sticking out of his skin.

And when Mr. Chang saw them, he shouted in horror:—

"You are a thief! You are a thief!"

Immediately the duck-feathers disappeared, and Wang stood up.

He thanked Mr. Chang over and over again; and you may be sure that he took good care never to steal or lie again.

THE POTATO–CHOOSING BOY

New Tale

ONCE upon a time, there was a boy who lived with his sister in a tepee made of vines. They lived on a large green island. Everywhere grew plants covered with scarlet flowers or delicious berries. A tree with big leaves like fans waved over the tepee, and birds, red, yellow, and blue, sang among the leaves. Oh, it was a beautiful island!

The brother and sister had no work to do, and they played all the day long, eating as many berries as they wished. But the sister was not happy. Each morning she got up when the Sun rose, and sang a sad song: —

> *"There are many berries on the bushes,*
> *There are many birds on our tree,*
> *There are many children in the big World,*
> *But only two in our tepee!"*

"Why do you sing so sadly, sister?" asked the boy.

But she shook her head and wept. And so it happened every day for months.

At last one morning the boy made himself a bow of yellow wood, and two arrows tipped with green and blue feathers; then he said: —

"Farewell, sister! I am going out into the big World to find your lost happiness."

The sister answered: —

"Know that my heart is breaking because there are no children on our island to play with me. Each month when the Moon is full I paddle the canoe down the river to the Big Sea Water, and visit a beautiful island where there are many children. I play with them, and they give me good things to eat. But when I get into my canoe to come home, the girls laugh at me and say: 'We will not go to your island because you have only berries to eat.' So I return home sorrowful"; and the sister wept again.

Well, the boy comforted her, saying: "I will go to the Medicine Man of the Black Rock, and ask him what to do."

So he launched his canoe in the river, and paddled down to the Big Sea Water. Then he hoisted a tiny red sail, and the Wind blew him, and blew him, night and day, across the waves. At last he came to a large black rock standing out of the water. From its top rose a cloud of white smoke.

The boy jumped out of his canoe, and sang a magic song, and a door opened in the rock. He stepped into a room with black walls. On a

Magic Deerskin in the middle of the room sat the old Medicine Man smoking his black pipe, while from its bowl went up a long line of snow-white Pigeons, that flew out of a hole in the roof, and away.

Stepping up to the old Medicine Man, the boy laid the yellow bow and the green and blue plumed arrows at his feet. Then the old Man, smiling, held out his pipe, and the boy took it and put it to his lips.

He softly breathed his magic song, and smoked the pipe. Then from its bowl went whirring up a long line of Bluebirds, Robins, and Thrushes; singing sweetly they flew out through the hole in the roof, and away.

Then the old Medicine Man smiled again, and said:—

"Mighty is your magic song, my Son, for you have smoked my black pipe and released my song-birds. I know what you want. You may choose a gift for your sister from my Magic Garden of Plants."

So saying, he rose from his Deerskin, and struck the wall with his pipe. Immediately the wall opened, and the boy stepped into a garden filled with waving green plants.

All their leaves began to rustle, and he heard little voices crying out around him: "Pick me!" "Pull me!" "Pluck me!"

He looked carefully about, but he did not know

which plant to choose for his sister. Some were covered with beautiful red flowers, and others had strange fruits growing on them.

Then a voice at his right foot cried out: "Pick me! Pick me! I will warm you when the cold, cold Winter comes!"

And the boy saw near his right foot a large plant hung with Red Peppers like big scarlet bells.

He thought to himself: "Peppers will burn my sister's mouth."

Then a voice at his left foot cried out: "Pluck me! Pluck me! I will refresh you when the hot, hot Summer comes!"

And he saw near his left foot a big plant hung with luscious Tomatoes, smooth and red.

He thought to himself: "Tomatoes will not strengthen my sister."

Then a voice cried out in front of him: "Pull me! Pull me! I'm sweet and brown! I'm mealy and white! Cold in Summer, hot in Winter! Eat me! Eat me!"

And the boy saw in front of him a homely plant with tiny white flowers staring up from its leaves. So he pulled and pulled. The plant came up, and there on its roots were many brown balls, each holding a secret.

He thought to himself: "I'll take this home to my sister."

So the old Medicine Man let him have the

plant, and he stepped into his canoe. He hoisted his tiny red sail, and the Wind blew him, and blew him, night and day, across the waves to his home.

His sister ran to meet him, and he gave her the plant. She picked all the brown balls off its roots, and buried some in the earth with hot stones.

When she dug them up again, they were puffy and hot, snow-white inside, and delicious!

Then the boy took the rest of the brown balls and buried them in the earth without the hot stones, and left them there. By and by, green plants grew up, their roots hung with brown balls.

Then the brother and sister made a great feast, and asked all the children from the island in the Big Sea Water. They came, and after they had tasted the puffy brown balls, they wished to stay for ever.

And they named the brother "Potato-Choosing-Boy," and so he was called all his life.

And his sister laughed, and sang:—

> *"There are many berries on the bushes,*
> *There are many birds on our tree,*
> *There are many children on our island,*
> *And joy in our tepee!"*

THE TURKEY–GIVEN CORN

Navaho Myth

AT the foot of the Encircled Mountain, in the distant Navaho land, there once dwelt a young brave named Natinesthani. He was very poor, for he had gambled away all his goods. And as he had nothing to eat, he was forced to go to the mountain to hunt Wood-Rats and Rabbits.

Near him lived his brother and his niece. They had plenty of food, but they would not give him any. They were angry because he had gambled away all that he possessed.

"Let him live on Wood-Rats and Rabbits as best he can," said his brother.

So things went from bad to worse with Natinesthani. One morning he rose early and said to himself:—

"My brother disowns me. My niece, whom I love, will not look at me. I will go away and never come back. I will go to a land where I shall be happy."

Then he put on his moccasins made of Yucca-fibre and grass, and flung over his shoulders an old blanket woven of Yucca-fibre and Cedar-bark. After which he went to his niece and begged her to roast him some Wood-Rats. She did so, and ground a quantity of meal, which she put into a bag made of Wood-Rat skins.

Now the niece had a pet grey Turkey — in those days all Turkeys had grey feathers — and it was roosting in a tree near the lodge. And Natinesthani said to her: —

"Dear Niece, give me your Turkey. I am going among strangers, and shall be lonely. I love the bird, and it will remind me of home. Yet I will not take it from you by force."

"Well, take my Turkey, then," said his niece, for she really felt sorry for Natinesthani.

So he took the bird and the bag of meal and the roasted Wood-Rats, and carried them all to a river called Old Age Water, that flowed near the Encircled Mountain.

He had no canoe, and he was just going to chop down a tree to make one, when he heard a voice close behind him crying: —

"Wu! Hu! Hu! Hu!"

He looked around and saw a stately Chief standing close to him. On his head was a bonnet of eagle-plumes tipped with Owl-Feathers. Over his shoulders hung finely dressed deerskins. His face was wonderfully painted, red and black.

This Chief stood for a moment in silence, then he shouted: —

"Wu! Hu! Hu! Hu!" and made a sign for Natinesthani to stand up.

The young man did so, holding his Turkey in his arms.

"My Grandson," asked the Chief, "what are you doing? Where are you going?"

"I am an outcast," replied Natinesthani. "I wish to go far away from my people. Take pity on me! Do not stop me! Let me go down this river with my Turkey, until I find a land where I shall be happy."

"No, my Grandson," said the Chief. "You must not go down Old Age Water alone. You will be drowned. I am the Talking Magician. I pity you."

Then the Talking Magician shouted again, "Wu! Hu! Hu! Hu!" and immediately there stood beside him a number of strange Beings.

"My People," said he, "cut down a tree!"

Immediately the strange Beings felled a huge tree.

"Do you, O Straight Lightning," said he, "bore a hole through it!"

Immediately Straight Lightning flashed through the tree, boring a hole from end to end.

"Do you, O my Winds, make the hole larger!"

Immediately Black Wind, Blue Wind, Yellow Wind, and White Wind rushed through the hole and made it larger.

"Do your duty, O my Clouds!"

Immediately a White Cloud wrapped himself around Natinesthani, and, lifting him gently, placed him inside the tree. Then Black Cloud crept into the hole and stopped up one end,

while Blue Cloud closed the other. So Natinesthani was tightly shut in.

Then they launched the tree, and as it floated
down stream, Natinesthani sang softly:—

> "*O the beautiful Tree, they felled for me!*
> *O the beautiful Tree, they bored for me!*
> *O the beautiful Tree, that carries me*
> *To the Land where I shall happy be!*"

But all this time he had forgotten his pet
Turkey. He did not know that the Talking
Magician had taken it from him, and that the
strange Beings were doing many marvellous
things to its wings.

So Natinesthani floated on and on, singing as
he went. The Four Winds guided the tree
gently along until it reached the end of Old Age
Water, where a whirlpool flung it high on land.
Then he crept forth and stood up.

He looked in all directions and could see no
one. He was alone. He sat down to think. He
was sad and desolate. He saw that the pet
Turkey was gone and began to weep.

But just then he heard the gobbling of a
Turkey sounding faintly in the distance. He
listened. It came nearer and nearer, and grew
louder and louder. At last he saw running
toward him his own pet Turkey, with outstretched wings, gobbling and gobbling with joy.
It sprang into his arms. It laid its beak against
his face, and caressed his cheeks with its wings.

"Welcome! Welcome! My Turkey!" cried he. "I am sorry for you, that you have followed me to this dreary spot! But I thank you for coming!"

It was now growing dark, so Natinesthani made a bed of dried leaves, and he and the Turkey lay down side by side. He spread his Yucca-fibre blanket over his pet, while the Turkey stretched one of its wings over its master. So they slept all night.

Next morning the Turkey sprang up and began to gobble in a peculiar manner. It ran before Natinesthani as if it wished him to follow. He did so, and it led him to a broad green meadow, through which flowed a clear sparkling stream. Here he sat down on the bank, while the Turkey gambolled joyfully around him.

"My Pet!" said he, "what a fine farm this would make, if only I had some seed!"

The Turkey gobbled loudly in reply, and ran around and around. It spread wide its wings and puffed out its neck. Then it ran to the East and shook its wings, and out of them dropped four grains of White Corn. Then it ran to the South and shook its wings, and out of them dropped four grains of Blue Corn. It ran to the West and shook its wings, and out of them dropped four grains of Yellow Corn; and to the North it ran and shook out four grains of Red Corn.

Then it flew to Natinesthani, and, flapping its wings violently, shook out Pumpkin seeds, Muskmelon seeds, Watermelon seeds, and Beans.

"Thank you! Thank you, my Pet!" he cried. "I hoped that you would give me something!"

Then he hastened and dug up the ground with a stick, and planted all the seeds. This took him the entire day. That night he and the Turkey ate roasted Wood-Rats, and lay down together again, and slept soundly.

Next morning, as soon as Natinesthani awoke, he got up and hastened to his farm.

Behold, all the seeds had sprung up in the night! The Corn was growing taller every minute, and its leaves broader, while small ears were sprouting from its sides. The vines were running fast over the ground. Yellow and white flowers were peeping from among their leaves, and little Pumpkins, Melons, and Beans were forming.

The Turkey puffed out its neck and began to dance and spread wide its wings. And Natinesthani laughed and sang with joy:—

> "*Oh, the beautiful Seeds they sent to me!*
> *Oh, the beautiful Seeds they gave to me!*
> *Oh, the beautiful Seeds that sprout for me*
> *In this Land where I shall happy be!*"

THE PET TURKEY WHOSE FEELINGS WERE HURT

Navaho Myth

Now after Natinesthani had planted his farm, and the magic seeds had sprung up in one night, he built a little lodge of branches for himself and his pet Turkey. And when it was dark, before he lay down to sleep, he sat by his fire looking eastward. He was surprised to see flames rising in the distance.

Next morning he said to his Turkey:—

"Stay at home, my Pet. I must go and see who makes that fire."

The Turkey drooped its wings, it felt so badly.

Natinesthani put on his moccasins of Yucca-fibre and Cedar-bark, and, taking his bow and arrows, started out. But though he searched everywhere, he could not find the fire or the people who made it. When he came home he said to his Turkey:—

"I must have seen a large Glow-worm!"

The next day he said to his Turkey: —

"Stay at home, my Pet. This time I shall surely find who makes that fire, or I will never try again!"

The Turkey swelled out its neck, and drooped its wings and head, and turned its back, it was so angry.

Natinesthani started out, and went on and on, until he came to a shelving rock. He climbed upon the shelf and saw two handsome lodges. He felt ashamed of his ragged blanket and moccasins of Yucca-fibre; nevertheless he approached the nearest lodge and pushed aside the curtain. He saw a lovely girl sitting inside. She was making a fine buckskin shirt trimmed with shells and fringe.

He entered the lodge and sat down. At that moment an old man came in.

"My Daughter," said the old man, "why do you not take my son-in-law's blanket?"

At that poor Natinesthani hung down his head and blushed, while the girl looked sidewise at him and smiled.

"My Daughter," said the old man again, "why do you not spread skins for my son-in-law to sit upon?"

But the girl only looked sidewise and smiled. Then the old man took some softly dressed sheepskins and deerskins and spread them next the girl.

"My Son-in-law," said he, "why do you not sit beside your wife?"

Thereat Natinesthani tried to get up, but sank back in confusion. Then he arose and sat down by the girl.

After that the old man spread a skin by Natinesthani's side and sat down. He took some Tobacco from a pouch ornamented with pictures of the Sun and the Moon, and filled a long pipe painted with Elk, Deer, and Mountain-sheep. He lighted his pipe and puffed the smoke to Earth and to Heaven each twice, and handed the pipe to Natinesthani, saying:—

"Son-in-law, smoke my Tobacco. It is good."

Now Natinesthani did not know it, but the Four Winds — Black Wind, Blue Wind, Yellow Wind, and White Wind — were with him. And when he took the old man's pipe, Black Wind whispered in his ear:—

"His Tobacco will kill you! It is bad magic! They who smoke it never wake again!"

So Natinesthani answered the old man:—

"I ask no one for a smoke. I gather my own Tobacco. It is here."

And he drew a small pipe from the bag of Wood-Rat skins and filled it with his own Tobacco. This he smoked.

The old man closed his eyes and nodded his head. Then, opening them again, he bade his daughter make a bed for their guest. She spread on the floor some finely dressed robes of Otter and Beaver skin, beautifully ornamented. Natinesthani lay down on these, and slept all night.

Next day, Natinesthani said to the girl:—

"My Wife, I have a pet Turkey and a lodge not far from here. Dress yourself for a journey.

I must go home to-day and take you with me."

So the girl hurried and dressed herself, and she gave Natinesthani a pair of handsome embroidered moccasins and the fine buckskin shirt trimmed with shells and fringe. These he put on. Then she ran to her father, and said:—

"I go with my husband."

And he replied:—

"It is well; go with him. He has withstood my magic, and no longer have I any power over him."

So together they set out, Natinesthani and his wife. And soon they came to the top of a little hill, and looked down on the farm in the meadow. Although the Sun was shining, a fresh Rain was falling. And over the farm gleamed a bright Rainbow. Then the Rain ceased, and Natinesthani led his wife down into the meadow.

Four times they walked around the farm. The Cornstalks were standing strong and tall. The yellow corn-fringe waved in the breeze. Bluebirds and Yellowbirds sang among the leaves. And on the vines were Melons green and gold, and large Pumpkins round and yellow, while Bean-pods hung there in thick clusters. Oh, it was a beautiful farm!

"Behold the Corn — our friend!" shouted Natinesthani with joy. "The food of my people!

We will husk it and store it for Winter!   We will shell it and grind it!   We will roast it or boil it!   We will save seed for the Springtime!

"But come, now, and let us pluck an ear of each colour.   We will go to my lodge and feed my pet Turkey.   I love the bird, and it is waiting for me."

So they gathered four ears of Corn, yellow, red, white, and blue, and hurried to the lodge. But, alas! the Turkey did not come running to meet them.   No Turkey was there.   All that they saw were turkey tracks.

Four times the tracks passed around the lodge, getting farther and farther away.   They then led toward a high mountain in the East.

"I will hunt until I find my pet Turkey," said Natinesthani, and he left his wife and travelled eastward.   All day he travelled, and the next, and the next, but still he could not find his Turkey.   On the fourth day he sat down and wept, saying: —

"O my Pet, it was all my fault!   If I had taken you with me, I should not have lost you!"

Then he rose up mournfully to return to his lodge, singing a magic song as he went: —

> "*O my dear, dear Pet!*
> *You were the black Cloud!*
> *You were the fresh Rain!*
> *You were the soft Mist!*
> *You were the keen Lightning!*
> *You were the bright Rainbow!*

You were the Corn,
Yellow, white, red, and blue!
The beautiful Bean were you!"

And so Natinesthani came back to his lodge and found his wife waiting there for him. But he never saw his pet Turkey again. For gobbling, gobbling sadly, it had flown far away.

And before that time the feathers of all Turkeys were grey. But since then, in their feathers are the black Cloud and the soft Mist, the flash of the Lightning, and the gleam of the Rainbow. The Rain is in their beards, and the Bean in their foreheads. And all the colours of the ripened Corn — yellow, white, red, and blue — are in every pet Turkey's wings.

PEACH BOY'S RICE–CAKES

Japanese Folktale

In far away Japan, in old, old times, there was once a poor woman who had no children.

One day, as she was washing her clothes in the river, she saw an enormous Peach floating by. She had never seen such a large Peach! It was pink and ripe, and she thought what a delicious meal it would make. But she had no stick with which to catch it. However, she remembered a magic song that she had learned as a child, and she sang it softly.

Immediately the Peach came nearer and

nearer until it stopped close at her feet. She picked it up, and, forgetting her washing, ran home as fast as she could.

She showed it to her husband, and he was as delighted as she at the thought of such a delicious meal. He quickly got a sharp knife, and was just going to cut the Peach in two, when, presto! it burst open of itself, and the prettiest little boy tumbled out on the table, and began to laugh merrily, and to caper around.

"Do not be afraid," cried the little fellow, running up close to the man. "I'll not hurt you! I am your little son, and will care for you in your old age."

Hearing this, the man and woman could scarcely contain themselves for joy. Each in turn picked the child up. They petted and caressed him, and called him "Peach Boy."

Peach Boy grew very fast, and in a short time was stronger, handsomer, and larger than any boy in the village. And when he was fifteen years old he came to his father and said:—

"I hear that a number of Demons live on a certain island in the Great Sea. They have seized many innocent people, whom they either eat or torture. I wish to rescue these captives and bring back some of the Demons' treasure to you. So give me your blessing, and let me depart."

At first the father would not hear of such a

thing, but when he remembered that his son was no ordinary child, he decided to let him go. So Peach Boy made ready to start, and when he was just setting out his mother gave him a bag full of Rice-Cakes, and bade him take good care of them, for they would help him safely on his way.

So he started, and at noon sat down by the roadside to eat a Rice-Cake. But no sooner had he taken one from the bag than up ran a great Dog, snarling and showing his teeth.

"Give me a Rice-Cake," yelped the Dog, "or I'll bite you!"

Peach Boy threw him a cake. And as soon as the Dog had eaten it, he drooped his tail and bowed his head and cried: —

"Peach Boy, I am now your servant and will aid you in anything."

"Follow me, then, to the Isle of Demons," said Peach Boy, and he got up and went on his way. And the Dog followed after.

They had not gone far, when a huge Monkey leaped from a tree, and stood in the way, rolling his eyes and gnashing his teeth.

"Give me a Rice-Cake," he howled, "or I'll tear you!"

Peach Boy threw him a cake. And as soon as the Monkey had eaten it, he knelt down in the dust and cried: —

"Peach Boy, I am now your servant, and will aid you in anything!"

"Follow me, then, to the Isle of Demons," said Peach Boy, and he went on his way. And the Dog and Monkey followed after. But it was some time before they stopped fighting one another and became friends.

They proceeded on their journey, and had not gone far when a bright Pheasant sprang out of a bush into the way, beating his wings together, and snapping his beak.

"Give me a Rice-Cake," he hissed, "or I'll peck you!"

Peach Boy threw him a cake. And as soon as the Pheasant had eaten it, he folded his wings humbly, and lowered his neck, and cried:—

"Peach Boy, I am now your servant, and will aid you in anything."

"Follow me, then, to the Isle of Demons," said Peach Boy, and went on his way. The Dog and the Monkey and the Pheasant followed after. But it was some time before they stopped quarrelling and became friends.

Well, Peach Boy went on and on, followed by his companions, until he reached the Great Sea. There a little green boat was waiting for him. Into it he stepped with the Dog and the Monkey and the Pheasant. Soon the little boat was spinning over the blue water.

Away! away! it sped over the waves until it drew near to the Isle of Demons. Then the Pheasant sprang out of the boat, and flew to

AWAY! AWAY! IT SPED OVER THE WAVES

the Demons' castle, and, alighting on its roof, told the evil ones that Peach Boy with his bag of Rice-cakes was coming. But the Demons only laughed scornfully and shook their shaggy red heads.

But when Peach Boy landed, with the Dog and the Monkey, he went straight to the castle and found a small door that the Demons had forgotten to lock. He and his companions slipped in very quietly, and as soon as the Demons knew that Peach Boy, with his bag of Rice-Cakes, was inside, they were terribly frightened.

Peach Boy fought with his sword, the Dog with his teeth, the Monkey with his hands, and the Pheasant with his beak; and all the Demons that they did not kill were so filled with terror that they fell off the parapets and were dashed to pieces — all except the Demon King. He surrendered to Peach Boy, and gave up his treasures.

Then Peach Boy bound the Demon King with strong chains, and, going through the castle, liberated the innocent people who were imprisoned there. Afterward the Dog, and the Monkey, and the Pheasant, carrying the treasure between them, and Peach Boy, leading the Demon King, set out for home.

Once more in the little green boat they sped over the blue water, and were soon in Japan. The whole country rejoiced, and the

Demon King was imprisoned in a black iron tower.

As for Peach Boy and his father and mother, they were now rich and powerful, and lived in a magnificent castle. With them were their three friends, — the Dog, the Monkey, and the Pheasant. And they all ended their days in plenty and happiness, for they always had as many Rice-Cakes as they wished to eat.

THE SEVEN CORN MAIDENS

Zuñi Myth

IN the days of magic wonders, in the Valley of the Zuñi Ancients, in the town called the Middle Ant Hill of the World, once dwelt seven Maidens more beautiful than any others on earth. They were the guardians of the Corn.

Every year the Zuñi tribes, even the People of the Seed and the People of the Dew, met together for a feast. Then the Seven Corn Maidens, in robes as white as Snow, danced before the people like seven bright Stars.

All the night through, backward and forward, danced the Maidens, waving their Magic Plume-Sticks above the growing Corn. And the stalks grew tall and strong, and the leaves spread like broad ribbons, while Corn-Ears sprouted from the sides of the stalks, each sweet and full of milk, and wrapped in soft green husks with yellow tassels.

And when Dawn drew near, the Chief of the People of the Dew played softly on his magic flute; and as he did so, the breath of flowers and the morning-song of birds came on the breeze. Then a white mist went wreathing upward from the folds of the Chief's garments, and the Seven Corn Maidens vanished in the mist.

After that the Chief turned to the People of the Seed and the People of the Dew, and said:—

> *"Be ye brothers, ye People! ye People!*
> *Be ye happy, ye People! ye People!*
> *Behold the seed of all seed-plants is here!*
> *Milk to the young is the Corn-Plant;*
> *Strength to the youth, and flesh to the aged!*
> *Gather and eat it. Cherish it true.*
> *Love our bright Maidens,*
> *Who guard well its sweet ears!"*

And as he finished speaking, the Sun rose, and the mothers of the tribes hastened to pluck the Corn. And some of the ears were blue, some red, some yellow, some white, and all were sweet and good.

And the People of the Seed and the People of the Dew feasted together, and grew stronger and handsomer and more contented. So it happened year after year, and the People turned their hearts to cherishing the Corn.

But as time went on, strange youths, who did not love the Corn Maidens, visited the tribes.

They said that they had seen far lovelier maidens. For each day at evening, violet rays rolled upward from a cavern under Thunder Mountain; and through the rays one might see the flutter of embroidered garments like painted spray, and the waving of white arms, and the streaming of soft, dark hair. For in the cavern danced the Seven Rainbow Sisters, hand in hand.

And the youths said, also, that the beat of drums and the low, sweet music that came from the cavern were like the liquid voices of hidden rivers, and were far more delicious than the sounds of the magic flute of the Chief of the Dew People.

So said the stranger youths, and the Seven Corn Maidens heard their words and were sad.

And when the time came again for the ripening of the Corn, the People of the Seed and the People of the Dew met together, as was their custom, for the feast. And while they sat waiting for the Seven Corn Maidens to appear, they heard the low beat of a drum from Thunder Mountain, and soft music. Then through the pale light of evening came floating the Seven Rainbow Sisters themselves, hand in hand and seven in number, their robes fluttering like painted spray. While from the tips of their Plume-Sticks quivered the violet rays.

The Sisters hovered over the heads of the people, and danced their magic dance. Faster and faster they moved, until they flashed like a circle of rainbow light. And the people shouted with joy, and held out their hands, and begged the Sisters to stay with them for ever. But the violet rays from the Plume-Sticks wreathed upward and hid the Rainbow Sisters from sight, while they floated back to the cavern under Thunder Mountain.

Then the people heard the sweet notes of the magic flute of the Chief of the Dew People as he led forth the Corn Maidens to the grain-field. But the Maidens moved silently. With pale, sad faces they passed among the people and laid down their Magic Plume-Sticks. Then, sobbing, they melted into a white mist, and drifted away to the South Summer-Land.

And when the Seven Corn Maidens were gone, a cold Wind from Thunder Mountain swept over the plain. The Corn-Stalks drooped, and the ears were blighted. The grain-fields grew bleak and barren.

The people wept, and hunger came among them. Then said they, one to the other: —

"We must send messengers after our beloved Maidens, and entreat them to come from their hiding place, so that the ears of Corn, that nourish all flesh, may ripen again."

First they sent out the Eagle, strong and swift; and he searched the rocks and mountains, but saw no trace of the Corn Maidens.

After that they sent out the Falcon, keen of eye; and he searched the cliff-shadows and hedge-rows, but found not the Corn Maidens.

The croaking Raven flew to seek them; and though he searched meadows and woods, he found them not.

Then the starving people, in their anguish, called to the Chief of the Dew People to save them.

In one hand he took the Magic Plume-Sticks of the Seven Corn Maidens, and in the other his flute. Swiftly he passed over the plain toward the South Summer-Land. And as he went farther southward, he planted the Magic Plume-Sticks in the ground, and, bending low, watched them. Soon their soft, downy feathers began to stir as if blown by the breath of a creature. Backward and forward, northward and south-ward, they swayed to and fro.

"Ha!" sighed the Chief, "'tis the breath of my Maidens in the South Summer-Land; the plumes stir to their breathings! I will hasten on, and scatter the bright beads of my Dew as I pass through the land. Soon again northward shall I fetch my beautiful Maidens!"

So said he, and hastened forward, scattering the bright Dew and playing on his magic flute.

And there, at last, in the warm Summer-Land, he found his Corn Maidens. He greeted them with a smile and a touch of his hand. And the white mists went wreathing upward from the folds of his garments. The wreaths of mist enveloped the forms of the Maidens, and, lifting them gently, wafted them northward.

And all the little birds of the South Summer-Land came flocking after, and Butterflies fluttered like bright flowers above the Maidens' heads. So came they all again to the Middle Ant Hill of the World.

Then were the starving people happy, and met for the feast. And the Seven Corn Maidens, in robes as white as snow, again danced in the corn-fields, and waved their magic Plume-Sticks above the growing Corn.

And so the People of the Seed and the People of the Dew once more turned their hearts to cherishing the Corn; and they fed their children with its sweet milk. And the Corn-Ears gave strength to the youth and flesh to the aged.

Thus it happened in the days of magic wonders, in the Valley of the Zuñi Ancients, in the Middle Ant Hill of the World.

So shortens my story.

LEGEND OF THE CORN

Iroquois Legend

LISTEN to the Iroquois Grandmother: —

Long, long ago, there lived a young brave who loved an Iroquois maiden, and she promised to

be his bride. She was very beautiful. Her hair
was not black like the hair of other Indian girls,
but silken and golden. She had many admirers,
and the young brave feared lest one of them
might carry her off. So, to protect her, he slept
at night before her lodge in the forest.

One night he was awakened by the sounds of
light footfalls and the rustling of branches and
leaves. He sprang to his feet, and saw the
maiden herself gliding all alone from the door of
her lodge. And though her eyes were wide open
and her hands outstretched, she could see nothing, for she was still in deep slumber, and was
walking in a dream.

Swiftly she moved among the trees and vanished into the forest. The young man hastened
after her. Faster and faster she sped before him,
as if fleeing for her life. And on and on he followed, through tangled thicket and along forest
paths.

Panting, at last he overtook her. He could
hear her quick breathing and the beating of her
heart. He sprang forward and clasped her
gently in his arms.

Lo! her form grew stiff and straight. Green
leaves sprouted from her sides. She raised her
hands to her head, and they were changed into
ears of Corn. And where her hands had touched
her hair, grew long, silken, golden threads.

And the young man no longer clasped a

maiden, but a tall plant, such as he had never seen before. He held in his arms the Maize — the Indian Corn!

WILLIAM W. CANFIELD (*adapted*)

THE RAM WITH THE GOLDEN FLEECE

Retold from Apollodorus, Ovid, and Other Sources

ONCE upon a time, there was a King of Bœotia who had two children, a boy and a girl. Phrixus, the boy, was very brave and handsome, while little Helle was gentle and beautiful.

But though they lived in a fine palace and wore silken robes, the children were not happy; for their father had sent away their dear mother Nephele, and they had a stepmother named Ino.

Now Ino was a wicked woman, and was jealous of Phrixus because she wished her own son to inherit the Kingdom. So she cast a blight on all the crops of the land, and told the King that unless Phrixus and Helle were killed there would be no Corn or bread for the people. Indeed, she even said that a Wisewoman in the cave of Apollo-of-the-Golden-Beams at Delphi had declared, unless Phrixus and Helle were sacrificed, that the Corn would never grow again.

So the King gave orders that the children should be led to their death.

Thereupon the servants of the wicked Ino took

poor Phrixus and Helle, and put their finest robes on them, and crowned their heads with branches, then led them to an altar where a priest stood with uplifted knife.

Now, Nephele, their dear mother, had not really left them, but was watching over them from the sky, where she floated about wrapped in a soft white Cloud.

When she saw her children about to be killed she spoke to a Ram with Golden Fleece who stood by her side: —

"Go quickly," said she, "and save my little ones."

The Ram, spreading his glittering wings, flew down to earth, and, standing before Phrixus and Helle, bowed his head and spoke with a human voice.

"Mount my back," said he, "and I will carry you to a place of safety."

The children sprang on his back, and held on to his horns; then the Ram, spreading his wings, soared up into the blue sky.

The priest and people shouted with wonder, while the wicked stepmother trembled from fear. But the Ram with glittering wings, flew rapidly away and vanished in the distance.

Over land and sea he flew, until he came to a wide body of water, rolling black and angry from shore to shore. Phrixus held on tightly by one of the horns; but poor little Helle looked down at the waves, and, growing giddy and faint, loosened her hold and fell.

In vain Phrixus stretched out both hands to save her, and almost fell himself; the Ram swept onward, carrying him far away, while he was still weeping, and calling his sister's name.

Across the sea, the Ram hastened to the land of Colchis, where King Æetes welcomed Phrixus gladly, and gave him his beautiful daughter in marriage. There the Ram died, and Phrixus presented his Golden Fleece to the King, who nailed it on an Oak in the midst of a grove.

As for little Helle, her brother mourned for her; but he did not know that she was become the bride of the King of the sea into which she was fallen. And ever since that day the sea has been called by her name — the Hellespont, or Helle's Sea.

HOW JASON BROUGHT HOME THE GOLDEN FLEECE

Now, in those golden wonder days, Pelias ruled over Iolcos, for he had dethroned its rightful King. He had even tried to slay the King's little son; but the baby had mysteriously vanished.

After this King Pelias lived in continual terror, because an Oracle had declared that a man wearing one sandal should bring him death and destruction.

Now one day, when the King was holding a feast for the people, he saw in the crowd a handsome youth dressed in a Leopard's skin and holding two spears. He wore but one sandal; his other foot was bare.

In haste, the King summoned him, and said: —

"Young Man, I have one question to ask you. Answer it wisely. If you had the power, and an Oracle had declared that a certain one of your subjects should be your death, what would you do to that man?"

"I would send him to fetch home the Golden Fleece from Colchis," replied the youth.

Scarcely were these words out of his mouth before King Pelias shouted: —

"Go, then, for you are that man! Make haste to depart, and bring back to me the Golden Fleece!"

So the youth was snared in his own words; for the famous Fleece was nailed to an Oak in a dangerous Grove, and was guarded night and day by a sleepless Dragon.

"I will fetch it," replied the youth. "But know that I am Jason, the rightful heir to this land. I was the babe whom you sought to slay. Yesterday I left my Schoolmaster Chiron the Centaur, to claim my rights from you. On my way hither I lost one sandal in a stream, therefore am I barefooted. Now will I depart on my quest, but when I return in triumph bearing the

Golden Fleece, I will demand from you the Kingdom of my fathers."

So saying Jason made haste to prepare for the voyage. Argus, the son of Phrixus, built for him a wonderful ship, in the prow of which Minerva-the-Wise-One set a piece of the Talking Oak of Dodona; which was a very wise Oak indeed, that gave always good counsel. Fifty oars had the Ship, and she was manned by fifty heroes. For with Jason sailed Hercules the Mighty, and his lad the beautiful Hylas; Orpheus the sweet singer went too; also the Twin Sons of Boreas the North Wind, — handsome youths they were, with long flowing yellow beards and hair, and wings that made a rushing noise like their father's. Fifty heroes went, all eager for adventures.

So the good Ship Argo, as it was called, set sail. While the joyful heroes grasped the oars, Orpheus struck his lyre, and the stroke of the oars kept such perfect time to his delightful harmony, that the ship seemed to speed magically along.

Many were the adventures of the heroes on their way to Colchis. They slew six-armed Giants, and the Twin Sons of Boreas saved King Phineas of Thrace from the Harpies.

Fearful were the foul Harpy-sisters, winged monsters, who swooped down on King Phineas's table, snatching his food, and making everything they touched so filthy and vile-smelling that

the King could not eat at all. So he was starving
to death. Then the Twin Sons of Boreas, rising
on their yellow wings, drew their swords and
chased the Harpies far across the ocean; and the
evil ones never returned again.

Many other exciting adventures the heroes
had ere they reached the shore of Colchis. At
last they landed in that country; and Jason,
presenting himself before King Æetes' throne,
demanded the Golden Fleece,

"That will I give you," replied King Æetes,
"if you will first tame the two brass-footed, brass-
throated, fire-breathing Bulls that Vulcan gave
to me. These you must yoke, and with them
plough a field. Then you must sow some
Dragon's teeth that I have."

All this Jason agreed to do, although he did
not know how he was going to accomplish such
a terrible task.

Now near King Æetes' throne his daughter
Medea, an evil Enchantress, was standing.
And when she saw how handsome Jason was,
she loved him. So she sought him out secretly,
and offered to aid him if he would wed her. This
he promised to do, if she would gain the Golden
Fleece for him.

That night by her magic arts he tamed the
two brass-footed, brass-throated, flame-breathing bulls, and yoking them, ploughed a field and
sowed the Dragon's teeth.

But King Æetes, when he heard what he had done, still refused to give him the Golden Fleece as he had promised. Instead he plotted to kill Jason and his comrades.

So when darkness came again, Medea cast the Dragon, that guarded the tree, into an enchanted sleep. Then she and Jason, seizing the Fleece, fled with it to the ship, and sailed away to Iolcos.

Thus after many adventures the fifty heroes returned in triumph from Colchis, bearing the Golden Fleece of the Magic Ram that had saved Phrixus and Helle from a cruel death.

But, alas for Jason! He wedded the evil Enchantress Medea; and she wrought destruction and death not only for King Peleas but for Jason and all his house as well.

THE ENCHANTED SWINE

Retold from Homer

IT was in those days of yore, when the Golden Apple of Discord caused so much mischief in the world, and when the Shepherd-lad, Prince Paris, brought destruction on his native city of Troy, that the wise Ulysses set sail from the Trojan shore with all his men, to return to his Kingdom of sunny Ithaca.

Many and fearful were their adventures ere

they reached a strangely wooded isle, where noisome herbs grew in the dark shade of gloomy trees. For two days and nights they rested on the shore, and, on the third morning when Aurora, the rosy-fingered Child of Dawn, threw open the Gates of Day, Ulysses arose, and climbed a height to view the isle.

In a deep vale he saw a thicket, above which rose the towers and spires of a noble palace-hall, from which smoke curled upward toward the sky. Returning to the ship, he pondered on the wisest course.

The next morning he called his men, and said: —

"My friends, amid your great sufferings listen to my words. We do not know the East from the West, nor what lies toward the rising or the setting Sun. We are lost on this isle, and surrounded by the boundless deep. Yesterday, I looked from a height, and saw smoke ascending from a thicket. Let now some of us go thither and inquire our way."

At his words the men remembered their fearful adventures with the One-Eyed Cyclops Polyphemus, who had eaten some of their comrades, cracking them like nuts, and with the giant Læstrigons, who had hurled great stones upon them. So the men's hearts sank with fear at Ulysses' words. They wept aloud.

But tears were of no avail to that unhappy

band! For the wise Ulysses, casting lots, sent the men thus chosen to the palace-hall; and the hero Eurylochus led them thither. Still weeping, they hastened on their way.

Soon they saw a stately palace-hall of hewn stone. Around it was a spacious park of noble trees. But as they drew nearer, there rose from the ground, Mountain-Lions and Wolves. With bristling hairs and rolling eyes they cringed, and in silence, with padded feet, circled round the walls. Then wagging their tails, and standing on their hind feet, they fawned upon the men like great Dogs well-fed by their master's hand.

The men, in fear, stepped beneath the portico, and heard from within the whir and clack of loom, while honeyed words of sweetest singing floated past their ears. Then through the half-open door they saw, within the hall, a bright-haired woman richly clad, who was singing sweetly while she threw the shuttle back and forth through a web as delicate and beautiful as if woven by Minerva's own hand.

She was Circe the Enchantress, the bright-haired daughter of the Sun, wily and watchful, and, though they knew it not, waiting for them. They called aloud. Forth she came, and throwing the shining doors apart, bade them enter. All followed her except Eurylochus, who stood without, for he suspected guile.

She led them in, and seated them on thrones.

Then mingling a drink of wine, cheese, fresh honey, and yellow meal, she poured into it a magic potion made of deadly herbs, and handed golden goblets full of the baleful liquor to the men. They drank.

She touched them with her wand, and cried: —

"Take your own forms, ye worse than beasts!"

And straight the men fell from their thrones upon their hands and knees. Their faces became snouts with pricking ears and reddish eyes. Bristles sprouted from their bodies. Their feet and hands were cloven hoofs. They were no longer men, but grunting Swine. Yet they had kept their human minds, and wept from terror and shame.

"Hence to your sties!" cried Circe, and drove them forth and locked them up in pens. Then flinging some Acorns to them, she went back into her hall.

As for Eurylochus, when he had waited long and the men did not return, he fled in horror to the ship.

Then when the wise Ulysses learned that the men had not come back, he slung upon his shoulder his silver-studded sword — a huge blade of brass — and his bow with it. He summoned Eurylochus to lead the way, but the terrified man clasped Ulysses' knees with both hands, and cried: —

"O take me not with you! Force me not to

go! Great Hero, leave me by the ship! You will never return, that I know! Nor can you ever deliver our comrades from their fate!"

"Stay here, then, Eurylochus," replied Ulysses. "Stay here by the ship, eating and drinking in comfort. I shall surely go!"

So he spoke, and left the ship. Soon he drew near to Circe's magic palace-hall. When, lo! a youth met him on the way, a sprightly youth, carrying in one hand a golden staff, and in the other a plant with black roots and a blossom as white as milk. So sprightly was the youth that he moved across the ground without walking, for little wings were on his cap and heels.

He took Ulysses' hand. "Rash mortal!" said he. "Why do you wander here alone? Your comrades are shut up like Swine in treacherous Circe's sties. A like fate awaits you, if you go thither without my aid. But that you may be safe from all mischief, take this flower, and bear it to the palace-hall of Circe. It will protect you by its magic virtue. She will bring you a goblet filled with mingled liquor. Drink it; it cannot harm you. When she smites you with her wand, draw your sword and rush upon her. Do not spare her, unless she swears to do you no hurt, and to restore your friends to their own shapes."

So spoke the winged youth, and placed the flower in Ulysses' hand.

"Take it," he said, "it is Moly, and blooms only for the Dwellers-on-Mount-Olympus. I am Mercury, the messenger of Jupiter sent from his Shining Palace to aid your quest."

Then back through the woody isle Mercury hastened, and flew away to Mount Olympus.

Ulysses took his way to Circe's palace-hall. With fast beating heart he pressed through the throng of fawning beasts, and stepped beneath her portico. He called aloud. Circe heard his voice, and flung apart the shining doors.

With voice so honey-sweet and with winning smile, she bade him enter. She seated him upon a silver-studded throne, and quickly mingled a magic draught. And pouring it into a golden chalice she presented it to him. He drank the liquor off.

Then Circe, rising, smote him with her wand, and cried: —

"Go to your sty, and wallow with your fellows!"

Ulysses drew his sword and rushed upon her, as if to take her life. She shrieked and fell upon her knees. With uplifted hands she pleaded piteously: —

"Who are you? From what great race are you? Wonders! You have drunk my magic potion, and it harms you not! No mortal being has ever done so before! Are you then that wise Ulysses come from Troy? Mercury — he of the golden staff — foretold to me that Ulysses should outwit me! Spare me now! spare me! And henceforth I will do you no harm!"

"O Circe," replied Ulysses, "do you ask me to deal gently with you, when here in your own palace-hall you have transformed my friends into Swine? Swear to me that henceforth you will not only do me no injury, but will change my friends back to men."

Trembling she swore as he desired. Then she arose and prepared a banquet for him. The Nymphs from fountains, groves, and streams, who waited on her, spread two thrones with gorgeous covers, and above them suspended canopies of richest purple. They set silver tables before the thrones, laden with golden plates and cups, and rich wine in silver bowls.

Around Ulysses' manly form they flung a princely cloak, and placed a foot-stool for his feet. Then came a fair-haired Nymph with a golden ewer, and poured pure water on his hands in a silver laver. Next they placed delicious viands upon the tables, and bade him eat and drink.

But the banquet did not please him, and he sat wrapped in gloomy thoughts.

"Why, O Ulysses," said Circe, "do you sit with dark thoughts gnawing at your heart? Why do you not eat and drink?"

Then replied Ulysses: —

"Think you that a good man and true would

be so faithless as to feast while his friends were miserable captives close at hand? If you wish me to enjoy this banquet, first set my comrades free."

Then Circe took her wand, and quickly led the way into the sty, and drove forth the grunting herd of Swine. They ranged themselves before her in a row. She threw upon them a magic drug, and they rose upon their hind legs. Their bristles fell away; their snouts grew shorter. And they were transformed into their own shapes again, only handsomer and younger than before.

They knew Ulysses, and crowded to his side. They pressed his hands with tears and sobs of joy. Even Circe was moved with pity, and bade them come as guests into her hall. She robed them in fresh tunics and fair cloaks. And all day, until the setting of the Sun, they feasted. When the Sun went down, they slept on sumptuous couches in her hall.

And when at last Ulysses and his men left that enchanted isle, Circe, the bright-haired daughter of the Sun, helped them with good counsel on their way. So once more they sailed across the boundless deep, to search for sunny Ithaca.

THE WINGED HORSE

Retold from Pindar and Other Sources

In days of yore there dwelt a young and handsome King in Corinth, named Bellerophon. He was about to set out on a strange adventure. He had vowed to kill the Chimæra, a terrible monster that was ravaging the land of Lycia.

She had three heads, — one of a Lion, one of a Goat, and the third of a Serpent. The front part of her body was like a Lion, the middle like a Goat, and the hinderpart like a Dragon. Her three heads breathed out fire and smoke. Such was the terrible monster that Bellerophon had sworn to kill.

One night while he lay on his couch, considering with what weapon he should slay the Chimæra, he fell asleep. He dreamed that a maiden stood beside him. Very tall and stately she was, and her large gleaming eyes regarded him steadfastly. A helmet covered her ringlets, and she bore on her arm the shadowy ægis — the shield of Minerva the Wise One — in the centre of which was engraved the snaky head of Medusa. In her right hand she carried a golden bridle.

"Bellerophon," said she, with sweet, calm accents, "arise, go to the Spring of Pirene. Take with you this magic bridle made of soul-subduing gold, and with it tame Pegasus, the Winged

Horse of the Muses. At dawn he will come flying from the Fountain of Hippocrene on Mount Helicon, and you shall find him drinking from the pure water of Pirene. With his aid alone may you slay the Chimæra."

Then Bellerophon awoke, and, though the maiden had vanished, he found the golden bridle lying by his side.

Hastily he arose and put on his brazen armor. Taking his bow he set out for the Spring of Pirene, which flowed cold and exceedingly clear from the side of a lofty hill near Corinth.

Quickly Bellerophon climbed to the spring, and approached it. Softly its waters fell, with musical murmur, into a beautiful marble basin, edged round with flowers and grasses. On its margin stood the Winged Horse drinking the pure water, while his silvery wings waved in the air, and his quivering hoofs seemed scarcely to press the sod.

A very wonderful horse was this Pegasus, for he was born from the blood that flowed from the neck of the Gorgon Medusa when Perseus cut off her head. Straight Pegasus had flown up from her blood, and had winged his way to Mount Helicon. There, with one stroke of his delicate hoof, he had cleaved the ground, and a fountain called Hippocrene — as bright and pure as the Spring of Pirene, had gushed from the earth and flowed down the mountain-side.

So on Mount Helicon in the grove of golden-beamed Apollo, Pegasus made his home, and was cared for by the Nine Sister Muses. Freely he came, and freely he went soaring into the sky, and no one ever sought to tame him.

Now, when Bellerophon saw Pegasus drinking from the Spring of Pirene, his wings glittering in the soft morning light, he stole noiselessly forward and clapped the golden bridle over his jaw.

Instantly a shiver ran through the animal's slender frame, his distended nostrils trembled; but as he felt the touch of the soul-subduing gold, he stood quietly and let Bellerophon mount him. Then upward he sprang, and soared into the sky, higher and higher, and away to the land of Lycia, where the Chimæra was ravaging, and destroying the people.

Terrible was the combat between Bellerophon and the Chimæra. He fought her from Pegasus' back, while the brave, Winged Horse hovered above her. One by one he cut off her flame-breathing heads; and so he destroyed her.

Then was Bellerophon filled with so great pride and presumption that he wished to ascend even to Heaven itself. So he urged Pegasus upward and upward, and higher and higher.

But Jupiter, looking from his throne on Mount Olympus, saw him ascending, and quickly sent a little insect to sting the Winged Horse. The insect hid under his wings, and stung him so badly that, goaded by pain, he flung Bellerophon from his back.

Down to earth Bellerophon fell, but he was not injured. And there he wandered about, sorrowful and lonely, until at last he died.

But the Winged Horse had flown into the sky and was become a cluster of Stars. There you may see him on any bright night if you search the glittering heavens.

THE SNOW–WHITE BULL

Retold from Moschus and Ovid

ONCE upon a time, in the land of Phœnicia, there dwelt a lovely young Princess named Europa. Often with her playmates, girls of her own age, she danced, or bathed in the bright water of the streams, or gathered the fragrant Lilies growing in the meadows by the sea.

One day at dawn, she rose from her bed, and putting on a purple robe, hastened out to find her playmates. Soon she met them, each carrying a basket for flowers. Together they ran down to the meadows by the sea, where they delighted to pick blossoms and to listen to the rolling waves breaking on the sand.

Europa carried a golden basket, on which were pictures, delicately engraved, telling the story of Io, the gentle maiden whom Jupiter once turned into a cow. And many and wonderful were the pictures that were wrought in brass and silver on the gold. Such was the beautiful basket Europa carried.

Soon the maidens reached the meadows by the sea. Hither and thither they ran, merrily plucking their favourite flowers. Some pulled Hyacinths, others plucked fragrant Daffodils, or gathered blue Violets and balmy Thyme, while still others tried to see who first could fill their baskets with yellow Crocuses.

But among all her playmates, the Princess Europa, breaking crimson Roses from their stems, shone radiant and beautiful like Venus, the Foam-born-One-among-the-Graces.

Now Jupiter was looking down from his ivory throne on Mount Olympus, and saw Europa gathering Roses. And as he looked, mischievous Cupid pierced his heart with a love-tipped arrow.

Then straightway Jupiter rose up, and changed himself into a Bull; not an ordinary one such as eats grass or is yoked for the plough, but a wonderful creature. He was snow-white, with a silver circle on his forehead. His horns were transparent and bright like gems, and his eyes mild and beautiful.

He hastened to the meadows by the sea. Lowing gently he approached the maidens. And when they saw the wonderful creature, they were not afraid, but longed to stroke his smooth white sides.

He stood before Europa, and, licking her hands, cast a spell over her. She fed him with Roses, and wreathed his horns with garlands. He skipped upon the grass, and, lying down, rolled his snowy sides among the flowers. Then, rising, he stooped at her feet, and, bending his head, showed her his broad back.

"Come, sweet friends and playmates!" cried Europa gayly. "Come, let us sit on the back of this Bull! He is not like other Bulls! See how mild and kind he is! Surely he will carry us gently!"

And, laughing, she took her seat on his back. But before her playmates could follow, up he leaped, and ran toward the sea.

In vain Europa stretched out her hands to her playmates, and called to them for help. The Bull reached the strand, and sprang upon the water. With unwetted hoofs he rushed over the wild waves. But the waves became calm beneath him, and sea-beasts gambolled around him. Dolphins, from pure joy, rolled in the foam. The Nereids rose up from their coral caves; while Neptune, King of the loud-sounding Deep, made a smooth, watery path to guide the Bull on his way. And the Tritons, thronging near the path, blew a bridal song upon their wreathed conch-shells.

But Europa, in great fear, grasped with one hand the Bull's glittering horn, while with the other she held up the folds of her purple robe lest it should be wet by the spume of the sea. The Wind, swelling out her robe behind her like a sail, lightly wafted her onward.

Soon she was far from her own land, and could see only the blue air above and the blue water around her.   Terror filled her heart.

"Whither are you taking me, O Bull?" she cried.   "Who are you?   Other Bulls fear the salt wave, but you run over the water with un-wetted hoofs!   Alas!   Alas!   poor me!   that I left my father's palace and followed this creature, who is carrying me away to lands unknown!"

"Fear not, beloved Maiden," answered the Bull gently.   "Take heart!   Fear not the ocean wave!   Soon you shall see that I am a man, not a Bull.   In the Isle of Crete a shining palace is awaiting you, where you shall reign over Crete and over my heart!"

So spoke the Bull and rushed on.   Soon he stood upon the shore of Crete.   He stooped, and Europa sprang from his back to the sparkling sand.

Then, lo! the Bull was changed, and was Jupiter once more!   Stately and bright he was, and crowned with Olive-like branches.   In his hand he held his eagle-tipped sceptre; while his robe, variegated like the flowers, was wrapped about his majestic form.

Then he took the wondering Princess Europa by the hand, and led her to the shining palace. And there the wedding feast was held.

And in honour of the lovely Bride, to-day men call the continent that lies to the west of Asia, — *Europe*.

THE GIRL WHO TROD ON A LOAF

OF course you have heard of the girl who trod on a loaf, so as not to spoil her pretty shoes; and you know all the punishment this brought upon her.

She was a poor child, but very vain and proud. She had a bad disposition, people said. As she grew older she became worse instead of better. But she was very beautiful, and that was her misfortune.

"You will bring evil on your own head," said her mother, "and when you grow up you will break my heart!"

And she did, sure enough.

At length she went into the country to be the servant of some very rich people. They were as kind to her as if she had been one of their own family. And she was so well dressed and so pretty that she became more vain than ever.

When she had been there a year, her master

and mistress said to her, "You should go and visit your relations, little Inger."

So she went in all her finest clothes. But when she reached the village, and saw her old mother sitting on a stone, and resting her head against a bundle of firewood that she had picked up in the forest, Inger turned back. She felt ashamed that she, who was dressed so well, should have a mother who was a ragged creature and picked up sticks for her fire.

A half year more had passed by.

"You must go home and see your old parents, little Inger," said her mistress. "Here is a large loaf of white bread — you can carry them this. They will be rejoiced to see you."

And Inger put on her best clothes and nice new shoes. She lifted her dress high, and walked carefully so that she might not soil her garments or her feet.

By and by she came to where the path went over a marsh. There was water and mud in the way. She threw the loaf of bread into the mud, so that she could step on it, and go over with dry shoes.

But just as she placed one foot on the bread, and lifted the other up, the loaf sank into the marsh, deeper and deeper, until she went entirely down, and nothing was to be seen but a black bubbling pool.

And what became of Inger?

She went down to the Moor-Woman, who brews below. The Moor-Woman is the aunt of the Fairies. But no one knows anything more about the Moor-Woman, except that when the meadows and marshes begin to reek in Summer, it is because the old woman is brewing.

Into her brewery it was that Inger sank. The kettles were filled with horrible smells, and Snakes and Toads were crawling around. Into this place little Inger sank; the bread stuck fast to her feet, and drew her down. She shivered in every limb.

"This comes from wishing to have clean shoes," thought Inger.

She stood there like a statue, fastened to the ground by the bread. Around her were many strange beings. How they stared at her, with wicked eyes!

"It must be a pleasure to them to see me," thought little Inger, "I have such a pretty face, and am so well dressed."

And she dried her tears. She had not lost her conceit. But the worst of all was the dreadful hunger she felt. Could she not stoop down and break off a piece of the bread on which she was standing?

No! Her back was stiffened; her hands and her arms were stiffened; her whole body was like a statue of stone. She could move only her eyes. The gnawing hunger was terrible to bear.

"If this goes on I cannot hold out much longer," she said.

But she had to hold out, though her sufferings became greater.

Then a warm tear fell upon her head; it trickled over her face and neck all the way down to the bread. Another tear followed, and still another, and then many more. Who was weeping for little Inger? Had she not a mother up yonder on the earth?

And Inger could hear all that was being said about her above in the world, and it was nothing but blame and evil. Though her mother wept, and was very sorrowful, yet she said: —

"Pride goes before a fall! That was your great fault, little Inger! Oh! How miserable you have made your mother!"

But Inger's heart became still harder than the Stone into which she was turned. She felt hatred for all mankind. She listened and heard people above telling her story as a warning to children. And the little ones called her "ungodly Inger." "She was so naughty," they said, "so very wicked, that she deserved to suffer." The children always spoke harshly of her.

But one day when hunger and suffering were gnawing her dreadfully, she heard her name mentioned, and her story told to a child — a little girl. The child burst into tears.

"When will she come up again?" she asked.

The answer was, "She will never come up again."

"But if she will beg pardon, and promise never to be naughty again?" asked the child.

"But she will not beg pardon," they said.

"Oh! I wish she would!" sobbed the child. "I will give my doll and my doll's house, if she may come up! Poor little Inger!"

These words touched Inger's heart; she wished to cry, but she could not.

Years and years went by on the earth above, and Inger's mother died. The child who had wept for her grew to be old — oh, very old indeed, and the Lord was about to call her to Himself. And as her gentle spirit was passing she remembered Inger, and wept once more for the fate of the unhappy one.

And her tears sounded like an echo in the abyss where Inger was. One of God's spirits was weeping for her! And remorse and grief filled Inger's soul, such as she had never felt before.

She thought that for her the gates of Mercy would never open. And, as in deep shame and humility she thought thus, a ray of brightness penetrated into that dismal abyss, a ray more vivid and glorious than the Sunbeams that melt the Snow-Figures children make in their gardens.

And this ray, more quickly than the Snowflake that falls on a child's warm mouth can melt, caused Inger's stony figure to dissolve, and a little grey bird arose, following the zigzag course of the ray to the earth above.

But the bird was afraid and shy of everything around it. It felt ashamed, and hid in a dark hole in a wall. There it sat, and it crept into the farthest corner, trembling all over.

For a long time it sat thus, before it ventured to look out at all the beauty around it. The air was so fresh, so soft. The Moon shone so clearly. The trees and the flowers gave out sweet odours. How all Creation told of love and glory! The little bird would willingly have poured forth its joy in song, but the power was denied it.

Then it flew out of the hole, and longed more than ever to sing in gratitude. Perhaps some day it might find a voice, if it could perform some deed of thankfulness! Might not this happen?

The Winter was a hard one. The waters were frozen thickly over. The birds and wild animals in the wood could scarcely get food. The little bird flew about the country roads, and, when it found a few grains of Corn dropped in the ruts, it would eat only a single grain, while it called to all the starving Sparrows to come and enjoy the rest.

It would also fly from village to village and look about. And where kind hands had strewed crumbs outside the windows for birds, it would eat only one crumb, and give all the rest to the Sparrows.

At the end of the Winter the little bird had found and given away so many crumbs of bread that they equalled in weight the loaf upon which little Inger had trod in order to save her fine shoes from being soiled.

And when it had given away the very last crumb, the grey wings of the bird became white, and expanded wonderfully.

"It is flying over the sea!" exclaimed the children who saw the white bird.

Now it seemed to dip into the ocean, and now it rose into the clear sunshine. It glittered in the air. It disappeared high, high above. And the children said that it had flown up to the Sun.

HANS CHRISTIAN ANDERSEN (*adapted*)

ALL THE HAPPY WONDER MONTHS

THE FOUR SWEET MONTHS

First, April, she with mellow showers
Opens the way for early flowers.

Then after her comes smiling May,
In a more rich and sweet array.

Next enters June, and brings us more
Gems than those two that went before.

Then, lastly, July comes, and she
More wealth brings in than all those three.

ROBERT HERRICK

THE FOUR SEASONS OF THE YEAR

So forth issued the Seasons of the Year:
First, Lusty Spring, all dight in leaves of flowers
That freshly budded and new blossoms did bear;
In which a thousand birds had built their bowers.

Then came the Jolly Summer, being dight
In a thin silken cassock, coloured green,
That was unlined all, to be more light:
And on his head a garland well beseen.

Then came the Autumn, all in yellow clad
As though he joyed in his plenteous store,
Laden with fruits that made him laugh full glad.

Lastly came Winter clothed all in frieze,
Chattering his teeth for cold that did him chill,
Whilst on his hoary beard, his breath did freeze.

EDMUND SPENSER (*condensed*)

OLD MAN COYOTE AND SUMMER
IN A BAG

Crow Myth

A LONG time ago, it was always Winter in the Northland. There was nothing but Ice and Snow. But in the Southland it was always Summer, and the beautiful birds were there.

Now one time Old Man Coyote stepped out of his lodge in the cold Northland, and saw a youth blowing on his hands to warm them.

"Why are you doing that, my Son?" he asked. "In the South is Summer, and young boys like you are chasing the Buffalo calves and running after birds. Why do you stay here where it is so cold?"

The youth did not answer. He was thinking of what Old Man Coyote had said, and it made him feel badly. He longed to see Summer, and to chase the calves and birds.

"I see you feel badly," said Old Man Coyote. "I can help you. I am going after Summer. Down in the Southland lives Woman-with-the-Strong-Heart, who keeps Summer and Winter tied up in bags. I am going to bring home Summer."

Then Old Man Coyote called his four servants, Wild Coyote, Deer, Wolf, and Jack Rabbit, and together they set out for the warm Southland.

Soon they reached the country of the Summer People, and Old Man Coyote said: —

"I will change myself into an Elk, and go into the wood. When the Summer People see me, they will come running to kill me. Then do you, Wild Coyote, who are so wise, go to the tepee of Woman-with-the-Strong-Heart, and, when she comes rushing out to see what the matter is, rub this magic medicine plant on her face. Then slip into her tepee, and you will see two bags — Summer in a dark bag, and Winter in a white one. Take the dark bag, but do not touch the white one."

So Old Man Coyote changed himself into an Elk, and went into the wood. Soon the Summer People saw him, and came shouting, and running to kill him; while Woman-with-the-Strong-Heart rushed from her tepee to see what was the matter.

Wild Coyote rubbed the magic medicine paint on her face, and it took her voice away so she could not call out. Then he slipped into the tepee, snatched the dark bag from its place, and ran away to the wood, where the Summer People were hunting for the Elk. But the Elk had run swiftly toward the Northland, and the Summer People were following after.

Wild Coyote ran with the bag, and when he grew tired he gave it to Deer.

Deer ran with the bag, and when he grew tired he gave it to Wolf.

Wolf ran with the bag, and when he grew tired he gave it to Jack Rabbit.

Jack Rabbit ran with the bag. And so they all came again safely to the cold Northland, and gave the bag to the youth.

And just as the youth was about to untie it, the Summer People came rushing up, and demanded the bag. But he would not give it to them, until they promised that the Northland should have it for half of each year.

That is the reason why the Southland and the Northland have each six months of Summer and six months of Winter, and why the birds fly Northward in the hot time, and Southward when the cold sets in.

As for Old Man Coyote, he kept his promise. He made a bird called Prairie Chicken. And a very wonderful bird is Prairie Chicken. His neck is a Buffalo's muscle. He has a Snake's head. In his tail is a Snake's rattle. His wings are the claws of a Black Bear. His legs are from Caterpillars.

And Old Man Coyote said to Prairie Chicken:—

"You are a bird. Go, now, and scare the people by the whirring noise you make when you fly up from the prairie grass."

So Old Man Coyote kept his word; and the Northland got Summer, and the youth had a bird to chase.

THE OLD WOMAN WHO MET
THE MONTHS

From the Island of Melos

ONCE upon a time, an old woman went out to gather sticks for her fire. It was very cold weather and she wished to warm herself. As she walked across a waste bit of land she saw a little house that had never been there before. She peeped through the door, and inside sat twelve handsome young Princes, richly clad.

"Come in! Come in! Old Woman!" they said.

So in she went. Now, she was a very polite, honest old woman, and she bowed low and said:—

"Good hour to you, my happy Princes!"

"The same to you, Old Woman," they replied. "But why do you come here in such very bad weather?"

"Ah, my Children!" she sighed, "I am a poor old thing, and am picking up sticks to warm my house for my little ones. But, alas! my house is tumbling down, the roof leaks, and the rain and cold come in."

Then one of the young Princes said to her, "Tell us, Old Woman, which of all the Months of the year is the worst."

"Why, my child," answered she, "all the Months are good. None of them is bad."

"But, my old Woman," said the young Prince, "how can January be so good as May?"

"My child," she said, "if January did not send us the Snow to cover the ground, all the little herbs and flowers would freeze. If April did not send us the Rain, May would have no beautiful blossoms!"

"Old Woman, have you a sack?" said all the Princes.

So she gave them her sack in which she had been putting sticks, and they filled it full of gold-pieces. And the next minute the old woman found herself in her kitchen with the sack by her side.

Well, when her rich neighbour — a greedy young woman — saw all the gold and heard the old woman's story, she took the biggest sack she could find, and went to the little house on the waste. She peeped in, and there sat the twelve handsome Princes, richly clad.

She entered without greeting them, and sat down.

"Why are you here, Woman?" asked one of the Princes.

"What is that to you?" said she. "The wretched Month of January is come, and I can't keep warm; that's why I'm here!"

"Come, then, tell us which of the Months you like best," said the Prince.

"I don't like any of them," answered she.

"They are all bad enough, except, perhaps, February; he has only twenty-eight days and is the shortest of all!"

"Woman, have you a sack?" said all the Princes.

So she gave them her big sack, joyfully. They filled it with Snakes, Vipers, and Toads. And the next minute she found herself in her kitchen with the sack beside her.

Then all the Snakes, Vipers, and Toads jumped out and devoured her.

THE REED THAT WAS A MAIDEN

Retold from Ovid

IN those wondrous golden times, Pan dwelt in the woods. And a very strange creature he was. His face and body were those of a man, while his long hairy legs ended in Goat's feet. From his flat forehead sprouted two little horns.

Sometimes with loud bursts of laughter he rushed through the woods, snapping twigs and trampling down leaves. At other times he bounded into the meadows, and noiselessly capered along the banks of streams where the Shepherds were watching their flocks. Often he thrust his ugly head through the bushes and grinned at the Shepherds, who, when they saw his wrinkled red face and little horns, deserted their sheep and ran away in a *panic*.

But above all things, this grinning mischievous Pan liked to frighten the maidens of Diana-of-the-Bended-Bow when they were hunting in the wood. He would spring at them from behind trees, and, shrieking, they would rush away in all directions.

Now it happened one day that Syrinx, the most beautiful of the maidens in Diana's train, was hunting Deer in the Forest. Her robe was tucked above her white knees, her hair flew in the wind, and her eyes sparkled with delight. She held her bow before her, with her sharp arrow ready to shoot.

Pan, peeping through the trees, saw her, and wondered at her beauty. Quickly he wreathed his ugly head with sharp pine-needles and, stepping into her path, spoke gently to her.

"O lovely Maiden," he entreated, "stay your swift footsteps. I am Pan, the guardian of Shepherds and of Bees. All living things in the woods and streams belong to me, the leaping fish, and the wild-wood creatures. They are all mine. I am Pan, their King. Stay, then, sweet Maiden, and be my Queen, and rule over them all with me."

But Syrinx fled away in terror. Pale and trembling she hastened through the woods, while Pan, shouting loudly, rushed after her.

Nearer and nearer he drew, until Syrinx heard his loud laughter explode close to her ears, and felt his hot breath on her hair. Alas! she knew not whither to turn! A gentle stream crossed her path, its bank overgrown with reeds. She sprang down the bank to the water.

"O my sister Naiads," she cried, "save me! Save me from Pan the goat-footed!"

And even as she cried out, Pan clasped her in his rough arms. But, lo, she was gone, she was changed! He no longer clasped a maiden, but a slender, trembling Reed growing up from the water's edge.

Then down among the Reeds sat Pan, sighing and weeping for his lost Syrinx. And the Wind, pitying his grief, stirred the Reeds gently, and they gave forth a murmuring sound like Syrinx' own voice sweetly lamenting.

"Beloved Reeds," said Pan, "you shall ever be with me, and for ever shall you charm away my sorrow."

So he made musical pipes of the Reeds fastened together with wax, and called them "Syrinx."

And night and day he wandered through the woods and pastures and along the murmuring streams, breathing on the Syrinx; and it gave forth such melodious, lamenting sounds, that all living things that heard them wept or laughed with sadness or joy. And the Shepherds, watching their flocks, said one to another: —

"Listen! Listen to Pan's Pipes!"

THE REEDS THAT TOLD A SECRET

Retold from Ovid

THIS is how the whole wide world came to know that King Midas had Asses' ears: —

All through the Happy Wonder Months, Pan wandered in the meadows where the Shepherds fed their flocks, or he slept in the mountain-caves, or he capered on his goat-legs along the banks of the streams.

And everywhere that he went, he played softly on his Syrinx. At the sound of his sweet strains Dryads peeped from their tree-trunks; and Naiads, rising up in the water-pools, wrung the bright drops from their azure hair, while they listened to his sweet pipings.

"Hark! ye Nymphs!" cried Pan. "Listen to the voice of my Syrinx," and then he piped so melodiously and sadly that the Dryads and Naiads laughed or wept from sheer joy or sorrow.

"Hark, ye Nymphs!" cried he again. "Listen while I pipe a tune more delightful and charming to the ear than any from the lyre of golden-beamed Apollo"; and then he piped louder and more sweetly than before.

But while he was speaking these boastful words, golden-beamed Apollo heard him. Quickly he flew down to earth from his Palace in the Sun. His yellow hair was wreathed with Laurel from the Daphne-tree; his long robe, dyed with Tyrian purple, trailed in the fresh green grass; while his lyre, adorned with ivory, glittered with a thousand gems.

"I am come, O goat-legged Pan," said he, "to hear you make good your boasting words. Let us have a musical contest. Old Tmolus, King of yonder lofty mountain, shall be our umpire."

To this Pan eagerly consented, for he thought: "Surely on my Syrinx I can play a more delightful tune than any that Apollo can strike from his lyre."

Then, upon his lofty mountain old Giant Tmolus seated himself. His blue hair was crowned with Oak-leaves, and Acorns hung about his hollow temples. He shook his ears free from huge trees, and cried out to Pan: —

"Ho! guardian of Shepherds and Bees! Let there be no delay. I am here to be your umpire, and will render a just decision."

Then Pan breathed softly on his Syrinx; and sang of snowy Lambs bleating in green pastures, and of Bees sipping honey from the flowers.

Apollo, holding his lyre in his left hand, struck its strings gently with his right, while from them gushed such delicious melody that the very stones danced and the trees bowed their tall tops.

"Stay! stay your music! O Pan!" cried King Tmolus. "The notes of your pipes sound shrill and ear-piercing compared with Apollo's ravishing music. To Apollo alone belongs the victor's wreath."

"Not so! not so!" said a hoarse voice near by, for while they were playing, King Midas had drawn near. "The noises Apollo makes may please the ears of a Mountain-King," said he, "but Pan's sweet pipings alone can charm my music-loving soul. To Pan belongs the victor's wreath."

"Stupid mortal!" exclaimed Apollo in fury, "may you, then, have ears suited to enjoy the rude pipings of goat-legged Pan!"

So saying, he seized King Midas's ears and pulled them out longer and longer, until they became Asses' ears filled with grey hairs and flapping on either side of the poor King's face.

Then, laughing scornfully, Apollo flew back to his Palace in the Sun.

But King Midas, in horror and shame, fled to his own palace, and hid his Asses' ears under a purple turban, so that no one knew he had them.

But it chanced one day that the royal barber, while cutting King Midas's long locks, saw the tips of the Asses' ears peeping out of the turban. Now he was a wise man, and knew that he must not tell what he had seen. But the secret troubled him more and more until he ran down to the river-bank, and, digging a hole, whispered into it:

"King Midas has Asses' ears! King Midas has Asses' ears!"

Then he filled up the hole, and went home more contented.

Soon afterward, a bed of quivering Reeds sprang up over the hole, and, whenever the West Wind blew through them, they shivered and sighed and shivered and sighed: —

"Hist! Hist! King Midas has Asses' ears!
Hist! Hist! King Midas has Asses' ears!"

And that is how the whole wide world came to know that King Midas had Asses' ears.

THE HUNDRED-HEADED DAFFODIL

From Ovid and Other Sources

In the long, long ago there dwelt in the heart of the earth a fierce King named Pluto, who reigned over the Kingdom of Hades. Dreary and dark was that subterranean Kingdom. Cerberus, the three-headed Dog, guarded its entrance, while the Shades of the Dead moaned through its hollow-sounding palaces.

There was not a single beautiful thing in all Hades. There were no flowers, no sunlight, no birds; and Pluto, with gloomy eyes and sullen brow, drove his black steeds from one end of the Kingdom to the other seeking gold and silver ore; for all the wealth of the underworld belonged to him.

Now it happened one day that Venus the Beautiful was looking down from Mount Olympus and saw King Pluto driving madly about. She called her winged son, mischievous little Cupid, to her knee, and, kissing him, said:—

"Dear Child! See yonder gloomy Pluto! He has no beautiful thing in any of his caverns. He has nothing to love. I will not have it so. So do you, my Child, take one of your love-tipped arrows — that wound but do not kill — and shoot him through the heart."

So spoke Venus. And Cupid, opening his golden quiver filled with a thousand sharp arrows, took from it the sharpest. Then bending his bow he shot King Pluto straight through the heart, wounding him sorely.

Now, high above on the sunny earth was a bright blue lake, and near it was a lovely field of flowers. There little Proserpina, the daughter of Mother Ceres, Keeper-of-all-the-Cornfields-in-the-World, was playing barefooted in the grass.

She tossed her curly hair and pelted her playmates with flowers. Then, gathering up the skirt of her little dress, she filled it with sweet nosegays of Violets, Roses, Lilies, and Marigolds. Her playmates did the same, and heaped their baskets with Hyacinths, Crocuses, Amaranth, and Rosemary, each trying to gather the most.

"Look! dear Girls!" cried Proserpina at last. "See this wonderful flower growing here in the middle of the meadow! It is a golden Daffodil and has a hundred heads!"

As she spoke she pulled the Hundred-Headed Daffodil, roots and all, from the ground. Instantly there was a roaring and a rumbling and the earth opened wide. And from its yawning chasm leaped Pluto's black horses, drawing his golden chariot. And in the chariot stood the fierce King himself, wrapped in his mantle and urging on his steeds.

Cupid's arrow was still sticking in Pluto's breast, and when he saw little Proserpina he straightway loved her. Then swiftly he grasped her and carried her off. The flowers fell from her lap, scattering upon the grass. She saw them fall and wept; then stretching out her small white hands, she cried: —

"Alas! dearest Mother! I am being carried away! Save me! Save me!"

But all in vain she cried, for King Pluto, guiding his steeds and calling each by name, shook the reins and plunged once more into the chasm that closed above his head.

Through rocky gorges and caverns the steeds rushed, and across black pools of boiling water, and over sulphurous lakes, until they reached King Pluto's subterranean Kingdom. And there he made little Proserpina Queen of all Hades.

But she was not happy, and sat weeping and wailing for her mother until the tops of the mountains and the depths of the seas rang with her cries.

Now Mother Ceres, Keeper-of-all-the-Corn-fields-in-the-World, heard her little daughter's cries, and leaving her fields and the ripening Corn-Ears hastened to the flowery meadow. But she could not find Proserpina, for her play-mates were all gone. Only the withered flowers and the empty baskets lay upon the grass.

Then Ceres beat her breast with despair and tore her Poppy-Wreath from her head. And over land and sea, throughout the wide world, she went, seeking her child, and crying as she went:—

"Proserpina! O my Daughter! Proserpina!"

By night she carried two flaming torches, by day she searched in the light of the Sun. But nowhere could she find her lost child!

"O Zephyr! Gentle Zephyr!" she asked the West Wind as he floated by, "have you seen my daughter?"

And when Zephyr whispered "No," she has-tened on.

"O Boreas! Strong Boreas!" she asked the North Wind as he rushed by, "have you seen my daughter?"

And when he roared "No" she hastened on.

And so she asked each thing she met, but no-where could she find her lost child.

Meanwhile, in her grief and anger, she neglected her cornfields. The birds picked the seeds out of the ground. The weeds grew up rank and thick. The hot Sun burned the blades of Corn. And soon all the Cornfields, the wide world over, were dry and barren. There was no Corn, and the hungry people cried for bread.

And so it was when at last Ceres reached a fountain that gushed from the earth. And Arethusa, the Nymph of the Fountain, raised her head from the water and tossed back her dripping hair. Then she spoke thus: —

"O Mother of the child whom you have sought throughout the whole world, cease your grief and tend your Cornfields once more! The world does not deserve to suffer so at your hands!

"Know that I, Arethusa, have seen your daughter. As my stream was passing through the caverns of the underworld I saw Proserpina seated on King Pluto's throne. She is sad but no longer weeping, for the King loves her tenderly, and has made her Queen of all Hades."

And as the Nymph Arethusa spoke, Ceres stood amazed, and as if turned to stone. Then swiftly she got into her chariot drawn by Dragons, and flew to Mount Olympus. Beating her breast and tearing her hair, she stood before Jupiter's throne.

"I am come, O Jupiter," she cried, "to beseech you to restore to me my little daughter, whom King Pluto has carried off to his dark

Kingdom! If he brings her back to me I will return to my cornfields and give bread to the people!"

Then Jupiter answered: "Gladly will I give back Proserpina to you if she has not tasted any food while in Hades. Otherwise, she must stay with Pluto for ever."

Then he bade his messenger, Mercury, hasten to Hades and fetch Proserpina.

So Mercury put on his winged hat and shoes, and taking his Staff of Sleep in his hand flew swiftly down to Pluto's Kingdom. And in a beautiful garden that Pluto had made purposely for her, he found little Queen Proserpina playing by herself. But, alas! she had already plucked one Pomegranate from a bending tree, and had eaten seven of its seeds! So she could not return to her mother Ceres!

But when Jupiter learned this he decreed that for seven months every year Proserpina should dwell in Pluto's dark Kingdom, while for five months she should live on the bright earth with her mother.

And so it was. Every year for seven months little Proserpina reigned as Queen in gloomy Hades, while Ceres, mourning her loss, neglected her cornfields. They grew dry and barren, the Snow fell upon them, and Winter ruled the earth.

But when the seven months were passed

Proserpina returned, and Ceres once more tended her Cornfields. They grew green, the Corn sprang up, the golden ears ripened in the sunshine. And Spring and Summer and flowers and joy came back to earth.

MARIORA FLORIORA

Moldavian Legend

IN all the wide Wonder Garden of Earth no Nymph was so lovely as Mariora Floriora, the Sister of the Flowers. She was as bright as a tear of joy, as light-footed as a Fawn. Her golden hair, soft as silk, fell in clusters on her white brow and in waves on her shoulders. On her lips was a scarlet blossom, in her mouth were Pearls.

When she went forth to walk in the meadows, the flowers laughed with joy, and, opening their hearts, bowed before her; while their voices rang out like chimes: —

"Good-morning, sweet Sister Mariora Floriora! What will you have of us? Will you have the scent of the Cowslip, or the perfume of the Rose, or the fragrance of the Violet? Take us, take us, Sister, and place us in your hair, or let us fall asleep upon your breast."

So, listening and happy, she passed on her way near the hoary mountain. And at her smile it grew young again, and dressed itself in a robe of green and crystal.

The birds woke and sang: —

"All hail, Mariora Floriora! What will you have of us? Will you have our sweet voices? Or shall we fetch you honey in dewy cups? Or will you listen to the sighing of the gentle breeze?"

So all Nature awoke and rejoiced, when Mariora Floriora, the Sister of the Flowers, walked abroad.

But one day she met a young stranger, mounted on a black horse with a white star in its forehead.

"Sweet Maiden standing among the flowers," said the stranger, "are you the daughter of a King or the shadow of a dream I once had?"

"If you would know who I am," she answered, "ask my sisters the flowers, ask the mountain, the torrents, the singing birds, the waterfalls, and the skipping Fawns."

"Then, truly," exclaimed the youth, "you are Mariora Floriora, the Nymph of the Flowers and the maid of Aurora. You are my destined bride! I will dismount from my steed. I will remain with you for ever."

Mariora Floriora listened with a blush and with laughter. She hid her face in her curls, and peeped through them like a Butterfly or a bird peeping from the leaves.

The stranger dismounted and seated himself beside her in the grass. She laughed again, and made a sign. A table loaded with delicious fruits rose from the ground. They ate and were happy.

Then she made another sign, and a chariot drawn by six white Horses sprang up before her. She took the stranger by the hand, and they entered the chariot. The enchanted steeds neighed, and swiftly skimmed over the surface of the meadow, and flew to and fro across the mountain-top.

The sister flowers, seeing that they were forgotten, drooped their heads and faded. The birds stopped singing. The mountain took off its robe of green and crystal, and hid itself in a Cloud, while all the leaves of the trees yellowed, withered, and fell.

But the lovely Mariora Floriora thought no longer of her sisters the flowers, or of the birds and the mountain.

Then the Sun, looking down, drank the bright drops of Dew from her golden hair, and transformed them into a Cloud that rose slowly to the sky.

"Mariora Floriora," said the Sun, "you are fair and lovely, but you are fickle. The sweetest dreams will end! Do you know that your sisters the flowers are faded and are returned to the Sky complaining bitterly? Your birds are silent, and your mountain is mourning. Punishment will surely overtake you, O Mariora Floriora!"

But she would not listen to him. She had thoughts for nothing but the stranger.

The air was soft, the mountain was bathed in pearly light. The little birds neither flew nor sang. Shadows were the only moving things.

Then came a plaintive sound through the air like a mother's voice mingling with the music of bells. The Earth trembled. Mariora Floriora gazed fearfully around. A black Cloud hovered dark and menacing above her head, like the Evil Spirit of the Storm. It spread its sombre and awful wings across the sky. It was the same cloud that was formed from the dewdrops in her hair.

Mariora Floriora grew pale, and leaned toward the stranger.

"Farewell! O Beloved!" she sighed. "The Evil Storm Spirit has come from the mountain to tear me from your heart. I have forgotten my sisters the flowers, and they have complained of me in the sky."

She wept as she spoke. And the Cloud became darker. The Thunder roared, and the Lightning flashed. The Winds moaned. And Mariora Floriora hid her face in despair.

The black Cloud swooped downward, and the Evil Storm Spirit, seizing her in his arms, flew away with her to the mountain. Then the Sun shone brightly once more, the Sky was blue again.

And where now is Mariora Floriora, the Nymph

of the Flowers, the maid of Aurora? Is she
wandering over nine lands and nine seas seeking
the Wonder Garden where dwell all the Nymphs
and the Stars?

When the silvery-white Moon rides high and
serene in the heavens, Mariora Floriora's plaintive murmurs are heard in the caverns of her
mountain.

THE WOOING OF POMONA

Retold from Ovid

ONCE upon a time, in the happy days of old,
Vertumnus, Keeper-of-All-the-Orchards-in-the-
World, crowned himself with flowers, and wandered about looking for orchards that needed
his care.

It happened that he strayed near a high wall,
above which he saw the tops of fruit-trees laden
with rosy Apples. Near the wall some Fauns
were dancing, their ugly horned heads wreathed
with pine, and their goat-feet trampling the
grass.

"Tell me, O Pans," said Vertumnus, "who
dwells behind this high wall?"

"The lovely Pomona, the Hamadryad, dwells
there!" they cried. "Alas! she loves only her
garden and fruit! Daily with pruning-knife
she trims her Apple-Trees; and she waters their
roots, and cares for the blossoms. But she has

no eyes for her poor lovers, who haunt this wall hoping in vain for a glimpse of her face! Many are her suitors, but she disdains them all; they may not even enter her garden."

"But *I* shall enter her garden!" said Vertumnus.

And straightway he dressed himself like a gardener, with a pruning-hook in his hand, and went into her garden. Pomona came forward to meet him, and eagerly begged him to prune her vines.

So fair and joyous was she, and so delicate like an Apple-Blossom, that Vertumnus, gazing on her, loved her with all his heart. But she, thinking that he was a gardener, scarcely looked at him at all, and watched him prune the vines. Then, when evening came, she paid him and sent him away.

But Vertumnus could not forget her. On another day he dressed as a reaper and carried a basket of Corn to Pomona. She bought some, and sent him away.

Again and again he returned to her, sometimes as a fisherman, and again as a pruner; but always she took what he had to offer, and paid him and sent him away. And always Vertumnus, as he gazed at her, loved her more and more.

At last, one day, he changed himself into an old woman, wrinkled and bent. And, wrapped in a cloak, he entered Pomona's garden.

"Fair Maid," said the old woman, "how beautiful are your Apples! How heavily laden are your trees with the glowing fruits of Autumn! Come, let us sit here on the grass, and admire their rich colours."

So Pomona sat down beside her, and the old woman, after giving her a few gentle kisses, said thus: —

"Look, dear Maid, at yonder Elm wreathed in a grapevine from which hang clusters of purple Grapes. What would the Elm do without the beauty of the vine that clings so tenderly to it? And if there were no Elm for the vine to lean against, the poor thing would lie upon the ground to be trampled under foot!

"Ah me! fair Maid! Why do you, then, send away all your lovers? Why not seek a strong husband, like yonder Elm, to lean upon? Be advised by me, an old woman! There is Vertumnus. Choose him for yourself. Of all your suitors he is the most desirable. He is handsome, he is graceful.

"You will be his first and only love! Then, too, your tastes are alike. You are devoted to your garden and your Apples. He, the Keeper-of-All-the-Orchards-in-the-World, holds rich gifts of all kinds of fruits in his hands. Never again shall the Frost nip your buds; and never again shall the rude North Wind, Boreas, strip the Apple-Blossoms from your boughs. Vertumnus will devote his life to you, doing anything that you may bid. He loves you dearly; have pity upon him!

"Listen, now, sweet Maid, and I will relate a story that shall move your heart: —

Story of the Stony Maiden

"Once upon a time, in the golden isle of Cyprus, there lived a maid named Iphis. The noble young Teucer loved her. He came daily to her house, but she would not open the door. He hung garlands wet with the dew of his tears on her doorposts, and, pressing his sorrowful face against the door, he implored her to listen; but still she would not open.

"Cruel she was, and deaf to his entreaties. At last in despair he sank down and died upon her threshold. Then Iphis went and gazed coldly upon him. But as she looked her cheek turned pale, her eyes became set, the warm blood stood still in her veins, her limbs grew numb and heavy. She tried to flee, but she could not move. She was turned into a cold, cold stone!

"So, lovely Pomona, learn from this tale not to be cruel. Lay aside your disdain, and give yourself to one who so tenderly loves you!"

So spoke the old woman, and, rising, she flung off her cloak. And before Pomona's astonished and delighted eyes Vertumnus himself stood in all his brilliancy, like the golden Autumn Sun.

On his head was a crown of bright flowers. In one hand he held rosy Apples and yellow Pears, in the other a great cornucopia heaped high with Grapes, Plums, and Peaches. So joyous were his eyes and so beautiful was he, that Pomona loved him straightway.

And ever after that the happy Pomona and her Vertumnus wandered hand-in-hand about the world tending all the orchards. They helped the fruit-blossoms to unfold in the Springtime. They guarded the green fruit from blight in the Summer. And when the Autumn came, they painted the ripe, delicious fruits with all the glowing colours of the Autumn trees.

THE NEW YEAR

I⊤ was the last day of the Old Year. The Snow was falling heavily, and twirling and whirling through streets and alleys. The windows were white with Frost. Snow slipped in masses from the roofs.

The people on the streets were in a great hurry. They ran through the blinding flakes, and bumped into each other, then ran on again. The Frost on the wagons and horses looked like powdered sugar.

But when night was come the storm died

down. The air was calm, the Sky was deeply dark and transparent, and the Stars shone brightly like silver. Midnight drew near, — the last minute of the Old Year slipped away, the New Year was born.

And when the Sun rose, it sparkled on the Snow that crackled under foot. In the street some little Sparrows were hopping about, searching for food; but the Wind of the Old Year had swept the Snow clean. It was terribly cold.

"Tweet! Tweet!" said one little Sparrow to another. "People call this the Happy New Year! I think it is worse than the Old! I am very sad! Last night people rejoiced because the Old Year was gone. They fired guns and made a great noise to welcome the New Year. I, too, was glad, for I hoped that warmer days were come. But it is colder and freezes worse than ever! I think people must have made a mistake — it is not the New Year!"

"When Spring comes, the New Year begins," said an old Sparrow with a white head.

"But when will Spring come?" asked the others.

"When the Stork returns," replied the old Sparrow. "No one in town knows when that will be. Only the country people know. Shall we fly away to the fields and wait? Surely Spring will come sooner in the country."

"That sounds very well," said another Sparrow, who had been hopping about, chirping. "But I have found too many comforts here in town. I should miss them in the country. Where I live the family have placed three flower-pots by the garden wall, with the openings against the wall and the bottoms of the pots pointed outward. They have cut a hole in each pot big enough for me to fly in and out. I and my husband have built a nest in one of them, and there we have brought up our children. The people strew bread-crumbs for us every day, so we have plenty of food. No! I think my husband and I will stay where we are."

"But we will fly away to the fields," said all the other Sparrows, "to see if Spring is come."

And off they flew.

It was really Winter in the country. It was much colder than in the town. The freezing Winds blew over the snow-covered fields. The farmer, wrapped in his coat, sat huddled in his sleigh. The reins lay on his knee. He beat his arms across his breast to warm them. The horses ran and their sides sent up clouds of steam. The Snow snapped and sparkled. And the little Sparrows hopped about in the road, shivering and crying.

"Tweet! Tweet! When will Spring come? It is a very long time in coming!"

"Very long, indeed!" sounded a loud voice over the meadow.

Perhaps it was an echo, or perhaps it was the voice of a strange old man who sat on a mound of Snow. He was clad in white. He had flowing white locks and a pale face. His eyes were large, and clear, and blue, like ice.

"Who is that old one?" asked the Sparrows.

"I know who he is," croaked a Raven. "He is Old Man Winter himself. He rules here still. He did not die when the New Year came. He is watching for the coming of little Prince Spring. Oh! how cold it is and how you shiver, my little ones!"

But the Sparrows did not answer; they only hopped about, still crying: —

"Tweet! Tweet! When will Spring come?"

Week after week passed by. The woods were dark and drear. The lake was frozen and grey. Icy mists hung above the land. Flocks of black Crows flew silently overhead. But one day a little Sunbeam touched the lake. The Ice softened and shone like silver. The Snow did not sparkle any more.

Still Winter sat on his white mound, ever gazing southward. He did not see that the Snow was vanishing and sinking into the earth, and that here and there green grass was springing up.

In the grass the little Sparrows hopped. "Tee-weet! Tee-weet!" they cried. "Surely Spring is coming."

"Spring!" And a joyous cry sounded over

the meadows and through the brown, leafless woods!

The moss freshened on the tree-trunks, and from the land of the South two Storks came flying with outspread wings, and on the back of each Stork sat a lovely child, a little boy and a little girl. They sprang to the earth and kissed the green grass.

They drew near to Old Man Winter, whose icy breath stirred the air. They threw their arms about his neck and kissed him. A thick, damp mist rose from the mound and like a veil wrapped itself about the two children. Then a soft Wind blew away the mist, and the Sun shone.

Old Man Winter was gone! And the lovely little children of Spring sat on a flowery throne. Then the little girl held her apron up; it was filled with blossoms. She cast white and pink petals over Apple and Peach trees, and showered the grass with spring flowers. Next, the boy and she both clapped their hands, and flocks of birds came twittering, and singing: —

"Spring is here!"

How beautiful it all was!

And the little Sparrows hopped with joy, and cried: —

"Now the New Year is really come!"

HANS CHRISTIAN ANDERSEN (*adapted*)

APPENDIX

NATURE MYTHS AND STORY-TELLING

As an aid to Nature-study, a nature myth or tale should be told the children at least once a week; for such stories are both practical and cultural. They may be used to arouse interest in botany, flower-raising, tree-planting, farming, school-gardening, bird-study, and art and poetry. Rightly told or read aloud, they will stimulate the imagination and fancy, and enrich expression.

Little poems for memorizing or for reading aloud, are included here; and the children may learn and dramatize the stories of which is offered a large variety to choose from.

There are myths, poems, and tales, about more than forty different kinds of flowers (garden and wild), as well as many about trees, animals, insects, birds, also about the Sun, Moon, Stars, Rain, Wind, Clouds, and Rainbow.

The classic myths will help to explain poetry and pictures; while tales like "Little White Daisy," and "Why the Frogs Call the Buttercups," will fix botanical names in the children's memories. The farm-stories and the bird and flower legends will prove most helpful to Vacation-School teachers and to mothers summering in the country.

The following Programme is merely suggestive. If so preferred, any teacher, librarian, or social worker, may make a new and attractive one to suit the fancy of her audience, by reading over the stories and consulting the *Subject Index* on page 469. For instance a charming *School-Garden Programme* may be planned, or one for a wild-flower excursion, for a picnic, or for a "birding" expedition.

This Programme follows the Seasons, from the time that School begins in the Autumn. It follows the progress of the Seasons in a temperate climate where Autumn, Winter, Spring, and Summer reign equally. Story-tellers in very cold or warm parts of the country should rearrange the Programme to suit their own Fauna and Flora.

"An Old English Calendar of the Flowers," is appended on page 452. Special material for Resurrection Day (Easter), Dominion Day (Canadian), Bird Day, and Arbour Day may be found on page 451.

PROGRAMME CALENDAR
FOR EVERY MONTH OF THE YEAR

To use this Programme, read over the stories for the week, and choose that one best suited to your audience. If too old for your children, read the story several times, and retell it simply in your own language. The stories may be read aloud instead of told. When a month has five weeks, use an untold story from a previous week.

Teach the children the little poems. Even young children who do not understand all the words, will delight in the rhythm and sound-colour. Gradually the full meanings of the words will come to them.

SEPTEMBER

FIRST WEEK. *Labour Day.*

Man who Brought Fire, p. 287; Why Unlucky Iron Kills, p. 290; In streams the gold, the copper flows (poem), p. 274.

SECOND WEEK. *Potato Wonders.*

Potato! Potato! p. 349; Potato-Choosing Boy, p. 355.

THIRD WEEK. *Corn Wonders.*

Legend of the Corn, p. 381; Seven Corn Maidens, p. 376; All around the happy village (poem), p. 338.

FOURTH WEEK. *Marvellous Adventures.*

Fisherboy Urashima, p. 223; Peach Boy's Rice-Cakes, p. 371; Boy whose Wings Fell Off, p. 249.

OCTOBER

FIRST WEEK. *In the Apple Orchard.*

Apple of Discord, p. 209; Idun and the Magic Apples, p. 215; Little Nymph who Rang the Bells, p. 114; Golden Apples of the Hesperides, p. 205; The Golden Apple, the Golden Apple (poem), p. 198.

SECOND WEEK. *Autumn Colours.*

Little Nymph who Loved Bright Colours, p. 11; Wooing of Pomona, p. 434; Legend of the Goldenrod, p. 136.

THIRD WEEK. *Wonder Fruits and Almond Flower.*

Why the Pomegranate Wears a Crown and Royal Robes, p. 202; Tantalizing Fruits, p. 204; White Flowering Almond, p. 319.

FOURTH WEEK. *Halloween.*

Witch Cat, p. 345; Old Witch who was a Burr, p. 137.

NOVEMBER

FIRST WEEK. *The Star Flower.*

Maiden White and Maiden Yellow, p. 50; Chrysanthemum Children, p. 47.

SECOND WEEK. *Unthrifty and Lazy.*

Nightingale and the Rose, p. 74; Lazy Boys who Became the Pleiades, p. 255; Girl who Trod on a Loaf, p. 404.

THIRD WEEK. *Greedy Ones.*

Erysichthon the Hungry, p. 323; Duck-Feather Man, p. 353.

FOURTH WEEK. *Thanksgiving Day.*

Cup of Thanksgiving, p. 31; The Pet Turkey whose Feelings were Hurt, p. 366.

DECEMBER

FIRST WEEK. *Winged Wonders.*

Magpie Maidens, p. 90; Winged Horse, p. 397; Ram with the Golden Fleece, p. 383.

SECOND WEEK. *Snow White.*

Snow-Blanche, p. 297; How the First Snowdrop Came, p. 303.

THIRD WEEK. *Gifts of Gold.*

Golden Gift of King Midas, p. 275; Wicked Fairies, p. 283.

FOURTH WEEK. *Christmas Day.*

Christmas Thorn of Glastonbury, p. 36.

JANUARY

FIRST WEEK. *New Year's Day.*

Old Woman who Met the Months, p. 416; New Year, p. 438.

SECOND WEEK. *Little Flowers for the Window-Box.*

Mignonette Fairy, p. 26; Forget-Me-Not, p. 39; **Legend of the Heart's Ease,** p. 28; A bit of the Sky fell down one day (poem) p.v.

THIRD WEEK. *When the White Snow Falls.*

Snowball Hares, p. 301; Garden of Frost Flowers, p. 304; Now you must know that in those early times (poem), p. 296.

FOURTH WEEK. *Magical Farm Animals.*

Enchanted Swine, p. 389; Snow-White Bull, p. 400; Why Dogs Have Long Tongues, p. 347.

FEBRUARY

FIRST WEEK. *Magic Music.*

Reed that was a Maiden, p. 418; Reeds that Told a Secret, p. 421.

SECOND WEEK. *St. Valentine's Day.*

Fairy Swan Song, p. 238; Morning-Glory Fan, p. 175; Adventures of Cupid Among the Roses, p. 55; Then came we to great breadths of shady wood (poem), p. 54.

THIRD WEEK. *Moon Folk.*

Sheep in the Pasture, p. 254; Jack and Jill, p. 252; Man in the Moon, p. 251.

FOURTH WEEK. *The Snowdrop Rises.*

Snowdrop Fairy, p. 7; Why the Snow is White, p. 302.

MARCH

FIRST WEEK. *Wild March Winds.*

Bag of Winds, p. 268; Halcyon Birds, p. 264.

SECOND WEEK. *St. Patrick's Day in the Morning.*

Why there are no Snakes in Ireland, p. 191; Last of the Serpents, p. 193.

THIRD WEEK. *March Hares.*

White Hare of Inaba, p. 181; Why Rabbits Have Yellow Hairs, p. 188; Little White Rabbit, p. 278.

FOURTH WEEK. *The Snowdrop's Neighbours.*

Legend of the Trailing Arbutus, p. 123; Legend of the Frail Windflower, p. 108; Legend of the Anemone and the Rose, p. 64.

APRIL

FIRST WEEK. *Whispering Waters.*

Arethusa, p. 148; Arethusa arose (poem), p. 144; Weeping Waters, p. 146; Stone that Shed Tears, p. 145; Little Hylas, p. 150; A Drop of Rain was falling (poem), p. 222; First April, she with mellow showers (poem), p. 412.

SECOND WEEK. *The Rainbow Bridge.*

Flower of the Rainbow, p. 246; Why the Iris Wears Rainbow Colours, p. 245; Colours of the Rainbow, p. 257.

THIRD WEEK. *Planting the Farm.*

Proud Buckwheat, p. 339; Farmer Mybrow, p. 342; Turkey-Given Corn, p. 360; All around the happy village (poem), p. 338.

FOURTH WEEK. *Flower Youths.*

Why Crocus Holds up his Golden Cup, p. 107; Echo and Narcissus, p. 16; Hyacinth, p. 14.

MAY

FIRST WEEK. *May Day.*

Old-Man-Who-Made-the-Trees-to-Blossom, p. 315; Mariora Floriora, p. 430; I bring fresh Showers (poem), p. 244.

SECOND WEEK. *Mothers' Day.*

Hundred-Headed Daffodil, p. 424; Maiden of the White Camellias, p. 40; Magic Strawberries, p. 199; Golden Strawberries, p. 201.

THIRD WEEK. *Buttercups and Daisies.*

Story that the Buttercups Told, p. 130; Why the Frogs Call the Buttercups, p. 132; Little White Daisy, p. 134; The air is soft, the dale is green (poem), p. 122; The Daisy scattered on each mead and down (poem), p. 106.

FOURTH WEEK. *Hidden in the Grass.*

Wood-Violet that was a Maiden, p. 127; Dandelion Fairies, p. 128; Fairy Cowslips, p. 140; Next followed on the Fairy Nobles (poem), p. 122.

JUNE

FIRST WEEK. *More Flower Youths.*

Cornflower Youth, p. 113; Pansy-Boy, p. 23; Primrose Son, p. 110.

SECOND WEEK. *Rose Legends.*

How Moss-Roses Came, p. 71; Blush-Rose and the Sun, p. 70; King Suleyman and the Nightingale, p. 73.

THIRD WEEK. *Flower Maidens.*

Princess Peony, p. 44; Little Princess White Chicory, p. 131; Bad Poppy Seeds, p. 24; Clytie, the Heliotrope, p. 21; Jealous girls these sometimes were (poem), p. 6.

FOURTH WEEK. *Queen-Rose.*

Rose-Tree Queen, p. 67; Fruit on the Rosebush, p. 118; Sultana of the Flowers, p. 72; I will not have the mad Clytie (poem), p. 54.

JULY

FIRST WEEK. *Lilies White.*

Lilies White, p. 111; Now all fair things come to light (poem), p. 6.

SECOND WEEK. *Blossom Visitors.*

Gleam-o'-Day and the Princess Lotus-Flower, p. 155; Prince Butterfly and Clover Blossom, p. 161; Marigold Arrows, p. 116; A Wild-Rose tree (poem), p. 154.

THIRD WEEK. *Wonder Wings and Webs.*

Anansi the Spider Man, p. 165; Ladybird! Ladybird! p. 171; Boy who Caught Flies, p. 172; Here are Sweet-Peas (poem), p. 6.

FOURTH WEEK. *Fairy Gloves.*

Pan's Lovely Maid, p. 142; Fox in Gloves, p. 141; The Foxglove on fair Flora's hand is worn (poem), p. 106.

AUGUST

FIRST WEEK. *Golden Fireflies.*

Prince Golden-Firefly, p. 158; Firefly! Firefly! (poem), p. 154.

SECOND WEEK. *Things in the Forest.*

Story of the Tiger and the Man, p. 183; Why the Deer Have Antlers, p. 190; Old Man Coyote and Summer in a Bag, p. 413; Her angel's face (poem), p. 180.

THIRD WEEK. *Moon Maiden and Dawn Maiden.*

Tithonus, the Grasshopper, p. 174; Robe of Feathers, p. 97; Maiden in the Moon, p. 256.

FOURTH WEEK. *Water Bright, Water Light.*

Arion and the Dolphin, p. 232; Prince Fireshine and Prince Firefade, p. 227; Jewel Tears, p. 234; A Drop of the Water of Light, p. 258; Full fathom five thy father lies (poem), p. 222.

FOR SPECIAL DAYS

RESURRECTION DAY (EASTER).

Beauty of the Lily, p. 32; Dragon Sin, p. 29.

DOMINION DAY. The Maple Leaf For Ever! p. 330.

BIRD DAY.

Bird Calls, p. 79; Boy that the Eagle Stole, p. 95; Greedy Blackbird, p. 83; King Picus the Woodpecker, p. 87; Pan's Song, p. 100; Spice Bird, p. 85; My old Welsh neighbour over the way (poem), p. 78.

See also *Birds and Bird Day*, in Subject Index, p. 472.

ARBOUR DAY.

Daphne, p. 333; Daughter of the Laurel, p. 317; Orpheus who Made the Trees to Dance, p. 320; Wind in the Pine, p. 326; Orpheus with his lute made trees (poem), p. 314.

See also *Trees and Arbour Day*, in Subject Index, p. 482.

STATE FLOWER AND TREE DAYS.

Look up names of flowers and trees in Subject Index.

AN OLD ENGLISH
CALENDAR OF THE FLOWERS

February   2. The Snowdrop in purest white array
First rears her head on Candlemas Day.

                14. While the Crocus hastens to the shrine
Of Primrose love on Saint Valentine.

March   25. Then comes the Daffodil beside
Our Lady's Smock at our Lady Tide.

April   23. About Saint George, when blue is worn,
The Blue Harebells the fields adorn.

May   3. While on the day of the Holy Cross
The Crowfoot gilds the flowery grass.

June   11. When Barnaby bright smiles night and day,
Poor Ragged Robin blooms in the hay.

                24. The Scarlet Lychnis, the garden's pride,
Flames at Saint John the Baptist's tide.

July   15. Against Saint Swithin's hasty showers
The Lily white reigns the Queen of the
Flowers.

                20. And Poppies a sanguine mantle spread
For the blood of the Dragon Saint Margaret
shed.

                22. Then under the wanton Rose again
That blushes for penitent Magdalen.

August   1. Till Lammas-day called August's wheel,
When the long Corn stinks of Camomile.

August   15. When Mary left us here below,
              The Virgin's Bower begins to blow.

          24. And yet anon the full Sun-Flower blew,
              And became a star for Bartholomew.

September 14. The Passion Flower long has blowed
              To betoken us signs of the Holy Rood.

          29. The Michaelmas Daisy among dead weeds
              Blooms for Saint Michael's valorous deeds.

October   28. And seems the last of flowers that stood
              Till the feast of Saint Simon and Saint Jude.

November   1. Save Mushrooms and the Fungus race
              That grow as All-hallow-tide takes place.

          25. Soon the evergreen Laurel alone is seen,
              When Catherine crowns all learned men.

December 25. Then Ivy and Holly Berries are seen
              And Yule-Clog and Wassail come round again.

STORY-TELLER'S REFERENCE LIST
OF NATURE MYTHS AND TALES IN OTHER
BOOKS

THIS list is practically an index to the volumes of the Story-Teller's Series: *Good Stories for Great Holidays; Story Telling Poems; Red Indian Fairy Book;* and *The Book of Elves and Fairies.*

It is also a reference list of nature stories to be found in various volumes useful to story-tellers in home, school, and library. It is merely suggestive for many good stories are not listed here because of lack of space. As a number of Hans Andersen's charming stories are not included in the volumes of his stories usually found on the children's shelves, references here are made to the two volumes of his fairy tales, *Wonder Stories Told for Children,* and *Stories and Tales.* They are quite complete, handy in size, and excellent for the story-teller's use.

A number of the books mentioned below are not for the children's own reading, but for adults; such as Davis, *Myths and Legends of Japan;* Leland, *Algonquin Legends;* Barker and Sinclair, *West African Folk Tales;* and Gordon Smith, *Ancient Tales and Folk-Lore of Japan.* They contain, however, many charming stories for adaptation.

KEY TO ARRANGEMENT

The arrangement follows closely the order of the stories in the body of this book.

I. Flower Myths and Tales (Garden and Wild).

II. Bird Myths and Tales.

III. Water Myths and Tales.

IV. Insects: Bees, Butterflies, Spiders, Etc.

V. Wild Creatures of Forest and Field.

VI. Fruit Myths and Tales.

VII. Sky Stories: Clouds, Wind, Sun, Moon, etc.

VIII. Fire Legends and Tales of Gold.

I

FLOWER MYTHS AND TALES

GARDEN FLOWERS. Amarakos the Marjoram, in Deas, *Flower Favourites;* A Yellow Pansy (poem), in Cone, *Chant of Love for England;* Bean Flower and Pea Blossom, in Tileston, *Children's Treasure Trove of Pearls;* Fairy Tulips, in *Good Stories for Great Holidays;* Fireflower (Poppies), in Beals, *Flower Lore and Legend;* Five out of One Shell (Sweet Peas), in Andersen, *Stories and Tales;* Flower Fairies (Peonies and Camellias), in *Book of Elves and Fairies,* also in Giles, *Chinese Fairy Tales;* Garden of Bluebells, in Wright, *With the Little Folks;* How the Carnation Came Red, in Deas, *Flower Favourites;* Legend of the Forget-Me-Not, in Skinner, C. M., *Myths and Legends of Flowers,* etc.; Legends of the Pansies, in Beals, *Flower Lore and Legend;* Lily of the Valley, in Lum, *Ancient Legends;* Lily Wife, in Skinner, C. M., *Myths, and Legends of Flowers,* etc.; Little Princess Sunshine (Lilies), in Wright, *With the Little Folks;* Little Violet and Proud Madame Tulip, in Deas, *Flower Favourites;* Snowdrop, in *Good Stories for Great Holidays;* also in Bailey and Lewis, *For the Children's Hour,* and in Andersen, *Wonder Stories Told for Children* (title, The Summer Gowk); Story of the First Snowdrops, in Holbrook, *Book of Nature Myths;* Story of the Iris, in Beals, *Flower Lore and Legend;* Tulip Bed, in Rhys, *English Fairy Book;* Wall Flower, in Lum, *Ancient Legends;* Why the Morning-Glory Climbs, in Bryant, *How to Tell Stories to Children.*

ROSES. How We Came to Have Pink Roses, in Bryant, *How to Tell Stories to Children;* Legend of the Christmas Rose, in Smith and Hazeltine, *Christmas in Legend and Story,* also in Harper, *Story-Hour Favorites;* Little Pink Rose, in Bryant, *Stories to Tell to Children;* Loveliest Rose in the World, in *Good*

Stories for Great Holidays, also in Andersen, *Stories and Tales;* Neighbouring Families, in Andersen, *Wonder Stories Told for Children;* Prince and the Nightingale, in Skinner, C. M., *Myths and Legends of Flowers*, etc.; Princess Beautiful, in *Riverside Third Reader;* Rose and the Lotus, in Skinner, C. M., *Myths and Legends of Flowers*, etc.; Rose Tales, in Beals, *Flower Lore and Legend;* Sir Galahad and the Rose Maiden, in Lum, *Ancient Legends;* Why Wild Roses Have Thorns, in *Red Indian Fairy Book*, also in Young, *Algonquin Indian Tales*.

WILD FLOWERS. Cañon Flowers (wild flowers), in *Good Stories for Great Holidays*, also in Connor, *Sky Pilot;* Daisy, in Andersen, *Wonder Stories Told for Children;* Goldenrod and Aster, in Beals, *Flower Lore and Legend;* Hans and the Wonderful Flower, in Bailey and Lewis, *For the Children's Hour;* How the Blossoms Came to the Heather, in Holbrook, *Book of Nature Myths;* Legend of the Primrose, in Skinner, A. M. and E. L., *Turquoise Story Book;* Legend of the Violet, in *Red Indian Fairy Book*, also in Canfield, *Legends of the Iroquois;* Meadow Dandelion, in *Red Indian Fairy Book;* One-Eyed Prying Joan's Tale (wild flowers), in *Book of Elves and Fairies;* Spring Beauties (poem), in Cone, *Chant of Love for England;* Spring Beauty, in *Red Indian Fairy Book*, also in *Good Stories for Great Holidays;* Star and the Water Lilies, in *Red Indian Fairy Book;* Story of the Fringed Gentian, in Beals, *Flower Lore and Legend;* Toinette and the Elves (Fernseed), in Dickinson and Skinner, *Children's Book of Christmas Stories;* Violet, in Lum, *Ancient Legends*.

II
BIRD MYTHS AND TALES
Useful for Bird Day

Birds' Ball-Game, in *Red Indian Fairy Book;* Boy Who Became a Robin, in *Good Stories for Great Holidays*, also in *Red Indian Fairy Book;* Buzzard's Covering, in Canfield, *Legends of the Iroquois;* Caliph Stork, in Lang, *Green Fairy Book;* Children in the Wood (ballad), in Scudder, *Children's Book;* Christmas Cuckoo, in *Good Stories for Great Holidays*, also in

Browne, *Granny's Wonderful Chair;* Christmas in Norway, in *Story Telling Poems,* also in Thaxter, *Stories and Poems for Children* (title,The Sparrows); Crow and the Pitcher, in Scudder, *Children's Book,* also in his *Fables and Folk Stories;* Dove Who Spoke Truth, in *Good Stories for Great Holidays,* also in Brown, *Curious Book of Birds;* Early Girl, in Brown, *Curious Book of Birds;* Greedy Geese, in *Good Stories for Great Holidays;* How Partridge Built the Birds' Canoes, in *Red Indian Fairy Book,* also Leland, *Algonquin Legends;* How the Hunter Became a Partridge, in *Red Indian Fairy Book,* also in Leland, *Algonquin Legends;* Jorinde and Joringel, in Lang, *Green Fairy Book,* also in Scudder, *Children's Book;* Kind Hawk, in *Red Indian Fairy Book;* King of the Birds, in *Good Stories for Great Holidays;* The King, the Falcon, and the Drinking Cup, in *Riverside Fourth Reader,* also in Dutton, *Tortoise and the Geese;* Kweedass and Kindawiss, in Kennedy, *New World Fairy Book;* Legend of the Swallows, in Young, *Algonquin Indian Tales;* Little Friend, in Brown, *Flower Princess,* also in Smith and Hazeltine, *Christmas in Legend and Story;* Little Owl Boy, in *Red Indian Fairy Book;* Magpie's Nest, in *Good Stories for Great Holidays,* also in Jacobs, *English Fairy Tales;* Masquerading Crow, in Brown, *Curious Book of Birds;* Mrs. Partridge's Babies, in Brown, *Curious Book of Birds;* Mrs. Partridge's Errand, in *Riverside Third Reader;* Nightingale, in Andersen, *Wonder Stories Told for Children;* Nightingale and the Pearl, in *The Jolly Book;* Old Woman Who Became a Woodpecker, in *Good Stories for Great Holidays,* also in Cary, *Ballads for Little Folk* (title, Legend of the Northland); Partridge and the Crow, in Dutton, *Tortoise and the Geese*; Princet and the Golden Blackbird, in Baldwin, *Fairy Stories and Fables;* Quails, in *Riverside Fourth Reader;* Rustic and the Nightingale, in Dutton, *Tortoise and the Geese;* Saint Kentigern and the Robin, in Brown, *Book of Saints and Friendly Beasts;* Sparrow's Wedding, in Rinder, *Old World Japan;* Story of the Oriole, in Holbrook, *Book of Nature Myths;* Sunshine Stories (Swan), in Andersen, *Wonder Stories Told for Children;* Swallow and the Other Birds, in Jacobs, *Æsop;* Tale of Woodpecker and Blue Jay, in Macmillan, *Canadian Wonder Tales;* Tongue-cut Sparrow, in *Good Stories for Great Holidays;* Why the Peacock's Tail Has a Hundred Eyes, in Holbrook, *Book of Nature Myths;* Why the Woodpecker's Head is Red, in Holbrook, *Book of Nature Myths;* Wild Swans, in Andersen, *Wonder Stories Told for Children;* Woodpecker Gray, in *Red Indian Fairy Book.*

III
WATER MYTHS AND TALES

BROOKS, STREAMS, AND LAKES. Ahneah, the Rose Flower, in *Red Indian Fairy Book;* Brook in the King's Garden, in Alden, *Why the Chimes Rang;* Hidden Waters, in *Red Indian Fairy Book; King of the Golden River,* Ruskin; Legend of Niagara and the Great Lakes, in *Red Indian Fairy Book;* Not Lost, but Gone Before, in Gatty, *Parables from Nature;* Silver Brooches, in *Red Indian Fairy Book;* Stream that Ran Away, in *Good Stories for Great Holidays,* also in Austin, *Basket Woman;* Ten Little Indians, in Kennedy, *New World Fairy Book;* Was it the First Turtle? in Holbrook, *Book of Nature Myths,* also in *Riverside Third Reader;* Who Killed the Otter's Babies? in Bryant, *Stories to Tell to Children;* Why the Water in Rivers is Never Still, in Holbrook, *Book of Nature Myths.*

FISHES AND THINGS IN THE SEA. Fisher and the Little Fish, in Jacobs, *Æsop;* Fisherman and his Wife, in Lang, *Green Fairy Book,* also in Scudder, *Children's Book* and in his *Fables and Folk Stories;* Fish Who Helped Saint Gudwall, in Brown, *Book of Saints and Friendly Beasts;* Greediness Punished (poem), in *Story Telling Poems;* How Kahukura Learned to Make Nets, in *Book of Elves and Fairies;* Star Jewels (Star fish), Brown; Story of the First Whitefish, in Holbrook, *Book of Nature Myths;* Thor's Fishing, in Brown, *In the Days of Giants;* Three Fish, in Dutton, *Tortoise and the Geese;* Why the Sea is Salt, in Thorne-Thomsen, *East o' the Sun and West o' the Moon;* Why the Sea-Turtle When Caught Beats its Breast, in Barker and Sinclair, *West African Folk-Tales.*

ADVENTURES IN THE SEA. Deep-Sea Violets, in Harrison, *Old-Fashioned Fairy Book;* Escaped Mermaid, in Rhys, *Eng-*

lish Fairy Book; Good Man of Alloa, in *Story Telling Poems;* Little Sea Maiden (The Little Mermaid), in Andersen, *Wonder Stories Told for Children;* Mermaid of the Magdalenes, in Macmillan, *Canadian Wonder Tales;* Mermaid's Child, in Brown, *Flower Princess;* Story of the First Emeralds, in Holbrook, *Book of Nature Myths;* Tide Jewels, in Davis, *Myths and Legends of Japan;* Undine, in Skinner, A. M. and E. L., *Turquoise Story Book.*

IV
INSECTS: BEES, BUTTERFLIES, SPIDERS, ETC.

Ant and the Cricket, in *Story Telling Poems,* also in *Riverside Fourth Reader;* Ant and the Snow, in Chandler, *In the Reign of Coyote;* Arachne, in Peabody, *Old Greek Folk Stories;* Bald Man and the Fly, in Jacobs, *Æsop;* Bees and the Flies, in Holbrook, *Book of Nature Myths;* Butterfly, in Andersen, *Stories and Tales;* Cobwebs, in Gatty, *Parables from Nature,* also in Rhys, *English Fairy Book;* Cricket and the Cougar, in Chandler, *In the Reign of Coyote;* Fairy Gifts, (Butterflies), in Lang, *Green Fairy Book;* Goats in the Rye Field (Bees), in Esenwein and Stockard, *Children's Stories and How to Tell Them;* Golden Cobwebs (Spiders), Bryant, *How to Tell Stories to Children;* Golden Grasshopper, in Skinner, A. M. and E. L., *Turquoise Story Book;* Great Mosquito, in Canfield, *Legends of the Iroquois;* How the Bees Got Their Stings, in Young, *Algonquin Indian Tales;* How Yogodayu Won a Battle (Bees), in Gordon Smith, *Ancient Tales and Folklore of Japan;* Jupiter and the Bee, *Æsop Fables;* Lesson of Faith, in *Good Stories from Great Holidays,* also in Gatty, *Parables from Nature;* Little Red Princess (Ants), in Bailey, *Tell Me Another Story;* Pitcher the Witch (Mosquitoes), in *Red Indian Fairy Book;* Princess Moonbeam (Fireflies), in Lyman, *Story Telling;* Queen Bee, in Young and Field, *Literary Reader, No. 3;* Spider and the Bee, in Young and Field, *Literary Reader No. 2;* Three Little Butterfly Brothers, in *Good Stories for Great Holidays;* What Happened to the Bees That Tried to Steal Honey, in Young, *Algonquin Indian Tales;* Why the Mosquito Hates Smoke, in Chandler, *In the Reign of Coyote.*

V

WILD CREATURES OF FOREST AND FIELD

Bears. Scrapefoot, in Esenwein and Stockard, *Children's Stories and How to Tell Them;* Three Bears, in Bryant, *How to Tell Stories to Children;* also in Jacobs, *English Fairy Tales;* and in Scudder, *Children's Book;* and Lang, *Green Fairy Book;* Ugly Wild Boy, in *Red Indian Fairy Book;* Why the Bear Sleeps All Winter, in Cowles, *Art of Story-Telling.*

Lions. Infant Heracles, and, Heracles the Lion-Slayer, Idyls 24 and 25 in *Theocritus, Bion, and Moschus,* trans. by Lang; Lion and the Mouse, in Esenwein and Stockard, *Children's Stories and How to Tell Them,* also in Scudder, *Children's Book;* Lion in Love, in Jacobs, *Æsop,* also in Scudder, *Children's Book;* Lion's Share, in Jacobs, *Æsop;* Saint Gerasimus and the Lion, in Brown, *Book of Saints and Friendly Beasts.*

Rabbits. Bad Wild Cat, in *Red Indian Fairy Book;* How Master Rabbit Went Fishing, in *Red Indian Fairy Book,* also in Leland, *Algonquin Legends;* Little White Rabbit, in Skinner, A. M. and E. L., *Nursery Tales from Many Lands;* Timid Hares, in Young and Field, *Literary Reader, No. 2;* Tortoise and the Hare, in Scudder, *Children's Book,* also in his *Fables and Folk Stories;* Why the Rabbit is Timid, in Holbrook, *Book of Nature Myths;* Witch That was a Hare, in Rhys, *English Fairy Book.*

Wolves. Boy Who Cried Wolf, in Bryant, *Stories to Tell to Children;* Gunniwolf, in Harper, *Story-Hour Favorites;* Little Red Riding-Hood, in Scudder, *Children's Book,* also in his *Fables and Folk Stories;* Saint Bridget and the King's Wolf, in Brown, *Book of Saints and Friendly Beasts;* Wolf in Sheep's Clothing, in Scudder, *Children's Book;* Wolf and the Kid, in Jacobs, *Æsop.*

Animal Friends, and Others. Adventures of Visu (Foxes), in Davis, *Myths and Legends of Japan;* Calydonian

Hunt, in Peabody, *Old Greek Folk Stories;* Elephant's Child, in Kipling, *Just So Stories;* Forest Full of Friends, in Alden, *Why The Chimes Rang;* How the Camel Got his Hump, in Kipling, *Just So Stories;* Meleager and Atalanta, in Storr, *Half-a-Hundred Stories;* Mowgli's Brothers, Kaa's Hunting, Tiger! Tiger! in Kipling, *Jungle Book;* Noisy Chipmunk, in *Red Indian Fairy Book;* White-Footed Deer (poem), in *Story Telling Poems;* also in *Riverside Fifth Reader;* Young-Boy-Chief, in *Red Indian Fairy Book.*

VI
FRUIT MYTHS AND TALES

Atalanta's Race (Apples), in Peabody, *Old Greek Folk Stories;* Elves (Strawberries), in *Good Stories for Great Holidays;* Fox and the Grapes, in Scudder, *Children's Book,* also in his *Fables and Folk Stories,* and in Jacobs, *Æsop;* How the Springtime Came (Idun and her Apples), in Baldwin, Story of Siegfried; Iduna's Apples, in Tappan, Myths from Many Lands; *Legend of the Blackberry,* in Skinner, C. M., *Myths and Legends of Flowers,* etc.; Magic Apples, in Brown, *In the Days of Giants;* Three Citrons, in Laboulaye, *Fairy Book;* Wonderful Pear-Tree, in Giles, *Chinese Fairy Tales.*

VII
SKY STORIES: CLOUDS, WIND, SUN, MOON, ETC.

CLOUDS AND RAIN. Aqua, or the Water Baby, in Wiggin and Smith, *Story Hour;* Cloud, in Bryant, *Stories to Tell to Children;* Hofus the Stone Cutter, in *Riverside Third Reader,* also in *Good Stories for Great Holidays,* and in Shedlock, *Art of the Story-Teller;* Little Niebla, in *Book of Elves and Fairies,* also in Hudson, *Purple Land;* Little Water-Drop's Journey, in Wright, *With the Little Folks;* Uncle Rain and Brother Drought, in *Riverside Fourth Reader;* Water Drop, in *Good Stories for Great Holidays.*

RAINBOW AND AURORA BOREALIS. Bag of Gold at the Rainbow's End (title, Buttercup), in Beals, *Flower Lore and*

Legend; Land of the Northern Lights, in *Red Indian Fairy Book;* Little Dawn Boy and the Rainbow Trail, in *Red Indian Fairy Book;* Northern Lights, in Macmillan, *Canadian Wonder Tales;* Rainbow Bridge, in Young and Field, *Literary Reader No. 2;* Pot of Gold, in Coe, *Second Book of Stories for the Story-Teller,* also in Scudder, *Dream Children.*

WIND TALES. Foolish Weathercock, in *Riverside Second Reader;* Four Winds, in Canfield, *Legends of the Iroquois;* How the Four Winds Were Named, in *Red Indian Fairy Book;* Lad Who Went to the North Wind, Thorne-Thomsen, *East o' the Sun and West o' the Moon;* Legend of the North Wind, in Coe, *First Book of Stories for the Story-Teller;* Sun and the Wind, in Bryant, *Stories to Tell to Children;* Wind-Blower, in *Red Indian Fairy Book.*

SUN AND MOON. Apollo's Sister (Diana and Endymion), in Peabody, *Old Greek Folk Stories;* Astounding Voyage of Daniel O'Rourke (Moon), in *Jolly Book;* Bamboo Cutter and the Moon-Maiden, in Davis, *Myths and Legends of Japan;* Boy in the Moon, in *Red Indian Fairy Book;* Crab and the Moon, in the *Riverside Third Reader; East o' the Sun, and West o' the Moon,* Thorne-Thomsen; Frog in the Moon, in Chandler, *In the Reign of Coyote;* How the Sun, the Moon, and the Wind Went Out to Dinner, in Coe, *Second Book of Stories for the Story-Teller;* Little Daylight, in Bryant, *How to Tell Stories to Children,* also in Macdonald, *Back of the North Wind;* Mouse and the Sun, in Macmillan, *Canadian Wonder Tales;* Phæton, in Peabody, *Old Greek Folk Stories;* Scar-Face (Sun), in *Red Indian Fairy Book;* Story of Little Tavwots (Sun), in Bryant, *How to Tell Stories to Children;* Sun's Sisters, in Bailey and Lewis, *For the Children's Hour.*

STARS. Coyote's Ride on a Star, in Chandler, *In the Reign of Coyote;* Great Bear and the Little Bear, in Coe, *First Book of Stories for the Story-Teller;* How the Fairies Came, in *Red Indian Fairy Book;* Legend of the Dipper, in Esenwein and Stockard, *Children's Stories and How to Tell Them,* also in Bailey and Lewis, *For the Children's Hour;* Legend of the

Morning Star, in *Red Indian Fairy Book;* Legends of the Pleiades, in *Red Indian Fairy Book;* Sky Elk, in *Red Indian Fairy Book;* Star and the Water Lilies, in *Red Indian Fairy Book;* Star Bride, in *Red Indian Fairy Book;* Star Dollars, in Bryant, *How to Tell Stories to Children;* Star-Lovers, in Tappan, *Myths from Many Lands,* also in Rinder, *Old World Japan;* Twin Stars, in Holbrook, *Book of Nature Myths.*

VIII
FIRE LEGENDS AND TALES OF GOLD
Useful for Labour Day

FIRE AND FORGE. Arms of Æneas, in Church, *Stories from Virgil;* Burg Hill's on Fire, in *Good Stories for Great Holidays,* also in Grierson, *Children's Book of Celtic Stories* (title, Good Housewife); Dwarf's Gifts, in Brown, *In the Days of Giants,* also in Tappan, *Myths from Many Lands* Firebird, in *Red Indian Fairy Book,* also in Gask, *Legends of Our Little Brothers;* Fire Bringer, in Austin, *Basket Woman,* also in Bryant, *How to Tell Stories to Children;* Forging of Balmung, in Baldwin, *Hero Tales;* How Fire Was Brought to the Indians in Holbrook, *Book of Nature Myths;* King of the Clinkers, in *Riverside Fourth Reader;* Making of the Hammer, in *Riverside Fifth Reader;* Mimer the Master, in Baldwin, *Story of Siegfried;* Tuba Cain (poem), in *Riverside Fifth Reader,* also in *Story Telling Poems;* Story of Prometheus, in Baldwin, *Old Greek Stories;* Wren Who Brought Fire, in Brown, *Curious Book of Birds.*

GOLD. Bad Boy and the Leprechaun, in *Book of Elves and Fairies;* Boy Who Found the Pots of Gold, in *Book of Elves and Fairies;* Curse of Gold-Regin's Tale, in Baldwin, *Story of Siegfried;* Dust Under the Rug, in Lindsay, *Mother Stories,* also in Coe, *Second Book of Stories for the Story-Teller;* Greedy Old Man, in *Book of Elves and Fairies;* Honest Woodman, in Cowles, *Art of Story-Telling;* Hoard of the Elves, in Baldwin, *Hero Tales;* Metal King, in *Good Stories for Great Holidays;* Ragweed, in *Book of Elves and Fairies.*

IX

WINTER: ICE, SNOW, FROST

Brother and Sister, in *Red Indian Fairy Book;* Cheerful Glacier, in Austin, *Basket Woman;* Ethelinda; or, The Ice King's Bride, in Harrison, *Old-Fashioned Fairy Book;* Frost Spirit, Whittier, in his *Poems;* Ice King, in Skinner, A. M. and E. L., *Pearl Story Book;* Jowiis, and the Eagle, in *Red Indian Fairy Book;* King Winter's Harvest, in Skinner, A. M. and E. L., *Pearl Story Book;* Little Match Girl, in *Good Stories for Great Holidays,* also in Andersen, *Stories and Tales;* Mother Holle, in Lang, *Red Fairy Book;* Shingebiss, in *Red Indian Fairy Book;* Silvercap, King of the Frost Fairies, in Bailey and Lewis, *For the Children's Hour;* Snow Image, in Hawthorne, *Daffydowndilly;* Snow Man, in *Red Indian Fairy Book;* Snow Queen, in Andersen, *Wonder Stories Told for Children;* Story of Bumps, in Phillips, *Wee Ann.*

X

TREE MYTHS AND TALES

Useful for Labor Day

Anxious Leaf, in Bailey and Lewis, *For the Children's Hour;* Balder and the Mistletoe, in Brown, *In the Days of Giants,* also in Tappan, *Myths from Many Lands;* Baucis and Philemon, in *Good Stories for Great Holidays,* also in Storr, *Half-a-Hundred Hero Tales;* Carob, in Skinner, C. M., *Myths and Legends of Flowers,* etc., also in Isaacs, *Stories from the Rabbis* (title, Rip Van Winkle of the Talmud); Christmas Tree, in Austin, *Basket Woman;* Dryad of the Old Oak, in *Good Stories for Great Holidays;* First Pine Trees, in *Red Indian Fairy Book;* Girl Who Became a Pine Tree, in Judd, *Wigwam Stories;* Horse and the Olive, in Baldwin, *Old Greek Stories;* How Maple-Sugar Came, in *Red Indian Fairy Book,* also in Young, *Algonquin Indian Tales;* Karl and the Dryad, in Brown, *Star Jewels;* Little Tree that Longed for Other Leaves, in *Good Stories for Great Holidays;* Maple-Leaf and the Violet, in Wiggin and Smith, *Story Hour;* Maple Seed, in Skinner, A. M. and E. L., *Emerald Story Book;* Mishosha, or The Enchanted Sugar-Maple, in *Red Indian*

Fairy Book; Old Pipes and the Dryad, in Stockton, *Bee-man of Orn,* also in Lyman, *Story Telling,* and in Young and Field, *Literary Reader, No. 4;* Plucky Prince, in *Story Telling Poems;* Proud Oak Tree, in *Good Stories for Great Holidays;* Silver Spoons in the Poplar Tree, in Skinner, C. M., *Myths and Legends of Flowers,* etc.; Simon and the Black Gum Tree, in Skinner, A. M. and E. L., *Nursery Tales from Many Lands;* Sugar Pine, in Austin, *Basket Woman;* Thunder Oak, in *Good Stories for Great Holidays;* Two Little Maple Leaves, in Wright, *With the Little Folks;* Spirit of the Willow Tree, in Gordon Smith, *Ancient Tales and Folk-lore of Japan;* Wakontas, in Young, *Algonquin Indian Tales;* Why the Juniper Has Berries, in Holbrook, *Book of Nature Myths;* Wonder Tree, in *Good Stories for Great Holidays.*

XI
FARM WONDERS

FARM DOINGS. Admetus and the Shepherd, in Peabody, *Old Greek Folk Stories;* Barney Noonan's Fairy Haymakers, in Esenwein and Stockard, *Children's Stories and How to Tell Them;* Blanche and Rose, in *Book of Elves and Fairies;* Boggart, in *Book of Elves and Fairies;* Elsa and the Ten Elves, in *Book of Elves and Fairies;* Farmer, the Sheep, and the Robbers, in Dutton, *Tortoise and the Geese;* Four-Leaved Clover, in *Book of Elves and Fairies;* Little One-Eye, Little Two-Eyes, and Little Three-Eyes, in Scudder, *Children's Book,* also in his *Fables and Folk Stories,* also in Lang, *Green Fairy Book;* Nail, in *Riverside Fourth Reader;* Piskey Fine! Piskey Gay! in *Book of Elves and Fairies;* Plowman Who Found Content, in Cowles, *Art of Story-Telling;* Tom Thumb, in Esenwein and Stockard, *Children's Stories and How to Tell Them,* also in Scudder, *Children's Book;* Toy of the Giant's Child, in *Story Telling Poems;* Wish Ring, in *Fairy Stories Retold from St. Nicholas;* Wood-Lady, in *Book of Elves and Fairies.*

HARVEST AND CROPS. Adzanumee and her Mother, in Barker and Sinclair, *West African Folk-Tales;* Ears of Wheat, in *Good Stories for Great Holidays;* Fairy of the Cotton Plant, in Skinner, C. M., *Myths and Legends of Flowers*, etc.; Flax, in Andersen, *Wonder Stories Told for Children;* Gift of Flax, in Skinner, A. M. and E. L., *Turquoise Story Book;* How Flax was Given to Men, in Holbrook, *Book of Nature Myths;* How Indian Corn Came into the World, in *Good Stories for Great Holidays*, also in *Red Indian Fairy Book;* How Wry-face Played a Trick (Potatoes), in Coe, *Second Book of Stories for the Story-Teller;* Jack and the Bean-stalk, in Scudder, *Children's Book*, also in Jacobs, *English Fairy Tales;* Legend of the Radish, in Skinner, C. M., *Myths and Legends of Flowers*, etc.; Little Corn Bringer, in *Red Indian Fairy Book;* Master of the Harvest, in *Good Stories for Great Holidays;* Quick-running Squash, in Aspinwall, *Short Stories for Short People;* Potatoes' Dance (poem), in Lindsay, *Chinese Nightingale;* Potato Supper, in *Book of Elves and Fairies;* Spirit of the Corn, in *Red Indian Fairy Book;* Why the Bean has a Stripe Down its Back, in Bailey and Lewis, *For the Children's Hour;* Wise Sachem's Gift, in Canfield, *Legends of the Iroquois.*

ADVENTURES OF BARNYARD FOLK. Billy Beg and His Bull, in McManus, *Donegal Fairy Tales*, also in Bryant, *How to Tell Stories to Children;* Chicken Licken, in O'Grady, *Story-Teller's Book*, also in Scudder, *Children's Book;* Curmudgeon's Skin, in *Book of Elves and Fairies;* Cock, the Mouse, and the Little Red Hen, Lefèvre, also in *Riverside Second Reader;* Cock and the Fox, in Darton, *Tales of the Canterbury Pilgrims;* Fox and the Cock, in Esenwein and Stockard, *Children's Stories and How to Tell Them;* Dumpy the Pony, in Lindsay, *More Mother Stories;* Eight-Footed Slipper, in Baldwin, *Wonder-Book of Horses;* Enchanted Pig, in Lang, *Red Fairy Book;* Golden Goose, Tappan; Goose with the Golden Eggs, in Jacobs, *Æsop;* Grandfather Pig's Spectacles, in Wright, *With the Little Folks;* Greyfell, in Baldwin, *Story of Siegfried;* Little Half Chick, in Bryant, *Stories to Tell to Children*, also in Esenwein and Stockard, *Children's Stories and How to Tell Them;* Miller, His Son, and Their Ass, in Jacobs, *Æsop;* Milk-White Calf, in *Book of Elves and Fairies;* Mud Pony, in *Red Indian Fairy Book;* Old Woman and her Pig, in Bryant, *How to Tell Stories to Children*, also in O'Grady, *Story-Teller's Book;* Piggywee's Little Curly Tail, in Wright, *With the Little Folks;* Poor Turkey Girl, in *Red Indian Fairy Book*, also in Cushing, *Zuñi Folk-Tales;* Story of Io, in Baldwin, *Old Greek Stories;* Straw Ox, in Skinner A. M. and E. L., *Nursery Tales from Many Lands;* Teenchy Duck, in Coe, *Second Book of Stories for the Story-Teller;* Three Little Pigs, in Bryant, *How to Tell Stories to Children*, also in Jacobs, *English Fairy Tales;* Three Billy Goats Gruff, in Esenwein and Stockard, *Children's Stories and How to Tell Them*, also in *Riverside Second Reader*, and in Thorne-Thomsen, *East o' the Sun and West o' the Moon;* Ugly Duckling, in Andersen, *Wonder Stories Told for Children;* White Cat, in Scudder, *Children's Book*, also in his *Fables and Folk Stories;* Why the Turkey Gobbles, in *Red Indian Fairy Book*.

XII
THE SEASONS AND THE MONTHS

Black Steeds of Aidoneus, in Baldwin, *Wonder-Book of Horses;* Boy Who Discovered the Spring, in Alden, *Why the Chimes Rang;* Chestnut Boys, in Poulsson, *In the Child's World;* How Summer Came to Canada, in Macmillan, *Canadian Wonder Tales;* How Summer Came to the Earth, in Holbrook, *Book of Nature Myths;* Mailcoach Passengers, in *Good Stories for Great Holidays*, also in Andersen, *Wonder Stories Told for Children;* Miss November's Dinner Party, in Dickinson, *Children's Book of Thanksgiving Stories;* Months, in Tileston, *Children's Treasure Trove of Pearls;* Nipon and the King of the Northland, in Skinner, A. M. and E. L., *Topaz Story Book;* Spring and Autumn Lover, in James, *Green Willow;* Summer Fairies, in *Red Indian Fairy Book*, also in Leland, *Algonquin Legends;* Twelve Months, in *Good Stories for Great Holidays;* Wood-Folk, in Peabody, *Old Greek Folk Stories*.

SUBJECT INDEX FOR STORY-TELLERS

SUBJECT INDEX FOR STORY-TELLERS

The Riverside Press

CAMBRIDGE . MASSACHUSETTS

U . S . A